The I

Emma Miles

Part one of Fire-Walker

Second Edition

Copyright Emma Miles 2021

This book is a work of fiction and is not based on any real persons (contrary to the concerns of my colleagues whenever I sit in the mess-room with my laptop) living or dead.

Contents

Chapter One

Kesta: Fulmer Island

'Mother, it has to be me.'

The Icante of the Fulmer islands regarded Kesta, her eyebrows drawn in tight above her mis-matched eyes; one blue, one brown.

'What I saw...' Kesta's words faltered. Images of her journey through the flames pressed themselves into her mind, and she shuddered. 'I can persuade them. I know I can.'

Kesta swallowed under her mother's continued scrutiny. As much as she ached to be the one to dare the unknown land, what she had seen in the flames still had her heart racing, and an intense headache was starting at the base of her skull. She had courage aplenty, but she wasn't foolish. There was every possibility the king of Elden would say no, every chance he would even be hostile.

'It makes sense for a *walker* to come with me,' her father agreed.

Kesta knew her mother well enough to read the concern behind her eyes. It wasn't Kesta she doubted, but she had to weigh up the consequences of sending both her husband and daughter across the sea.

Dia Icante closed her eyes, breathing out slowly. 'All right. But be wary. They have no magic in Elden, don't be too quick to show yours.'

Kesta nodded, although hiding who she was would be easier said than done. Like her mother, her eyes were mismatched, though hers were differing shades of green. Dark emerald, and new leaf.

Arrus touched his wife's arm. 'I'll get things ready.'

He hurried from the room and Kesta looked again at the chart, her finger tracing the edge of the Elden coast. Some of their fishermen traded with the Eldemen out at sea, and even ventured into the harbours of Burneton and Taurmouth, but relations between the insular Fulmer Islands and the much larger Kingdom of Elden were frosty.

'I should send the twins with you,' her mother said.

Kesta shook her head. 'They will be needed here. We'll be fine. Anyway, we are a diplomatic party, we can't appear too aggressive.'

Her mother took a step closer. The leader of the Fulmer islands was always so elegant, so perfectly poised, but today her shoulders were hunched and worry lines creased the skin around her eyes. 'Don't pay too high a price.'

'Of course not.' There was a tingling dance of nerves within her. They had no idea what the King of Elden might want for his help. Her father was a clever negotiator, brilliant at disarming people, but it wasn't the king himself who worried them. For years they had heard rumours of the powerful sorcerer who sat at the king's side, a menacing figure whose shadow lay across Elden. 'The Dark Man' they called him, and as much as that name evoked fear, it was he who would be their best protection against what she had seen coming from the north.

'You have a headache, my honey?' Dia reached out to press her fingers to the sides of Kesta's head. 'Let me get you some willow tea.'

Kesta nodded distractedly. 'Mother, those Borrow raids we had earlier this month...'

'You are thinking it was not an attempt at conquest, but a desperate attempt to flee to safer land,' Dia finished for her as she prepared the tea.

Kesta smiled. Her mother had a gentle manner, but an incredibly quick mind. She could also be fierce when she wanted to be.

Kesta's anxiety grew, her headache blossoming through her skull. The body of the Chemmish sorcerer who'd led the raid they'd put down only yesterday still lay in the hold's cellar. Some men who'd fought with him had indeed been from the Borrows, but most had been as Chemmish as their leader. Marks about the wrists, ankles, and necks of the Borrowmen suggested they had been slaves.

The worrying revelation had led to both herself and her mother attempting a *walk* through the flames to see what was happening on the far-off shores of the Borrow Islands. Kesta had pushed herself further, and what she'd seen...

Her mother handed her a steaming cup, and Kesta gratefully curled her fingers around it.

'You are still lost in the flame.' Dia stroked her hair. 'Please try not to worry, we can survive this.'

The door opened and her father strode back in. Arrus was a large man. His muscular frame and paler complexion suggested some Borrow blood in his own heritage. His long beard contained small plaits held with silver beads, his dark-brown hair cut short.

'Worvig is arranging a fishing boat to take us as soon as it gets light,' Arrus told them. 'And Pirelle is organising supplies. We'll need to buy or hire ponies when we reach Elden.'

'And what did your brother say about your going to Elden?' Dia's mouth curled up in a smile.

Arrus barked out a laugh. 'There was more swearing and growling than actual words, but you know Worvig, he'll follow an order.' He crossed the room to hug his wife. 'He'll also keep you safe.'

Dia made a noise in the back of her throat, and Kesta smiled. Her mother could take care of herself.

'Kesta, why don't you get some sleep?'

Kesta nodded, knowing it was her mother's way of politely dismissing her. Her parents no doubt wanted some time to themselves before she and her father left.

'I'll see you in a few hours.'

Instead of going to her room, she hurried down the stairs and through the large doors leading into the great hall. Two warriors sat beside the enormous fireplace at the side of the hall, talking quietly. A third man was cutting a slice of meat from the sheep hanging over the central firepit. Kesta screwed up her nose, feeling a pang of nausea. As a *walker* she touched no meat at all, but her people did rather than waste a fallen or injured animal. This ewe had slipped over a cliff yesterday.

'Silene,' one man greeted her, using her title. She had earned it not by being the daughter of the Icante, and later her apprentice, but by proving herself a capable leader. She couldn't deny that in her parents she had been lucky to have the best teachers – not to mention her uncle Worvig – but she liked to think gaining the title of defender of the Icante at her young age of twenty, was also down to herself.

She left the hall, gazing around the small settlement that stood within the crowning walls on the peninsular. There were forty small houses, and a barn to shelter their animals in the winter. Fulmer Hold wasn't the largest hold on Fulmer Island, but it was their heart, the Icante's home.

The tall gates were closed, four warriors on guard and another half dozen patrolling the high wall. Kesta gave the men a nod, and they lifted the bar to let her through.

Braziers lined the narrow causeway leading from the hold to the mainland. Far below, the surf broke against the cliffs, telling Kesta the tide was high. She paused halfway across, leaning over the rope rail to peer left toward the beach and the small bay. She knew more warriors patrolled down there, along with the twin scouts who guarded her mother. No fires were lit, nothing that might help an enemy land.

'Kesta.'

She spun on the balls of her feet, seeing the reassuring brawny figure of her uncle Worvig, as he hurried back to the hold. She took his hand and kissed his whiskery cheek. Even she had to admit she had a somewhat fiery nature, and it sometimes caused her to clash with her patient parents.

Worvig was different, though. He was a quiet and calm man, and one around whom Kesta felt she never had to hide her feelings.

'What are you doing out here?' Worvig demanded, glancing toward the hold. 'It isn't safe.'

'I needed some air. I needed... I needed to watch the beach for myself.' She shuddered.

Worvig frowned, bending a little to better see her eyes. 'Your father told me what you saw. It fair made my skin walk off my bones. But at the end of the day, a raider is a raider, and we'll see them off as we have always done.'

I wonder.

Kesta didn't want to contradict her uncle, but she knew this was different. They'd held off one Chemmish sorcerer, but there were many more. Four tiny islands against a continent.

'Your mother is strong,' Worvig said, seeing her hesitation. 'We don't need some heartless foreign sorcerer. But... I can see there is some prudence to it. Sending you, though...'

'I want to go. I want to learn about our neighbours, to understand them. And I also need to learn every way to defend our people, including negotiation.'

She could tell by the expression on his face he thought she'd never have the patience and tact for diplomacy.

'I can do it,' she insisted.

Worvig nodded, putting his arm around her shoulders. 'Come back in the hold, try to get some sleep. Your boat won't sail for another six hours yet.'

'I can't sleep.' She didn't want to admit even to Worvig that she was too scared to close her eyes, afraid she'd see the images she'd glimpsed through the flames again.

'Well, let's sit in the hall, then. I can tell you tales of your father.'

She grinned at that and reached up to touch his hand. 'Yes, please.'

***

Everyone on the island learned to sail, and Kesta was no exception. The boat carrying them across the ocean to Elden was a single-masted vessel with a small hold and a tiny cabin at the stern. To keep herself busy, Kesta offered to take the rudder, leaving her father and the fisherman to gossip and exchange stories. The fisherman's son was perhaps two years younger than Kesta and had the typically dark complexion of an islander. He did his best to impress her, but she remained politely indifferent. She had to admire his courage though, flirting with her right under the gaze of Arrus Silene.

The fisherman took over from her as the day wore on, and they swapped again as light faded. Kesta had only rarely been at sea and out of sight of land at night, and it was both frightening and exhilarating. She perched at the prow, leaning back to stare at the stars. The longer she looked, the more she seemed to find, pressing further and further away into the infinite.

Her father sat inelegantly beside her, placing his jacket around her shoulders. 'Still can't sleep, Urchin?'

She shook her head.

'We'll be fine. If my training and your mother's doesn't serve you, then just fight dirty like your uncle Worvig.'

She laughed, some of her tension easing.

They knew a little about Elden, enough to know the people differed from them. In Elden they had an odd social structure, where those who ruled held all the wealth, and from what Kesta could tell, did little of the work. On the Fulmers, the Icante and her Silenes were expected to work harder than anyone else. And their king was born to his position, not chosen for his strength or ability as the Icante was.

She frowned. If the rumours were true, the king's sorcerer was the one who held the power.

'It will be well, stop your worrying.' Her father gave her a nudge.

'Do you know what worries me the most?' she said slowly. 'That mother is asking for help. She's very strong, and... and pretty clever. Asking for help from a land we have avoided for many years, generations even, suggests she is afraid. I have never seen her afraid.'

Arrus turned to face her. 'Your mother had been afraid many times, my honey. She just hides it very well. She also knows that pride is worth less than the lives of her people. Trust her.'

'I do.' Kesta nodded, but she couldn't shift the fear in her belly.

***

It was evening when they arrived at the harbour of Burneton. Instinctively Kesta reached out her *knowing*, only to withdraw her magic with a gasp. There were so many people, so many burning emotions, she'd felt for a moment as though she were drowning. She was relieved when her father suggested she wait on the boat whilst he and the fisherman looked for an inn, and someone to hire ponies from.

'Do we have to stay in an inn?' she asked. 'Could we not keep going for a few hours and find somewhere to camp?'

Arrus regarded her with a worried frown. 'What is it, my urchin?'

She pulled a face, embarrassment making her squirm. 'There are just so many people here.'

Her father studied her for a moment, his shoulders sagging. 'Aye, Urchin, there are. I'll just get us some ponies then.'

As much as she wanted to hide away in the small cabin and wait, Kesta forced herself to stay on deck and watch the people. They had paler skin than the islanders, some of them with hair the colour of straw, or even butter. But they were just people, working, surviving, sometimes laughing. A young couple shared a kiss, and Kesta smiled, relaxing a little.

Her father returned with three ponies, broader than the hardy equines that lived on the largest of the Fulmer Islands. They loaded one with their supplies, then set off through the town.

From the maps they had, they knew to find the river and follow it upstream to the large lake on which stood castle Taurmaline. They rode for a while until it grew too dark for the ponies to see. Kesta's back and leg muscles were already sore. She'd rarely ridden in her life, and only ever for a short time.

They stopped in a narrow copse close to the water. Arrus lit a small fire, and they ate whilst quietly sharing their observations on Burneton.

A pony snorted, and Kesta reached out her *knowing* to soothe it.

Her magic touched something else. Malice.

She leapt up, drawing her sword with her right hand and calling power to her left. Her father was on his feet an instant behind her.

Five men crept toward them out of the darkness, all of them armed.

'On your way, friends,' Arrus warned with a growl. 'There is nothing for you here.'

As much as the emotions of these men made Kesta feel sick and her heart pound, she reached out again. They were wary, but not afraid. Despite their weapons, they'd taken Kesta and her father as easy targets.

Kesta's nostrils flared, and she turned her head slightly towards her father. 'They won't back down.'

Arrus responded by sweeping his sword up and leaping at the men. Despite her mother's warning not to use her magic, Kesta didn't believe this was the time for discretion. She called flames to her palms and sent a bright flare toward the men. Two of them staggered back, but another darted in, thrusting his blade toward her stomach. She blocked with her own sword, disengaging quickly and stepping aside. He was much stronger than her.

Arrus had already hacked deep into the shoulder of one thief and was engaged in a ferocious battering of swords with another. The whicker of the ponies warned Kesta there were more men behind them. As the man before her made another sweep with his blade, she dropped her sword and called her full power. With a cry, she threw the three men before her several feet through the air, the wind she created swaying the trees of the copse. As the men scrambled to get up, she called fire again, this time a blaze that appeared to engulf both her outstretched hands.

The thieves needed no more incentive, but fled into the darkness.

Arrus skewered the last man, using his foot to push him back off his sword.

Kesta stood frozen for a moment, breathing hard, her heart still racing. She swallowed, facing her father.

'You all right, Kes?'

She nodded and turned to the ponies.

Her eyes widened, her mouth falling open as she sucked in air.

They were gone.

Arrus swore. 'Those sneaky—'

'We could track them,' Kesta suggested.

Arrus growled. 'They'll be long gone, and probably in the wrong direction.'

Kesta picked up her sword and sheathed it, grinding her teeth. 'We'll have to go back to Burneton. It will take us forever to get Taurmaline on foot and without supplies. We'll just have to buy more ponies.'

'Ah.'

Kesta turned to stare at her father, at his flushed cheeks.

'I left our gems for trading in the saddlebags.'

Kesta closed her eyes and let out a frustrated cry.

'Sorry, Urchin.'

Guilt clawed at her.

They should have stayed in an inn.

'I think we both underestimated this spirit's-forsaken land.' She sighed. 'I guess we might just as well follow this river, then. It's a shame it's too small for a raft.'

Arrus cleaned his sword and sheathed it. 'Come on, then.'

***

It was one of the most unpleasant times in Kesta's life. They tried a few farmhouses to ask for help, but if Kesta went with her father to the door, one look at her mis-matched eyes had it slammed in their faces. If Arrus went alone to ask for food or the shelter of a barn, most of the time the door wasn't even opened. Despair crept through Kesta. How could they expect help from such a people who would turn away strangers in need? It was nothing like the Fulmers here.

They found a few things to eat in the countryside, and Arrus caught some tiny fish in the river, but they refused to steal. By the time they came within sight of the vast city of Taurmaline, they were starving, exhausted, and filthy. Just to make matters worse, a storm blew its way across the lake and it emptied a deluge of icy rain upon them.

Kesta had to clamp down tight on her *knowing*, but even so the buzz of life from the engorged population was overwhelming, distressing. Arrus kept his arm around her as they forced their way through the crowds toward the castle.

Despite the gates to the city being guarded, they'd been let through without so much as a question. The castle was a different matter, and Kesta saw the guards eyeing them up before they even reached the gatehouse.

'Let me try,' Arrus said. 'Keep your eyes hidden if you can.'

Arrus straightened up, calling on his years of authority. 'We are messengers from the Fulmer Islands and need to see the king.'

'Messengers?' One guard's lip curled in disgust. 'You look like beggars.'

Arrus put his hand on his sword. 'Would a beggar carry steel like this?'

Kesta tensed, ready to call power if she needed to.

One of the other guards stepped forward. His eyes narrowed as he carefully studied the Silene. 'They are from the Fulmers.' The man turned to his fellows. 'And he's right about the sword. Messengers, you say?'

'I do,' Arrus replied calmly. 'We bring news of dire import from the Icante.'

The guards exchanged a glance before the more amenable of the four gestured for them to follow him. 'Okay, then. His majesty is still seeing petitioners in his audience room. I'll take you as far as the steward there. He can decide if they'll allow you in.'

Chapter Two

Kesta: Kingdom of Elden

Her father gave a shout of protest as a hand shoved her in the back; she fell forward onto her hands and knees hitting the ground so hard her teeth clacked together. Kesta breathed out sharply, heart pounding, her muscles tense. Her dark hair fell forward over her face in wet tails and peering carefully from under her lashes she made a quick scan of the room. There were four other guardsmen beside the two who had dragged them in so rudely.

Before them stood the throne.

The Elden king was younger than she'd expected; his hair was sandy, almost red, and grew down below his shoulders. Her eyes widened, and she froze when she saw the man seated beside the king. There was no mistaking who he was. The Dark Man. It was said a storm had washed him up on the northern shores of Elden …

'If this is how Elden treats its guests, your majesty, it's no wonder the Fulmers refuse to treat with you!'

Her father stood and shoved away the guard who tried to stop him.

'Randle!' King Bractius warned the guard and waved him back with a hand. 'And you are …?'

'Arrus, Silene of Fulmer and husband to our ruler, the Icante.'

There was a gasp from the guards and Bractius leaned forward, looking her father up and down. The Dark Man didn't even blink. His pale blue eyes reminded Kesta of river ice on a sunny day. His hair was just long enough to start to curl but his black beard was cut close to his chin. His skin wasn't as dark as her own but didn't have the paleness of a man of Elden. His trousers and jacket were perfectly tailored and the gold embroidery on his green shirt caught the torchlight. She called up her *knowing* as gently as she could and the emotions of the others in the room hit her. Her father's anxiety overlaid by courage, the excitement and caution of the king. The Dark Man stiffened and turned from her father toward her. She withdrew her magic quickly, swallowing and biting her lower lip.

'Lord Fulmer.' Bractius got to his feet but a frown still marred his face. 'It is a long time since we have had a delegation from your islands. We have had no warning of your visit and – no offense – man, but such a small party might be mistaken for—'

'I'm no imposter.' Her father drew himself up and glanced at the Dark Man who leaned forward to whisper to the king. Kesta narrowed her eyes.

Bractius's face lit up in a wide and genuine grin and he held out his hand. 'Be welcome; what on earth happened to you, man? Who is your companion?'

Arrus Silene took the king's hand cautiously and then reached down to help her up. 'This is my daughter, Kesta Silene.'

She stood as gracefully as she could, and pulling back her hair, looked the king in the eyes. She pretended not to notice as he recoiled and hid her own expression with a curtsey. There was no ignoring the hiss from one of the guards though.

'Fire-Walker!'

The king recovered quickly and forced his smile to remain. 'Randle go and see to some refreshments for our guests. Come and sit, man, my lady; tell me why you're here.'

The Dark Man got slowly to his feet, watching Kesta like a hawk watching a vole. Her eyes widened, and she looked from him to her father, realising that the sorcerer was the taller of the two. There was no denying that he was a striking man, but the relaxed muscles of his face gave away no emotion and his eyes were so cold. She shivered.

'It is a … matter that might best be discussed privately.' Arrus sat at one of the benches toward the side of the room and to Kesta's surprise Bractius joined him. She seated herself at her father's other side and noted that the Dark Man had gone back to sitting beside the throne.

Bractius didn't hesitate and dismissed his guards at once. 'Go on.'

'As you know,' Arrus began slowly with a glance at the Dark Man. 'We have always been raided by warriors from the Borrows. Recently their attacks have become somewhat fiercer and more frequent and they've attempted to take more of our people captive. Some have tried to dig in and stay rather than just raid.'

Kesta forced herself to relax her muscles. Elden and the tiny Fulmer Islands had never actually been enemies; but they hadn't been friends either. They were all well aware that had Elden had more warlike kings, the islands would have been conquered long ago.

'If it were just the raiders, we would have dealt with it ourselves,' Arrus went on.

'Not just raiders, then?' Bractius focused on Arrus so intently he barely blinked.

Arrus shook his head. 'The last party had a Chemman sorcerer leading them.'

'A Chemman!' Bractius leapt up and looked over his shoulder at the Dark Man. It was widely whispered that the Dark Man was himself from Chem.

Arrus nodded as the doors were opened and the glowering Randle ushered in some servants. Bractius waved a hand for Arrus to stay quiet until all the food and the jugs of ale had been set out and the servants gone again.

'A one off?' King Bractius asked, narrowing his eyes at her father.

Arrus sat back down slowly, ignoring the food.

Kesta gave her father a chance to evade answering by standing to pour a cup of ale for the king and then for him. With only the slightest hesitation she poured another and took it to the Dark Man. She forced herself to meet his eyes and show no fear, although she could hear the rush of her blood in her ears. Neither of them spoke, but he gave a slight nod of thanks.

Arrus sipped his ale and glanced at Kesta. 'My wife, Dia, was able to help us defeat the sorcerer, but it was no easy task.'

'The Icante?'

All of them turned to look at the Dark Man.

'Yes, Lord,' Arrus replied. 'If the Borrows have allied with Chem instead of fighting them like they do everyone else, then the Fulmers are doomed. We ... I am not sure how many more sorcerers we could fight off alone.'

'So, you have come here for help?' Bractius looked her father up and down.

Arrus sagged. 'I had to swallow a lot of pride to come here, trust me. Then we were set on by thieves less than a day across Elden.'

'Your daughter wasn't hurt?' Bractius looked at her in concern. She was hardly surprised he'd assumed the worst considering the sorry state of them.

'She was not; nor I, except my pride. I hadn't realised your country was so hostile.'

'I am ashamed to admit we have our … difficulties. And my guards treated you like vagabonds when you got here.' Bractius sighed. He glanced at the Dark Man. 'I'm going to have to think about this. I won't not help you, but I'm going to have to consider what steps to take and their consequences. You will accept my hospitality of course and stay here until we have something resolved? You will join me for dinner tonight?'

Kesta saw her father glance down at his soaking wet and muddy clothes. The muscles of his jaw moved. To save his pride, she spoke first.

'Sire, we have only what you see us in. We would not wish to dishonour you by turning up to your table looking like this.'

Bractius stared at her for a moment and then shook himself. 'Of course, my lady, we will recompense you for your poor reception in our kingdom.'

The king's sorcerer had slipped away to a door and was speaking with someone outside. Moments later he let a middle-aged woman through.

'Ah!' Bractius beamed. 'This is Rosa, one of my wife's ladies-in-waiting, she will see to your comfort.'

The older woman smiled and curtseyed. 'My Lord, my Lady, if you would follow me?'

'Jorrun and I will see you soon.' Bractius dismissed them.

***

'What did you think?' her father had come to her room wearing a heavy woollen robe as soon as they were left alone. She looked longingly at the hot bath that had been filled for her. She quickly picked up a small pastry and contented herself with trying to quell the pain of hunger from her belly. The small mug of ale had left her feeling a little light headed, and she tried not to show it.

'I couldn't use my *knowing*,' she apologised. 'The Dark Man sensed it straight away. I like Bractius but ...'

'But?'

She studied her father's face, knowing that he wouldn't like what she was going to say. 'I like him, he is friendly and seems kind, but I fear he may also be weak. As we have seen ourselves, he allows brigands to roam his land. Is he strong enough to stand up to what we have seen coming from the Borrows? I'm not so sure. But ... the Dark Man now, he is another matter. I felt it was he who controlled the throne room.'

Arrus nodded. 'Sadly, that's my surmise also. I wonder if Chem, or the Borrows even, would have tried to conquer Elden long ago if that sorcerer hadn't washed up on their shores. Jorrun did he call him? That certainly sounds Chemmish. I wonder what he'll demand for his aid.'

'Are we going to have any choice but to pay it?'

Arrus looked at her thoughtfully. 'If it were no more than that one sorcerer then I would have faith that you and your mother could keep us safe.'

'You should have told Bractius of our *walking*.'

He absently picked up a pastry. 'You saw how they reacted when they saw what you are; not to mention the townsfolk we've passed. I'm not sure they'd trust what you and Dia have seen in the flames. I think we should keep your magic as secret as possible for now.'

Kesta recalled the images she'd seen in her *fire walking* and put her pastry down, all appetite gone.

'Bractius trusts the Dark Man with his life and his kingdom,' she said. 'That much I sensed.'

'Yet the Dark Man is hated and feared. I must admit he made me feel incredibly uncomfortable. Yet what can we do? If Elden will not help us, we will become another island of the Borrows and slaves to the necromancers of Chem.' He chewed on his pastry and then without warning bent and kissed Kesta's forehead. 'I'm keeping you from food and warmth. Learn what you can at dinner and we'll talk again in the morning.'

She waited until he left and then after cramming a pastry into her mouth, she peeled off her wet clothes and sat with a splash in the bronze bath. She let out a long sigh and closed her eyes, trying to ignore the sting of her blisters and the ache of her bruises.

Realising that she was starting to veer towards self-pity she ducked her head down under the water and scrubbed at her hair. The sensation of being clean and warm again was beyond bliss. It was a few hours until evening, so she risked laying down on the soft bed and letting herself drift into sleep.

She awoke to soft knocking and Rosa opened the door and called, 'My Lady?'

Kesta got up quickly and beckoned Rosa in.

'I've brought a few of my gowns that I think might suit you.' Rosa backed into the room almost hidden by a mound of glimmering taffeta.

'*Your* gowns?'

Rosa halted, and her face started to redden. 'Your pardon, my lady, I didn't mean to offend. I haven't had time to have anything bought. I'm afraid they may be a bit short for you but should fit otherwise—'

'I meant only that you are kind,' Kesta said hastily. 'I am grateful for anything you can lend me.'

Rosa smiled, but she fidgeted and avoided looking Kesta in the eye.

'What would you suggest?' Kesta asked.

'Oh! Well; you have such beautiful eyes that I'd have said green, but your dark hair and skin would really suit red.'

Kesta turned sharply to look at her, thrown by the unexpected compliment. 'Oh.' She swallowed. 'I think green will do; I most often wear green.'

'What is Fulmer like?' Rosa asked with genuine interest as she dropped the gowns on the bed and picked out the two green ones.

'I live on the north side of the main island where the forest grows thick and the cliffs are high,' Kesta said as she combed out her hair. She didn't really feel like talking but this woman didn't deserve rudeness. 'We have a fortified holding that stands on a small peninsular on the cliff edge and nearly a hundred warriors. The islands are less cultivated than what I've seen of Elden, most of it is left alone to be wild.'

'I hear that there are dangerous animals there and that ...' The woman faltered, and her face reddened.

'*Walkers* tame the animals?' Kesta glanced at her and took one of the gowns. 'Animals don't harm us; we don't harm animals.'

'So, you really can control animals, Lady Silene?' Rosa handed her one of the dresses.

'It's just Silene. *Silene* is my title, we put our titles after our names as they are *what* we are and not *who* we are.'

Rosa regarded her with wide eyes, her shoulders drawn in tight toward her body. Kesta sighed. A few days and this would be over, and she'd be able to go home.

'Thank you for the dress,' she tried.

Rosa gave a shrug. 'Would you like me to help you into it?'

What she really wanted was to be left alone and not have to deal with the court of Elden.

'Yes, please.' She tried to give a friendly smile, but it felt false even to her. She hesitated a moment and then called up her *knowing.* The emotions she felt from Rosa were the slight nausea of embarrassment and a tang of fear. As gently as though she were unpeeling a spider web one strand at a time, she eased away the woman's anxieties and sent her tendrils of warmth.

'This is a lovely dress; did you make it?' It was a simple robe with a long, full skirt and straight sleeves. It laced at the back and had a sensibly high neck line, but it wasn't far off the right size, just a little short and loose about the waist.

'No, Queen Ayline bought this one for me. It matches one of your …' Rosa faltered and bit her lip but Kesta laughed and Rosa soon laughed nervously with her.

'It would be a strange dress that matched both my eyes.' Kesta squeezed the older woman's arm reassuringly and then looked at the door, her heart sank.

'Let me see how your father is doing and I'll walk you both down.'

***

Kesta could hear the noise of the main hall long before she reached it and she instinctively clamped down tight on her *knowing*. A herald stood at the entrance and she could smell a boar roasting. Musicians were playing, and she heard the loud, rolling laughter of the king. The hairs on the back of her neck prickled, and she turned to come face to face with the Dark Man. He looked down at her; his expression perfectly controlled and giving away nothing. Daringly she challenged him by calling back her *knowing*. She sensed at once the shift in his own power; it was almost as though the man before her was made of a cold wind. She'd never felt anything like it before. His gaze did not so much as flicker.

'Lord Arrus, Silene of the Fulmer Islands, and his daughter; Kesta Silene.'

She turned quickly to take her father's arm as he strode into the room. His borrowed clothes stretched across his broad shoulders. He made his way confidently toward the high table. Bractius stood to meet them and came around to clasp Arrus' wrist like an equal. She wondered how much of that greeting was politics and how much the king's own warm nature. She started when she realised that the Dark Man was standing right beside her. She tried to hide how unnerved she felt; even another *fire-walker* couldn't do that. The slightest of smiles touched the corner of his mouth and she turned away clenching her jaw and fists.

'This is Queen Ayline,' Bractius introduced as he offered Arrus the seat to the right of the Queen. She was no more than seventeen but possessed a polished confidence that suggested she'd been raised for her role. She was a little shorter than Kesta and pale as cream with hazel eyes and chestnut hair.

'Welcome to Elden.' She smiled. 'I was sorry to hear that you had such a bad journey.'

Bractius pulled out the chair to his left and offered it to Kesta as the queen chattered away to her father. The Dark Man sat to Kesta's left and watched her as though waiting for her to protest at his proximity. Gritting her teeth and ignoring him she focused on the king.

'So; have attacks from the Borrows increased here in Elden?' she asked.

Bractius grinned. 'Straight to the point! You were right, Jorrun!'

'Right about what?' Kesta demanded.

Bractius's smile faded a little, and she felt his uncertainty as he tried to gauge how much he'd offended. She tried a smile herself and Bractius visibly relaxed.

'Jorrun said that the women of the Fulmers are as involved in the defence of the islands as the men. I was going to seat you next to Ayline as I thought you might have things to talk about; but Jorrun suggested you would be more at home with us.'

Kesta still couldn't sense anything from the Dark Man and the urge to turn around and look at him was incredibly strong. She could imagine his cold blue eyes on her and she suppressed a shiver.

'As only woman are *fire-walkers* and the Icante rules the islands, it makes sense to involve us in all things,' Kesta replied politely. 'Please excuse me if we are not meant to talk politics at dinner, it's just that the matter is so urgent to us.'

Bractius opened his mouth to speak but Jorrun interrupted him. 'As it is to us. Am I right in surmising that there's more to your story? Have you *seen* something?'

She hesitated, gazing into Bractius's brown eyes and refusing to turn to the Dark Man. 'Yes, I have,' she said slowly, going against her father's advice. 'When I *walked,* I saw a Chemman necromancer overseeing the loading of a ship on the rocky shores of one of the Borrows.'

Jorrun spoke again. There was a very subtle accent to his voice, a purr to his rs. 'Then your fears of the attacks not being a one off are well founded.'

'They are,' she turned slightly toward the Dark Man.

'What do you think?' Bractius asked his friend over her head.

'I think I have a lot of work to do tonight.' Jorrun snorted. 'But you have not said all.'

Kesta heard the Dark Man move toward her. Her muscles tensed, and she still refused to turn.

'What else did you see? What is it that keeps you awake at night and set your father running for Elden?'

She spun about in her chair to face him. 'How do you know that? How do you know …' She clenched her teeth and fought to keep her temper under control. With her *knowing* loose she could accidently transfer her feelings to those around her and start a fight in the king's dining hall. Jorrun raised an eyebrow, and she felt an overwhelming urge to punch his perfectly poised face. She drew in two slow, deep, breaths and closed down her magic. Turning her back on the Dark Man again she addressed Bractius and saw that both her father and Queen Ayline were watching her.

'I saw … I saw that the men boarding the ship were Borrow men; but they were dead Borrow men.'

'Dead?' Bractius shook his head with a frown.

Kesta bit her lip and then tried to describe them. 'They had wounds they shouldn't have survived. They moved as though they'd forgotten how to do so. There was little colour to their skin, and I thought that perhaps their blood did not flow.' She drew her arms tightly around her body and swallowed. Her throat constricted, and she had to force her next words out. 'My *knowing* does not work that well over distance and while *walking* the flame but even so, I felt no life in them. Nothing.'

'Please excuse me.' The Dark Man got to his feet and strode out of the hall.

Kesta's mouth fell open a little, and she sat back in her chair, her eyes following him out of the room. Bractius placed a hand on her arm. 'Don't mind him. Tell me; it took you how long to get here?'

'Nearly seven days.' She turned her attention back to the king, her eyes flickering across his face.

'So, this ship could already be attacking the Fulmers. And why did you not tell us your full plight?'

'We were concerned that our magic would worry or offend you.' Arrus answered for her. 'I'm sorry, but we don't know you but by rumour and Elden has little reason to help us. We are a self-sufficient people and there's little we can offer in payment, as I'm sure you know.'

Bractius looked away and his face coloured slightly. 'I'm sure that we can come up with something; besides, we're all very well aware that conquering the Fulmers would be but a step toward attacking Elden.'

Arrus nodded. 'This is something big, we're sure of it.'

'Please, Arrus, Kesta, I know it's easier said than done but trust me a few hours longer. Come on, eat, drink, try to enjoy the music. We are all friends here.' He lifted a chalice of wine and saluted Arrus.

Kesta looked at her father and nodded. There was nothing else they could do but wait to hear what the king of Elden was willing to offer them.

She noticed that Jorrun's plate had been left unused and empty. The discomfort in her stomach reminded her that she hadn't eaten either. She looked about the table at the dishes and spotting an aubergine stuffed with cheese, olives, and tomato, moved it onto her plate. Queen Ayline was doing a good job of drawing her father away to safe topics and she could feel him relaxing. Kesta's eyes kept going to the empty seat to her left, and she noticed Bractius doing the same.

'Kesta, you look as though you're asleep with your eyes open.' Bractius gave her a polite nudge and in that unguarded moment, as she met his eyes, she felt an overwhelming warmth for the Elden King. 'Go on to your room; I'll not be offended.' He squeezed her hand.

'Your majesty, I apologise—'

'No, I apologise. I apologise that the Fulmer Islands felt they had to wait until they were desperate to come to me for help. Go and sleep, my lady, in a bed that is safe.'

Kesta swallowed and refused to let herself give in to emotion at the king's kindness. With a smile at her father she stood and gave the king and queen a curtsey before retreating from the hall.

A young page who was waiting beyond the door offered to light her way to her room with his torch and she accepted. As good as she was out in the wilds at finding her way, she felt completely lost within the stronghold of Taurmaline. Once in her room, she slid the bolt forcefully across the door and going to the shutters, opened them wide. She was perhaps four stories up and high enough to look over the stone walls of the city toward Lake Taur. The storm was still blowing, and rain lashed through the open window. Thunder growled somewhere to the north and her thoughts flew to her people and especially to her mother. She was a long, long way away and whatever the fate of her people there was nothing she could do for them now; nothing except beg from a king who was the puppet of a sorcerer of Chem.

The page had lit a branch of candles for her and moving away from the window she sat and gazed into the flames. Calling up her power she lost herself in the flickering light, and concentrating hard on a point inside her skull, she triggered the 'switch' in her brain that allowed her to *walk*. She thought of her home and moments later she could see the walls of Fulmer Hold from the watchfire set above it on the cliffs. She tried to force the image closer, and the pain made her gasp; she almost lost her grip on the vision. It felt as though someone had inserted a huge needle through her skull and was continuing to twist and push it. There was always a small amount of pain involved in *fire-walking,* but she hadn't experienced anything like this since she'd first attempted it as a child. She could only guess that it was down to the distance.

Forcing herself to take slower breaths she defied her body's attempts to shut down her consciousness and with a sudden jolt, her vision moved to the nearby beach. What she saw hurt more than pain. Warriors of the Fulmers lay strewn along the shore with jagged wounds in ripped flesh and scattered limbs. The sea foam appeared almost golden and looking up she saw that it was reflecting the light of a burning ship. It was not a ship of the Fulmers. Movement caught her eye and her heart gave a leap of joy when she recognised her mother moving carefully toward the trees, supported by her uncle.

Something huge lurched toward them. It was man-shaped but there was something horribly wrong with the way it moved. It swung a monstrous hand toward her fleeing family and her uncle spun about with his sword and took the creature's arm off at the elbow. It didn't even pause. It grabbed her uncle and threw him across the shingles. Birds flew up out of the forest to flap about it, but it paid them no heed as it jerked after her mother. Kesta watched helplessly, her heart pounding and her nails digging into her palms. Then a bright light shot toward the man-beast and it caught fire in an instant. Her uncle had scrambled to his feet and both he and her mother vanished into the trees. As the monster crumpled and burnt, the small light moved away; it altered shape and for a moment it almost looked like a tiny man.

'Demon!' Kesta gasped.

The candles went out, and the room was plunged into darkness.

***

She awoke with her brain pulsing inside her skull. Her cheek was pressed against the carpet, her head too heavy to lift.

'My lady? Oh, my goodness!'

She heard Rosa fighting to close the shutters and the sound of the wind and rain became fainter. She tried to rise, and she felt hands slide beneath her torso to help her.

'What happened? I'll fetch the healer!'

'No.' Kesta's tongue was dry and too large for her mouth. 'No, I'm all right. I was just so tired after my journey I fell asleep right there in the chair and must have slipped off.'

Rosa narrowed her eyes but chose not to argue. 'Shall I at least tell your father?'

'No; honestly, I am fine. What time is it?' It was hard to tell in the stone room with the shutters closed.

'It's yet four hours until midday. I thought I'd pop in early to leave you the day dresses Ayline ordered from the city; they are not tailored I'm afraid.'

'I am very grateful for anything. Do you know if the king will see us yet?'

'Her majesty was getting ready to go down to the audience room when I left her. Is there anything I can get you? Some hot water or some breakfast?'

Kesta almost retched at the thought of food. 'No, I best dress quickly and wake my father. I want to know ...' she looked at the older woman realising that she'd been about to confide in a stranger. *Well, why not?* 'I want to know if the king will help us.'

'Of course!' Rosa drew herself up straighter. 'Red for today?' She went to the pile of four dresses that she'd all but dropped on finding Kesta on the floor.

Kesta nodded and patiently allowed the woman to help her get ready.

Rosa led her to her father's room and Kesta knocked on the door. Her father had been lent a page by King Bractius and it was the boy who let Kesta in. Her father was striding up and down the room. He took one look at her and shooed the boy out.

'Kesta?'

'I *walked* last night! Fulmer Island was attacked, and I think mother was hurt; though she was alive the last I saw. Those creatures were there – the dead Borrowmen; many of our warriors are dead, but our enemy's ship was destroyed and ... there was a demon there. It killed our attackers!'

'A demon?' Arrus gripped her arms and looked down into her face. 'Describe it.'

'It looked to be a tiny man made of flame.'

'Chem magic!' He growled. 'But it makes no sense for them to attack us and help us. Unless it was a Borrow raid and—'

'No, father, they were the dead men that I saw before.'

'Let's get to the king.'

Arrus almost bowled the poor page over as he flung the door back open and strode down the hall to the stairs. The boy tried to scurry ahead but ended up being caught awkwardly between Arrus and Kesta on the stairs before choosing to run when they reached the bottom. He got to the audience room about half a minute before them; enough time for them to be announced and invited to go straight in. Several people were waiting outside the audience room and Kesta saw their angry and curious looks. The guards closed the doors behind them and from the expressions on the King and Queen's faces Kesta could see that this meeting was to be entirely formal. The Dark Man sat in his usual seat to the king's left and Kesta's feet faltered when she saw his face. His skin was pale and dark circles traced his eyes; he looked as though he hadn't slept in weeks.

'Lord Arrus, Lady Kesta.' Bractius looked down on them without standing. 'You deserve nothing less than a direct response to your petition. I've thought very carefully over the implications of the attacks on the Fulmers and I can't imagine that Chem will stop at conquering the islands. We received further information last night that confirmed your fears that Chem has set out to conquer the Borrows.'

Arrus nodded grimly. Kesta's eyes narrowed as she wondered what the information was and how they'd gained it. Instinctively she reached for her *knowing*, but with a glance at the Dark Man she stopped herself.

'However.' Bractius leaned forward. 'We would be better served saving our resources to prepare to defend Elden than send them to aid a people who have declined, for years, to ally with us or even make official trade agreements.'

The king's words hit Kesta like a punch to the stomach. She drew in a sharp breath and bit down hard on her lower lip. Her father clenched his fists and took a step forward.

'Hear me out, Lord Arrus.' Bractius raised a hand quickly. 'Despite that, I cannot stand by and allow innocent people to be slaughtered. We may just as well fight off the Chemmen on the Fulmers as here in Elden. And there is one trade we can make that will bind our countries without the need for fancy drawn out agreements. If she marries Jorrun and ties your family to Elden, you will have five hundred warriors and two ships to take back with you to Fulmer. The price for our aid is your daughter.'

Kesta stopped breathing. For a moment, the room seemed to swim away from her and her vision blurred, nausea crawled through her stomach. She spun around to look at her father who stood frozen; his face turning red. She couldn't even find her voice to protest; they were trapped, and they knew it. She forced herself to look up at the sorcerer, but his face gave nothing away.

'You don't know what you're asking.' Her father's voice came huskily through his tightened throat muscles. 'On the Fulmers we do not give away our daughters.'

Bractius shook his head and gave a puzzled smile. 'We are granting you both a great honour, as well as our aid. Your islands, although dear to you, have little to offer Elden in real terms. Your daughter is the only thing of value that you can offer. Such an alliance makes sense. If you want my help, that's the price.'

Kesta clenched her fists, she felt her throat constrict and her nostrils flare as she forbade her body to betray her. Blood seemed to leave her fingers and muscles to burn at her face and neck. It felt like an eternity that she stood there with her blood roaring in her ears. Although he had no right to make the decision for her, Kesta couldn't move her tongue and so her father spoke.

'We have no choice,' Arrus said through gritted teeth. 'You know that.'

Then he gave way to his unhappiness. He grabbed Kesta's hand, and they fled the audience hall.

Chapter Three

Kesta; Kingdom of Elden

She knew her father needed to speak with her, but she didn't care. She went straight to her room and slammed the door behind her. Tears sprang to her eyes, and that made her even more furious and grabbing blindly at the edge of the table she flipped it over; the dishes and candles making a satisfying crash. Her eyes fell on the dresses and snatching one up she gripped the fabric to tear it, her teeth clenched in a snarl. It refused to rip and hurling it across the room gave no relief.

Trapped.

She sat heavily on the edge of the bed, her heart pulsing against her lungs.

But what else could they do? Without help the Fulmers would be conquered; even with Elden their chances looked bleak. But to be forced into marriage ... she was aware such things still happened in Elden but in her own islands it had always been for the woman to choose. And to the Dark Man! She shuddered, wiping her eyes roughly with the heal of her hand. Was there any honourable way out of this without condemning her people to death? If it had been Bractius himself, she could possibly have lived with it.

She went to the window and opened the shutters; breathing in the cold air in deeply. She realised she was shaking, and she wrapped her arms around herself. The rain had finally stopped, but the wind was still fierce. She looked down at the courtyard below; a wagon full of eggs was being unloaded and laughter drifted up in snatches. All of a sudden it hit her hard that she might never go home again. The strength went out of her muscles and she sagged against the stone wall, her vision obscured by sparks of red, and pain stabbed behind her eyes.

There was a timid knock, but she ignored it, growling deep in her throat. The door opened, and she heard a small gasp.

'May I bring you anything?' Rosa asked.

Kesta glanced around briefly but her throat muscles tightened. She heard the older woman grunt as she righted the table and then the glug of liquid into a glass. Rosa approached her as cautiously as she would a wild animal and held a glass of brandy out to her.

'I heard that you have been offered a political marriage,' she said. 'I might be wrong … but I'm guessing you're not too happy?'

Despite herself Kesta laughed. She reached out and took the brandy.

'Thank you. I'm sorry for the mess.'

'His majesty is talking to your father at the moment.'

'Is the D … is Jorrun with them?'

She shook her head. 'May I talk freely to you, my lady?'

'Always.' Then out of the corner of her eye she saw the mess she'd made of the room. Tentatively she called up her *knowing;* understandably Rosa was nervous, even a little afraid, but she could sense nothing but a desire to help. She wondered what in the spirits' name she'd done to deserve sympathy; especially considering her behaviour.

'Lord Jorrun is … he is quite daunting.' Rosa looked out of the window rather than at her. 'He's powerful, but no one knows anything about the magic he uses except maybe the king. He's very ... solitary. It's said he spends hours, days even, hidden away in his Raven Tower and no one knows what he does there. If it's any consolation to you, I've never heard of him treating anyone badly. He is strict in adherence to the laws of the land and expects the same of everyone and as such, his rulings in court are often harsh. But that said, he and the king are close, and I don't think Bractius would be friends with a bad man.' She looked at Kesta earnestly with her large brown eyes. Fine wrinkles lined her face and there were strands of grey in her tawny hair.

'Thank you.' Kesta took a swallow of the brandy, savouring the burning sensation in her throat. It was sweet, and she could taste honey. Rosa's words had not reassured her at all, but the woman's kindness had left her feeling a little calmer; almost numb. 'I hope the queen doesn't mind me borrowing you?'

'Not at all,' Rosa gave a wince. 'She has ladies her own age. Shall we see what we can salvage of this room?'

They re-set the candles and picked up the pieces of broken crockery and scattered fruit. The pastries had made more of a mess and they dropped the pieces into the fireplace. They were just shaking out the dresses when the door shook with an abrupt knocking. With a scowl, Rosa went to open it and stepped back as Arrus strode straight in.

'Kesta, I'm so sorry!'

Rosa hesitated in the doorway and Kesta gestured for her to come back into the room as her father enveloped her in a bone-breaking hug. He lifted her chin to look at her red, swollen eyes and shook his head.

'Bractius thought he was doing us a great honour offering you such a powerful marriage and his aid. He tells me that he didn't know what an insult it would be in the Fulmers to force a woman to marry, let alone a *walker.*' He sighed. 'Despite that he won't change the offer and I—'

'We can't say no.' Kesta tried to reassure him despite her own feelings. 'The islands come before one woman; even a *walker.*'

Her father looked at her, the muscles in his face moved as he ground his teeth, his cheeks flushed. 'There is something else. I need to get back the Fulmers as soon as possible. Bractius tells me that he can have his men mustered and ready to travel with me in two days. Jorrun also insists that he has important work to do and cannot tarry here. The wedding is to take place in two days.'

Rosa quickly grabbed the decanter off the table. Kesta didn't miss a beat and snatched up the candlesticks instead.

'Two days!'

Arrus took a step back.

'Did you not at least insist that they save the Fulmers first before you hand me over?'

He took another step back and dropped a heavy pouch onto the table. He cleared his throat. 'Thane Jorrun has sent you some money so that you can purchase what you need for the wedding.'

She picked up the pouch and threw it straight out of the window. Rosa gave a cry of alarm and even her father gasped.

'I'll give you a moment to take it in.' Arrus, for all his size and strength, almost scuttled to the door. 'I'm afraid we are expected at dinner tonight.'

The candlestick struck the back of the door as it closed.

Rosa ran to the window and looked down as Kesta clenched her teeth and fists. She took in short deep breaths but couldn't stop the hot tears flooding her vision and spilling down her cheeks.

'Hey you!'

Kesta startled at the volume from the older woman.

'Bring that money up here at once and you'll be rewarded; try to take it and you'll lose both hands!'

She turned to see Kesta looking at her with her mouth open; she blushed and then shrugged. 'My lady, I hope you don't mind me saying ... I respect your independence and pride; but there is more than one way to show it. When you marry Jorrun, you must look and act like a queen and show him from the start that is how you expect to be treated. Do you understand what I mean?'

Kesta clamped her mouth shut and tilted her head to regard the older woman. As much as she wanted to let her anger out and show her defiance, she could see that what Rosa suggested was a much more mature and reasonable way of handling things. No amount of candle throwing was going to change her situation. But she needed an outlet for her turmoil of emotions.

'I really need some air.' She exhaled loudly.

'If you give me a moment to fetch you a cloak and make sure that man is on his way up with your money, we could take a walk around the lake? If we go northward away from the wharves, there should be fewer people; especially on a wild day like this.'

'I would be grateful.' Kesta nodded.

While she waited for Rosa to return, she placed the candlestick back on the table and swapped the soft black slippers she'd been lent for her sturdy walking boots that reached almost to her knees. Rosa came back in with the barest of knocks. She was already wearing a long grey cloak, and she handed Kesta a black woollen one and then held out the pouch of coins.

'I gave that scoundrel two gold; though I'm sure he would have made off with it all if I hadn't caught him.'

'I did throw it away.' Kesta shrugged.

Rosa bit her lip and regarded her cautiously 'Will you be willing to let me take your measurements later?'

Kesta smiled and snorted. 'I promise to behave.'

They made their way down through the castle ignoring the curious looks they received.

'What would you wear for a wedding in the Fulmers?' Rosa asked.

She really, really didn't want to talk about it. She closed her eyes and clenched her teeth, drawing in a deep breath. She knew it wasn't fair to take it out on Rosa. 'Usually something quite simple but we dress it up with flowers and vine leaves; or berries in the autumn. What about here?'

'The more lace, silk, and jewellery the lovelier the bride is considered.' Rosa frowned. Their eyes met, and both women laughed nervously.

Rosa opened a door into the kitchen courtyard. Kesta almost coughed at the smoke and metal tang of the air.

'It will be better away from the city,' Rosa said, seeing her expression.

They left through a wooden gate and followed a narrow, cobbled, road downward. They passed a loaded wagon and a group of women carrying baskets of fish. Rosa turned off the path and descended a set of steep steps to a wider street that followed the city wall. It was lined with houses, made of the same stone as the wall and the castle, that backed against the hill. Some people had built awnings outside their homes and sat beneath them plying their trades. There was a cobbler and a net mender, a baker, and a potter. Three women sat together sewing and Rosa wished them a good morning.

The way became busier and Kesta clamped down tight on her *knowing*. Rosa moved closer to her and steered her toward a wide set of steps that led down to a plaza in the centre of which stood a well.

'That's the way down to the wharves.' Rosa pointed. 'But we'll take the Forest Gate to the north rather than Lake Gate.'

They crossed the plaza, zigzagging through the crowd. Despite not using her *knowing*, Kesta felt goose bumps run up her arms and twice she glanced over her shoulder. She could see nothing amiss and put it down to being surrounded by so many people.

When eventually they squeezed their way through the Forest Gate, Kesta's nerves were completely on edge. Rosa took them straight off the gravel road and onto the grass and headed toward the lake. There were a few small boats pulled up on the muddy shore and a group of young children ran through the lacy edge of the shallow water; but for the most part it was as quiet as Rosa had promised.

'Is it far to the forest?' she asked, searching the horizon with her eyes.

'About a day if you rode; just a few hours by lake. The Raven Tower is deep within the forest,' she added hesitantly.

'Well at least that's something,' Kesta murmured. She glanced back toward the road; there was a man standing there looking down toward the lake. He appeared to be wearing a guard's uniform of some kind and she dismissed him as harmless.

They wandered along the shore in companionable silence. Kesta tried not to let her mind wander to her future or dwell on what she might have to endure. Instead, she fell to wondering what had become of her mother and uncle and if they would send word by messenger to Taurmaline. *Fire-walking* too far and too often was incredibly dangerous and could lead to a coma; part of her thought it would serve everyone right if she was unconscious for her wedding!

'I should have thought of organising a picnic, so we could go further,' Rosa said.

'Oh, are you hungry? We can go back, I don't mind.'

'Oh, no, I'm fine!' Rosa reassured her. 'I was just thinking of later. Perhaps it's something we could do tomorrow if the rain stays off?'

Kesta nodded; reminded at once that tomorrow would be her last day of freedom. She gazed across the open lake, so wide that she could not see the further shore. The water was a sullen grey matching both the sky and her spirits. As she turned to look back toward the castle, she exclaimed, 'That man is following us!'

Rosa stepped forward to stand beside her. 'He is wearing the livery of the Raven Tower.'

Kesta strode toward him. The man visibly startled but drew himself up to stand his ground. He was perhaps in his mid-forties with thinning hair shorn close to his scalp. He was about five feet ten inches and erring toward broad; muscle softening toward fat.

'Why are you following us?' Kesta demanded. 'Who are you?'

'I am Merkis Tantony, my Lady.' He rose up onto the balls of his feet and gave a slight bow; his grey eyes never leaving hers. 'Thane Jorrun asked me to see to your safety'

'My safety!' she glanced at Rosa who was almost hiding behind her. 'You mean he wanted to make sure I didn't leave.'

Tantony cleared his throat, politely lifting a fist to his lips. 'No, ma'am, his orders were to make sure that no one bothered you.'

'Is he expecting someone to bother me?'

Tantony blinked but didn't look away. 'I was led to believe that you and your father were attacked on your way across Elden?'

'That was out in the wilds. Surely you don't expect bandits right here in Taurmaline?'

'Not bandits, no,' he replied evasively.

Kesta's eyes narrowed, and she called up her *knowing*. The stocky man was uncomfortable and nervous; he wasn't used to dealing with what he considered a 'highborn women' and he wasn't sure what to expect from her. More than that, there was a real fear of failing the Dark Man. A real fear.

'Well, the only person who has bothered me is you, so you had better go.'

Tantony's skin reddened and Kesta felt a twinge of guilt; after all it wasn't this poor man's fault that Jorrun was being so controlling even before they got married.

'Maybe we should just pretend he isn't here,' Rosa suggested.

Kesta tried not to let herself be affected by the hope in Tantony's grey eyes.

'Has he told you to stop me doing anything?' she demanded.

He shook his head. 'No, I was just to follow you and keep you safe.'

'And if I was to set off right now for the Fulmers?'

'I'd have a long walk, ma'am,' Tantony replied quickly with a straight face.

'And why would he send his Merkis and not a mere warrior?'

'He ... trusts me, ma'am.'

'Well I don't,' she replied sharply. 'Come on, Rosa, we'll do as you say and ignore him.'

Kesta was fuming; how dare Jorrun treat her like a possession even before they were married! And did he really think that a woman of the Fulmers was defenceless? Then she remembered their supplies had been stolen by a gang of petty bandits and she felt a wave of shame. No wonder they thought she was weak and helpless.

She gave a shake of her head. 'Let's go back.'

'My Lady are you sure?' Rosa looked at her in concern. Even Tantony halted and watched her with a frown.

'Yes, it's getting cold.'

They skirted back along the lake and up to the gate, Merkis Tantony keeping a respectful distance behind. As they crossed the plaza Kesta became acutely aware of a sentient creature in distress. It battered against her *knowing* even though she'd closed it down. She heard the squeal of the pony before she saw it; it had collapsed on the ground beneath a load of heavy sacks. Its owner was trying to drag it up by its halter at the same time as lashing it with a thin stick. Kesta darted forward, grabbed the stick, and struck the man in the face with it.

'Let it go!' she snarled.

The furious man made to grab her, but she stepped aside and caught him by the wrist. At once she summoned her *knowing,* and she transferred all the pain and distress the pony was feeling into the man. He collapsed to the cobbles, clutching at his stomach and chest.

'Demon!' he accused through gritted teeth.

'That is what this poor creature is feeling!' Kesta spat. 'You have not fed her in four days. The load's too heavy and not evenly balanced! She's shoed poorly and on the verge of going lame!'

'Come away, ma'am, please!' Tantony appealed to her, aware of the growing crowd.

'She has so many bruises she can't remember when she last didn't hurt!' Kesta threw the stick at the man. 'I am buying this pony.'

The man tried, but failed, to get to his feet. 'It isn't for sale! How will I get the salt to my buyer?'

'I don't care.' Kesta took a step toward him and he shrank back. 'Do you know what we do to people who abuse animals on the Fulmers? We make them live for a year as that animal. If I *ever* hear of you hurting an animal again, I *will* come and find you.'

She held out her hand and Rosa hastily took out the coin pouch and placed two coins on her palm. Kesta threw them at the man.

'Your knife, Merkis.'

'My knife?' Tantony stared at her in alarm.

'Cut the load off that pony, man!' she ordered him.

Tantony scrambled to obey although she could make out a few mumbled curses as he worked. Kesta crouched by the pony's head and opened her *knowing* to it, letting it understand who she was and what she intended. She removed the halter and as soon as it was free of its load it stood, with some difficulty, and then followed behind Kesta as she made her way toward the castle. Both Rosa and Tantony stared after her open-mouthed for a moment, before glancing at each other and hurrying to follow.

'What are you going to do with it?' Tantony asked carefully after a while.

'*You* are going to see that it's stabled and fed and cared for by a good farrier. Then you can tell Thane Jorrun that it's coming to the Raven Tower.'

'I'm not sure—'

She spun around to glare at him and he closed his mouth quickly.

'Yes, ma'am.'

***

They left the reluctant Tantony, and the rescued pony in the kitchen courtyard and Kesta returned to her room with a heavy heart. It was hours yet until she had to face another dinner with Jorrun and the king's court and the room was already taking on the feel of a prison to her. Rosa seemed to sense her despair.

'My lady, I must make some arrangements for your dress. Can I get you some books, perhaps? Is there something that you would like to do to occupy your mind?'

'What I most want is to know how things fare in the Fulmers.' She sighed. 'I would be grateful for some books. I carve sometimes; but I'm not that good.'

'Leave it with me.' Rosa smiled, although she radiated concern. 'I will try not to be long.'

'I'll be fine.' Kesta forced a smile of her own.

When Rosa left, she dragged a chair over to the window and sat gazing over the wall to the lake. It was almost impossible not to let herself dwell on what her life would become but she fought again to turn her thoughts aside. As strong and adept as the warriors of Fulmer were, they were outnumbered many times over by the raiders of the Borrows. Add to them the necromancers and soldiers of Chem and they had the same chance of survival as a shrew in a bonfire. No matter which way she looked at it, no matter how she might wish she was somehow powerful enough to turn the tide, it all came to the same answer. Leaving in the night or even taking the drastic action of ending her life might free herself from an unhappy existence; but it would condemn her people to death not to mention bring shame and grief to her parents.

She was startled by a knock at the door. Whoever it was didn't open it, so she crossed the room to do so herself. Two young girls stood there bearing trays of food. They both looked terrified of her, so she threw out an aura of calm and invited them in. They placed the food out for her with shy smiles and then hurried back out of the room.

It was almost half an hour later when Rosa returned with her arms full. She'd brought a selection of books as well as some wood and a whittling knife.

'You are very resourceful.'

'It is a good idea to be indispensable at court.' Rosa pursed her lips.

'I don't think I could ever fit in here.' Kesta threw herself into a chair.

Rosa took in a deep breath and then sat down beside her. 'Queen Ayline looks out for her ladies; young as she is. However, Thane Jorrun usually only comes to Taurmaline once a week, if that. My Lady … Queen Ayline has agreed to allow me to go with you to the Raven Tower as your companion until you're settled. That is if you would like my company?'

Kesta looked at the older woman feeling overwhelmed and struggled hard not to show any weakness. 'That is a kind offer, but you don't have to come.'

'I want to.' Rosa glanced at her and then picked up one of the books. 'Would you like me to read to you while you try some carving?'

'I would like that very much.'

* * *

Rosa walked behind her and her father as they went down to the main hall for dinner. As before, King Bractius greeted them and Rosa slipped away to sit at one of the lower tables. Jorrun stood politely as she was seated but she avoided looking at him. For a while she made polite conversation with the king and queen and her father, but they were interrupted several times by Thanes and Jarls of the nearby strongholds of Elden who had been summoned to Taurmaline.

'I hear you were down in the city today.'

She started as the Dark Man spoke beside her. She glanced at him but refused to reply.

'We will not be able to take the pony with us on the ship.'

'I'm sure your man is resourceful enough to get her to the tower.'

'You do know that Tantony is a Merkis? He is the leader of my warriors and runs my stronghold for me.'

'I wouldn't care if he was king of all the world,' she retorted.

'No, I don't think you would.'

She looked up at him, but his focus was somewhere across the room. Instead she turned to Bractius.

'Your majesty, I must ask that you do not invite me to dine with you tomorrow night. I need to spend the time alone and would not wish to offend you by declining an invitation.'

The king's eyebrows went up, his eyes widened, and then slowly narrowed, but he nodded. 'Of course, it's your prerogative. This … must seem a very busy place compared to the islands.'

'It is indeed. You have had no word?'

'If I had I would have informed your father at once; of that I promise.'

She nodded and turned back to her plate, willing the king to finish his food and retire so that she could be released.

* * *

52

When she returned to the refuge of her room, she went straight to the window but could see nothing on this moonless night. Not a single star shone through the thick cloud. She knew that she shouldn't even try but as alone and desperate as she felt she couldn't resist the temptation to *walk*. She turned to the candles on the table and flexing the muscle within her skull and between her eyes she slipped her consciousness into the fire, focusing on her far away and beloved home.

The pain that hit her knocked her backward and off her chair, smacking her head hard against the floor. She managed to roll over onto her hands and knees and drag herself onto the bed. The anger she had clung to gave way to her fear, and a tear tickled her cheek. She tried to ignore the nausea in her stomach. One more day and then her life would no longer be hers. Only one more day.

She woke slowly; becoming aware of Rosa moving about the room. She'd opened the shutters and cool air breezed in with the scent of recent rain. She could smell porridge and sweet fennel tea and despite the throbbing of her head, hunger began to stir.

She sat up groggily and tried to get her mouth to work.

'Good morning, Rosa.'

'Oh, good morning, my Lady. I hope I didn't wake you?' She quickly fetched a dressing robe and helped Kesta into it.

'No, not at all. Is it late? I don't want to waste the day.' She looked out the window and saw that the sun was trying to peer between fast-moving clouds.

'It's early yet.' Rosa poured her some tea and after offering a pot of honey, sat to finish her own. 'I found that man Tantony lurking about at the foot of the stairs. He says he's sent someone with your pony on ahead to the Raven Tower. I've asked the kitchens to put a lunch together for us, so we can walk further out today. They can spare us a boy to carry it.'

'Why bother with a boy when we have a Merkis Tantony?' Kesta grinned.

Rosa tried to look concerned, but she couldn't help laughing. 'I'm not sure he'll put up with that.'

'He will if he wants to come with us.'

'Before we go, can I take some more measurements? I'll quickly pop down to the seamstress and be back within an hour.'

Kesta sighed and looked down into her cup. 'I know you're right and I should show some dignity, but it goes against my nature to go along with this meekly.'

Rosa snorted. 'My Lady, from what I've seen you do nothing *meekly*! I'm sure Thane Jorrun is well aware of your feelings on the matter. I wonder ...' She stopped herself and her eyes widened.

'No, go on,' Kesta reassured her.

'It makes me wonder what the king and Thane are truly planning,' she said carefully. 'The queen and her ladies are speculating that it must be the magic of the Fulmers that prompted their bargain for aid.'

'Because spirits know why any man would want to take on a demon-eyed harridan like me.' Kesta finished sourly.

'I think your eyes are amazing.' There was a hint of hurt in the older woman's tone. 'And I love that you're not afraid to show how you feel.'

'Well that's something I could never be accused of.' Kesta smiled wryly. 'I think it's safe to say Thane Jorrun didn't choose to take me on for my diplomatic skills. Come on, let's get these measurements done before I think about it too much and change my mind.'

***

Rosa hadn't yet returned when her father knocked urgently at the door. He stood looking at Kesta awkwardly for a while until finally, feeling sorry for him, she relented and stepped forward to hug him.

'Any news?' she asked.

'Nothing.' He shook his head and Kesta noted the dark circles around his eyes. 'Although the Dark Man says there has been no further attack on the Fulmers.'

'You have seen him today?'

'I met him and the king early to discuss our plans for the defence of the islands. You know, King Bractius is more astute than I first gave him credit for. They're just dealing with a merchant who is making a complaint, so I thought I'd pop up to see if you wanted to join us? I would value your input.'

Kesta hesitated. Ordinarily she would have jumped at the chance to be involved; however, she'd been looking forward to spending her last day of freedom out in the open with Rosa. Her father frowned at her in confusion.

'I had made plans for today ...'

Her father's smile faded, and she held back her desire to use her *knowing* on him to see how he was coping with their situation. Respecting a person's privacy was an important part of being a *walker* and sometimes it didn't pay to look too closely at what a person truly felt about you. Her father's anger and grief weren't things she could face at the moment, anyway. Guilt squirmed inside her belly, there wasn't much time left to spend with him, but the thought of having to speak with the Dark Man made up her mind.

'I'm so sorry, but I really need to be outside.'

He nodded and sighed. 'I understand.'

'Let me walk down with you.' She took his arm, and they made their way down toward the main hall.

Rosa was waiting outside, and Kesta had to stop herself from laughing out loud when she saw Merkis Tantony was carrying a large basket; the face he pulled would make anyone believe it was full of dung. Kesta kissed her father's cheek.

'May I call on you this evening before I go to dinner?' her father asked.

'Of course!' Kesta forced a smile but couldn't meet his eyes. She turned to Rosa and Tantony. 'Are you ready?'

'Yes!' Rosa replied enthusiastically.

'I don't see why we can't take a servant,' Tantony muttered as he followed them.

They took the same route as the day before down through the city to the Forest Gate. Rosa pointed out some of the traders, telling Kesta which ones were reliable, who charged too much, and which sold the best goods. Tantony trailed behind them and they ignored the occasional snort he made when he disagreed with something Rosa said.

The sky was a little overcast still as they skirted the lake but by the time they decided to sit and eat, patches of sunlight were breaking through. Rosa flicked out the blanket they'd brought and laid out the food. As Rosa described each dish, Kesta was surprised at how much had been packed and delighted that, other than a selection of sliced cold meats, it was all things she could eat. Rosa pulled out a flagon of wine and three small pewter chalices. Kesta looked up at the hovering Merkis to see his reaction as Rosa handed him some wine.

'Thank you for thinking of me.' He gave a small bow.

Kesta picked up a strange shaped parcel of batter and biting into it found it was a pleasant mixture of cheese and vegetables; the batter itself was slightly spicy.

'So how long have you been at court?' Kesta asked Rosa to make conversation.

'Thirty years.' Rosa winced. 'I was eight when I was sent to court to serve the old queen, Bractius' mother. I am the second daughter of a minor noble; one who had not managed to retain his fortune. I was of little value as a wife as things stood and a burden on my father's limited resources. Queen Myrtle agreed to take me on as a lady-in-waiting as she had a fondness for children. She taught me much, and I learnt to make myself indispensable.' Her shoulders rose as she took in a deep breath. 'When Myrtle died, the king dismissed most of the ladies back to their families but some of us were allowed to remain at court to help run the household and see to the things the king didn't want to have to bother with. When Bractius married and the new queen came to Taurmaline, she arranged to bring in her own ladies. There are only two of us left that once served Queen Myrtle, the rest have been married off to widowers who valued a woman who can run a household over the attractiveness of youth.'

Kesta looked at her and wondered how lonely her life must have been in a court of young women; always worrying if she'd be sent away or sold off to some man. No wonder she felt so much sympathy for her and was willing to travel with her to the Raven Tower.

Kesta glanced up at Tantony and saw that he was regarding Rosa intently.

'And what of you, Merkis?' she demanded. 'Don't just stand there blocking out the sun; have some food and tell us how long you've been at the Raven Tower.'

'Well.' He knelt awkwardly and Kesta saw that the position caused him pain. 'I was a Hirsir commanding a hundred men for King Dregden. Eight years ago, I was injured in a Borrowman raid and it took me a long time to recover.' He tore a hunk of bread in half and layered meat on it but Kesta could tell that he was hiding his discomfort at telling them of his weakness. 'I was awarded the position of Merkis for my services and sent to Northold – the Raven Tower – to command there on the king's behalf.'

'So, you were not originally Thane Jorrun's man?' Kesta asked in surprise.

'No.' Tantony's expression became guarded. 'He was given the Raven Tower at Northold when Thane Ragfin was killed alongside the late king.'

Kesta wanted desperately to ask more but part of her was afraid of the answer and she got the impression that the Merkis didn't want to speak about his Thane. Her heart gave a jolt when Rosa asked for her.

'Is he a hard man to command under?'

Tantony continued to chew his bread and stared off into the distance. 'He is a very private man. If things run smoothly, he's happy to leave us to it; he doesn't tolerate deception, theft, or fighting. When he first came to the stronghold, he sent away several servants and some of the warriors. One man he killed outright for something he heard he'd done. He is ... a cold man; but strangely easy to be loyal to.'

They sat – and in Tantony's case stood – in silence eating the food although Kesta had lost much of her appetite. She gazed out at the lake where small boats lifted and dipped on the wind-stirred water. She'd lived all her life surrounded by the sea; her life tied to the rhythm of its tides. The lake didn't smell the same; it smelt of mud and rotting leaves.

'Oh, ma'am.' Tantony turned to her. 'I arranged for some of my warriors to go ahead to the Tower and they are taking your pony with them. The farrier was happy for it to travel.'

'Thank you.' She shook herself out of her melancholy and smiled at the Merkis.

'Do you know the history of the Raven Tower?' Rosa asked her, perking up as well.

'No, I have never heard it,' Kesta admitted.

'It started life as a village and then grew to a stronghold.' Rosa poured them all some more wine. 'Many, many years ago the Thane of that stronghold was called Dagcarr. He was a great warrior, of course, and had not only driven off many raids from the Borrows but had led raids against them. It was even said that he'd led a successful raid along the coast of Chem. The king honoured him by making him a Merkis and then a Hersir of his warriors. The king had three daughters and the youngest of them had hair the colour of butter and eyes like a summer sky. Asta was only fifteen when Dagcarr persuaded the king to let him have her for his wife. Dagcarr was a very jealous man, and he didn't like his young and cheerful bride talking to other men. He killed one of his own warriors when he caught him gazing after her. It was he who commanded the building of the Tower to keep Asta locked away. For years she was kept there alone with only Dagcarr allowed to enter the Tower. The only other company Asta had were the ravens that came to settle in the rafters.

'The confinement turned Asta mad and one day she threw herself off the Tower. The king accused Dagcarr of causing her death and sent his warriors to slay him. Since that day they say that Asta's ghost haunts the Raven Tower and Dagcarr haunts the strongold. Allegedly the ravens still cry both their names.'

'Is that true?' Kesta demanded.

Tantony laughed out loud; it was a warm, deep sound. 'No, it's not true. The Tower was built purely for military purposes. The stronghold where the Raven Tower stands is actually called the Northold. It was a defensive position chosen to protect Taurmaline from invaders who might follow the river south. The Tower was built to overlook the forest and give a better view of the lake and the land all around. There was indeed a Thane Dagcarr who was Hasir to the king; he actually kidnaped the king's daughter after the king refused to let him have her. Dagcarr had designs of his own to become a Jarl and be elected king himself; as in the old ways. The king and his warriors pursued him and killed Dagcarr and all his warriors. They were too late to save the girl; she'd killed herself with a dagger rather than submit to Dagcarr.

'The Northold does have some dark history; but there are no ghosts, my lady.'

'Thank you, Merkis.' She looked at the man's weathered face more closely. His nose was a little crooked as though it had been broken and badly set, scars across one side of his jaw made his short grey beard uneven; but if you looked beyond his rough appearance, there was kindness in his grey eyes. She felt guilty that she'd sought to make things difficult for him, but she wasn't about to admit it. 'But I hope I am not expected to live locked away in that Tower; because I won't put up with that!'

'No one is allowed in the Raven Tower but Thane Jorrun.' Tantony's eyes went hard, like flint. 'Not even the servants can go in. My warriors carry instructions from Thane Jorrun to prepare the best room in what we call the Ivy Tower in the main stronghold for you. It's a nice room that gets much light.'

She looked down at her hands; trying to force away the rush of emotion as she pictured a cold stone room in an isolated forest stronghold full of strangers.

'Have you tried the hazel cake there?' Rosa reached over and squeezed her hand. 'It is made with mead and one of my favourite things.'

'I'll try it.' Kesta nodded and took in a deep breath.

***

They stayed until the sun made long shadows and the clouds began to cluster in gloomy knots. They packed away the remnants of their food and the three of them walked side by side back to the Forest Gate. The plaza was busy with stalls closing and people making their way home or looking for bargains among what was left of the now not so fresh foods. Merkis Tantony went ahead of them to push a path through the diminishing rush of people and back to the kitchen courtyard.

'Ladies.' Tantony gave a low bow. 'I have a quick errand to run and then I'll be back to lurk in the corridors.'

His face remained perfectly serious but Kesta knew him well enough now to recognise that he was being humorous.

'Well, we will be sure not to let ourselves be attacked or try to run away before you return.'

'I would be most grateful.' He turned and stalked rapidly away, the slightest of hitches in his gait.

'What would you like to do this evening?' Rosa asked cautiously as they made their way up the stairs to the castle guest rooms. 'Did you want my company, or do you want to be on your own? We … could join the queen and her ladies if you wanted.'

'I imagine it would be a good idea for me to make friends and allies here in Taurmaline.' Kesta sighed. 'But I really can't be doing with small talk and trying to be sociable; not tonight. I would be happy if you did stay and read to me for a while and maybe we could take dinner in my room?'

'I would be happy to.' Rosa turned to smile at her. 'I have a couple of errands myself that I must see to, so I'll pop to the kitchens on the way past to make arrangements. Shall I see if your father is about and let him know you've returned?'

'Yes; thank you.'

Kesta barely had time to build up the fire in the grate and take off her cloak before her father knocked and came in. He strode straight to her and gave her a hug that lifted her off her feet. He smelt of old leather, wood smoke, and the herbs of the cleansing scrub her mother made. She clung to him as she hadn't since she was a child and when he let her go, he turned to hide the glistening in his eyes.

'Thank you for doing this, Kesta.'

She knew how much it was twisting him inside that he had to let her, so despite her growing anger and fear, for once, she kept a firm hold on her temper. Instead she told him of the two tales she'd heard about the Raven Tower in order to try to amuse him, and of the room she was to have in order to reassure him.

'I will make the best of it that I can,' she said firmly and looked her father in the eye.

He forced a smile, but she couldn't completely hide her misery; not from him.

'And Rosa is coming with me.'

'You seem to have made friends with that woman rather quickly.' Her father frowned.

'I am capable of making friends.' She punched him softly in the arm.

'Of course, it's just that usually you're such—'

'Sea urchin! Go on, say it!' She grinned at him and he responded in kind. Then his face turned serious once again. 'My little Kesta; you'll be okay?'

'Mother raised me to be a *Walker;* you raised me to be a warrior. I'll be fine.'

There was a tentative knock at the door and Rosa opened it. 'Please excuse me, there was a page on his way up to fetch you for dinner, Lord Silene. Oh! Your pardon, I meant just *Silene.* I told him I'd let you know he's waiting outside your room.'

He nodded and turned to Kesta. 'You're sure you'll not come down for dinner? People will wonder why you're not there.'

Kesta drew herself up and opened her mouth for a sharp retort but Arrus laughed like a barking bull-seal and raised his hand. 'My daughter,' he said proudly. 'I'll see you tomorrow.'

Rosa set about lighting some candles as Arrus left but knew better already than to close the shutters to keep out the cold. Instead she moved the chairs closer to the fire so that she could read to Kesta there. Two firm knocks interrupted them, and Rosa frowned.

'Maybe they're bringing dinner early,' she said as she put down the book and went to the door. She stood back in surprise when she found Merkis Tantony standing there. He looked everywhere but at them and for a moment Kesta feared he'd been sent to force her to attend dinner after all.

'Forgive my intrusion.' He bowed and held out a large wineskin to explain his presence. He addressed Rosa, 'When we crossed the Forest Market you mentioned that you thought the best wine came from Renjal's stall. I myself love this red wine from Calina's small shop on the wharves. I know the wharves are not a place you ladies like to go,' he added hastily at Rosa's expression. 'However, I thought you might like to try it and would be interested in your opinion. It comes from Woodwick.'

He handed Rosa the skin.

'Oh, well, thank you.' Rosa turned to look at Kesta and shrugged.

'Thank you, Merkis.' Kesta stood. 'We will certainly let you know what we think.'

Tantony stood there awkwardly for a moment before bowing again and wandering slowly off. As Rosa closed the door Kesta let out her laughter.

'What?' Rosa demanded.

'I think the Merkis is a little taken with you!'

'What? No!' Rosa shook her head.

'If you say so.' Kesta grinned. 'Let's try that wine then.'

The wine was indeed very pleasant; almost velvety to drink with no bitterness. They had a companionable meal and for the most part Rosa did a good job of distracting her from thinking too much of the day to come. For the most part.

Chapter Four

Kesta: Kingdom of Elden

From the moment she awoke Kesta's heart began to race and although she felt unnaturally warm, a chill shivered across her skin. Her eyes searched the room and her desire to smash everything fragile was intense. Instead, she poured herself some wine and gulped it down. She went to the window and drew in several long breaths of cold air until the dizziness started to fade. She'd never before in her life felt so much like an animal in a trap. She swallowed and pinched hard at the bridge of her nose, forcing back the tears although her vision blurred. Pressure built against her throat, she wanted to roar everything out from her lungs, but her pride made her hold it back. By the time Rosa came to her door she was composed and also a little drunk.

'Is it okay if the servants bring in your bath water and breakfast?' Rosa asked, glancing around the room. She was wearing a dark-green velvet dress and her hair was coiled up on her head. She looked beautiful in a warm-hearted way; like someone you couldn't resist hugging.

'Yes, come on in.' For Rosa's sake she smiled.

The servants bustled about, clearing things away and replacing them with other things. Rosa sat in her chair by the fire and read to Kesta while she soaked herself in the hot water and washed her hair with rose oil and lemon juice. When she was dry, Rosa combed out her hair; humming softly to herself.

'If you put on your gown, I'll dress your hair for you,' Rosa said.

Kesta could almost feel the woman holding her breath to see if she would protest.

'All right.'

Rosa went to the bed and moved aside some soft cloth. Kesta sat up straight and her eyes widened when she saw the material beneath. It was a dark emerald green on which were embroidered many tiny leaves in a lighter, glittering, green. Rosa lifted it and she saw the cut of it was as simple as she'd suggested. It had a long, full skirt that trailed just a little behind, a low 'v' at the front that was filled with a dark-green lace, and long narrow sleeves.

'You made a dress that matches my eyes!'

Rosa nodded, and her own eyes crinkled in a smile.

'That must have taken hours to stitch!'

'I had four ladies working on it. Well try it on then!'

Kesta smiled despite herself and Rosa helped her into the dress. It was heavier than she'd expected but very soft. Rosa looked her up and down.

'Well?' Kesta demanded.

'Perfect.' Rosa breathed out. 'Now sit down and let me do your hair. Are you happy if I pin it up in coils? I have some snowdrops to dress it with.'

Kesta swallowed and nodded. A stone sat in the bottom of her stomach and she wished she hadn't eaten as her food was telling her in no uncertain terms that it wanted to come back up.

The door rattled a little with a light knock and two giggling young ladies-in-waiting stuck their heads around it.

'Can we come in?' one of them asked shyly.

'Kesta?' Rosa prompted.

She shrugged. 'Why not?'

The two girls came in and looked her up and down. They themselves were dressed in layers of silk and lace with jewels at their throats and ears. Kesta steeled herself for their scorn.

'You look very elegant,' the younger of the pair said seriously.

'Your hair is so shiny and soft,' the other added.

Kesta murmured a thank you and tried not to look cross or miserable. Her nerves were so all over the place that she couldn't even begin to call on her *knowing* to better assess these two young women.

'Right, out of the way then!' Rosa shooed them. 'Go report back to the queen!'

With more giggling the girls retreated from the room, closing the door behind them.

'Weddings are exciting things for young girls who dream of handsome warriors and Jarls.' Rosa sighed.

'I'm going to be sick.'

Rosa grabbed a half-filled bucket of cold water and held it in front of Kesta just in time. She put the bucket down and held Kesta's hands for a while saying nothing.

'I'm sorry.' Kesta felt a hot, embarrassed tear snake down her cheek.

'You were being so quiet; I should have realised you're more upset than you were letting on. Do you want to talk about it?'

Did she? In all honesty yes, she did; but she wasn't about to admit any weakness even to Rosa.

'I drank some wine before breakfast to calm my nerves; I must have had too much on an empty stomach. I'll be fine.'

Rosa obviously didn't believe her, but she squeezed her hands and went back to finishing her hair.

'I would suggest some brandy; but maybe that wouldn't be such a good idea,' Rosa said.

'Probably not,' Kesta replied, thinking the opposite.

There was another knock at the door and both women sighed. When no one entered Rosa went and opened it.

'Silene.'

'Is she ready?' The huge man sounded almost timid.

'Just,' Rosa replied. 'Come on in.'

As Arrus looked at Kesta, his eyes seemed to light up. 'I hope Elden realises how much it has gained. Are you ready to do this?'

She held his eyes but couldn't bring herself to reply.

'Oh!' Rosa exclaimed. 'Just one last thing. Um ...' She lifted a wooden box from the bed and opened it. She winced as she handed it to Kesta. 'Thane Jorrun asked me to give you this.'

Kesta stared at the contents of the box. It was a chain made of delicate silver leaves. It was plain. It was beautiful. It was perfect.

She wanted to hate it.

Her father looked over her shoulder and gave a grunt. 'Would you like me to do it up for you?'

She could see Rosa looking at her hopefully out of the corner of her eye. She wanted to rebel and refuse to wear it; to let him know that he didn't own her and couldn't buy her. But to shun his gift might start their marriage on a higher level of hostility and she couldn't help but wonder how far he would go to make her do as he wished. Hadn't Tantony said the Dark Man had killed a warrior for doing something he didn't like?

'Kesta?'

'Yes.' She nodded sharply.

The metal was cold against her skin as her father did up the clasp. He stood back and smiled sadly. 'You look lovely, Kesta.'

She drew in a breath. 'Let's get this over with.'

Lifting her chin, she strode to the door and opened it. She turned and reached out her hand toward her father and he offered her his arm to escort her down to the great hall. Rosa followed behind them. A page who had been hovering saw them and darted away. She wished that she'd thought to demand something private rather than have to endure the eyes of all the Elden court; at least it had been so quickly arranged that only those within a day's travel had been able to attend. Even so, the great hall was crowded but for the narrow corridor left for her and her father.

Kesta clamped down tightly on her *knowing* and concentrated on taking deep and even breaths. She held lightly to her father's arm but in truth she clung to his strength. Ever since she could remember, Arrus Silene had made her feel safe; he'd been patient with her temper and encouraged her fierce independence. To be taken from him when he needed her to help fight for the Fulmers was almost harder to bear than the thought of what the Dark Man might do to her.

Then she found herself standing below the throne of the great hall. She drew in a sharp breath and bit her lower lip. The king himself stood there. Her heart still hammered against her ribs, but the tightness of her lungs eased a little when she realised the ceremony wouldn't be performed by some empty priest of Elden. The Dark Man stood perfectly still; he was dressed in an immaculately tailored suit, all black apart from tiny silver leaves embroidered on his shirt. He didn't even glance toward her.

The king reached out his hands, palms upward, and Jorrun at once placed his elegant left hand on the king's. Arrus hesitated a moment before stepping back and leaving Kesta alone. She met Bractius's eyes as she reached out her own small hand and let it rest gently on his. The king moved his hands together and then placed hers on Jorrun's. She gritted her teeth angrily when she saw that she was shaking. Then the king turned and picked up a long strand of ivy and she took in a sharp breath. This was no wedding of Elden; the king was performing a simple Fulmer ceremony! She looked up to regard Bractius fully for the first time, meeting his eyes and feeling a little warmth return to her skin.

Jorrun's hand was cool and perfectly steady beneath hers as the king bound them together. Bractius's voice rang out clear and confident.

'From this day you are bound together, pledged to work together to make your lives a better one; a happy one. You will listen to each other, respect each other, and support each other; being patient with each other's differences and imperfections. You will remain truthful, loyal, and faithful to each other in all aspects of life. Do you agree to these terms?'

The Dark Man's voice was firm. 'I agree.'

Kesta swallowed, and it hurt, her throat and chest too tight for her to draw in a breath. She was still shaking, but she refused to let Jorrun's hand take the weight of hers to rest her arm. Could she agree to those terms? They were the pledge of a Fulmer marriage and there was nothing in them to which she could disagree; they were fair and perfectly reasonable. It was the particular man to which she didn't want to pledge herself. Behind her she heard people shifting and looking up, Bractius's eyes had narrowed, his brows drawn in tight and his lips pressed in to a thin bloodless line.

She held his gaze. 'For the Fulmers, I agree.'

The king's face reddened, and his frown deepened but he forced a smile. She felt the slightest hardening of the tendons in Jorrun's hand. She lifted her chin and straightened her back defiantly. It was a tiny victory, but she'd made her point clear nonetheless.

Even so, she'd given her life to a man that she disliked; a man she feared.

'This is an important day in our history.' King Bractius raised his voice to the crowd. 'Where Elden and the Fulmer Islands stand side by side united not just in marriage, but in their determination to see off raiders of the Borrows and our old enemy; Chem. Together we are stronger; our combined heritage and unique ways will come together to make us more powerful. Join us now in a feast to celebrate the marriage of my closest friend and loyal Thane, Jorrun of Northold, and the beautiful Lady of Fulmer; Kesta Silene.'

Kesta jumped at the loudness of the cheer and the king reached out to clasp Jorrun's free wrist before bending to kiss Kesta's cheek and whisper in her ear; his breath a tickle against her neck. 'You will not regret this.'

A page stepped forward to hand them both an extravagant glass chalice of wine. In Fulmer tradition their hands would remain bound until the marriage was consummated; however, Jorrun raised their hands and a pale blue light consumed the ivy. With a quick movement he pulled his hand away, and the ivy remained hanging loose, but completely intact, along Kesta's wrist and arm. She stared at it wide-eyed and shocked for a moment before quickly lowering her arm to hide it. Possibly no one but her father knew of the full Fulmer ceremony, but she burnt with a blush and wondered at Jorrun's meaning. The man himself had already wandered away at the king's side to clasp wrists and speak with one of the Jarls who had attended.

'Are you all right?'

Rosa's voice was soft at her side and she was overwhelmed with relief and gratitude.

'Better for you being here.' She shook loose the ivy and clasped the older woman's hand. She felt a small amount of satisfaction when she stepped on the vine and turned her heel on it.

'Kesta.' Her father placed his huge hand on her shoulder.

She smiled but couldn't meet his eyes. 'I'm fine. Go mix with the Jarls and see if you can forge any useful friendships or trade agreements!'

'Kes—'

She stood on her tiptoes and kissed his cheek. 'Father, you have made me a strong and capable woman. Don't worry for me; I'll make sure that I'm happy and that I find my own way to fight for the Fulmers. Just promise me that if I'm not ... if I'm not able to come home, you and mother will come here when you're able.'

'Of course, we will!'

He enveloped her in a bone-breaking hug that squeezed tears out of her; then set her at arm's length to look into her eyes.

'Don't!' she said, feeling emotion surge up from her stomach.

Rosa stepped between them, lightly touching both their cheeks and then taking Kesta's arm. 'My lady, you should have something to eat; you have a long journey to make soon.'

Then they were surrounded by a flock of brightly coloured ladies in all their silk and lace. Kesta curtseyed to the queen and forced herself to smile at the ladies.

'Congratulations on a most prestigious marriage,' the queen said coolly.

Intrigued, Kesta called up a little of her *knowing* despite the proximity of so many people. From the ladies-in-waiting came a flighty mix of emotions and snippets of surface thought, including, to her surprise, jealousy. It seemed that two of the girls had hoped to be the ones to catch the Dark Man's eye. There was a small amount of reserved hostility from Ayline; she didn't trust Kesta and wondered how much of a rival she would become at court.

Kesta almost laughed; as far as she was concerned the girls were welcome to Jorrun, and she had no desire whatsoever to spend another moment at the court of Taurmaline.

'Thank you, your majesty,' she replied. 'Thank you also for your hospitality and for the gifts you bestowed on myself and my father.'

'You are most welcome.' The young queen hid her true feelings very well. 'No doubt you will want to spend time settling into running your new household; but we look forward to you coming back to visit us here in Taurmaline.' She picked up her long skirts and whisked her ladies away. Only the two youngest paused to give her a shy smile and a courtesy which she returned.

'Will you eat?' Rosa badgered her again. 'Jarl Hadjer of Taurmouth keeps glancing this way and it would be as well to move away and avoid that old octopus.'

Kesta nodded and she let the woman guide her past several polite well-wishers and toward the tables. She searched the crowd but couldn't spot

Jorrun anywhere. An agonising hour of polite conversation followed as Kesta tried to make her way back to her father, with Rosa faithfully hovering at her side. Then, as she excused herself from the Thane of Ferryford, she turned and found Jorrun standing before her. She flinched and then cursed herself.

'We are leaving,' he said.

She stared at him, her teeth and fists clenched. How dare he order her like that?

'I will say goodbye to my father and then collect my things from my room.'

Rosa opened her mouth to speak but Jorrun beat her to it. 'Your belongings have already been sent down to the ship. We can speak to Arrus Silene on the way out.'

She stood frozen in anger; and a little fear. As much as she wanted to flee the great hall she really didn't want to go with this man. However, she was not about to let him embarrass her in front of all these people. Standing on her toes she caught sight of where her father had moved to and walked slowly toward him. With Jorrun just behind her, everyone moved out of her path and no one tried to waylay her.

Arrus took one look at her face. 'You're going?'

'Yes.'

He hugged her, lifting her off her feet and then putting her down. He turned to the Dark Man. 'Treat her well,' he warned him.

Jorrun nodded and then turned to look at Kesta expectantly.

Feeling sick, she made her way to the large arched doorway and down the steps to the long hallway where Jorrun moved forward to walk at her side. She almost laughed at the thought of what they must look like to people; her with her angry scowl and him with his cold eyes and mirthless mouth. Her father had followed behind with Rosa; as had several curious others from the hall. The king and queen had already positioned themselves at the castle door. The king clasped Jorrun's wrist and then hugged him. For a moment, Kesta thought she imagined a smile on the Dark Man's face.

'Good luck,' Bractius told his Thane. 'Send me news.'

'Of course.' Jorrun bowed, and taking the queen's hand, kissed it. Was that the slightest trace of a blush on her face and throat?

Then the king was taking her hands to kiss her lightly on the cheek and he himself led Kesta down to where two horses waited. Jorrun sprang onto one of them and then turned to look at her. She stared at the other horse in growing horror. She hadn't ridden anything this big before, and never side-saddle. Humiliation stared her in the face, but she forced herself forward to greet the horse. She breathed in deeply and expelled her fear; refusing to let it back in with her next breath. She called up her *knowing* to let the horse understand her and gauge its temperament. There was a brightness to its mind, and it was curious about a human who could form a connection with it. She sent warmth, calm, and curiosity of her own.

'Lady Kesta?' The king stepped forward; at the same time Jorrun raised a hand, and the king halted.

Kesta placed one hand on the horse's shoulders and the other on the back of its saddle; placing one foot in a stirrup she pulled herself up and managed to twist around to sit sideways. She gathered up the reins and held them very loosely in one hand.

With the slightest of smiles toward the king, Jorrun set his horse forward at a fast trot. Kesta's horse quested toward her and she gave her assent that they should follow. She could feel how aware the horse was of her on its back and adjusted the way she was sitting. She felt its gratitude and satisfaction. She looked around her, hissing out through her teeth and sitting up straight and tense when she saw that Rosa was hurrying along behind and turned off at the steps down to the lower level of the city. She couldn't believe that the lady-in-waiting had been left to make her own way. The horse lifted its head to try to look back at her.

'Nothing to worry about.' She touched its neck.

Jorrun remained silent for their entire awkward journey down to the wharf. A small ship with two sails and a large cabin awaited them. Two servants came forward to take the horses and Kesta slipped to the ground while trying to prevent her dress hitching up. Her horse refused to be led away, and she felt its disappointment; she reciprocated and stopped holding back on her feelings of sadness and apprehension. To her surprise the horse turned to nip at the unfortunate servant and then trotted forward to nudge her.

'Are you going to bond with every animal you meet?' The Dark Man stood glowering at her from the boat's gangway. 'Come on.'

Reluctantly, she stroked the horse's cheek and then closing off her *knowing,* turned to follow Jorrun. She looked around and was relieved to see that Rosa had made it on-board. Without another word Jorrun strode to the cabin and went in. The door swung shut behind him.

The gangway was removed, and ropes were hauled in. Kesta realised that they were in the way and grabbing Rosa's hand, squeezed past the cabin to the front of the ship. She sat on the deck and let her legs dangle over the edge; Rosa sat tentatively behind her.

'Maybe you should talk to Thane Jorrun,' Rosa suggested.

Kesta stubbornly dismissed the idea. 'If he wants to shut himself away that's up to him. I want to be out here in the open air.' She closed her eyes and felt the wind first against the side of her face and then behind her as the boat slipped out onto the lake. She heard the whoosh and crack of the sails filling and took in a deep breath. She wished that she were out on the open sea heading back to the Fulmers. The two women leaned back against each other and watched the lake water flow past them. Farmland gave way to forest as the miles drifted by. One of the men brought them some wine and some pastries. Glancing up, Kesta saw that Merkis Tantony was hovering beyond the cabin and she guessed the kindness was down to him.

As daylight began to fade Kesta spotted the dark shape of a tower through the trees. It was narrow with a sharply pointed roof.

'Is that it?' she asked Rosa quietly.

Rosa followed her gaze. 'Yes, that's the Raven Tower.'

Kesta's heart gave a leap against her ribs.

The boat was steered to a long, narrow, landing dock and two of the sailors jumped across to tie up the ropes. There was a row of four small houses and a large shelter filled with timber. Smoke curled up from behind the houses and from the smell Kesta guessed they were smoking fish. A small crowd had gathered to meet them and Jorrun had already emerged from the cabin and jumped across to the dock. He strode forward to shake hands with one of the men; his clothes were simple and worn and although he appeared muscular, he was clearly a labourer and not a warrior.

'That's Kurghan.' Tantony stepped up beside Kesta. 'Shipbuilder, wheelwright, cooper; if it's made of wood, he can build it. Most of those with him are family. He has two brothers who are fishermen and his sister is married to one of the stronghold's warriors.'

Tantony stepped across onto the dock and held out his hand; Kesta took it and followed him over. The Merkis helped Rosa, and they caught up with Jorrun. Kesta felt everyone's eyes on her but she could see only curiosity and no hostility.

'My wife,' Jorrun said. 'Kesta Silene of the Fulmers.'

There followed some clumsy but well-meaning curtseys and bows; Kesta forced a quiet hello and a genuine smile before Jorrun was striding off again. They followed a rough path through the trees to an overgrown clearing. She halted as they stepped out of the trees and Rosa almost walked into her. The outer wall was far larger than she'd expected. Thick wooden stakes encased some tall earthworks crowned with a narrow walkway. There was a wooden barbican and the gate itself was reinforced with stone. Several warriors watched them from above and Tantony raised a hand in greeting. Kesta had to quicken her pace to catch up with Jorrun as he passed through into the outer circle. Several buildings, some of stone and some of wood, but all thatched, stood between the outer and inner walls. The inner wall was constructed completely of stone and the gate which stood ajar, was augmented with strips of iron.

As she slipped through the gate Kesta stopped again but this time her feeling was not one of awe but of consternation. Before her stood the keep, a square building of possibly four levels with a rounded tower at each corner. One of the towers was completely wrapped in ivy. Around the keep was an overgrown wilderness through which chickens pecked and goats wandered untended. Ahead and to her left stood two long buildings which, from the smell, she guessed to be stables. Before them stood the grey-stone Raven Tower whose summit caught the last rays of the sun. Some grunting to her left drew her attention to a rooting pig.

'Oh!' Rosa exclaimed beside her.

Merkis Tantony shifted his feet, looking a little embarrassed. 'It is a little neglected I suppose,' he muttered.

'This is a fortress, not a lady's garden.' Jorrun turned to address them with a frown. 'If you'll excuse me, I have something important to attend to. Merkis, you'll take them in.' With that he strode on toward the tower.

'Well.' Tantony took in a deep breath. 'Welcome to Northold.'

They followed him around to the front of the keep; Kesta glanced left but Jorrun had already vanished. Above, a single raven circled.

'There are a few of us live in the keep,' Tantony said as he walked up the steep steps and pushed open the heavy door. 'Myself included. There is the cook who is the wife of one of the warriors; she is very good. She pretty much runs the household for me. Four of the other wives assist her and they have various children who run errands and look after the animals. There are others who come in a few times a week to clean and help, but they live in the outer circle.'

'And does your wife work in the keep?' Rosa asked.

The Merkis turned away and coloured slightly. 'I am a widower, ma'am.'

The door opened straight into the great hall and fading light spilled in from a large, high window at the opposite end. To either side stood a huge fireplace in which a dozen men could have stood; only one was lit, and a boy stood turning a carcass on a spit while steam rose from a large cauldron. The boy froze, his eyes widening when he realised who these ladies must be; but Tantony waved a hand at him to indicate that he should get on with what he was doing. There was a raised dais with a long table and decoratively carved chairs below the window. Two long tables stood on the lower level and ran from the dais as far as the fireplaces. At each corner of the room stood an arched door and Tantony headed to the one at the far left. He lifted the latch and pushed the door open; smiling when he saw that candles had been lit in sconces along the wall.

The room at the base of the tower was larger than Kesta had imagined but dark despite the candles as there were no windows at all. The room was empty but for a few chairs pushed against the curving wall and an old dusty tapestry of a stern-looking woman reclining in a garden.

'These two southern towers are set aside for guests, normally,' Tantony told them as he started up the steep stairs. 'When the king stays, he's given the south-west tower. This first room here is more often than not used for storage when not in use. The room above has a small fireplace, two bronze baths, and a garderobe. Above that is a room for entertaining and then a bedroom on each of the remaining three levels.' He looked back over his shoulder. 'Jorrun thinks the highest tower room would suit you best – and to be honest I think he's right – but if you find the climb up the stairs too much, you can, of course, use whatever room you like. This whole tower is yours.'

'So ...' Kesta bit her lower lip and forced herself to ask. 'Does Thane Jorrun use one of the other towers?'

Tantony gave an audible sigh. 'Jorrun lives in the Raven Tower. My room is in the main building on the level above the great hall; just above the door. You can get to the two upper levels of the main keep from the stairway in the north-east tower. The kitchen and storerooms are below the keep and the stairs down to them in the north-west tower. Now then ...' he opened the final door at the top of the stairs. 'I will leave you to settle in; your belongings will be on their way. I need to catch up on things, so you will probably find me down in the kitchen or stores, or in the steward's room above the stairs to the kitchen. We normally only have a formal dinner in the great hall when we have visitors or on feast days; but Reetha, our cook, will set out food in there for whoever is about. Jorrun has his meals taken to the Raven Tower; you are of course welcome to have yours brought up here. Jorrun has instructed that if you so wish you may take over running the household and I am to hand over the relevant keys and funds to you.' He looked at her expectantly.

'We can talk about that later when I've had time to get my bearings,' she replied. 'Thank you for showing us around. We won't keep you any longer.'

He gave a small bow and then hesitated. 'Just one thing ... no one is allowed in the Raven Tower except Thane Jorrun. Not even I've set foot in there since he came to the stronghold. Well ... find me if you need me.' With that he squeezed past them and headed down the stairs.

What was it he got up to in his tower? Kesta shuddered.

She walked cautiously into the room and was surprised at how light it was despite the fact dusk was now upon them. There was a chill breeze that raised goose bumps on her skin and she saw there were three windows facing east, south, and west. There was a four posted bed with heavy green and brown curtains and a large clothes chest covered in the same fabric. There was a stunning table cut from a thin section of a gigantic tree's trunk and polished with a red-brown sheen. Kesta ran her fingers across it, looking down at the swirling pattern of rings. Four chairs were set about it cushioned in dark-green velvet. A long window seat curved with the tower below the west window and on the north side was a small fire grate.

'It will be cold in here in winter,' Rosa said.

Kesta went to the windows. To the west most of the view was blocked by the southwest tower but when she strained her eyes against the gathering night, she thought she could make out the lake. To the south there was the slightest of silver and orange glows where the clouds were thin low on the horizon, against which the vast forest was a black silhouette. To the east was the imposing solid shape of the tall Raven Tower. In one of the narrow windows yellow candlelight flickered.

'Shall we look at the other rooms?' Rosa asked.

'Much as I hate to admit it, Jorrun was right.' Kesta winced. 'I love this room. If only it looked out over the sea! But yes, let's look at the other rooms and see which one you would like.'

As they were exploring, a young nervous woman, barely more than a child but rounded with pregnancy, found them and knocked softly at the open door.

'Excuse me, my lady, miss.' She bobbed; more crouch that curtsey. 'Mum – I mean Reetha, the cook – sent me t' ask. She says that she 'asn't 'ad much call to cook for a lady who ... um ... a lady from the islands, but that she 'as done 'er best until you let 'er know what y' like. She says is mushrooms in white wine and cream, with 'erbs an' early greens, an' scrambled eggs with goat's cheese an' dried tomato any good to y'?'

The young girl pulled a face as though expecting to be yelled at.

'That sounds lovely.' Kesta tried not to laugh and said seriously, 'And what is your name?'

'I'm Trella, my lady. Miss, my lady?' she turned to Rosa. 'Are you a d ... from the Fulmers too?'

'I'm not, but I am happy to have the same.'

'Rosa would also like some of the meat off the spit and a little of that stew I smelt in the great hall.' Kesta glanced at her companion. 'No one else needs to go without and be hungry because I'm a *fire-walker*. Would you kindly have someone bring it up to this receiving room?'

'Of course.' Trella's smile was sudden and brief. She turned to go and then remembered. 'There are some men downstairs with trunks of yours, shall I let 'em up?'

'Please do.' Kesta nodded.

The girl spun away and scampered down the stairs.

***

Rosa decided on the room below Kesta's and she wondered if it were because the woman didn't like the idea of being alone in the tower. Kesta herself wished with all her heart that she could be left alone; she thought of the candlelight in the window of the Raven Tower and fear squeezed all of her muscles.

'I hope you stay in there forever,' she whispered under her breath.

As they'd begun to unpack her things, she'd found her belt knife and had placed it under her pillow. She had agreed to the marriage and that meant she'd agreed to what came with it; but the idea of allowing the Dark Man to have use of her body against her will filled her with equal measures of fury and terror. One minute she felt as cold as though all the blood had drained from her and the next so hot that sweat trickled down her back. She knew that she could never go through with it willingly; did he know that too?

Voices heralded the arrival of dinner and they made their way down. Trella was back, with another woman almost Rosa's age, and two boys of perhaps eight or nine years. They set out the food on the long table and poured some wine and then all but Trella backed away.

'Is there anything else you're needing?' Trella searched their faces.

Kesta's eyes glanced over the room without taking anything in. She sagged against the wall but couldn't draw the strength from her unresponsive muscles to pull herself upright. Her appetite had fled, and she felt sick at the thought of putting any of the food in her mouth.

'That's all, thank you,' Rosa said for her.

The four servants scuttled out.

Rosa regarded her and said softly, 'Sit down Kesta, before you fall down.'

Kesta did so, and she looked forlornly at everything set out on the table. Rosa picked up the wine and poured more into Kesta's chalice.

'Drink that; all of it.'

Kesta's stomach flipped, but she picked up the chalice and forced all the wine down her throat. Rosa winced and leaned over to pour her some more before sitting back in her chair.

'I'm sure it won't be as bad as you fear,' Rosa tried, picking up a thick slice of bread and ladling some stew over it.

'*You* don't even sound convinced!'

'Well ... then get really drunk and you might not care so much!'

'That's the best plan you can come up with?'

They stared at each other across the table; then a laugh burst from Kesta at the same time as a tear slipped from one eye.

'It's not a bad plan.' She shook her head and took another sip of wine. Getting too drunk to care was probably more rational than stabbing Jorrun. A lot more beneficial to her people too. She wondered what the repercussions would be if she did murder the Elden's sorcerer and the king's best friend; they certainly wouldn't be good. She drank more wine and picked at the eggs.

Rosa cleared her throat. 'It seems that Jorrun is quite happy to give you lots of freedom and responsibility. There are plenty of men in Elden who wouldn't hand over their purse to their wife.'

'In the Fulmers all women are free, and responsible for their own choices and lives.' She gazed down into her chalice.

'Tell me more about the Fulmers,' Rosa demanded, sitting up straighter.

Kesta did so; describing her clifftop stronghold home, the forests full of wild animals and tantalising fruits. She picked at the food and sipped at the wine while she told of the treetop pathways made of narrow swinging ladders; of the fierce fishermen, and the enigmatic foresters.

'Kesta.'

She jumped and dropped her chalice; it left a dark red trail across the table that reflected the candlelight. Jorrun was standing in the doorway; he held a bottle of wine in one hand and two ornate glasses in the other.

'Come with me.' He didn't wait but walked on up the stairs.

She stood, and Rosa stood with her. *It was too soon!*

Rosa walked around the table to squeeze her hand and kiss her cheek. Kesta realised she wasn't breathing and forcing in air she made her knees lift and carry her to the door. She could feel her skin burning but she was freezing cold inside; the stairs seemed infinitely steep but the stairway not long enough.

He had poured her some wine and moved around to the other side of the beautiful table to pour himself some.

'Sit, please.'

She did so; her hands clenched into fists on her legs beneath the table. She couldn't look up at his ice eyes.

He sat down. 'You are happy with your rooms? Did Merkis Tantony explain that you may take over the running of the household if you so wish?'

She cursed herself for her dumbness; this was no time to become a frightened prey animal. Drawing herself up she found her voice. 'Yes.'

Even to her own ears she sounded angry and rude. She swallowed and tried again. 'I am looking forward to seeing the views from these windows in the daylight.'

'I have some rules for you.'

She glanced up then but could not hold his gaze.

'Well, one rule; the other is more a request. This is the same command I give to everyone who comes to the stronghold; even the king. Do not *ever* enter the Raven Tower. You know that I am a sorcerer; the Raven Tower is a dangerous place.'

He studied her face, and she did her best to meet his regard steadily as she nodded once. She was too numb to feel any curiosity.

'My request is that you accept a young girl of this stronghold as your maid. I understand that it's not the custom of the Fulmers, but it would mean a lot to me. She is ...' He turned toward the window and his eyes became distant. 'She is a somewhat difficult young woman, but I have seen a kindness in your nature and I think you might be able to help her if you can find the patience. If you will not do it for me, then consider that Rosa will be used to having a maid or a younger lady-in-waiting to attend her.'

Kesta frowned. She didn't want a maid, and she didn't want to do anything to help the man before her; however, there was no good reason to turn away a young woman who apparently needed help. Not yet anyway.

'Very well.' She lifted her chin and tried to muster a small show of pride. 'I will give her a chance at least.'

'That is all I ask.' Jorrun stood and Kesta flinched. 'You look exhausted. I know that it has been a difficult day for you. I'll leave you to rest and settle in; we will speak again tomorrow evening.' He walked to the door and then paused there. Kesta could not so much as blink never mind turn around. 'Just so that you understand me; I am not in the habit of forcing myself on any woman – not even my wife. Goodnight.'

The door closed and every muscle in Kesta's body turned to liquid; she almost wet herself. Anger rose up from her toes at the same time as overwhelming relief rushed up from her stomach to her tingling scalp. She picked up her wine and swallowed it down; vowing that she would never, ever, allow herself to feel that afraid and helpless again. She moved around the table and picking up Jorrun's glass hurled it against the wall. She felt satisfaction and release at the wonderful sound of shattering glass.

Slowly, she went to the window and looked across the overgrown inner circle of the stronghold toward the east. It was too dark to see anything; but the soft light of a candle danced still, high up in the window of the Raven Tower.

Chapter Five

Osun; Covenet of Chem

Osun sighed and turned his head to look at the woman next to him. She had her back to him with one small rounded shoulder above the blankets and appeared to be asleep; but he could never be certain. As quietly as he could he slipped out of the bed and stooping under the sloping fabric of the tent, pulled his robe over his head. The sharpness of the air hit him as soon as he lifted the flap and he snatched up a lantern and hurried to the wagon. A lock of his long, black hair was blown across his eyes and he impatiently pushed it away. The bullocks were hobbled nearby and one of them snorted at him in the darkness. He placed the lantern on the floor of the wagon and clambered inside, wincing as the pendant around his neck seared his skin a second time.

'I'm coming!' he said through gritted teeth.

He went to one of the chests and taking out a large flat obsidian bowl, he filled it with water; then from the flask that nestled beside the bowl he let three small drops fall. He reached beneath his robe, grasped the blood-red amulet, and clenched it in his left hand as he held the lamp high with his right and peered into the water. It began to cloud as the dark droplets dissolved and then cleared to show the face of a man with startling eyes.

'Yes, Master?'

The reply came not from the bowl but from the amulet in his fist, the deep timbre of the voice vibrating in the bones of his fingers.

'What do you know of raids against the Fulmers? Why have I not heard of this before?'

Osun shook his head. 'Master, I know nothing of such raids. Rumour has it that all the islands of the Borrows have now been conquered but there has been no word of the Fulmers.'

'All of the Borrows? You're sure? Why haven't you contacted me before now?'

Osun couldn't help but flinch back from the water. 'Master, I am yet two days outside of Margith where I can gain certain news; I didn't want to furnish you with false information. Let me speak to the other traders there and listen in at the temple; I will confirm the truth as soon as I am sure it is truth and not rumour.'

'Very well. You're sure you've heard nothing of plans to attack the Fulmers or Elden?'

'Elden! Gods, no! I'd have told you at once! You think that is their intent?'

There was a long silence.

'See what you can find out in Margith. You'll contact me within three days?'

'Yes, Master.'

The water seemed to thin, and the image of the man vanished. Osun rocked back on his heels and put down the lantern. Even after all these years, travelling to Margith made him nervous; too many priests, not to mention the fact it was the ruling seat of one of the necromancers. At least his master had not asked him to go into the palace!

He tipped the water over the back of the wagon and stowed everything carefully back in the chest. He slipped back inside the tent and hung up the lantern, pulling his robe back up over his head. Anxiety gnawed at him and instead of returning to his side of the blankets he shook the woman's shoulder; she made no protest but lay unmoving as he used her body to try to alleviate the knot of anxiety in his chest.

***

He awoke to the smell of boar and mushrooms and cursed when he saw how much light was seeping through the tent. He grabbed his long coat, struggling into the sleeves as he pushed out through the thin hide flap.

'You should have woken me.'

'Sorry, Master.' Milaiya glanced up as she turned the thin strips of meat on a long metal plate balanced over the fire. Her voice sounded contrite enough but, as ever, he thought he caught a glimpse of contempt in her eyes. Her sullenness grated on his nerves. She had no need to be so miserable; he treated her well enough, never beating her and giving her a fair share of his meagre rations. He even ensured that her clothes were reasonably warm, and that she had shoes.

Milaiya had too wide a nose and too narrow a face to be considered beautiful, although her curling copper hair redeemed her a little. Her bloodlines were insignificant, she had no particular skills, and he'd bought her cheaply as a general slave two years ago. His previous slave had been an old pleasure slave in her thirties, pretty enough still but useless for the chores he required. He'd made a loss on her sale, but he had to admit that Milaiya had made up for it.

'Get the tent packed away and harness the bulls.' Taking his knife from his belt he took the meat off the cooking plate and put it on his own. As he chewed, he considered the road ahead. Margith was on his regular route and he usually made a small profit there before heading further north toward the mountains and the glacier field. There was money to be made taking simple necessities out to the farther villages in the coldest part of the north but there was little news to be gathered there. What he did gain were snow bear pelts and sea-cow fat all of which made even a lone merchant like him a tidy profit. The best place to sell such goods was Arkoom, but he'd avoided the capital city for three years now. Every time he looked in the mirror he saw the face of his father; a face that he thought must be unmistakable. If anyone asked, he told the tale that his mother was a skin slave from a cheap house and he never knew who his father was; he'd worked his way free and set up as a trader. For the most part no one particularly cared who he was; but things were changing.

He shook himself from his daydream and saw that Milaiya had finished stowing away their belongings and was leading the long-haired, red bullocks over to the wagon. That was one thing he could say about her; she was efficient and could somehow pack an amazingly large amount of goods into a small space.

'Eat something, then we will be on our way.'

Milaiya glanced up and nodded, stroking the long, coarse hair and softer ears of one of the bulls. A smile ghosted her face as the bull leaned into her, then her head lowered as she turned and walked over to Osun to finish the two small strips of meat he had left.

'Drink your tea and we'll get going.'

He pointed to the small bundle of herbs that sat beside her cup. It was a concoction that supposedly ensured she wouldn't fall pregnant although it apparently damaged her chances of conceiving in the future. There might be some money to be made by selling a slave's baby, but the inconvenience of having his only slave pregnant and useless would outweigh any gain in coin.

***

Although the night had been cold, the ground was already boggy with snow thaw that had not dried up or run off. He couldn't help but sigh when he thought of the all too brief springs he'd spent across the sea in a warmer land. The two red bulls strained at first but soon got into a steady pace and he didn't try to push them; he knew that abusing his animals wouldn't bring him gain in the long run. This part of Chem was hillier with many deep river valleys racing down from the mountains. He preferred the rough but milder coast and had to admit he missed the coastal city he'd grown up in – although not the life he'd had then. If he'd had a choice, he would have set up shop as a trader in luxury goods, sending someone else out to do all the fetching and travelling for him. If he'd a choice he would settle, make real friends, maybe even buy a woman with good bloodlines to bear him a son.

But he didn't have a choice, he wasn't a slave, not exactly, but he wasn't free. Between his master and constantly looking over his shoulder to be sure he wasn't recognised or discovered, he lived his life always on edge. He never dared stay anywhere too long or let anyone get too friendly. The covens of the Arkoom sorcerers had spies of their own and despite their bond of friendship, he feared his master. As a child his master had been powerful, now the Gods only knew what the man was capable of. He had never been offered the choice of what he wanted or where he wanted to be; he was to be a spy in Chem, caught between his master and the Covens of Arkoom.

***

Sleet hit them hard on their second day and they were forced to make camp early before night fell. It took a lot of will, but mostly fear of recrimination, for Osun not to curse at the Gods for the inconvenience; he was so close and yet frustratingly kept from comfort and warmth. Not for the first time he was tempted to throw away the tube of blood around his neck and be free from this life of lies and constant fear. But a promise was bound around his soul and sealed by his mother's blood. Milaiya stirred a little as he moved away from her warmth. He was used to being alone, it had been his life since he'd been sent back to Chem, but that didn't mean that loneliness didn't hurt.

His heart lifted as he sighted the walls of Margith the next day, black against the slush and snow. It was said that the city walls were made from the vomit of a fire mountain and he didn't doubt it. The stone was jagged and sharper than teeth, mostly black but swirled with iron red, sulphur yellow, and pumice white. Legend said that the blood of a thousand slaves bound the rock together from hands torn to pieces by the harsh, serrated surface. Above the walls tall towers peered, as black as the walls but polished and sheer. The sun refracted off them, distorting the towers' shape. Osun flicked his long whip at the bulls to bid them hurry. Excitement and anticipation warred with anxiety as they reached the gates. He recognised two of the guards and gave them a wave as they approached.

'Oswan, ain't it?' One of them said, eyeing the wagon.

He didn't correct him. 'Yup. Got held up by that sleet last night so I'm late for the market.'

'Ah.' The guard spat. 'They won't let you set up now.'

'More time for pleasure before work then!' Osun grinned.

The guard showed his crooked teeth back with a chuckle. 'Aye, go on with ya, save some ale for me!'

Osun nodded and flipped him a coin. It never hurt to have a guard or two on side. 'Have one on me!'

They drove on through the gate and Milaiya shifted beside him, securing her small veil. He made a decision and his spirits lifted still further.

'We'll go to the Sunset Inn.'

Milaiya turned in surprise but said nothing. The Sunset Inn was the best in Margith, in the heart of the city and close to the palace of the resident coven. Osun felt proud of himself at the bold and dangerous move and also somewhat pleased that he was more than able to afford it. He might be a spy for his master, but he was still a very adept merchant and had accumulated a tidy sum in secret.

The inn was a massive four stories tall and even boasted a tower on one corner. It was frequented by the most prosperous of merchants, particularly those who dealt in slaves with sorcerous bloodlines, and sometimes members of the covens themselves. There were secure underground pens for holding valuable slaves as well as ample stabling. The food was talked about all over Chem. Osun's mouth watered just thinking about it. They drove up to the impressive iron gates and a well-dressed young man opened them and gave a small bow. He wore a simple copper collar to show that he was a paid servant and not a slave.

'What is your requirement, master?' the young man asked without looking up.

'Stabling and safe storage for my wagon.' He hesitated, a desire for luxury and to elevate his status momentarily warring with his natural inclination to be thrifty. 'I need only one room, but I'd like something spacious.'

'Come in, master, I will send the lodging manager out at once.' He pulled the gates open wide to allow them to drive in.

Osun had only just stepped down from the wagon when he was presented with a mug of hot, dark wine, by a young female slave. Her short veil and severely tied back hair denoted her as a domestic slave rather than a pleasure slave. She bowed and without speaking indicated for him to follow; in Chem a woman could not speak unless spoken to first. Behind them Milaiya had picked up his bag of personal effects which she'd packed for him; he trusted her implicitly to have picked the right things and had learnt that she was better at remembering and anticipating what he would need than he was himself. They passed a trader coming out of the building followed by three women and a well-armed guard – most likely a less wealthy relative. The women were short and slight and covered from head to toe, a gauzy veil obscuring even their eyes marking them as valuable virgin merchandise. The guard watched Osun with narrowed eyes, but the trader gave him a nod and a smug smile, clearly pleased with whatever transaction he'd made.

The inn's expansive reception was full, and the noise of conversation and the clang of cutlery rattled against Osun's nerves. The Lodging Manager came hurrying over at once with a low and flustered bow.

'Master, I am so sorry not to greet you at once, but a Lord of Arkoom Coven was just leaving and had my full attention.'

Osun felt his blood freeze and his face burn, but he kept his voice calm as he replied, 'I quite understand. May I ask which venerated Lord I had the misfortune of missing?'

'It was Lord Feren, Master. Sadly, he did not stay here at my wonderful establishment but some of his party did and he blessed me by joining them here to break their fast before departing back to Arkoom.'

His father's uncle, then, someone Osun would not have wanted to bump into; even so his rapid heartbeat began to ease.

'Did they bring exciting news from the Seat of Arkoom? I heard that we have at last conquered those raiding dogs of the Borrows.'

'Yes, it is true.' The Lodging Manager leaned forward to confide excitedly. 'There is to be an official announcement at midday and we are requested to celebrate wholeheartedly.'

'And what of Elden?'

'Elden?' the man looked puzzled and Osun felt a pang of disappointment. He would have to seek further information elsewhere.

'I just wondered what their reaction would be, in a way we have done them a favour, but we have also shown them how powerful we are.'

'Indeed. With the Borrows' fleet we could take the world. These are great times, Master. Please, would you follow my slave to your room?' He seemed to recall that he was very busy.

'Of course.' Osun smiled. 'I'd like a bath filled please and some provisions sent to the room.'

'I will see to that at once, Master.'

Osun followed after the silent slave and didn't even glance over his shoulder at Milaiya. They ascended two flights of stairs and were taken to a solid looking pine door. The inn slave opened it wide and then stepped back, freezing in a low bow and holding out a key in her open palm. Osun snatched it without a word and looked around the room. The walls were a glossy dark-green, the furniture intricately carved pine, stained to the colour of oak. The heavy curtains at the window and around the bed were a leaf patterned brown and a copper bath stood in one corner partially obscured by a tapestry screen. He flicked his fingers out toward the slave to indicate that he was satisfied, and she could leave.

'I'm going to the temple after my bath and then to the market to see if there are any deals worth making,' he told Milaiya as he went to the window to look out. His room overlooked the busy street and was high enough up that he could peer beyond several rooftops toward the temple and the Palace of the Coven. He gritted his teeth against his fear and instead focused on his resentment that his simple life of trading and passing on information had been interrupted by the Seat of Arkoom and his overly ambitious father. He owed Elden nothing, but unfortunately, he did owe his master, was indeed owned by his master as surely as he owned Milaiya. These recent events scared him far more deeply than having to risk himself more than usual as a spy. Chem was his home, his culture, and yet his time in Elden had left him feeling somewhat discontent and somehow unfulfilled in his mind and in his soul. It wasn't just his being a spy that meant he had to watch every word and every action, this land was full of jealousy, resentment, hunger for power, and fear of the powerful. Since the rise of his family and necromancy, blood was all.

He shivered and turned to see that Milaiya had set out his best jacket and a deep blue shirt. He nodded his approval. Three slow knocks announced slaves and Milaiya hurried to the door to let them in. Three of them carried two buckets each of hot water and a fourth, two buckets of cold for mixing. Two others brought in trays of food which they laid out on the table; they hovered for a moment until Osun flicked his fingers at them to indicate it was sufficient. After Milaiya had scrubbed him in the bath and helped him dress, he ate just enough to settle his stomach.

He didn't need to tell Milaiya that she could help herself to the food and left-over bath water, it was understood that she was allowed when they stayed in an inn. He did however remind her to get his clothes laundered and not to leave the inn. The last thing he needed was someone damaging or stealing a good, if sullen, slave. An unaccompanied woman outside a building was considered as belonging to no one and therefore belonging to anyone.

He secured his purse and a knife to his belt and then fastened his jacket over them. Having no guards, he carried his own sword and prided himself that he was more than capable of using it. He stopped off at his wagon to collect a string of beeswax candles and a bolt of good red cloth as offerings for the temple and set off across the city.

The main street was crowded with many licenced food vendors having set up along the flag-stoned pavement; despite having just eaten the rich aromas were tantalising. The best of the city's shops lined either side of the street, but despite his longing for such a shop of his own, Osun didn't pay them much attention; he was unlikely to be able to sell any of his goods at those shops and any items he purchased would have their prices marked up so high he would never make a profit.

The temple was the largest building in the city. It had to be to hold so many Gods. Osun wasn't sure he believed in any of them but concluded it was prudent to visit often, both to hedge his bets and be seen to show the proper devotion. It also gave him a chance to gather information. Which Gods were the most popular told him a lot about the state of Chem, about its political and economic climate. One of the reasons that Chem looked down on Elden was that they were a country of only two Gods and one of them was female – Sky Father, Earth Mother. All Chem's Gods were male; if any of them ever wanted to procreate and produce another God, they just kidnapped a suitably attractive human woman. As for the barbaric people of the Fulmers, they worshipped anything and everything, and had some odd idea about everything having spirits. Osun almost chuckled to himself when he imagined a dark Fulmer warrior worshipping a tree.

He assumed a suitably sombre face and ascended the long steps. The temple, like much of the city, was built from black volcanic rock. The huge doors were of rare oak as smooth and flawless as the stone. They stood open wide but not invitingly; the inside was dark and full of whispers. He nodded at a fellow trader who came scurrying out; they made no eye contact. Stepping over the threshold was like stepping out over a cliff edge the contrast between where light was and wasn't was so great. Sounds echoed in the deep alcoves. When his eyes adjusted, he made out the long corridor and hidden rooms from which candlelight seeped and wavered. Priests stood waiting to greet the worshippers and accept their offerings, ready to pounce on anyone who hesitated in their choice of God. He trod carefully on the glistening, polished floor.

Domarra was the God of prosperity and of merchants. Not surprisingly Domarra's popularity rarely wavered. His alcove was the fifth on the left and Osun was sure to peer into the other alcoves on his way past as discreetly as he could without lifting his head. He walked purposefully enough that none of the hovering priests did more than glance at him. In the distance, there was a queue for the alcove that housed the alter of Hacren, God of Death, the God of the necromancers. Hacren was feared more than any other God and had once had very few worshippers; now he had worshippers that could only be described as fanatical as well as those that went in the hope of currying favour from the Seats of Arkoom. His neighbour, Monaris, God of War, was less busy and the alcove of Warenna, God of Magic, was empty. Osun's feet almost faltered. Chem's was a society based on magic and its economy based strongly on those who carried magical ability in their blood; for Warenna's worshippers to have abandoned him was startling. His eyes went back to the line awaiting the alter of Hacren and he went cold inside.

He reached Domarra's alcove and smiled at the priest, handing him the cloth and candles.

'Domarra's blessings.' The priest bowed.

There were two other men in the alcove, both kneeling at the altar so Osun politely waited. The God's effigy was carved from white marble and was a stark contrast to the darkness. The God the stone depicted was four times the size of a mortal man and strongly muscled. He had a wild, curling beard but a bald head. He held out one hand from which dangled a bounty of fruit, his other hand held a set of scales and a sword was at his hip. He was dressed in a shirt open almost to the belly and trousers tucked into long boots. The statue's expression seemed to change in the light of the flickering candles from benevolent to threatening and back again.

'He looks angry today,' Osun mused under his breath, just loud enough that the priest could hear him, but not so loud that he would disturb those praying. 'Have we not prospered from our victory over the Borrows?'

'War costs money.' The priest sighed. 'You have not traded today?' A priest was one of the very few people of Chem that did not address anyone as 'master'.

Osun shook his head. 'I was delayed by the weather.'

'They have put the traders' tax up again at the market.'

Osun's shoulders slumped. 'There goes my profit. I would have thought an increase in tax would have swelled our worshipper's numbers; it seems quiet today.' He looked around at the priest.

The priest frowned and hugged the cloth closer to his chest. 'In times like these people will turn to the God they fear the most, losing faith in the one who has sustained them.'

'Or perhaps the God of the *ones* they fear most.'

The priest shuffled his feet and glanced around. 'There are rewards to be had in this life by following a popular God, but it is the next life and our own souls we should concern ourselves with. Keep your faith, Pilgrim, Domarra looks after his faithful.'

'He does indeed.' Osun smiled grimly.

One of the worshippers got to his feet awkwardly; he was in his fifties and thin in a way that proclaimed a terminal illness. He regarded Osun steadily before bowing to the priest and making his exit. Osun took a candle and lighting it, knelt and set it on the alter at Domarra's booted feet. He knew he was being a hypocrite by praying. People were what he believed in; they had enough power and evil between them to outdo all the Gods. Even so, he asked for Domarra's protection and thanked him for bringing him prosperity; even though he'd done all the work to gain it himself.

So; people were abandoning their own Gods and those of their families to curry favour with Hacren and the necromancers of the Dunham family. They were afraid.

Osun stood and gave the priest a nod and smile. 'Blessings, Holy One.'

'Blessings, Pilgrim.'

The light when he got close to the door was so bright he had to squint and his eyes watered. He jumped as someone moved to his right.

'I'm sorry, brother, I didn't mean to startle you.'

Osun turned, raising his hand to shield his eyes from the sun, and found himself facing the sickly worshipper from Domarra's alcove. The fact that he'd called him 'brother' meant that he considered them to be equals.

'Can I help you?' Osun straightened up and hid his anxiety.

'Pardon my intrusion; I couldn't help but overhear you had not been to the market yet to trade.'

'That's so,' Osun replied uneasily.

'May I ask what you have to sell? Forgive me, you do not recognise me; I am Farkle Worne. We have done business in the past, be it a few years ago.'

'Farkle!' Osun's jaw dropped. He recalled a large and fit man with a generous head of hair.

'Time has not been good to me.' Farkle smiled wryly. 'Not to my health, or to my business. My shop is closed, and my son now runs a stall in the market.'

'I am sorry to hear it,' Osun said genuinely. He had traded maybe two or three times with Farkle when his shop was a new venture and he still took his goods from the traders that came to market. He had always been a fair and friendly man. 'Come, brother, let's get off the street and catch up somewhere that does a decent meal.'

Farkle hesitated.

'My turn to pay, I'm sure,' Osun reassured him; he couldn't help but feel some sympathy and if there was a chance of a good deal out of it that avoided a few market taxes so much the better. 'You can host me next time I visit to talk business.'

Farkle seemed to relax. 'That is very generous. There is a nice little place off the main way just beyond the palace.' Farkle indicated with his hand and they descended the steps and into the street.

This part of the city gave way from shops to the most splendid of houses; most donning the stark style of the temple. The street widened out and several wells stood along its length from which male slaves came and went with buckets. Up ahead, the palace stood behind high walls and a small crowd had gathered outside.

'What's that all about?' Osun wondered.

'Adelphy Dunham is parading the wealth he won from the Borrows.' Farkle grimaced.

Osun recalled Adelphy from his childhood; he was the son of his father's cousin and strong in magic. Like most of those with power Adelphy was a bully and he also took pleasure in causing physical pain and humiliation. Osun himself had received a fractured cheekbone from the man for allegedly not getting to his knees quickly enough when he'd come to look over the female slaves to make a purchase. He was a tall, thin man, with a nose that seemed too large for his face. He was also the son of the man who had killed Osun's mother. Adelphy had invaded the palace of Margith six years ago, slaughtering all within it and taking the Seat of Margith for the Dunhams, taking their tally of seats up to eight and ensuring the necromancer's dominance. Osun's jaw began to ache from gritting his teeth and he forced himself to relax.

'I might take a quick look.' He didn't wait for Farkle's reply but strolled up to the edge of the crowd. Despite being quite tall he couldn't see over all the gathered men, so he edged his way forward as politely as he could. Several guards in metallic red armour stood guarding a row of chained slaves; all women and none of them covered. Most of them had the curling brown hair and dark eyes of the Borrows but in all of them there were varying signs of some Fulmer heritage. Darker skin, straight black hair, lighter eyes, and a taller, willowier, build. Each one of them could produce several more powerful sons for the Dunham family. Adelphy was showing them that the Dunham's hold over Chem was unchallengeable.

He drew in a sharp, deep breath, glancing around at the crowd and feeling his pulse quicken. There was a tightness across his chest and he pushed clumsily between the gathered men to get outside their circle and into the open where he could breathe. He almost bumped in to Farkle.

'Let's get that food.' He forced a smile although Farkle's expression showed nothing but hopelessness.

The older man led him off the main street and down a narrow road, turning right down an even smaller ally barely wide enough to walk single file. Osun would never have thought of looking for an eating establishment down here, but a small sign did indeed hang out over the black cobbles. Farkle pushed open a battered wooden door and walked confidently in. There were only two, small windows, so the interior was dark but more comfortable than the blackness of the temple. There were three tables, and none occupied, a man looked up from polishing cutlery with a delighted smile on his face.

'Master Farkle, I didn't expect to see you again this week.'

'I have business with my friend here and trading can be hungry work.'

'Please, sit!' The grey-haired man barely gained more height as he leapt down from his stool and rushed to pull out two chairs. 'Today I have roast snow hare with honeyed parsnips or a stew of beef.'

'Gunthe is a fine cook,' Farkle reassured Osun as he sat.

'The hare sounds good.' Osun nodded.

'And for me.' Farkle agreed.

'At once, masters.' The cook bustled off behind a dividing curtain.

'Gunthe, like me, has the misfortune of having connections with an out of favour family,' Farkle said cautiously. 'Business is not good if you're related to someone who has crossed the Dunhams. You are lucky that you have no ties.'

Osun cringed; *if only he knew!* 'Is that why your shop failed?'

Farkle glanced at the curtain and door before replying; his grey eyes both sad and angry. 'As you know, the Coven of Telanis was the last seat to hold out against the Dunhams. I only have distant links with that now extinct family; they provided the gold for the decorative mammoth tusks I sold in my shop. It was enough to bring me trouble and make people fear being seen in my shop. I had no choice in the end but to gift all my stock to Hacren and publicly denounce the Coven of Telanis. With no stock, I had to sell the shop and start again at the market.' He sighed and shook his head. 'For me, as you can probably see, it's too late to start again. I think only of my son.'

Osun couldn't meet his eyes. Farkle's story was all too common and he couldn't afford to associate too much with someone who had been disgraced by the Dunhams; he couldn't risk drawing attention to himself. He gritted his teeth in annoyance at the pity he felt and the urge to help. He cleared his throat.

'I am not sure if my goods would be suitable for your stall, but I do have a small selection of ivory and gold pendants.'

It would be risky for both of them to trade without declaring it to the city tax officials but Farkle was obviously in desperate straits and Osun wasn't averse to saving a bit of money. Farkle could also prove a useful source of information in the city; market traders heard much.

'I could make you a fair offer.' Farkle regarded him.

The cook emerged from behind the curtain and with a friendly smile placed a jug of well water and two cups on the table. 'Can I get you some geranna?'

Osun winced, he wasn't a fan of the very sweet fruit liquor. 'Do you have a pale beer at all?'

'I do, master.' He bowed and ducked back behind the curtain.

'I am staying at the Sunset Inn.' Osun told Farkle. 'If you walked that way with me, you could take a look.'

'I don't carry much money with me, but if we are able to come to a deal, I could meet you again in the evening for a drink in the Sunset?'

Osun hesitated. It would not be good to be seen in such a popular establishment with someone so out of favour. 'I have other plans for the evening,' he said diplomatically. 'Perhaps we could have an early lunch here before I set off tomorrow.'

'Yes, that might be better,' Farkle said sadly.

Gunthe brought out their drinks and, very quickly after, their food. They talked of people they knew in the city and of who was doing well and who, like Farkle, was doing badly. It was as Osun feared; the Dunham's control of the city was now absolute. Gunthe, overhearing some of their conversation, told them that he'd heard there was to be a hanging at the end of the month.

'A captain of the guard,' Gunthe said quietly as though fearing to be overheard even in his empty establishment. 'He had been favoured by the old coven and had been allowed to buy a breeding woman of good blood, one that was supposedly sired by the coven's Lord himself. The fool bragged about the bloodline of the son he got from her and that he might grow to be powerful.' He shook his head sadly. 'The son was slaughtered, the woman too along with the two daughters she'd born.'

'A waste of good blood.' Osun shook his head. *And the Dunham's ensure no rivals with power are born.*

'Well, I am glad that my bloodlines are plain.' Farkle drank down his geranna. 'And even had I made my fortune I don't think I would purchase a woman with magical bloodlines; it's just not worth it. Live in a little comfort, that's all I want.'

'Aye.' Gunthe nodded and jumped up to take their empty plates. 'And being left alone to live without fear, that would be something to be prized.'

***

Osun and Farkle walked in silence through the city back toward the Sunset Inn, both deep in thought. Osun glanced at the people he passed; no one really knew him, but he wondered if anyone noted who he was walking with and if it would draw unwanted attention. He shouldn't have taken such a stupid risk. When they reached the inn, he showed his key to the slave manning the gate.

'I will take a look at my wagon and see that it's securely kept,' he said.

The slave bowed and gesturing another slave over – a young boy. He instructed him to show Osun where his wagon and team of bulls were being kept. Osun was more than a little impressed with the inn's security. The wagon was locked into a large room and a guard checked the number of Osun's key before unlocking it and allowing him in. The guard kept the door open but waited outside; it would be hard to have a private conversation.

'The chest is here, just inside,' Osun said loudly. Farkle looked startled; then realised what he was doing. 'It is heavier than traditional chests, but like I said I find it preserves perishable goods better than pine.'

'It's a good size,' Farkle replied as he climbed up into the wagon behind him.

'Take a look at the lining.' Osun took out a key and went to a small strongbox hidden behind some bolts of cloth toward the back of the wagon. He unlocked it and taking out a roll of velvet unfolded it to reveal several ivory pendants on gold chains.

'It's very fine,' Farkle said, running his finger over the links and lifting a pendant to check its quality and craftmanship. Under his breath he said, 'I can only offer twenty gold.'

'They're thirty,' Osun replied.

'Thirty!' Farkle said a little loudly. 'That is a lot of money for a chest!'

'But worth it to preserve rare spices and herbs.'

'Twenty-three,' Farkle whispered.

Osun thought about it. Twenty-three was actually a reasonable offer, especially if he wasn't going to pay a trading tax on it. 'Twenty-seven.'

'Still, I don't usually trade in such goods, so I don't think I'll be hurrying south to buy one any time soon. It's a fine piece of craftmanship though, for a chest. *Twenty-four.*'

'Twenty-five.'

Farkle winced. Osun felt guilty for pushing to take advantage of someone so down on his luck. 'Go on, then, twenty-four.' He sighed, knowing it was still a good deal.

Farkle's face broke into a smile and he reached out his hand for Osun to shake. Osun put the pendants back in the strongbox.

'There is a man on Copper Street who deals with fine wooden items,' Farkle said as he jumped awkwardly down from the wagon. 'He might be interested if you're willing to haul chests up here.'

'Maybe I'll pay him a visit.' Osun followed him out of the room, past the guard, and in to the courtyard. 'Anyway, I will be at market early tomorrow so no doubt I will see you there. Maybe we could even find something to trade!'

'Ha ha, maybe we could! I will see you tomorrow, brother.'

'Blessings to you, brother.' Osun didn't stay to watch Farkle leave but instead headed into the inn and found a quiet-ish corner to have a drink and watch the room. For the first time he noticed how many people wore symbols of the blood God, Hacren, on their person. Brooches, pendants, a small earing, or subtle button. He resolved to buy himself something in the market the next morning, silently apologising to Domarra.

As darkness fell, he ordered himself a meal but had to admit that despite its price and fancy arrangement, it was not as good as the flavoursome cooking of Gunthe. When he'd finished, he went back out to the courtyard and cringed when he saw it was the same guard as before still looking after the guest's transportation. Then an idea came to him.

'I am embarrassed to admit I dropped my key somewhere in my wagon earlier. I need to retrieve it.'

The guard narrowed his eyes, then seemed to recognise him. 'Of course, master, would you like me to help look?'

'No, no, I'm sure it will only take a moment.' Osun climbed up into the wagon and quickly drew out his scrying bowl and filled it with water, listening hard for any sign of the guard. He took out a small vial of blood and let three drops fall before pulling out the long pendant from beneath his shirt. Relief washed through him when his master answered at once.

'It is not safe for me to talk for long,' he whispered hastily. 'I can confirm the Borrows are taken. Adelphy parades captives with Fulmer blood for all to see. Hacren is in strong ascendancy and people openly wear regalia of necromancy. Even weak blood rivals are being executed.'

'Thank you, Osun. I still need to know of their plans for the Fulmers and Elden. We will have to think about how to get that information. You may have to go to Arkoom.'

Osun's heart skipped a beat. 'I'll see what more I can find here, first, Master; I will be in touch soon.'

He jumped and nearly upset the bowl as the guard called out, 'Are you all right, master?'

'I should have brought a light,' he called back. 'Ah! Wait a minute.' He quickly tipped the water back into the jug to dispose of later. 'I have it!' He put the scrying bowl away and taking the key from his purse, clutched it in his hand. He jumped down from the wagon and gave the guard a rueful smile.

'Do you need a slave to help you to your room?' The guard looked him up and down, clearly thinking that he was drunk, stupid, or both.

Osun waved his fingers in dismissal. 'No, I know the way.'

He walked steadily back in to the inn and up to his expensive room; though his nerves were far from steady. Arkoom; his master wanted him to go to Arkoom.

Chapter Six

Dia: Fulmer Isle

Dia peered through the darkness to the flames beyond the breakwater. Smoke stung her throat and made her eyes water. She tried to silence and steady her breathing, stretching out a leg slowly to get more comfortable among the wet undergrowth. Water dripped down from the leaves above, landing with heavy splats on her clothes and skin.

'What in the dark deeps was that?' Worvig hissed beside her.

Dia held up her hand to quiet him and shook her head. Her side throbbed with its own fire from the slash the dead Borrowman had given her. There was a cry from deeper within the forest – the unmistakable sound of a man dying. There was still at least one of their undead enemies on the island. She could feel Worvig's frustration but as a Silene he was family, chieftain and protector to the Icante of the Fulmers. The fact that he was more injured than she didn't come into it; the warrior wanted to be fighting, not cowering. Pressing her right hand to the wound, she pushed herself up with her left; knife still clutched within her fingers.

She crept forward, bowing beneath the trailing branches and feeling Worvig's anger and fear pulsing behind her. Usually her *knowing* would have been invaluable in tracking down a hidden enemy, but from the undead Borrowmen there were no tendrils of emotion. She was about to shut her magic off when she felt the metallic tang of panic away to her right. She signalled to Worvig and the big man nodded, moving ahead of her with his sword gripped at his side. They were heading back toward the sea and the burning ship.

Worvig raised a hand but plunged on himself, erupting from the undergrowth to swing his sword at a grey-skinned Borrowman. He grunted with the effort of the blow and it took the creature's head off its shoulders; no blood sprayed out, only rotten flesh. Its arms flailed and Worvig barely ducked in time to miss the sweep of its mace. Dia darted forward to thrust her knife into its spine but it didn't so much as flinch.

'You have to burn them!' A young warrior with his already dark skin blackened with soot splashed back from the shallows onto the narrow beach. Dia saw at once what he was heading for and ran for the dropped torch while Worvig fended off the flailing creature. She snatched up the torch and the young warrior shadowed her protectively, despite having no weapon, while she pushed it against the creature's tattered clothing. The flame caught and all three of them retreated back toward the water and watched as the dead Borrowman burnt. It made no attempt to save itself, continuing to fight and flail until its body lost the muscle and sinew to stand.

'Dorthai, where are the others?' Worvig demanded of the young warrior.

He shifted his feet and didn't look up at them. 'I think most went back to the stronghold when the demon came.'

Dia turned to look at the ship, it was drifting now, moving out on the tide. 'That fire demon seemed to be on our side; or against the Borrowmen at least. It saved me and Worvig.' A wave of dizziness swept through her and she clutched tighter to the wound at her side. 'Whatever it was we have no choice but to retreat to the stronghold ourselves. We'll have to sweep the island at first light and make sure none of our enemy have survived.'

'What of the Chemman necromancer?' Dorthai asked in concern.

Worvig's teeth flashed in a grin. 'I took him out when he swam ashore to escape the fire.'

Dia didn't add that she'd disabled the pale man by transferring fear and pain into his soul when he'd grabbed her thinking her an easy hostage. Let the warrior have his moment.

'That thing's head is still looking at me!' Dorthai's eyes were wide in the torchlight.

Dia looked to the beach and spotted the severed head. It did indeed appear still animated; if not alive. It made her skin crawl.

'We'll burn it tomorrow. We'll burn everything tomorrow. Come on.' She gritted her teeth against pain and exhaustion and cut into the forest toward the stronghold at a fast trot.

***

They heard raised voices long before they came to the causeway. Braziers were lit along the narrow cliff path to the hold, the walls themselves were dark. The braziers had been Dia's idea; they allowed clear sighting for their own archers of any approaching enemy while spoiling their enemy's night vision and leaving the defenders on the wall almost invisible. They heard the gates open and several men came running out.

'Icante! Worvig!' The first man to reach them was Venon, a veteran warrior in his fifties.

Worvig swung his fist at the man and lay him flat on the ground. 'I didn't command a retreat!' he roared.

Dia pulled herself up and glared at the others. 'I don't want to hear excuses. We think we dispatched all the Borrowmen but we will sweep the whole island as soon as the sun rises. Has anyone arrived from the other strongholds?'

'Not yet, Icante,' one of the men muttered.

'Let me know when they do. In the meantime, send the healer to me and see that Dorthai and Worvig get a good meal and as much ale as they can hold.'

She wanted to crawl, but she held herself upright as she made her way across the outer ward to the longhouse that held the great hall. A very young woman was waiting for her and walked with her to the private chambers at the rear of the building. Pirelle was not a strong *Walker*, but she was as sharp minded as a crow so Dia had taken her on as an apprentice, anyway.

'Did you see much?' Dia asked, collapsing onto the bed.

Pirelle lifted Dia's hand from the wound and pulling away the fabric of her shirt gave a hiss of concern. Like Dia, Pirelle's eyes were brown and blue but her hair was dark-brown rather than black. 'Not much,' Pirelle replied with a shake of her head as she set water to boil. 'I could see no other ships, just the one aflame. I ... I lost sight of you, Dia, and when the men came back—'

Dia waved a hand in irritable dismissal. 'The fact they will feel themselves cowards will be punishment enough; though it took more than courage to face those dead men and that fiery demon. I've never seen anything like it; nor heard tell of one. I would think it a creature of Chem except that it helped me and defeated our enemy.'

'It helped us?'

Dia nodded, staring up at the roof beams. With a wave of almost-grief she missed her feisty daughter intensely in that moment. Kesta was always learning and loved the old tales and might have heard something of fire demons; but Kesta was many miles away with Arrus.

As though reading her mind Pirelle said, 'Arrus will go mad if he hears the warriors retreated and left you out there with Worvig.'

'Worvig will handle it in his own way.' Dia sighed. 'It was … not an ordinary battle. But the young man, Dorthai from Dolphin Isle, discovered the dead creatures are vulnerable to fire. That will be very useful.'

Someone knocked on the door a bare instant before it opened, and an elderly woman stepped in. Her hair was the silver-grey of a rabbit's fur but without its softness.

'You needed me?' The healer went straight to Dia and 'tsked' over the wound. 'That will poison.' She shook her head. 'I'll put you into as deep a sleep as I can and clean it up. It will be hard to stitch.' She glared at Dia as though it were her fault she'd received such a jagged wound instead of a neat, clean one.

'I know you will do your best,' Dia replied tiredly. 'Worvig will need you when you finish here.'

'That lump can wait.' The healer pulled a small bottle out of one of her many pockets and handed it to Dia. 'Two swigs.'

Dia gritted her teeth and forced herself to swallow two mouthfuls of the foul-tasting concoction. Its sweetness was almost rotten. She settled back against her pillow and gratefully drifted into sleep.

***

Dia awoke slowly; the sound of deep voices, not quite raised, leaking into her dreams. Pirelle was standing in the doorway softly directing the men outside to wait a little longer. She recognised one of the voices as Worvig's and the other as the chieftain of Eagle Stronghold.

'Pirelle! Tell them to get on with searching the isle for any remaining enemies. Send for Dorthai; I want him to come with me to search the beach. I want to see any remains before they are burnt.'

Pirelle nodded; but Worvig shoved the door open and called in, 'I'd like to give you more warriors than just Dorthai.'

'I'm sure you would,' Dia replied, swinging her legs out of the bed to stand. 'This is a job for *Walkers,* you warriors have your own work. Dorthai proved himself last night, and he is the man I need to assist me.'

Worvig grunted his disapproval but nodded; there was no point arguing with the Icante. 'I'll send him – and leave ten men here at the stronghold.'

Dia smiled. 'Very well.'

Dia changed her shirt for one that was not torn and bloodied, pausing briefly to wash with the warm water Pirelle had left out for her. She strapped on her boots and tied her hair back with a leather thong. Pirelle held her cloak out and handed her a crust of bread as they hastened out into the great hall. Two women stood waiting for her; they were not *Walkers* but Dia gestured for them to follow. Both women carried bows and had knives at their hips, they were about the same age as Dia and looked so alike it was hard to tell them apart. Their hair was dark but with the bluish sheen of a magpie's feathers; their eyes hazel.

'The others are collecting wood for pyres,' one of them said as she thrust open the doors and stepped out into the daylight. Clouds still bunched together tightly in the morning sky but silver light seeped through and the rain had ceased. A warrior stood at either side of the door and they stood up straighter as the women passed.

'Heara, you go ahead and read the path for me.' Dia instructed the woman who had spoken. Her lifelong friend was the best there was at reading a trail, better even than her twin Shaherra. 'Shaherra, grab us a couple of torches.'

She turned to regard Pirelle. The young woman's eyes were wide and her breathing rapid; Dia couldn't blame her for being nervous. Pirelle had not left the stronghold during the raid but observing while *walking* was just as real as being there and the emotions you read from others just as brutal.

'Use your *knowing*,' she instructed softly. 'I don't think we can feel anything from the dead men but there may have been more than one Chemman on that ship. Also, there is a chance that some of our missing warriors are yet alive.'

'How many are we missing?' Shaherra asked.

'Eleven we know are dead,' Pirelle replied. 'Eight more are unaccounted for. There are no reports from the other strongholds of raids elsewhere; it seems they struck straight at us.'

'This wasn't a typical Borrowman raid,' Dia said. 'Not by a long way. Last night's raid was meant to take the Stronghold of the Icante.'

'They sought to conquer us?' Pirelle asked in alarm.

'And might have succeeded if it were not for that fire demon,' Dia admitted reluctantly. 'Despite Kesta spying out the ship being loaded with "strange, grey, Borrowmen," I, for one, was not prepared for the horror and intensity of their attack.' She shuddered. 'And I foolishly anticipated them attacking elsewhere.'

'We have never had a direct attack on this stronghold!' Pirelle leapt to her defence.

Dia felt a wave of warmth toward the young woman and Pirelle blushed as she picked up the emotion with her *knowing.*

'Not for many years but it has happened,' Shaherra mused. 'Now and again an ambitious Chieftain emerges in the Borrows and tries his luck.'

'But when was the last time we were attacked by Chem?' Pirelle asked.

'Never.' Both Dia and Shaherra answered at once.

'Chem attacks to conquer, not to raid.' Dia went on. 'It is not a harsh place of limited resources like the Borrows. We have little that they would want in terms of material goods; they would achieve more by going for their traditional target; Elden.'

What is it they might want from us though? Dia mused. *A base from which to supply themselves and attack Elden? But then surely the island of Mantu would have been a better choice? Unless they had hoped to keep it secret from Elden for as long as possible and were relying on the fact that the Fulmers liked its isolation from its much larger neighbour?* She shied away from thinking of her husband and daughter; she had no time to spare for worrying over them when there was nothing she could do about whatever they might be facing in Elden.

'Icante!' Dorthai came running to join them as they reached the gates of the defensive wall. 'Should I not search the island with the other warriors?' The young man sounded offended.

'I need someone I can rely on.' Dia told him. 'Worvig needs to coordinate the chieftains; you have proved yourself to be someone that I can trust. Tell me of your experience with the dead man last night.'

Dorthai hesitated; Pirelle moved ahead to walk beside Shaherra.

'I am obviously not a *walker* but ... even to me they *felt* wrong. They didn't quite move like men; like they'd forgotten how to use their bodies at first. They had no expressions.' Dorthai shuddered. 'They made no sound. They were incredibly strong. The first strike of one tore the sword from my hand and near broke my wrist. When I struck with my knife, it didn't bleed. I … I was at a loss as to how to defeat it. I saw other warriors struck down around me and I almost ran. But then I saw that their ship was in flames and it gave me courage. I wondered if they would burn. I did run then but only to start a fire and gather torches. I set light to as many as I could while they fought the warriors who had remained. Someone said we should get back to the stronghold to defend from there with fire arrows.'

Dia sensed he knew very well who had given that command, but she didn't press him. 'But you stayed.'

'There were still several of those things left … *alive*. I had thought they were easy to sneak up on, but I think I'd only been able to do so when they were distracted and engaged in fighting. That last one you found me with seemed to sense me right away. It moved so quickly! Like it had just then learnt not only how to use its body again but how to do it better. It knocked the torch from my hand and, well, you and Worvig were there then.'

'Thank you; that is useful.'

'Dia!' Heara appeared on the path in front of them. 'I have a trail. Seems to be an injured man pursued by one of those creatures.'

Dia nodded, and they followed the scout through the tall bushes. Heara slowed her pace when she got back to the trail, bending now and again to better read the marks she found. She held up her hand, and they all stopped to wait while she stepped slowly ahead.

'He is dead.' Heara turned to speak over her shoulder. 'It's Onwin.'

Dia gave a shake of her head. Onwin was – had been – one of their most experienced warriors.

'Looks as though the creature that killed him headed back toward the beach.'

'We will do the same,' Dia said.

Heara went ahead again and Shaherra stepped back to Dia's side with her hand on her dagger hilt. There was a strong smell of smoke and burnt wood long before they stepped out of the trees and onto the beach. The ship had been broken up by the sea and a large part of it had washed up against the rocks. Planks and long crates had been thrown up onto the pebbles and sand along with several bodies. Gulls and crabs swarmed the beach, but one area was notably empty of carrion hunters.

'That's the head,' Dorthai whispered.

Dia's skin tingled and itched as though she'd walked through an invisible spider's web. She shuddered and then asked Pirelle, 'anything?'

'I ... I want to say no but that isn't quite the case. I don't feel the emotions of a person but there is a *wrongness* here; it makes me feel queasy.'

Dia called up her own *knowing* and immediately tasted the sour fear from Pirelle and Dorthai. The twins were uneasy but alert, concentrating more on their surroundings than their emotions. She picked up on what Pirelle had tried to describe at once; it was a feeling of impending danger such as a lone person might feel on hearing a large predator growl. Life pulsed in the severed head at the same time as death ate at it. For a moment Dia found herself rooted to the spot in dread, but she forced herself to move.

'The head is alive, it's watching us,' she said.

Shaherra drew her dagger and Heara nocked an arrow to her bow. Dorthai gripped the torch he carried in both hands like a club. Pirelle shrank back behind them as Dia stalked forward. The eyes of the head followed her as she approached, the slack mouth contorted as though attempting a grin.

'Who are you?' Dia demanded. 'Why have you attacked the Fulmers?'

'I've come for you, Icante,' The head slurred. 'I intend to put a child in your belly myself!'

Dia stepped back, mouth open and eyes wide, her hand going to her stomach. Her muscles tightened over her lungs so she had to fight to draw in air. She snatched at Dorthai's torch and reached for the wind; flame billowed forward and engulfed the head. It laughed as the flesh melted away.

'I am coming, Icante!'

Chapter Seven

Kesta; Kingdom of Elden

Rosa watched her with amusement and curiosity as she ate her breakfast like a starving cub.

'You're much happier today. I noticed that Thane Jorrun left rather quickly last night?'

Kesta looked up and almost laughed at the burning curiosity on Rosa's face.

'I admit he surprised me a little. I wonder ...'

'What?' Rosa demanded.

'He is so secretive up in his tower; I wonder if he has a mistress – or a man even – hidden away up there. It seems that this marriage is purely political to him.' She laughed at Rosa's scandalised expression. 'Is that such a rare thing in Elden?'

Rosa sat back. 'No, I suppose it isn't.' She fastened back a loose strand of her hair. 'So, what are we going to do today?'

'Today,' Kesta stood up and pushed back her chair. 'We are going to turn this hovel into a stronghold! Let's go pester Tantony.'

They found Tantony in the great hall with a few warriors and keep staff. He was mopping up some stew with coarse oat cakes and quickly wiped his mouth with the back of his hand when he saw Kesta.

'My lady?' He looked wary.

Kesta came straight to the point. 'This stronghold needs to be more self-sufficient. I may no longer be able to help my own people in the Fulmers, but I can at least get us readier for war here. I need the land around the stronghold cleared and timber cut; the ward also needs clearing to make room for growing food.'

'Well now.' Tantony wiped his hands on his trousers. 'That might not be such a bad plan, but it would take a lot of labour and a lot of coin.'

'I see plenty of men about the stronghold with nothing better to do than eat and sleep and lean against the walls!'

Tantony winced and glanced back at the warriors who were seated at the table watching the exchange. 'Ma'am, there are a few labourers and tradesmen whom we could get to do the work but mostly the men here are warriors. When they are not on duty, they have weapons practice and hunting to do. I cannot spare any warriors.'

'A shame; I was thinking of holding a feast and bringing out some kegs of ale for anyone willing to help me with the work.' She saw several of the warriors sit up straighter. 'Never mind, us women will have to do the best we can and hold our own celebration.'

'Merkis!' one of the men tried to whisper, but it came out a sharp hiss.

'Look, maybe I can ask for volunteers among the warriors.' Tantony sighed. 'We can offer a couple of coins and this feast of yours. It's about time we cleared away some of the encroaching trees, anyway; too many hiding places for raiders. I'll put the word about. I take it you want to start on this right away?'

'Tomorrow will do; thank you Merkis.'

'Indeed.' He looked at her reproachfully. 'I'll get any of the bondsmen who are not engaged in more urgent duties to report to you tomorrow morning.'

'Thank you.' She gave a slight bow of her head and the most charming smile she could muster. Her *knowing* told her that most of those in the room felt intrigue and even a little excitement. Only one or two projected stinging resentment. 'Come, Rosa, let us see Reetha next.'

Word had obviously gone ahead as Reetha was waiting for them at the bottom of the tower stairs. She was a tall, sinewy, woman with flint-grey hair coiled in plaits about her head. She looked unabashedly at both Kesta's mismatched eyes.

'How would you feel about a herb garden and a large vegetable plot within the keep?' Kesta came straight to the point.

'I think I would feel it was about time.' Reetha folded her wrinkle-skinned arms. 'For as long as I've worked here people have kept their animals in the keep. There are still some herbs and onions to be found out there if you're willing to wade through brambles and stickles.'

Kesta nodded. 'I intend to have a proper barn built with pens and storage space. When the land around the keep is properly cleared, we can pasture the animals there.'

'It would take a lot of fencing or animal herds to keep them safe; and since they are all owned by different karls and warriors, there—'

Kesta waved a hand. 'Animals are not a problem; I am a *walker*. Can you find me a handful of trustworthy children who can mind them? It need be only during the day, the animals will all come back into the keep at night if I ask them.'

Reetha's eyes narrowed. 'As long as y' witchcraft harms none I can find y' the workers from among the children of the owners. Some of them could do with more honest work.'

'Have them report to me when we have finished clearing the ward. Also, I've promised a feast and ale for those who help me clear the land and dig the plots; is that something we are in a position to provide?'

Reetha gave a slight shake of her head. 'We brew our own mead and have some stores but our next supply boat from Taurmaline is due three weeks hence. How long do you think this work will take?'

'I'm not sure.' Kesta's shoulders sagged. 'Can you send to Taurmaline for an earlier delivery of extra goods?'

'If y' got the coin, I can send someone to the city to make the purchases and secure a boat to deliver.'

'I'll have coin for you this morning.'

Reetha raised an eyebrow but unfolded her arms. 'Do you want to see the kitchen and cellars?'

Kesta tried to hide her disinterest; cooking was something her mother had never been able to involve her in. 'Yes, I should see it all; but be assured I've heard good reports of how you run the keep household and I have no desire to interfere.'

A tension that had hung between the two women evaporated almost at once and Reetha's thin mouth turned upward into a smile. 'Well, of course I will need to change a few of our supply orders to take into account what you like to eat; but I am sure your garden will be a Goddess-send.' Reetha chattered away as she showed them around the main kitchen with its huge fireplace, stone bread oven, and dry and cold cellars. There was a well in the wine cellar and Reetha told them there was another out in the ward close to the stables. As they came back through, Reetha picked up a freshly baked bread roll and splitting it in half with her long fingers slathered both pieces with butter. She handed Kesta and Rosa a half each.

'My thyme bread.' She nodded at it proudly. 'I was going to send you some up with your noon meal but it's so much nicer hot.'

Kesta took a bite; it was soft and slightly sweet and the thyme subtle but delicious. She wiped a drip of butter from her chin and laughing declared, 'That must be the best bread I've ever tasted! Thank you, Reetha, if you could send me some up warm with breakfast each day I will be delighted!'

Reetha gave a satisfied nod and held back a smile. 'I will do that, Lady.'

'And I will be sure that there is plenty of thyme in the herb beds.'

***

'Where next?' Rosa asked as Kesta headed out of the keep.

'I want a proper look around the grounds to see how much work will need doing and choose a site for the barn. Then we will go and see the man that Jorrun spoke to yesterday to see if he will build it for us.'

Rosa looked down at her feet and Kesta saw that she was wearing a pair of dainty court shoes.

'I think I may need to adjust my attire while I stay with you!'

Kesta lifted her day dress to reveal her own sturdy boots. 'We'll see if there is a cobbler anywhere about. You might want to stick to the paths in the meantime.'

'No, I'll manage.' Rosa smiled and to show her determination she set off around the keep.

While most of the ward was cropped grass, in places the ground was churned up by the rooting of pigs, and in others it was so overgrown they could not find a way through it. They discovered several goats that made both of them jump when they started up their eerie bleating.

'They sound like dying babies!' Rosa exclaimed.

'I can't believe the place has been left to go so wild.' Kesta shook her head and looked up at the Raven Tower. They had come within a few yards of it and another two steps would bring them under its shadow. 'I wonder what so preoccupies him up there that he doesn't even see what has become of the ward.'

Determinedly Kesta strode toward the tower and walked around to its entrance. She heard Rosa gasp, but she didn't try to stop her. The door was set deep in the grey stone and looked disappointingly plain. Her eyes were drawn to the large keyhole, and she reached out a finger to touch the metal edge of it. She crouched just a little to move her eyes closer to it but bit her lower lip and straightened up again. The handle was a large hoop of iron on a hinge which had been oiled and showed no signs of rust. Would the door be locked if she gave it a pull?

'So where do you think you want the barn?' Rosa asked anxiously behind her.

Kesta sighed and turned her back on the door. 'Near the well so water doesn't need to be hauled too far; close to where the stables are, I think. Let's take a look at those and then go on down to the lake.'

'These stables are almost as big as at castle Taurmaline.' Rosa lifted her skirts to keep up with her. 'Did Tantony say how many warriors man the stronghold?'

Kesta frowned. 'I don't think so; I guess I should ask.'

Two men stood outside the stables; one holding the halter of a roan gelding while the other worked at a hoof with a file. They looked up but didn't pause in their work.

'Master's inside,' the farrier said.

Kesta nodded and pushing aside one of the double doors went in. After a moment she realised that she was staring with her mouth open and quickly closed it. It was airy, light, spacious and absolutely spotless; a complete contrast to the ward outside. It went back a long way with stalls to either side and storage space in the rafters accessed by ladders and narrow walkways. She could smell the warmth of the horses and hear the rustle of straw and the snuffle of curious nostrils. Several windows let in light; the shutters thrown back against the whitewashed walls. There was an underlying smell of vinegar and lavender and she guessed they used both to scrub out the stalls.

'Ma'am?' A startled boy, stepped out of a stall pulling a cart full of soiled straw behind him.

'I'm Kesta Silene; the Thane's new wife. I am just looking about the stronghold and I must say these stables are … well, they are very well kept.'

A huge grin took over the boy's face, and a man walked out behind him. He was a good six inches taller than her, wiry with a long grey beard and moustache, both plaited and clipped with steel rings. His hair was a lighter grey and also clipped neatly back. A huge pink scar covered one side of his face and sealed shut one eye; from the dip of the skin Kesta guessed that the socket was empty. *Fire.*

She called up her *knowing*. The boy seemed excited and there was an uncomplicated friendliness about him that she took to at once. The man was guarded, and she sensed a lot of pride there. She became aware at once of the different personalities of the horses also, some like still pools, others like bright darting dragonflies.

'Are you master here?' Kesta broke the silence. 'I am Kesta Silene and this is my companion, Rosa.'

'I heard.' The man folded his arms. 'The Thane leaves me to run things.'

'I can see why; I can't imagine anyone doing a finer job. I'm having the ward cleared and the land about the stronghold. Tell me, where do you pasture the horses?'

The man's eyes narrowed but she could sense more curiosity than hostility. 'We winter the warhorses here; but when they are not being used elsewise, they get taken across the river to the pastures north-west of here. What are you thinking?'

'That once cleared, we make more use of the land around the stronghold; it will take a lot of work, but I'd like to take the forest back several yards.'

'That would be a lot of work.' The man took a step back and let his arms drop to his sides. Kesta tried not to smile when she felt his grudging approval. 'About time someone took more interest in the hold 'stead of stargazing in towers. You'll need horses. Couple o' old warhorses here could take a run out hauling logs. Ricer and his brother Kine, down at the dock, both have plough horses they loan out. My names Nerim, by the way; the boy is Nip.'

Kesta gave the slightest of bows in acknowledgement. 'An herb garden is among what I plan for the ward; anything in particular you need grown for the horses let me know.'

'I'll draw up a list. By the by, your pony is just down there. Not in the best way when she got here, but I heard what you did for her. She is coming on well and should make a nice lady's mount; however, we are clearing out this stall as the Thane says he has bought a horse for you in Taurmaline. On its way here, so it is. Nip will take you down to see the pony if you like?'

Kesta opened her mouth to speak, but hesitated, folding her arms across her chest. Why would the Dark Man be buying her a horse after complaining about her bonding with animals? She gave her head a quick shake, realising she was being rude. 'Thank you, I'd love to see the pony.'

Nip quickly pulled his cart out of the way, and looking around for something to clean his hands on, settled for the front of his tunic. He had curly hair in mousy ringlets and dark grey eyes that Kesta found it hard not to be captivated by. Few had eyes of that colour in the Fulmers.

'This way!' Nip grinned, showing a chipped tooth; but the grin fell away, and the boy's eyes widened. Kesta spun around to see the only man who could hide from her *knowing* standing a few feet away.

'My Lord?' she tried to hide how startled she was, but her heart was pounding.

'A raven has returned from Taurmaline.' Jorrun lifted his left hand and uncurled his long fingers to show a tiny roll of paper. 'I thought you would wish to know at once that your mother, Dia Icante, is alive and well, as is your uncle Worvig. King Bractius says that they lost nineteen warriors but held off the attack from Chem.'

'It's definitely Chem and not the Borrows?' Kesta held her hands together to stop them shaking.

'So it seems,' Jorrun replied coolly, closing his hand over the small scroll. 'We have sent messengers ahead of your father, but your mother is a very clever woman, she will understand much already. I won't keep you from your work; I will see you later.'

Jorrun turned and stalked out of the stables. Kesta watched him like a kestrel watching a cat leave.

'Nip, run and get these ladies a glass of wine,' Nerim growled.

'Kesta?' Rosa touched her arm while Nip darted away to one of the ladders.

'I'm fine.' She shook her head. She hadn't realised how tightly her fear for her mother and uncle were coiled in her belly until relief had released the knot. She drew back her *knowing*; not wanting to taste any pity from those around her. Then she saw Nip coming back down the ladder with a glass of deep red wine in each hand; gripping the wood with his forearms only as he scampered down as surefooted as any goat. She laughed, and the cramping tension eased from her back and shoulders. 'That is a boy worth keeping.' She smiled.

'He is a good boy.' Nerim's eyes lit although he did not smile.

'Your son?' Kesta asked.

Nerim nodded.

Nip handed them the wine, and they sipped at it while they went to check on the pony. Kesta ran her hands over its ribs and winced at the sores from the old ill-fitting harness. It snuffled into her shoulder while she stroked its cheek.

'Do you ride, Rosa?'

'I rode out with the queen sometimes.' Rosa held her glass with both hands.

'Then if you'll ride out with me sometimes, I'll give you this pony. What will you call her?'

Rosa looked startled. 'Oh, well; I would think she would be called Nettle. She's tough but has a wild beauty.'

'I like that.' Kesta stroked the pony's soft nose. 'Nettle. Come on then; we have more work to do today.' She turned to Nerim. 'Thank you for your hospitality; I think I will enjoy working with you.'

'My Lady.' Nerim gave a small bow and, after kicking his son, Nip did the same.

***

They took a slow stroll around the outer circle of the stronghold between the two walls. They were greeted by open stares; some of curiosity and some of hostility. Most of the women acknowledged Kesta and Rosa with a curtsey or 'good morning'; but the warriors and the few tradesmen among the houses barely grunted. She could feel that Rosa was uncomfortable and nervous, and she had to fight to stop it infecting her too. For the most part the houses seemed to be in good repair. The amount of thatch concerned her, and every building was constructed out of wood, except the blacksmith's forge, which had a three-sided building made of stone and a roof of slate.

Completing their circuit, they left through the gateway and followed the track down toward the lake. Kesta heard one of the warriors guarding the gate speak behind her.

'Look, she's had enough of Jorrun already.'

The other warrior snorted in amusement and she gritted her teeth, pretending not to have heard. So; not all the warriors at the stronghold respected their Thane. That was certainly something to think about.

As they approached the small cluster of cottages, they saw a woman emerging from the smokehouse. She was dressed in dull grey with her hair gathered up under a scarf. She stopped when she saw them and waited for them to approach.

132

'Good morning.' She gave a small curtsey. 'May I help your ladyships?'

'Good morning; we are looking for Kurghan. I have some work for him.' Kesta studied the woman. Lines creased the corners of her brown eyes that were underscored with dark shadows. She radiated composure and confidence and Kesta felt no sense of pre-judgement or expectation from her. 'May I ask your name?'

'Aven, Lady. Kurghan is just finishing off a fishing boat; I'll take you to him.'

'Are you his sister?' Rosa asked to make conversation as they followed the path to the large work shed. Kesta could hear wood being sawn and the voices of two men.

'I am indeed. I hear you're from the Fulmers?'

'Oh, I'm not!' Rosa replied quickly. 'But Kesta is. I'm from Cainridge but have been at the court of Taurmaline for most of my life.'

'You might find it a little quiet and … rustic here.'

'Not with Kesta here.' Rosa laughed.

Aven raised an eyebrow and glanced around at Kesta. 'There were some of us thought that Jorrun would never marry; he never seemed interested. You were quite a surprise, Lady Kesta.'

'It was purely political,' Kesta murmured.

'Oh, I'm sorry.' Aven winced. 'Still, I don't think you will be treated badly. The Thane is somewhat protective of the women of this hold.'

Kesta and Rosa looked at each other but before they could ask more Aven called out to her brother. The sawing stopped and Kurghan came out of his boathouse; gesturing for his companion to join him. He held out his hand and Kesta took it, gripping firmly, before he realised his error and flushed with embarrassment.

'Lady, what brings you out here?'

'I'm getting a feel for the stronghold and its people; but to get to the point I'm here to offer you a large job.'

Kurghan gave a pull on his beard. She could feel his curiosity and excitement; this man loved to work and was eager for something challenging. 'What kind of job?'

Kesta grinned and it caught all those around her. 'Well; to start with I'm having the ward cleared out and several areas for planting dug. I'll need some fencing to segregate the animals while you build me a large barn with storage for hay and crops. I'm having the area around the hold taken back in all directions so there will be plenty of wood. I'll need more fencing then to separate pasture. The land outside the hold will remain common, of course, with areas designated for haymaking. Does anyone here grow wheat or corn?'

'Only in very small quantities,' Aven supplied. 'More is grown across the river beyond the mill.'

Kesta nodded. 'So, other than the excellent boats you build, what is the industry of the hold? A lot of supplies are obviously brought in but what do you exchange for it?'

Aven and Kurghan looked at each other and she picked up both awkwardness and surprise.

'Why, the Thane is paid in gold for protecting Elden with his magic,' Kurghan said.

Kesta's face warmed with a blush and she tried hard not to let her smile slip. She should have known that; now she'd revealed her ignorance to these people. Rosa shifted beside her. She was relieved when all she felt was sympathy; these were good people.

'I would be happy to hear any suggestions you have for anything else the hold needs,' Kesta said. 'We start tomorrow but I understand if you have other work that you're committed to first.'

'We can get this boat finished in a couple of days. I can send you my two eldest lads to start with some sawing and fencing; feed them and slip them a wheel of cheese and a bottle of wine to take home and they'll be happy.' Kurghan's mouth curled upward to show his teeth in a grin. 'My niece is as good at fishing as either of them and can catch enough to make up the loss; if Aven can spare her?'

'Aye, I'm up together with the smoking and we're out of wool to weave.'

'I am happy to take on women to work with me, if you can spare a little time and are interested?' Kesta told Aven. 'I shall be clearing and digging myself.'

Aven looked from Kesta's earnest face, to Rosa and Kurghan's shocked ones and placed her hands on her hips. 'Well now, that's something I wouldn't miss! I'll nip by between smoking the catch. I might see if any of the other girls want to tag along if that's okay?'

'I would love that,' Kesta said genuinely. 'I intend that the gardens – especially the herb garden – be something to benefit everyone.'

'Hey now,' Kurghan grumbled. 'I hope my supper will still be on the table when I finish my day's work!'

'Supper will be in the great hall for anyone working late with me,' Kesta said firmly. 'Nothing special, just filling; but there is to be a big feast when the work is done.'

'Well then.' Kurghan threw up his hands. 'We'll be with you in a couple of days!'

Kesta held out her hand, and he shook it with a chuckle.

'Aven; see you tomorrow.' She turned and walked back toward the hold and Rosa hurried to catch up with her.

'I like what you're doing,' Rosa said slowly.

'But?'

'But; have you spoken to the Thane about your plans?'

Kesta stopped and looked at the earthworks and wooden ramparts that protected what was now her home. 'He told me I could have the running of the household but that isn't enough. I should be in the Fulmers, fighting for my people. I should be at my mother's side using my powers to fight off the necromancers of Chem. I was raised to rule, Rosa; raised to lead and defend. Jorrun doesn't rule this stronghold; he neglects it to do whatever it is he spends his days doing in that tower. Even Tantony, much as I like him, seems to do nothing more than keep the place trundling along. If this is to be my home, if this is to be where I have to stand and defend, then I will do it to the best of my ability and Thane Jorrun will just have to put up with it.'

Rosa slipped her hand around Kesta's arm and squeezed it. 'I can't wait to see all your plans come to be!'

Sadness seeped from Kesta's heart into her blood, but she refused to let it push at her eyes. Instead, she turned her thoughts away from the Fulmers and her family and considered how much she'd achieved that morning. It was a good start.

'Let's grab something to eat and then go let Tantony know how much of the hold's funds we have spent so far.'

***

They found Tantony behind a desk piled with parchment. The Merkis stood and knocked the desk with his thighs, his chair scraping back. 'Have you been told of the message we received from Taurmaline?'

'Jorrun found me,' Kesta told him and seeing a chair, pulled it toward the desk to sit down. 'Has there been news on my father's progress?'

'He is only a day into his journey back to the Fulmers. I hear you've had a busy morning.' There was a hint of reproach in his voice and Kesta felt a moment of guilt that she might have shamed the old warrior.

'I've come to discuss my plans with you and to ask your advice.'

Tantony looked up sharply.

'You know the hold and its people better than me. I've made some progress and most reactions have been positive; it will cost us in time, labour, and of course gold, but most people see the benefit. What do you think we should do?'

'Well, there is strategic benefit to what you have suggested,' Tantony said slowly, studying her face. 'Although it has been several generations since any enemy has struck this far inland. It'll be expensive but in the long run will save us money. We should also gain enough extra timber to float some down to Taurmaline to sell.' He sighed. 'Some will take umbrage at a foreigner – and a woman at that – coming here and instantly making huge changes. I presume that you wouldn't want to make the changes more slowly and subtly?'

'Actually, Kesta has been quite clever and diplomatic,' Rosa spoke up.

Tantony looked at them both. 'That may be so among the woman and tradesmen, but you will find some of the warriors a bit … set in their ways.'

Kesta placed a hand on the table. 'Do you really believe that if Chem has truly taken all the Borrows we won't see war this far inland? Even if they don't come here, the chances are our warriors will be sent to the coast. The work needs to be done while we have the people to achieve it; do the men want their families to starve or be less than adequately protected?'

Tantony nodded reluctantly. 'You put forward a strong argument. I'll get the warriors on board but be prepared for some ... muttering and resentment from some quarters.'

Kesta gritted her teeth, trying not to let her anger rise. The men of Elden would just have to put up with the fact that she was used to commanding.

'Thank you for your advice, Merkis. Was there anything else that needed my attention today?'

'Well, young Catya came here asking after you and I suggested she await you in your receiving room.'

Kesta felt a twinge of annoyance; she really didn't want to take on this woman of Jorrun's. She wondered again who she was and what she meant to the Dark Man.

'I'd best go and see if I'm willing to take her on. Good day to you, Merkis.'

***

When they passed through the great hall to return to their tower, there were still several warriors seated at the tables. Kesta made a point of meeting their eyes and two of the older men stood briefly to bow; most of the others quickly followed suit but Kesta noted that three young men remained seated. She chose to ignore it although her anger rose, and she felt a strong desire to march over and remind them who she was. But then, who was she? Not a queen, not here. In Elden women did not command. Still, it galled her that they showed her so little respect and through her, Jorrun as well.

When they walked into the receiving room, they found a young girl standing by the window. She couldn't have been much more than thirteen years old and looked as thin as a wheat stalk. She had long brown hair that hung down over her face and she peeped out at them with expressionless blue eyes. There was a stillness to her that shouted and Kesta suppressed a shudder, for some reason afraid to use her *knowing*. The table had been set with food and everything had been placed with precision. The girl gave a curtsy without lifting her eyes.

'Are you Catya?' Kesta asked.

The girl nodded.

Kesta regarded her with narrowed eyes but lifted her chin and took in a breath; the girl was shy, not rude. 'I am Kesta and this is Lady Rosa. Have you eaten?'

The girl glanced up, surprised by the question; or perhaps wary of an accusation. Catya's face was as hard to read as Jorrun's. She wondered if they were related. Perhaps an illegitimate daughter?

'Pour us some wine and then sit down and join us.'

Catya didn't stir until both women were seated, then she cautiously crept forward and poured wine from the jug. She froze when Kesta spoke.

'Usually I like to take hot tea with my noon meal. Nettle is a favourite of mine, but I also love fennel and mint. Could you see to that for tomorrow?'

Catya glanced at her and nodded.

'Very good. Now sit down and eat, you look half starved.'

Catya waited until both Kesta and Rosa were eating before reaching out tentatively for some bread. Kesta handed her the butter without looking at her.

'If I can get some parchment, I'll draw up some plans this afternoon and we can list what tools and materials we need,' she said. 'I'll present them to Jorrun and see what he thinks.'

'Will he get a say?' Rosa grinned.

'As long as his answer is yes.' Kesta grinned back. 'But I was thinking about what you said, and I think you're right; I should have discussed it with him first.'

'I know you're angry, and I don't blame you, but your life will be much more pleasant if the two of you do get along.'

Kesta became aware of Catya in her peripheral vision, hunched over her bread like a squirrel. Just what was this child to Jorrun? Would she report back all that was said? Slowly she opened up her *knowing,* but it was almost as though no one was sitting there. It was not the same as when she tried with Jorrun; with him it was like being brushed by cool, empty air. Catya was like bumping into a stone wall.

She'd met someone like that once before in her life; years ago...

She drew her *knowing* back quickly and swallowed some wine to hide her discomfort. It was not something she wanted to remember.

'Catya; what would you like to learn?'

The girl flinched and glanced up briefly; there was a storm of anger and hatred in her eyes and Kesta drew in a sharp breath.

'Learn?' The girl dipped her head and let her hair fall over her eyes again.

'Yes. You also Rosa. I don't know what ladies-in-waiting are taught in Elden but in the Fulmers we learn all we need to survive and fend for ourselves. For example.' She leaned across the table. 'Archery, knife fighting, fishing, horse-riding ...'

'Knife fighting?' Catya sat up and her gaze was steady as she stared at Kesta.

'Yes Catya. Even a woman who is not a warrior should be able to defend herself. Generally, we are not strong enough to wield a sword against a man but knowing how to use a knife could save your life.'

A complex series of emotions swept across the girl's face and out of the corner of her eye she saw Rosa look from Catya to her and back again. The older woman had a sharp mind and Kesta couldn't help but think Queen Ayline had been a fool to undervalue her.

'I can already ride,' Rosa said. 'And since the horse Jorrun has purchased for you is not yet here perhaps we could start with knife fighting?'

'Very well.' Kesta smiled. 'Fetch me the paper and inks and see if you can pick up a couple of knives.'

Rosa nodded and stood to leave; Catya also got up but Kesta raised her hand. 'You stay, Catya, Rosa can manage on her own.'

The girl sat back down reluctantly and Kesta studied her until Rosa had left the room.

'Who are your parents?'

'Dead,' Catya murmured.

'Who is your guardian?'

'Jorrun, now.'

'And before?'

Catya hesitated and Kesta didn't need to be a *walker* to feel the anger building against the girl's emotional wall.

'Uncle. He is dead now too.'

There was satisfaction in that statement.

'So where do you live?' For a moment Kesta thought that the girl might say that she lived in the Tower.

'Kitchen storeroom.'

Kesta sat back. 'Well, that won't do. Go and fetch your things; you will have the room above this one.'

Catya stared at her wide-eyed.

'Well get going!'

Catya got up and scampered to the door not even pausing to close it. Kesta stood slowly and went to the window to gaze up at the Raven Tower. Just who *was* the Dark Man?

***

Catya was patient at first while Kesta and Rosa drew out their plans, first using slate and chalk and then transferring everything onto parchment. The girl scowled over the letters that Kesta made her shape on the slate but Kesta was pleased to see that the girl had not been entirely neglected in her learning. When Kesta put her plans aside and stood to stretch, Catya followed her avidly with her eyes.

'Well, we have been cooped up long enough!' Kesta declared. 'Help me move this table and we'll make a start. Now; there are lots of things to consider about each situation as to how you approach and where you attack.' They moved the table aside and Kesta handed an eating knife to both Rosa and Catya. 'Hold out your knives as though you're defending yourselves.'

Kesta smiled as both of them extended their arms and held the knives out toward her.

'Well, waving a knife about at full stretch might put some people off attacking you but there will be little strength in any slash you make, and you certainly can't stab anyone like that unless they stand still and let you run at them!'

They looked at each other and Kesta laughed. 'Let me show you. You need to bend your elbow and pull your arm back a little to give yourself some power and thrust …'

They were still practising when Trella and the children that assisted her brought up their evening meal; Catya retreated almost to the corner as they put the table back and laid out their meal. Trella's expression changed from shock to disapproval but Kesta ignored it and dismissed her civilly from the tower.

'Pour us all some wine and then sit and join us,' Kesta instructed Catya.

Rosa chatted away, changing subjects rapidly and trying to involve Catya; she showed not the least offense when the girl didn't speak. Kesta took the opportunity to learn all she could about life in Elden from the older woman and was happy to listen. She wasn't surprised, but was slightly annoyed, when Jorrun appeared in the doorway. With a loud sigh she sat back from the table and stood.

'Excuse me, ladies.' She picked up her plans and followed the Dark Man up to her room, noting that he had only one glass in his hand with the bottle of wine. He placed both on the table next to the glass that had survived the previous night.

'I will be sending a reply to Bractius tomorrow, would you like to include something for your family?' he asked as he poured the wine.

Not the King, *but* Bractius, *she noted.* 'I would be grateful. Just let them know that I am well and glad to hear that my mother and uncle survived the attack.'

He looked at her and then sat slowly as though faced by a snake that was unnaturally friendly. She sighed, and after pulling out another chair with a scrape, sat heavily in it.

'You probably know what I've been doing today.' She pushed the plans toward him across the table. 'I should have spoken to you first, I see that, but I'm used to commanding and just getting on with things.' It was as close to an apology as she could allow herself; after all the man had forced her to be here against her will. 'This is what I was hoping to achieve. What do you think?'

Jorrun studied her for a while before looking down at the parchment and flattening it out. He regarded it in silence and Kesta dearly wanted to call up her *knowing,* but she didn't want him to catch her prying.

'You would have made a great Queen for Elden,' he said, picking up his glass and taking a sip. 'Or Icante for the Fulmers; but bringing you here was more important than you know.'

'We could have made an alliance without this.' She burst out angrily.

Jorrun regarded her with his ice eyes and then pointed at her plans. 'This will be very good for Northold. I've left the place to itself for too long while I tended to my work. I'm happy for you to continue and trust that I'll not have to intervene. You may face resistance from some of the men; how will you handle it?'

The change of direction and question left her floundering; her emotions still high but unable to continue displaying her anger without coming across as childish. It made her seethe all the more. She gritted her teeth.

'I am aware that women do not rule or command in Elden. However; I have no intention of doing anything other than show my authority. If you're not happy with that then you shouldn't have married a woman of the Fulmers.'

The slightest of smiles pulled at his lips but vanished quickly. 'How do you find Catya?'

Kesta took a long swallow of wine while she considered her answer. 'She is difficult; but I believe there will be good reason for that, so I'll reserve judgement until I've found out who she really is inside. Is she your daughter?'

Amusement danced in his eyes and momentarily they didn't seem so cold. 'No, she is not.'

Kesta sat back and dared to study his face. Every muscle was relaxed, no smile, no frown, no tightness to his jaw. The way his eyes never left hers made her feel intensely self-conscious, and she looked away, shifting in her chair. 'Is there any more news on what's happening in the Borrows or Chem?' she asked, eventually.

Jorrun's chest rose in a silent sigh that gave away his frustration. 'Nothing as yet but it's hard to get news from over the sea from countries with which we do not trade. I begin to wonder if the fact no Borrowman has escaped your warriors is because they are instructed to fight to the death rather than be captured and give away information. And, of course, the dead sent by the Chemman necromancer can tell us nothing.'

'I hadn't thought of that.' Kesta sat up straight. 'We must let my mother know it's imperative to try to catch someone alive if they attack again.'

'I've already sent word to that effect. How far can you *walk*?'

'I can just reach the edge of the Borrows from Fulmer Ilse and reached the Fulmers from Taurmaline.'

'That far?' Jorrun raised an eyebrow.

'My mother is stronger.' Kesta admitted. 'I can't *walk* those distances without blacking out after a few minutes.'

Jorrun rubbed at his closely trimmed beard and then got to his feet. 'There might be something I can do to help you with that. I must get back to work; we will speak again tomorrow.'

'What *is* your work?' Kesta sprang up also and stood between the Dark Man and the door. Her heart was pounding, and she expected anger or even a physical blow.

Instead Jorrun paused and put his glass carefully down. 'Kesta, I will never lie to you but at times there will be things that I will not tell you. I realise that's a poor way to win your trust, but my reasons are good.'

He moved around her and left without waiting for a response; however, she heard his steps pause, and she wondered if he were waiting for the sound of smashing glass. She was tempted to yank open the door and say, 'Well?' But she found she didn't dare. The muscles of her stomach and chest itched as though wanting her to laugh at the same time as pressure built behind her eyes and nose. She sat down and drank her wine.

Chapter Eight

Kesta: Kingdom of Elden

A small group had gathered the next morning, mostly women and bondsmen. Despite Tantony being there, few warriors had joined them. Kesta tried not to be disheartened but talked through what she needed doing, and what her small team were able to achieve of it. Then she shocked them all by picking up a scythe and getting straight on with clearing herself.

By midday Kesta had bound her hands against blisters and switched from cutting to piling up all the debris ready to burn later. Rosa not only brought them water but also organised lunch to be taken out to them and the men working on the edge of the stronghold's clearing. They sat together in companionable silence as they ate, Kesta surveying the progress they'd made. Everything had been cut back from around the keep and a large swathe had been cleared almost to the defensive wall on one side. She turned to look up at the Raven Tower, realising she was almost in its shadow. One raven circled it to land and was greeted with a harsh chorus from its roost.

'You must be the new lady of the stronghold.'

She turned around to see a warrior addressing Rosa. He had blonde curling hair and short stubble rather than a beard. His eyes were dark brown, and his mouth was curled up in a friendly smile.

'Oh no!' Rosa stood and brushed down her dress. '*This* is Lady Kesta.'

Kesta stood more slowly, holding the man's eyes and calling up her *knowing*. He continued to smile but there was an underlying tension about him; he was like a predator deciding whether she was a victim or a threat.

'I never expected the Thane to marry, let alone such a useful woman; beautiful too. Such lovely dark skin.'

He reached out a hand toward her cheek and she flinched back; but instead of touching her face he pulled a twig free from her hair.

'I am from the Fulmers,' she said.

'So, I hear. Perhaps I should follow my Thane's example and look there for a wife.' He continued to smile charmingly and Kesta gritted her teeth, not allowing herself to feel flattered. He really was a handsome man, but she knew instinctively that he was dangerous too. 'Has he told you what he does all day up in that tower? All night too from what I hear. Such a shame to neglect a new bride.'

'Have you come to help or just stand there and chatter?' Despite her best efforts he'd flustered her, and he knew it.

'I just got back from my mission, so my men and I will be taking a well-deserved break. Find me work worthy of a strong man and we might consider helping you tomorrow; after all I would be delighted to have more of your company, my Lady.'

Kesta drew herself up straighter. 'Prove yourself a strong man and I will find you plenty of work; reward it too. Be here tomorrow morning and if you can clear more land than me by the end of the day, there will be a keg of dark beer in it for you.'

'I can think of better prizes.' He raised an eyebrow.

'That is the one that's on offer.'

'Well, I can't turn down a challenge! I'll see you tomorrow.' He turned away with a wink and strode off.

'Be careful there.' Rosa touched her arm.

'I know.' She waved a hand dismissively. 'I have us extra workers tomorrow and I have a feeling some of the other warriors will follow him; that's the main thing.'

But her heart was pounding faster, and she watched him walk away.

***

That evening they hauled up water to heat so that they could all take a hot bath. Catya was disappointed that they'd left no time for lessons, but she'd worked as hard as Kesta during the day and was almost asleep in her plate when Jorrun walked up the tower steps. Instead of wine he held a small package in his hand.

'My apologies; you were working late, and I should have given you more time.'

'No, it's fine.' Kesta stood and ascended the three flights to her room. Her muscles ached, and she knew she would regret how hard she'd worked in the morning. 'How is your work going?' She glanced over her shoulder in time to catch a smile on his face. She was so startled she nearly tripped. When she looked again, he was perfectly composed and emotionless; she decided she must have imagined it.

'Frustrating actually,' he confessed. 'But I found the incense recipe I recalled might help you. I keep a large store of ingredients in the tower.' He placed the package on the table. 'Burn it in the fireplace and it should stave off the worst of any pain you might be subjected to in *walking*. There is a side effect though; it can bring vivid dreams.'

She touched the string that held the waxed linen closed and sat down. 'So, you have no more news from Chem or the Fulmers?'

'Not none, just nothing of use.' He sat down opposite her and rubbed at his bearded chin with one finger as he watched her. She waited, wondering if he were deciding what he could tell her. 'I saw the work you've done down in the ward; you made a lot of progress in one day. I haven't had a chance to speak to Tantony yet; how did the warriors take to it?'

She winced. 'Not that well at first but I think I've won some reluctantly over. I'm expecting more to join us tomorrow.'

'How is Catya doing?'

'She works hard. Talks little. I wondered if she might be from Chem, like you, but she's so pale.'

'She is from Elden; the natives of Chem are as pale as the people of Elden.'

'But ...'

'I am of mixed blood. On my mother's side.'

'How do you know it's on your mother's side? I thought you were a baby when you were found in the sea; that you were alone?'

He sat back in his chair and for a moment it seemed he would refuse to answer. 'It is not common knowledge and has been kept quiet for good reason. I was eight years old when I escaped from Chem and I remember a great deal of the place in which I was born.'

'Escaped?'

'Yes. I escaped.'

'Will you tell me more?'

'I imagine so.' There it was, that ghost of a smile. 'But not yet.'

She didn't bother to hide her annoyance. 'You know I'll just try to guess and make up all sorts of things.'

'But I trust you not to tell those things to others. Bractius knows everything if that reassures you?'

'Not really. Does he know what you do in the tower?'

'Yes.'

'Has he ever been in the tower?'

'Yes.'

She sighed loudly and picked at the knot on the parcel. 'Is there anywhere in particular you would like me to try to *walk* tonight?'

'Chem or the Borrows would be good; but I understand if you need to look at the Fulmers or check on your father's progress.'

'I could try Chem.' She sat back in her chair and drew in a deep breath. 'But I think it will be too far and often the flame will take me where it wills and not where I want if I stretch too far.'

'Really?' He leaned forward and looked at her with renewed interest. 'I've studied Fulmer magic but there is nothing written by the *walkers* of the isles themselves. Tell me in your own words what the flame is to you.'

She hesitated. The ways of the *Fire-Walker* were a closely guarded secret that wasn't shared with outsiders and much not even with those of the Fulmers who could not *walk*. She'd sworn a vow to keep those secrets, but even had she not, she was reluctant to share anything with this man who hid so much.

'Fire is one of the Great Spirits,' he said. She found she couldn't tear her eyes away from his. 'Like Earth, Wind, and Water. The Earth is one, Water is one, and the Wind is all one. Only fire can be made by man, but it all comes from one Great Spirit. You would think that the woman of the Fulmers would be closer to the Earth, like the women of Elden once were. Or living on an island you would expect a connection with the sea and Water to be their choice in magic. To *walk* it would make more sense to harness and travel the winds to see afar – but no; it is Fire that they choose. Or perhaps Fire chose them. You call the sorcerers of Chem 'Necromancers' but in truth they are masters of elemental magic like you. Necromancy is the province of a particular sect, a powerful clan who use the once forbidden blood magic. At the moment they rule Chem.'

'I …' she found herself at a loss for words. How had she managed to lose herself in eyes that only moments before she could hardly bear to look at? Somehow, they were no longer cold. She realised that she was breathing faster and clenching her fists momentarily she looked away and slowed her lungs. 'We do not master the Spirits but seek to work *with* them. We are close to the Earth, Wind, and Water but it was Fire that granted us the gift of *Walking.*'

He waited, but she shook her head.

'I'm sorry, I can't tell you more.'

He smiled, and he seemed to become a different person right before her eyes; but only for the briefest of moments before he stood and said formally, 'That is only fair since I have also held much from you. Perhaps that will change one day; but not yet. I wish you luck tonight walking the flame. Oh, and tread carefully with Adrin.'

'Adrin?' She felt her cheeks and throat tighten as her blood rushed there.

'The warrior you challenged. Good night.' He left the room abruptly, and she remained staring at the door for some time after.

Shaking herself she went to the fireplace and adding a large log stirred it up into a strong blaze. She opened the parcel and an aromatic scent was released out into the room. There were dried petals and whole flowers, small amber beads of resin, and seeds of varying size and shape. There was a sharp, almost citrus, tang to it that tingled her nostrils but was softened by the perfume of the flowers. She hadn't asked Jorrun how much she should use.

'Oh well.' She grabbed out a handful and flung it into the fire. The fire sparked blue and green and scented smoke curled upward. She took in a deep breath of the pleasant aroma and then settled herself to look into the flame. She found her connection almost at once and gave the ritual thanks and greeting. Already the room around her had melted away and there was nothing but the elemental dance of light before her. She pushed at the point within her skull and behind her eyes and, falling into the flame, willed herself far across the sea.

Sharp pain stabbed deep in to the centre of her skull, but she ignored it and pushed forward. She felt the flame give way and at once she was flowing away from herself. The pain increased and part of her registered that her body was struggling to draw breath but below her was land, a coast with sandy shores and ... and what was that? Further inland on the high hills all was white! But below her there was movement and flickering torches. The fire pulled her down to it and she was on a wharf filled with a fleet of ships. It was night, but they were being loaded. Barrels and long boxes.

Long boxes?

Salt leaked from a gap in the planking of one leaving a tiny trail that the fire illuminated so that to her it was a ribbon of diamond. A door opened a crack and a young woman peeped out, only to for the door to fly open as a man grabbed her to pull her inside.

Then the fire threw her back, scorching her skin as it had not done for many years. She fell back onto the rug and unbearable pain seized her skull. So much for Jorrun's incense!

But already it was easing, and she pulled herself up, taking in slow, deep breathes.

'Mistress?' She opened her eyes to see Catya standing in the doorway. 'Are you all right? I was just checking if you needed anything before I went to bed.'

All at once it hit Kesta. The fury behind those young eyes, the desire to hide, the tightly controlled denial of emotion. She realised she was staring and finding her voice said, 'No, thank you, Catya. I see to myself for the most part so please don't feel obliged to run after me. If I need something of you, I will ask.'

Catya bobbed her head and left at once, hiding behind her long hair.

Kesta rubbed at her temple though the headache had lost its intensity. She lay back gratefully on the soft pillow without bothering to undress.

It had been many years before when she'd seen a young girl like Catya. She'd been a girl herself and learning the ways of a *walker*. As was her duty she'd been *walking the flame* to watch over the islands when she'd sighted raiders. She'd called the alarm, and the warriors were mobilised, but against the advice of her mentor she'd gone back to watching; wanting to see if they were in time to stop the raiders. They weren't, not for some. They'd hit a small settlement and smashed in the gate. As they slaughtered the men and women who fought, one Borrowmen punched a young girl to the ground and proceeded to rape her right in the middle of the fighting; the shock and brutality of it had sent Kesta reeling from the flame and left her shaking and crying herself sick. She'd refused to *walk* again for several weeks. The girl had been rescued, but too late. Two weeks later she'd thrown herself off the tall cliffs onto the rocks; but Kesta had never forgotten the overwhelming despair and fury she'd seen in the girl's eyes and not dared to feel through her *knowing*.

Kesta got up and filled her glass with the remainder of the wine Jorrun had left the night before and drank it down quickly to drown the anxiety in her stomach. She threw some more of the incense onto the fire and its soothing scent enfolded her and before she knew it, she was asleep. Images of the verdant forests of the Fulmers assailed her, and she kept going back to the small holding, seeing the raiders from above, seeing that arm swing toward the girl.

The door to her room opened, and she froze; where had she left her dagger? Jorrun stepped in dressed in shadow, his face a mask without life. He came straight to the bed and lifting the blanket got in. Kesta tried to protest but her voice was frozen; she tried to move, to get away, but her body wouldn't respond. Panic flowed through her limbs like hot water as Jorrun straddled her and taking hold of the cloth of her shirt ripped it open.

Then the door opened and Jorrun stepped in. He was at the bed in an instant and with unnatural strength he grabbed the first Jorrun with both hands and flung him against the wall. A sword materialised in his hand and with a sigh he walked over to the fallen Jorrun and stabbed him through the chest. He walked back toward her and said, 'Wake up, Kesta, I will be there in a minute.'

With a start she woke, sitting up and gasping for breath. The fire had all but gone out and the room was chilly. She looked quickly to the floor where the Jorrun had fallen and then chastised herself for her foolishness. She hadn't had a nightmare like that in years! Jorrun had certainly been right about the vivid dreams.

She jumped when someone knocked softly on the door and her heart pounded as it slowly opened and Jorrun stepped in. At once she called up her *knowing* to feel if he was real, to check his intent, but as always, she could read nothing from him. She swallowed, her muscles tightening.

He walked around to the far side of the table, keeping a distance between them, and sat in his accustomed place. 'Is that what you think of me?'

For a moment she was confused, then she realised he must be able to see how frightened she was. 'No! Of course not! Well ... well, I suppose I did fear that possibility when I first was forced to marry you.'

Jorrun winced and looked down, leaving his eyes shadowed. 'That's understandable. You don't know me and things in Elden are different from in the Fulmers. I'm sorry that I did not alleviate your fear sooner.'

She wasn't sure why his apology unsettled her so much, but she got the impression that Jorrun was not someone who apologised often – or lightly. She quickly changed the subject. 'What happened to Catya? Who hurt her?'

Jorrun rubbed at his neatly trimmed beard. 'She was orphaned at just six years old. Her only relative was an uncle, a warrior here at Northold. She was sent to him, but he abused her. When I came here, I found out. I killed him and told everyone that I would not tolerate women at this hold being treated in such a way. I brought Catya into the keep and the women here take care of her as much as they can; but I think they are frightened of her because of what I did.'

'I would have hoped that any of them would have done the same thing and gutted the man,' Kesta said vehemently. 'Rape carries a death sentence on the Fulmers – not that any man there would do such a thing.'

'Your dream, that was something you saw?'

She drew up her legs to hug her knees. 'Yes. Hey! How do you know what I dreamt? How did you ... how did you know to come here?' She regarded him wide-eyed, her heart still racing.

'I'm a *walker* too, Kesta,' he said it so quietly that she thought she must have misheard him.

'But men can't be *walkers*,' she said after a long silence.

'I don't walk fire, Kesta, I walk dreams.'

She stared at him. *He walked dreams?* There were stories, old stories told by grandmothers, of the magics of long ago. It was said that once even the people of Elden had magic but their magic had died even before the explorers who were her ancestors had come to the Fulmers. 'There is a myth,' she said slowly. 'Of *dream-weavers*. People who could enter your dreams and change them. It was the magic of Elden. No one in Elden has magic anymore.'

'No, not for a long time,' he replied. 'But the magic of Elden lives on in Chem – and in me.'

'Your mixed blood,' she said tentatively, wondering how much she could get from him, concerned she might offend him. 'It is of Chem and Elden I am guessing, yet you say the people of both lands are pale skinned. Your blood, is it also of the Fulmers?'

He stood, and she flinched despite herself.

'It is. You should sleep, Kesta, you have much to do tomorrow and I would hate to see you lose your challenge.'

She scowled at him and there it was again, the briefest of smiles that changed his face completely.

'Good night, Kesta.'

'No wait! I haven't told you yet of what I saw when I *walked*. I got to Chem; I'm sure it was Chem, but the hills were all white.'

'Snow. Yes, there would be snow still this time of year.'

'They were loading ships. Barrels and long boxes of … I think they were salted bodies.'

Jorrun's hands clenched into fists. 'How many ships?'

'At least ten, probably more. It was hard to count from where I was watching.'

'Thank you, Kesta.' He grabbed the door handle and left without another word.

Kesta lay back on the bed.

A dream-walker.

A man with the blood of all nations.

***

Despite everything she did manage to sleep and awoke feeling groggy and heavy-bodied. Rosa was in the room, quietly tidying, and she opened two of the windows a crack. Kesta drew in a deep breath of the cold air; there was just a hint of frost.

'Hello, Rosa.' She yawned. Her muscles protested as she climbed out of bed.

'Sorry to wake you.' Rosa winced. 'But some people have already started work again out in the ward and I didn't think it would look good if we arrived late.'

'No, you're right.' She grabbed for her trousers and tunic, tying her belt and dagger around her waist. 'I'll grab something to eat and then we'll head out. Is Catya up?'

'She is, and I told her to get on with her own breakfast.'

Kesta nodded and was about to tell Rosa about her eventful night but bit her tongue. As frustrating as Jorrun's secrecy was, he and Bractius obviously had their reasons. She trusted Rosa and longed to discuss her thoughts with someone, but they weren't her secrets to share. She did however think it a good idea to let her know what had happened to Catya.

'It was obvious the girl has been mistreated in some way.' Rosa sighed as they made their way down the tower stairs. 'And I've seen both pity and indifference shown by the other women of the hold, but no sign of bullying or abuse. So, Thane Jorrun is a protector of women?' She looked at Kesta to gauge her reaction.

'Thane Jorrun is a frustratingly hard man to know.'

'But you're finally trying to know him.'

'Finally?' Kesta gave her a shove but her frown turned quickly into a grin. 'Tell me, what do you know of his history? All we know on the Fulmers is that he was washed ashore by the sea as a baby and the late king made him his sorcerer.'

Rosa stopped on the stairs. 'To be honest, I don't know much more. I know he was fostered with Bractius in Eyre with Jarl Ceren in his younger years, away from the court, and the two have been close as brothers ever since. He was about thirteen when they came back to court and he was always a very serious boy; he never got into trouble and was always polite. Bractius on the other hand was trouble.' Rosa smiled and shook her head. 'The two of them were sent to serve as warriors on Mantu for a year when they turned sixteen and when they came back Bractius had grown up immensely.'

'Mantu, that's the island to the north of Elden?'

'Yes. Little more than a harbour for the warrior and fishing fleets but of great strategic importance.'

Kesta thought of the ships being supplied in the harbour somewhere in Chem and shuddered. She drew in a deep breath and brought her mind back to the present. 'Breakfast.'

She ate quickly and standing, put her arm around Catya's shoulders to give her a brief hug. 'Come on, ladies, let's get to work.'

As Rosa had warned her, several people were already out working. A group of women were cutting back the long grass while some warriors, led by Tantony, were hacking at and uprooting some brambles. Adrin was also there before her and was lounging against a cart full of uprooted brambles with four other men. Kesta's heart sank; it would have been better for her to have arrived here first. Adrin saw her and stood up straight but he held back as Tantony headed straight for her.

'Good morning, Lady Kesta, Lady Rosa.' He wiped his hands on his tunic. 'Kurghan's sons are out cutting trees, we thought we'd get on with clearing.'

'So I see.' Kesta nodded. 'Have you seen Jorrun today?'

'Very early, yes.' Tantony looked worried. 'He sent a message straight to the king. It said that …' He glanced at Rosa. 'That we are to expect a strong attack, but we don't know where yet.'

'That's so. I might be able to determine where once they set out as long as I have a landmark to set them by.'

'You can do that?' Tantony asked in surprise.

'Yes, I... I think so. As long as they have fire somewhere on the ships.'

'And if they don't?'

'Then I am blind.' Kesta winced. 'In the meantime, we can be as prepared as we can be here.'

'Yes indeed.' Tantony led her back toward where he'd been working. 'It's good to be keeping everyone occupied, busy men are less trouble and there are only so many hours a day I can get them to practice with their weapons or stand guarding unthreatened walls. Are you happy for us to just carry on as we are?'

'Yes, that's fine. I, on the other hand, have a contest to lose.'

'Lose?' Both Tantony and Rosa asked at once.

Kesta ignored them and walked over to where Adrin waited for her with a warm smile. She felt, rather than saw, Catya following her so she turned to the girl and said, 'Are you happy to help the other women with the clearing?'

Catya didn't look happy, but she nodded, narrowing her eyes at Adrin before walking away.

'My lady.' Adrin gave a small bow.

'I hope I didn't keep you waiting long? The Thane and I were working late last night.'

Adrin glanced up at the tower and his smile slipped just a little. 'Not at all. Would you like to choose your patch of ground?'

'I thought I'd start at the east wall and work toward the Raven Tower.'

'Very good.' Adrin grinned. 'I'll work to your right. How wide a plot shall we clear?'

'Five feet?'

'Six!' Adrin challenged.

Kesta held out her hand and Adrin shook it, squeezing only gently and holding it a little longer than was necessary. 'Let's get to it then.'

Kesta selected a scythe and a fork from the cart, checking that the former was sharp. Adrin did the same. Some of his hangers on picked up some tools, but they were more interested in watching than helping. They walked to the wall and one of the men lay down some rope to mark off where their two strips would start. With a grin, Adrin began swinging his scythe at once although it was clear that he was not used to using such a tool. To his surprise Kesta leaned her scythe against the wall and walked the length of her strip to the tower. In all it wasn't too bad, the grass was long with stalks as high as her shoulders. There were a few saplings that had taken root, large patches of nettles, and clumps of thistle. She decided to start with the saplings, putting all her weight onto the fork to loosen the roots as much as possible. At first, she felt self-conscious, aware of the warriors watching her, but she focused her *knowing* deep into the earth and away from the people and sank herself into her task.

Adrin had already cleared a considerable area by the time she'd taken out all the saplings and the largest of the shrubs. She began gathering up everything she'd uprooted and taking it to the cart. Rosa joined her, bringing her some water.

'He thinks he is beating you,' Rosa said. 'They think you're not even trying.'

'He is beating me.' Kesta sighed. 'There was never any getting away from the fact that he is far stronger than I; but they'll learn that I plan, and I think.'

Rosa smiled and nodded. 'I'll bring you both some food shortly. When do you think you'll need a break?'

162

'I think that might be cheating.'

'No; as you say it's planning, thinking, and using the assets that you have.' Rosa's smile became a grin.

'With the worst already done I shall get straight on with cutting now. When I've cleared a third, or he has reached the tower with his cutting, bring us food then.'

Rosa nodded and went on to offer water to Adrin.

Kesta picked up the scythe and with nothing more resilient than grass to cut she fell into an easy rhythm. On the Fulmers everyone helped with the harvest and Kesta had learnt to handle a scythe as a girl; back then the tool had been almost as big as her, now it was like an extension to her arms. Even so she was only about a quarter of the way down her strip of land when Adrin reached the Raven Tower. Here and there though, saplings still stood, some hacked off near the base, others still whole.

Kesta hopped up onto the cart, throwing on an armful of cut grass before sitting down. Rosa handed her a bowl of vegetable stew and some bread and then stepped back out of the way as Adrin jumped up onto the cart to sit beside Kesta. He held out a hand and Rosa stepped forward to give him his food.

'I've taken a look at your plot,' Adrin said between mouthfuls. 'You're a clever woman.'

'Thank you.' She tried not to smile too much. 'But you have the advantage still. I have no doubt that with your strength you'll have those roots up and the debris cleared away before I can finish cutting.'

'I wondered if you might use your magic.'

Kesta paused. There was nothing in a *walker's* skills that could clear land for planting, unless she burnt everything down, but he didn't need to know that. 'That would be cheating,' she replied.

Adrin nodded. 'You are a very interesting woman.'

'Chieftain!' Tantony barked as he came striding over; glancing up at the Raven Tower.

Adrin gave Kesta a wink and a grin and hopped down off the wagon. 'It's only fair that we both rest our feet, Merkis!'

Tantony glared at him and the man's smile faded a little. 'Yes, Merkis. Apologies, my Lady,'

Kesta decided it would be best to say nothing. It was the first time she'd seen Tantony assert any authority and Rosa was watching him avidly.

'My Lady,' Tantony turned back to Kesta. 'We have had a reply back from the king already; he intends to sail here first thing tomorrow to consult with the Thane. It's a military visit not a court one so he'll be arriving with just a few warriors. As you're busy would you like me to see that his rooms are readied?'

'Well, yes.' Kesta was taken aback a little. Surely the king ought to summon his Thane to him, not go rushing across the lake himself. No wonder Jorrun had gained the reputation of being the real power in Elden. 'I'm sorry but I must finish this.'

Tantony scowled, but he nodded and walked away with a warning glance at Adrin.

'Well, something has got the king stirred up!' Adrin stated.

Kesta was shocked to find herself eager for her evening talk with Jorrun; she glanced up the tower and Adrin mistook her reason.

'Don't worry about him, he's too busy with his sorcery to worry about what we're doing.'

'Well, shall we?' She smiled at him and he beamed back.

'After you, my Lady.'

Even though she knew she would lose, Kesta threw herself into cutting the rest of her plot. Adrin tried his best to look casual, but he showed a spark of temper at one small tree whose roots he couldn't pull up until he'd dug down a substantial way. Kesta had only just finished cutting and begun clearing when Adrin threw a tangle of roots onto the cart; covering himself in loose earth as he raised his arms with a cry of triumph. Kesta was exhausted, but she held herself straight as she walked over to the cart.

'Congratulations. Rosa, would you have a barrel of beer brought from the cellars please?'

'Yes, my Lady.' Rosa walked away, seeming reluctant to leave Kesta alone with Adrin and his warriors.

'We thought you might catch him.' One of the men grinned.

'Aye! We thought that stump had bested him!' Another agreed.

Adrin growled and thumped the man's arm playfully. 'I'd like to see you do better, Pagna!'

'Well I'd love to have another contest, but with the king coming tomorrow I think I'll be busy.' Kesta told them. 'Although I am happy to provide another prize if you want to compete among yourselves?'

'No, we have had our contest, and it was a pleasure; now fair is fair and we'll get some more work done for you tomorrow. This place should never have been so neglected. Tantony is a great commander in a battle, none better, but administrating a stronghold takes a different kind of planning. The Thane—'

'Barrel is coming!' One of the warriors interrupted quickly.

'It's good to have you here, Lady, is what I mean to say.' Adrin gave a small bow and then hurried off toward his barrel with his retinue of warriors in tow.

'What do you think?' Rosa asked as she re-joined her.

'I'm not sure yet,' Kesta said slowly. Her eyes followed Adrin and while she did feel a flush of attraction, the hairs on her arms also prickled warningly. 'Come on, let's go find Tantony and see what we need to do for the king's visit.'

***

Kesta found herself standing in her room looking across to the Raven Tower. As always, light flickered behind the glass. Reluctantly she tore herself away and went down the tower stairs to join the other two.

'You look nice this evening,' Rosa said.

Kesta touched her red dress. 'I should probably do something about getting myself some more clothes.'

'Talking of suitable clothing I made these while you were working.' Rosa went over to a chair and lifted up some trousers. 'If any of the ladies of the queen's court catch me wearing these, I'll be ostracised for life!'

'Can you make me some?' Catya asked at once.

'Well, I should think so.' Rosa looked from the girl back to Kesta.

'Wear what you want.' Kesta shrugged. 'I won't be ostracising anyone! I'm not interested in the court or what people think of me.'

'Queen Ayline ...' Rosa bit her lip.

'Go on,' Kesta prompted.

'She keeps a tight hold on the ladies of her court and her influence over who has favour and power changes fortunes and lives. I would just ... I would just warn you to be wary not to make an enemy of her. Even though Bractius and Jorrun are close, she could make life very unpleasant for you.'

'And for you,' Kesta said quietly. 'I will be mindful of that.'

She heard a door close below and the barely perceptible sound of Jorrun's steps on the stairs. For such a tall man he walked very lightly, more like a hunter or scout than a warrior. She stood at once and met him in the doorway.

'Any more news?' she asked.

'Some.' He gestured for her to proceed him up the stairs and didn't speak again until they were in her room with the door closed. 'We've received a longer, more detailed missive from the Fulmers. The Icante, it seems, had a disturbing confrontation with one of the necromancers.'

Kesta tensed. 'Is she all right? She wasn't hurt?'

Jorrun held up a hand. 'She is well. I'm going to tell you a little about Chem. I want you with me tomorrow when I talk with the king and it will help you if you know more about the necromancers.'

Kesta nodded, although all she wanted to hear was what had happened to her mother.

Jorrun drew in a deep breath. 'In Chem political power and magical power amount to the same thing. There are several powerful families and many more of lesser ability, all competing to rule Chem. In the capital City of Arkoom there is a palace with a council chamber of fifteen Seats; those that hold the Seats rule Chem. To take a Seat the sorcerer who holds it and all, or most, of his followers and family must be killed by the challenger and his 'coven'. Through planning, deceit, and pure power all of those Seats are now held by what you call 'necromancers'; ones who use blood magic.

'There is no one strong enough to oppose them and take from them a Seat, anyone who did would be dead in moments as the other necromancers would destroy them. It's the first time there has ever been an alliance between covens and it was engineered by a Lord called Dryn Dunham. It was not he that your mother confronted but his nephew, who himself has a coven, and holds a seat in Arkoom; Argen Dunham.' He paused to look at Kesta and her blood ran cold. 'Whether now or later, Chem intends to take the Fulmers.'

Kesta leapt to her feet with her hands clenched into fists.

'Kesta, I won't let it happen.'

'But how can you stop them? Just you! Just you against fifteen necromancers that their own people can't depose!'

'Two assaults on the Fulmers have now been repelled. My guess is their plans for the Fulmers will now be put on hold until Elden is conquered, and I am dead.'

'Who *are* you?'

'I am a slave, Kesta.'

'A slave?' She shook her head, but his expression remained perfectly serious. 'You helped my mother and our warriors defeat them, didn't you? How did you do that? Not by dream-walking.'

'No, not by dream-walking.'

'Why won't you tell me anything? I hate you!'

Jorrun flinched as though she'd struck him and Kesta bit her lip in shock that she'd gone that far. She was so angry though that lights danced before her eyes and her blood pounded in her ears.

Jorrun closed his eyes. 'I will tell you everything when I can, Kesta, more than you will want to hear, that I promise you.'

'If I find that anything you hold back has put my people at risk—'

'I am doing everything I can to protect our people.'

'How can I believe that?'

He didn't reply, and she took a moment to look at him, really look. He looked exhausted.

With a cry of exasperation, she went over to where Rosa had tidied away their glasses and poured what she guessed to be brandy from a decanter. She placed a glass in front of Jorrun and sat back down.

She took in a deep breath. 'Why are you not able to tell me things?'

'It is the command of King Bractius and his father before him that what I am and what I do remain a secret. It is also self-preservation on my part. Knowing even as much as you do would turn people in Elden against me and … warn Chem that I am alive. Already I am sure they suspect.' He paused to study her face. 'So, you hate me.'

Kesta felt her blood burning her throat and cheeks and she looked away. 'I didn't mean that. But why would Chem care that you're alive if you're just a slave?'

He looked at her but didn't speak.

Kesta growled at him, then laughed and drank back her brandy. 'Very well. You look like you need to sleep, and I certainly do. Will we speak tomorrow with the king visiting?'

Jorrun sat back in his chair and rubbed at his beard with two fingers. 'I'll probably not have a chance to come here but as I said I intend for us both to take council with the king.'

'Thank you for that much.'

'You should have been a queen, Kesta, or an Icante as you call them. I will always give you the respect owed to such.'

She swallowed and shifted in her chair, looking down at her hands.

'I will leave you.' He stood. 'We will entertain the king privately. It's not unusual for he and I to consult one another and dine alone. Good night, Kesta.'

'Good night.' She found herself wanting to apologise for losing her temper but couldn't find the words. It was so frustrating though, being kept in the dark, but despite everything there was a rebellious part of her that couldn't help starting to like Jorrun, slave or no.

Chapter Nine

Dia: Fulmer Isle

Dia read through the crumpled letter again; her temper hadn't subsided in the two days since she'd received it. She stood up and paced the room, trying to understand her husband's decision but no matter how many times she re-read it she couldn't forgive him. Other than confiding in Worvig, she'd managed to keep her temper under control and hadn't as yet revealed to the clans that they'd lost their intended Icante heir. It would not go down well.

One of her gulls had reported that Arrus was less than an hour away from the islands. As yet they'd sighted no other ships and the location of the necromancer who had spoken through the severed head hadn't been found. The chieftains of each clan were getting restless and irritable, wanting something to fight and hating that their quarry was hiding behind magic. Was this necromancer alone somewhere? Or was he on a ship with an army of undead warriors?

She crumpled the letter and tossed it into a chest in the corner of the room. She looked around again, her room seemed suddenly dark and enclosing.

'Fetch Worvig; we'll go and meet Arrus,' she told Pirelle.

The young *Walker* put down her sewing and left quickly without a word. Dia found the twins outside her door and gestured for them to follow.

'What's happening?' One of the warriors demanded as the three women crossed the main hall.

'Just going to meet my husband; we'll hold counsel when I return. Ah, Worvig!' The broad-chested man was strapping a large axe to his back as he stepped up to join her. 'Your brother is on his way with the Elden ships.'

'Should we not get some of the warriors together to meet theirs?'

'Considering what has occurred, I wish to demonstrate the importance of our women to these Eldemen.'

Worvig glanced back at Heara and Shaherra, both heavily armed with their gleaming black hair tied back in long braids.

'And I wish to speak with Arrus before all is revealed to the chieftains.'

'As do I,' Worvig grumbled.

Dia gritted her teeth. She couldn't bear to begin to think what her daughter might be going through, left alone in Elden and sold off to that sorcerer. Kesta was strong and clever, she knew that, but she was her little girl; her fire-hearted child. She felt the heat of her own anger on her skin but even so, a chill ran down her spine. Was Kesta even still alive? Or had her explosive temper got her in trouble? Her breath caught, and she almost stumbled, her hand going to her chest. Would that man use sorcery to subdue her, beat her, kill her?

Beside her Pirelle gently touched her arm, and she drew in a deep breath, glancing at her apprentice with a smile of thanks. She clenched her hands into fists and then forced them to relax.

***

The stronghold had a small harbour far below it in a wide cove, but it was too shallow for the two large Elden ships to come in. Dia stood proud and unmoving as three small boats rowed in toward her. She recognised her

172

husband's shape at once, his hair blacker than any of the Eldemen around him, his shoulders broader. For the most part the people of the Fulmers were willowy, but not Arrus and his brother. They were giants on the Isles, a throwback to some Borrow blood somewhere in their ancestry. She opened up her *knowing*, welcoming the familiar and comforting feel of her husband at the same time as feeling furious with him. His dark skin looked almost grey; his head was bowed, shoulders slumped. He didn't look like a triumphant warrior who had succeeded in his mission; he looked like a father whose heart had been broken.

'Dia.' Her name was said with so much emotion as he leapt from the boat to the sand that, despite their audience, Dia hurried forward to take his hand. He could barely dare to look at her and yet he was a strong man, and honest, so he did. 'I lost our daughter.'

'I know,' she whispered, her own pain sharp in her chest.

He drew in a deep breath and straightened his back. 'Icante, may I introduce to you Merkis Vilnue, he commands the men the king has sent.'

One of the men from the boat came forward and gave a low and polite bow. 'Icante, it's my honour to fight with you. I've been instructed by my king that until he calls for my withdrawal, I am under your command.'

'The islands thank you for your assistance.' Dia drew upon all her pride and authority, pushing it out with her *knowing*. She saw the man's pupils widen a little. So, he liked a powerful woman. 'We've made room in our stronghold to house thirty of your men and a chamber that might suit you unless you intend to remain on your ship? The rest of your warriors will have to camp here on the beach.'

'I'd be grateful for a room in your stronghold,' Vilnue replied. He looked curiously at the twins and Pirelle, nodding politely to Worvig. He had long sandy hair and a short beard that showed streaks of grey; he was almost as tall as Arrus and Worvig but didn't have their bulk. 'I'll let the men stretch their legs on shore until you give us our orders to sail out; but we'll maintain a small camp here when the ships go.'

'I will have food and drink sent down here,' Dia replied. She'd expected a little more resistance from the Elden warriors to being commanded by a woman, yet this Merkis seemed to take it in his stride. He'd been assigned to her command, and he accepted that; a soldier through and through.

'We've brought our own rations, but fresh provisions would be gratefully received.' The corner of his mouth quirked up in a smile.

'If you'll follow me, I'll show you to the stronghold.' Dia remained straight-faced. 'Worvig Silene will remain on the beach to direct your men.'

Worvig opened his mouth to protest but Arrus elbowed him in the ribs.

'The chieftains of the islands have gathered here to take counsel.' Dia gestured for Vilnue to walk with her.

He quickly turned to one of the warriors. 'Get the men to set up camp here, but leave the ships crewed. Graph, Borra, you two come with me!'

Two of the Elden warriors scurried forward and fell in somewhat awkwardly behind Heara and Shaherra. Shaherra made a show of flicking her long braid back over her shoulder and flexing her muscles, resting her hand on her belt near one of her knives.

'We'll give you a couple of hours to settle your men and then we'll commence our council of war.' Dia went on as she walked. Arrus stepped up beside Pirelle but remained silent. 'It's a bit crowded in the stronghold at the moment, but it's a necessary discomfort.'

'I'm not much of a diplomat, I'm afraid, Icante.' Vilnue gave a shake of his head. 'I don't know much of your chieftains and strongholds.'

'There are thirty-two chieftains on the islands.' Dia told him. 'That includes Arrus and Worvig who are Silene. And there are seventeen *Walkers* now that Kesta is gone. All are encouraged to speak what is in their heart. I will think tonight on what is said and make my plan by the morning. You are welcome to speak your mind also; here you will be considered a chieftain.'

Vilnue was silent a while as he contemplated her words. 'I thank you for including me in your council.'

'It's only prudent. You know your men and ships and what they can do better than we.'

Several temporary camps had been set up around the stronghold by the warriors that had accompanied the chieftains of the islands. They eyed the Eldemen with a mixture of curiosity, disdain, and hostility. Dia couldn't help but fear their reaction when they learnt that they'd taken their future Icante. Vilnue seemed to take the warriors reaction as expected and wasn't offended or intimidated.

'This is the main hall,' she indicated with her hand, her eyes sweeping over the large open room, the firepit in the centre, the benches and tables that formed a large rectangle around it, and the curtained alcoves behind which the guesting chieftains had claimed beds. Many of them were seated at the long tables, talking, drinking, dicing, or listening to the singer who had set up in the corner. The bard was an older woman with steel in her dark hair but whose voice was strong and pure. Some of the chieftains stood but Arrus gestured for them to settle and wait. Dia continued through the hall and out of the wide door at the far end. There, a set of steps went up; they led to her own quarters and those of Pirelle, the twins, and of Worvig. She tried not to think of Kesta's empty room. Instead she took the flight of steps beside them that led down and turned about to go under the great hall.

Here was mostly storage but also the healer's quarters and a few small rooms for guests. She stopped at one that had horizontally slit windows high up near the ceiling, allowing in a shaft of light.

'This is for you. Also, the room next to it which has three beds. There is a guest house outside the main building that will accommodate twenty comfortably, twenty-seven at the most.' It could squeeze in more, but she wasn't willing to accommodate more than thirty Eldemen within the stronghold. 'Shaherra here will be your guide until the council. I'll leave you to organise your men.'

She didn't wait for a reply but strode off at once with Pirelle, Arrus, and Heara. Shaherra remained behind with a wicked smile on her face and her hand on her dagger hilt.

'Dia ...' Arrus touched her shoulder as they ascended the stairs, but she shrugged him away. She glanced back at Pirelle and Heara and the two women discreetly backed away; Pirelle to her room, Heara to stand guard outside the Icante's door. As soon as she gained their private chambers, she slammed the door shut and shoved Arrus hard in the chest.

'Why?' she demanded, tears springing to her eyes and the word catching in her throat.

Arrus stood dumb for a moment, swaying slightly, he blinked rapidly as his eyes watered. 'To save us all. We cannot defend ourselves against Chem. What was I to do? To say no would be to allow all our people to die! Kesta understood. Our brave girl ...'

Dia shut down her *knowing*, unable to endure her husband's pain. She slipped her arms around him and hugged him fiercely. 'Our brave girl,' she repeated. 'If they hurt her, I will kill them all.'

'If she leaves any of them standing.' He laughed, although no smile touched his eyes. 'So; what's the plan?'

Dia pulled away to look at him. 'We have learnt much. Their dead men can be destroyed with fire. It seems their reason for attacking us is to capture those with *walker* blood and ...' she hesitated, bile rising in her throat. 'Use them to produce children.'

Arrus pulled away from her in shock, his face turning red.

'We've killed another necromancer but there's one remaining that I believe must be nearby. We've been trying to track him but so far, he has eluded us. Perhaps he fled by ship and is long gone ... but my instinct screams at me that he is still near.'

'Then he is near.' Arrus nodded.

'There's something else. There was a demon, made of fire; it burnt the Chemman ship and drove all the creatures and one of the necromancers that led them to shore. He was weak and frightened when he crawled out the sea; I incapacitated him by exacerbating his fear and pain and Worvig stabbed him through the heart. The demon creature has not been seen since, but it helped us, of that I'm sure. I've been talking to the other *Walkers* about the old tales. Arrus; we think it may have been a fire-spirit.'

'But none have seen a spirit for generations!' He ran his fingers through his thick, black hair. 'Not since our ancestors settled on the islands.'

'I know.' Dia sat down heavily in a chair. 'But I think it's what we saw. At first, we all thought it was a demon of Chem sorcery; but then why would it help us? I've asked the fire over and over, but it doesn't answer. I'm thinking of calling all the *Walkers* to join and *walk* the fire together.'

'Such a thing has not happened in our lifetimes.' Arrus frowned. 'Is this one necromancer so dangerous?'

'Yes!' Dia said vehemently. His threat still made her skin crawl.

'But you defeated the others.'

'I think this one is stronger,' she said slowly. 'The first attack we faced from a Chemman seemed badly organised and they seemed ill prepared for our defence. This second one was a larger attack, with thought and cunning. If it weren't for the fire-spirit, we would have been defeated here at Fulmer Hold.'

Arrus made to protest but Dia raised her hand and shook her head. 'Despite Kesta's warning of what she saw we could never have prepared ourselves to face the horror of those dead men, and the one that made them is still somewhere out there. He could have hundreds more. He could *make* more.'

'We have the Eldemen now,' Arrus tried to reassure her. 'And the fire-spirit might help us again—'

'We can't count on that.' She shook her head. 'I'm going to write a letter to King Bractius and his sorcerer. In the mean time you should get changed and get ready for council.'

'Don't forget we need the king and his men.' Arrus winced.

'I won't say anything that they don't deserve.' Dia narrowed her blue and brown eyes.

***

The council hadn't needed much encouragement to gather; they'd been waiting to do so for hours – some for days. Of the *Walkers,* only four were missing. Two from the furthest and smallest of the islands who didn't wish to leave their homes unprotected, Siphenna; who was nearly ninety years old and did not travel far anymore. And Kesta.

Food and mead had been served around the tables and Shaherra had cleared a space for Vilnue and his three chosen warriors to sit. Worvig diplomatically placed himself beside the Merkis leaving Shaherra to stalk back to her place close to the Icante. Dia didn't keep them waiting but took a sip of mead before standing. It took but a moment for the room to hush.

'My people of the Fulmers, you know why we are here. This spring we have endured desperate attacks from the Borrows followed by two attacks led by Chemmen. We know now that their intent was not just to raid, but to conquer.' A loud rumble of angry retorts erupted around the hall. This wasn't new information, but their fury was far from subsiding. 'We have discovered that necromancers are behind the attack. They have used their vile blood magic to raise dead men to fight against us; but we know they can be destroyed with fire. We know the necromancers can be killed by simple steel.'

She nodded her head toward Worvig, letting the warrior take the credit for the kill. Worvig looked uncomfortable, but Arrus led the deafening cheer from warriors and *walkers* alike.

'Only six days ago I received a chilling message from our enemy.' She paused, struggling to find a way to speak the dead head's message out loud. 'There is still a necromancer alive and free somewhere. He intends to attack. His plan is to steal *Walkers* to give him heirs with strong magical ability.'

This was new information, and it was received with shock and outrage. Several of the *Walkers* visibly turned pale; Pirelle couldn't look up to meet anyone's eyes. Arrus leapt to his feet and banged his fists on the table, his voice silencing the room. 'We will not let this happen! They will not take a single one of our *Walkers* or women!'

Oh the irony. Dia kept her face frozen. She glanced at Merkis Vilnue; the Eldeman was observing the room and taking everything in silently. His men looked less comfortable.

She raised a hand and slowly the room settled. 'Our very own Silene, Kesta, has remained in Elden to work with the king and his sorcerer. In her place, King Bractius has generously sent us two war ships and five hundred men.'

If Arrus's raucous cheer was a little too forced and accompanied by a watering of his eyes, no one seemed to notice; no one but Dia and Merkis Vilnue who looked down at his hands.

'Kesta has secured a trade deal with Elden that will help to protect our islands. Now, then.' She paused, looking around at all of their faces. So much emotion. 'We have a necromancer loose and threatening us. Our whales and birds have not found him. Our *Walkers* have not found him. Our trackers have not found him. But he is here; I know it. We have to assume there will be another attack. Tell me your thoughts.'

At once several of the chieftains leapt to their feet. As Dia sat, Arrus remained standing and pointed to one of the chieftains. 'Ufgard, what do you say?'

Ufgard was the chieftain of Otter Hold on the north-west side of Fulmer Isle. He was in his late sixties and a veteran of both Borrow raids and raids against the Borrows. His hair had turned a dark, iron-grey, and his scars told his tale of hard-fought victories.

'We should strike back! Hit the Borrows where they recruit their dead and burn their ships!'

'The Elden King believes the Borrows may be conquered and under the rule of Chem,' Arrus said. That brought the room to silence, but one woman stood. 'Walker Tarlos.'

Tarlos was of Eagle Hold in the south. Both of Tarlos' eyes were brown, but one was like honey and the other dark as the earth.

'You have asked the flame of course?'

Dia nodded. 'I've dared to let myself go in the flame in the hope I might be shown something, or that the fire-spirit that helped us might make contact. I've had no success. I was going to suggest that we might all try to make a *walk* together.'

'It is a thing not done in an age, but worth trying.' Tarlos gazed at her thoughtfully. 'We should make the *walk* at Otter Hold though, I think in this Siphenna's experience will be invaluable.'

'If another stays here to assist Pirelle, I will make that journey.' Dia agreed. It was only a day's walk across the forest paths to Otter Hold and would be worth the risk.

None of the men chose to speak against it; this was *walker* business.

'Now, then; we have two warships and many warriors at our disposal.' Arrus indicated the Eldeman Merkis. 'It would make sense to keep one close to here and have the other patrol near the smaller islands; but these are not traditional attacks and we also have this craven necromancer hiding out somewhere.'

'We need to do a full search of all the islands!' One of the men broke formality and called out.

'Such a search would mean bringing men back in off the patrol ships,' Worvig warned him.

Merkis Vilnue stood slowly; a little unsure of his welcome.

'Speak, Merkis.' Arrus waved a hand toward him.

'You may use some of my warriors in your searches; or if you prefer, they could replace your warriors who come back off the boats.'

'It might be better if our own warriors search the islands,' Dia replied. 'Only because they know the land better. I will consider placing some of your warriors on our longships.'

There were some grumbles of disapproval, but Vilnue gave a smile and a nod and sat back down.

'*Walker* Dinue.' Arrus invited a small woman in the early months of pregnancy to speak.

'Do we know how far these necromancers can extend their magic?' she asked.

'Unfortunately, not.' Dia shook her head. 'But I've written to the Elden King to ask for any information he has on Chem magic. Dinue, I recall that there was a Borrow boy, about twelve when he was left here injured on a failed raid of Dolphin Isle. Would you see if he knows anything of Chem magic?'

'Of course; I'll ask him.'

'Does anyone else have any ideas or any updates?'

The council went on until late in to the evening as the holds discussed ways of defending themselves. They exchanged news of food supplies, births, deaths, the strength and upkeep of each hold. Throughout, Dia observed the Elden warriors growing restless, while Vilnue watched and listened with patience and interest.

'Tell your brother to stay close to Vilnue and make a friend of him if he can,' Dia said quietly to Arrus while a loud chieftain was diverting attention to himself.

'You don't trust him?'

Dia put her hand over her mouth to hide her words with the pretence of rubbing at a tired eye. 'After what they demanded in return for their aid? No, I don't trust any of them.'

***

Dia spent a sleepless night gazing at the night sky through the crack in the shutters. The waves shushed over the rocks below the cliff, the wind barely stirring the trees. Beside her Arrus was still and his breathing almost silent, so she guessed he was also wakeful. Most of her anger at him had subsided; she couldn't deny that he'd had no choice in his decision. Would she have made the right choice? Could she have left Kesta in the hands of an Eldeman sorcerer? She didn't think so; perhaps she was not as strong as her husband and daughter.

'We'll find him,' Arrus said. 'I think we need to ensure every *walker* has an escort of warriors with them until we do.'

'Yes,' she agreed, turning to put her arm around him. 'And as much as I hate to take away anyone's freedom, we should advise all women not to leave their homes alone.'

'Should we get all of those living in isolated houses to move to the strongholds?' He took her hand in his larger, calloused one.

'We should advise it; but not everyone will be in a position to leave their homes or livestock.'

Arrus gave a low growl of frustration. 'Even with the Elden warriors we don't have enough people to man the ships, search the islands, and stand guard over all our people.'

Dia took a long, slow breath in and out. 'We will just have to do our best.'

Fulmer Hold was as busy as a kicked ant's nest when dawn came creeping along the coast. The chieftains and their warriors were packing up to return to their own holds, some on foot and some by sea. Dia chose Worvig and Pirelle to command the stronghold and Shaherra to keep an eye on things. Arrus, Heara, and Dorthai were to be her escort along with ten warriors and those of Otter Hold who were making their way home. All the *Walkers* except Pirelle and Dinue were to travel with them. Dia was painfully aware that she would be leaving the people of Fulmer Hold vastly outnumbered by Eldemen. If Elden was going to betray them, she was making it easy for them.

Heara ghosted ahead as they took the path along the clifftop. The sea breeze had picked up and there was briny water in the air. Arrus walked ahead, talking with Chieftain Ufgard, leaving Dia to walk among the mostly silent *Walkers*. As they turned from the sea and followed the path into the dense forest, Heara appeared momentarily at Dia's side to give her a nod and smile of reassurance, before quickly vanishing again. No *Walker* was afraid of the forest or the animals within, however Dia noticed a chill to the air as she stepped into the shadows and pulled her jacket more tightly around herself.

'It's because we can't feel them,' one of the *Walkers* said behind her.

Dia turned to see a woman just a little younger than herself with rare red hair and lighter skin. Larissa of Argent Hold. Her grandfather was an Eldemen fisherman. The story went that her grandfather and grandmother met in their boats on the sea between their lands. They met every week to argue about who had the right to fish there; until one day the Eldeman climbed across into her boat and never went home.

Dia nodded, glancing around at all the *Walkers* and realised they were as on edge as herself. 'We should be able to sense this necromancer though.'

'I wonder.' Larissa's mismatched blue eyes were troubled. 'We do not know their powers.'

Dia couldn't deny it. There was no history of conflict between the Fulmers and Chem, being separated as they were by the Borrow Islands and flanked on the south-east by Elden. All they knew were second-hand stories from their few Borrow captives and from occasional trade with Eldemen. She'd certainly felt the fear and panic of the necromancer who had leapt into the sea and struggled to shore when the fire-spirit had torched his ship. She'd assumed he was their leader, their strongest; until the head. Larissa was right; this other man might be much stronger. They didn't even know if he was alone.

She took in a deep breath and drew herself up. 'We know we can kill them,' she said firmly. 'That's what matters.'

Even so she couldn't help feeling a vulnerability in the forest that she'd never experienced in her life, even before her *fire-walking* abilities had materialised. It still felt the same, the flicker of life that were birds, the darting tickle of squirrels and rodents; the deep thrumming of trees. It still sounded the same; the churr of insects, the rustling of leaves so similar to the sound of the sea, and the stirring birdsong. Even so there was a heaviness over Dia's heart that wouldn't lift and she found herself desperately missing her daughter's fire.

They stopped just after midday to rest and Heara came to sit with them.

'I looked down on Comfrey Farm from the ridge,' she said softly for Dia's ears only as she nibbled at some fish and flatbread. 'I couldn't see their animals and no sign of life.'

Dia felt dread settle like a stone in her stomach and she put down her own food. 'I'm glad you didn't investigate alone. We must do so, of course, but I am loath to send all these *Walkers* down there; it's dangerous enough for us all to be in one place.'

'I could go back with some men when we reach Otter Hold.'

It would be the sensible thing to do, Dia knew, but if there was trouble on the island the sooner they found out, the better.

'Take Dorthai and get closer,' she said. 'Don't put yourself in danger but see if the farm really is empty.'

Heara popped the rest of her bread into her mouth and nodded. She made her way over to the young warrior and tapped him on the shoulder, speaking a few swift words. He looked around to Dia, and she gave a single firm nod. Dorthai quickly gathered up his things and followed the scout between the trees.

'Trouble?' Arrus asked.

A ripple of concern spread through the *walkers* and warriors.

'Heara has spotted something that might be of concern.' She forced a smile, willing Arrus to understand that this was not the time to discuss it. 'She's going to take a quick look. Come on, we shouldn't be dawdling, let's get on our way.'

Arrus frowned but didn't argue. They packed away their supplies swiftly and Arrus sent two of the Fulmer Hold warriors out to scout in Heara's place. He remained at Dia's side as they followed the sun westward. The path took them back out of the forest and through hilly meadows where a few curly-furred cows grazed; young calves unsteady at their sides. Campion and gorse splashed the harsh coastal grass with pink and yellow; a single small hut standing among them. A man sat outside watching them as he turned the handle of a butter churn.

'Larissa, Corvun, pop down and warn that cowherd we may have an enemy loose on the island and catch us up as quickly as you can,' Dia commanded the *walker* and one of the warriors.

'I'll go with them,' Arrus offered.

She watched anxiously as the three of them hurried away, glancing back over her shoulder frequently until they were lost to view as the path took them down a steep incline toward a river valley. It was only moments later that movement caught her eye and she spun quickly to see not just her husband, but Heara and Dorthai jogging toward them.

Dorthai's face was grey and her best friend looked no better.

'Heara?' She hurried back to meet the scout.

Heara shook her head; a little out of breath. 'It's not good.'

'Not good!' Dorthai exclaimed. 'It's—'

Heara gave him a shove to quiet him as the others gathered around.

'Comfrey farm has been attacked.' Heara looked at them all. 'I found some of their animals wandering in the forest and circled around to check for tracks. I found signs of fighting; signs of a slaughter. No bodies remain but for one—'

Dorthai made a retching sound.

'There was a baby. What was left of a baby. It had been eaten.'

'By animals?' Dia asked, praying to the spirits that her friend would say yes.

'The teeth marks were human.'

Dorthai turned and vomited. Dia had to grab for Arrus's arm as the ground seemed to pull out from under her.

'The other bodies,' Arrus said through gritted teeth. 'Could they have been eaten?'

Heara shook her head. 'The other bodies walked out of there.'

'Then they were not dead.' Ufgard said.

'They *were* dead,' Heara said emphatically. 'The blood on the ground told of their deaths. The tracks that left were like those of the creatures that came ashore on Fulmer Beach. Dragging, sporadic, occasional signs that they had fallen. The tracks become surer as they go along; as the creatures learnt to walk again. Only one set of footsteps are sure and purposeful; they arrive, move about, then depart with the dead.'

'The necromancer,' Dia breathed.

'He is building a new army with our people. Women and children too.'

Arrus drew his sword. 'Men! With me!'

'No!' Dia cried out, raising an arm to stop him. 'We must get all the *walkers* safely to Otter Hold! Ufgard, send four of your men ahead to gather your warriors and send out messages to the other holds. As loathe as I am to delay, we must make our *walk* tonight, and after that I and two other *walkers* will join your warriors to hunt the necromancer. Your warriors should not try to engage the necromancer himself lest they be taken and turned against us—'

Ufgard went to protest but Dia shut him down with a glare.

'This is no time for hurt pride! And I am aware that I'm leaving families out there in danger.' The words caught in her throat. 'That will be the task of your warriors. They must evacuate the area and keep the necromancer from turning more. If they get a chance to kill any of those turned, they must do so; but I say again, do not engage the necromancer.'

'But the others were killed with steel. You said so.' Ufgard looked from Dia to Arrus.

'Only after I crippled his power with fear,' Dia replied softly. 'Tread carefully. We do not know what other magic they have or how much stronger this man is.'

Reluctantly, Ufgard pointed at four of his warriors. 'Be quick. We don't want to lose any more lives.'

'I should go.' Heara touched Dia's arm.

Dia's heart clenched. She didn't want to risk her friend, but Heara was the best there was. 'Be careful.'

'That goes without saying.' Heara kissed her cheek and then beckoning at the chosen warriors with a wave of her hand she set off at a fast run.

'We need to go too,' Dia said.

Arrus nodded, looking around to judge the *walkers* and assess their fitness. 'Let's go.' He set off at a fast walk and the others fell in with him.

***

They reached Otter Hold with the sun low off the west coast. Ufgard's wife, Kerin, came out to meet them.

'The warriors and scout, Heara, set out two hours ago,' she told them, her eyes darting from one *walker* to another and her hands fidgeting before her. 'Siphenna is waiting and we've nearly finished building your ritual fire.'

'Thank you.' Dia hugged the older woman.

'We've fetched water for you to refresh yourselves, would you follow me?' She invited the *walkers*.

Dia turned to Arrus. 'I'll see you later.'

He nodded, remaining with Ufgard as the women followed Kerin.

Every hold had a guest house by tradition and Otter Hold's had been set aside for the *walkers*. Dia was grateful as it allowed more privacy, if less safety, than the alcoves of the great hall. Siphenna was sitting silently in a chair outside the door with a young girl of twelve attending her. Siphenna had soft white hair, as fine as down, that contrasted strongly with her walnut skin. She was small and dainty looking as though made of tiny bird bones. Her skin was as lined as pine bark and her stunning eyes – grey and dark blue – had dulled with age. She smiled at the *walkers* as they approached, and holding to the arms of her chair stood carefully.

'It is good to see you, my girls,' she said, as fondly as though she were mother to them all.

Dia was first to kiss her wrinkled cheek, careful of the silky thinness of her skin. She smelt of sweet honeysuckle. The others lined up behind to greet her, the last offering her arm so they could walk into the guest house together. Dia gasped at the coldness of the water as she splashed it over her face and neck and pulled her fingers through her hair to tidy it. Kerin offered her some nettle tea and some oat cakes sweetened with honey.

'I'll leave you.' The lady of the hold gave a small bow and gestured for Siphenna's assistant to come with her.

'Thank you!' Dia called after her. She took a moment to gather her thoughts and sipped at the tea, looking over her mug at the women who remained in the room. Outside the sun had set, and the light had taken on a blue-grey hue.

'You are afraid, Icante,' Siphenna said gently.

'I am afraid,' she admitted, causing a ripple of concern to sigh through the other *walkers*. With these women there was nothing to be gained by pretending to be stronger than she was, or surer than she was. 'The first

190

Chemman we killed was easy. He came with mortal warriors and seemed to have little power himself. He used elemental magic, drawing flame to his hand. Kesta and I drew wind and water against him and Shaherra put an arrow though his heart.

'The second Chemman, as you know, was much stronger; his army larger and included the dead. We killed him because the fire-spirit burnt his ship and he came ashore disorientated; afraid of burning and drowning. I caught him off guard, fed his fear to incapacitate his power. Worvig finished him.

'But there was another man with him. One we did not know of. Either he was not on the burning ship or he got away unseen. As we now know he seems to be recruiting himself a new army of dead by killing our men, women, and children. Heara can track him; but I'm afraid that if our warriors attack him, they will become *his* warriors. I propose that we *walk* the flame together to petition the spirits of the fire to give us wisdom and grant us aid.'

'Such a thing was done when I was very young,' Siphenna's eyes grew distant. 'The spirits did not come forth to speak, but our enemies were destroyed. I did not know I was a *walker* then; I watched the ritual fire from a distance and prayed to the spirits that I might one day join those women.' She sighed and straightened up. 'The light is gone. It is time to ignite the flame.'

The fuel for the fire had been set several yards away from the stronghold and close to the cliff edge. Several warriors stood a respectful distance away, facing outward, to keep watch for danger. Dia went to check the small bonfire's construction and be sure that everything was there that should be. Among the kindling and logs were plaited wreaths and ropes of prayer grass along with the dream herbs; mugwort, mint, burdock, asparagus and valerian roots.

She walked around it twice to quell her nerves and then took a seat beside Siphenna on the cold ground. Without prompting all the women touched their hands to the earth, palms down, then reached forward to lift the bowl that had been placed ready before them. They drank down half of the cool water and placed back the rest. Dia took in a long deep breath, feeling the air swell her lungs and then reaching out both hands she took that of the woman to each side of her, forming a circle with their limbs. Calling on her magic she agitated the air just within the piled wood, creating heat until fire burst forth and ate hungrily at the kindling. Smoke began to rise and Dia triggered the part of her brain that allowed her to slip free and *walk.*

She became aware of the other women in the flame, at once part of her and separate. Of all of them Siphenna's presence was strongest, like a spark of lightning that did not dissipate. Instead of seeking to move to a place, Dia strengthened her awareness of the fire in which they were immersed.

'Great flame, we petition for your guidance and aid. Your *Walkers* are in danger and our people are being enslaved by blood magic. Hear our prayer, spirits of fire.'

'Hear our prayer, oh spirits of flame,' the other women chorused.

For a long moment Dia feared that there would be no reply; but she felt something slowly grow stronger and larger as though it were liquid squeezing through a small portal. Excitement and fear flowed from the other *walkers* mirroring her own. On many occasions she'd sensed the presence of a spirit within the flame, some even guided her in what to see. None had ever communicated with her.

'Speak, daughters of the flame,' it crackled and spat.

Dia hesitated, but another voice took her place, sounding infinitely young. Siphenna spoke, 'Flame father, one has come to our island to steal your daughters of flesh and murder the people of the *fire-walkers*. He is from another land and uses the magic of blood to command the dead. We fear his power and know not if we can defeat him. Can you help us?'

'I have already done so, at the behest of another.'

With a mixture of excitement and apprehension Dia realised that this must be the spirit that had burnt the ship.

'We thank you!' But who was it that had petitioned the spirits before them? Could it have been Kesta?

'The *dream-walker* of Elden sent word.' The fire-spirit sighed and softly hissed. 'Bad things awake with the blood. No one is safe, not even ancient spirits. We will help, but you must help us. The blood sorcerer you seek knows that we are against him and set a trap. He has a fire-spirit caught in his possession and will force it to cause destruction against its will. I cannot defeat him alone this time. I am Doroquael. I will come through into your realm; but for me to stay long we must keep a balance. A spirit for a spirit.'

'Done!' Siphenna said at once.

'And done!' Doroquael replied before Dia could protest.

'Now see with me,' Doroquael breathed.

Dia was pulled deep within the flame, the vortex through which they hurtled so bright in hues of orange and red that it hurt. Fear gripped her at the speed at which they moved, and awareness of her physical self tattered away. On they dove, swirling patterns too quick to make sense of assailed her senses. Then they slowed and as her eyes adjusted, she saw through a window the ward of a stronghold far below her in which figures moved. Her heart gave a leap of joy when one turned, and she knew it was her Kesta; but she was torn away almost at once as the image spun about and they looked within the small room of a tower. A man lay upon the floor, one hand flung out as though reaching for help. He had skin too pale for the Fulmers, but too dark for Chem, Elden, or the Borrows.

Then, as though picked up by a fierce wind, she was dragged out of the tower and once again they tumbled through the fiery funnel. There was a sickening sense of unravelling and her ears roared. For the briefest of moments, they looked upon a man in his early thirties with long black hair and a short, neat beard. He glared at them with cold blue eyes ...

Then Dia found herself thrown backward against the hard ground, her head slamming against the earth and her teeth clacking together. The prayer fire exploded upward in crackling sparks of blue and she pulled herself up onto her elbows to scramble back. She looked around quickly to check on the others and saw that Siphenna hadn't moved. The eldest *walker* sat still, facing the subsiding bonfire, slumped forward slightly as though dozing. Dia crawled across the hot, scorched grass and took hold of Siphenna's shoulder, crying out as the woman fell back.

Her eyes looked emptily up at the night sky.

Siphenna was dead.

Chapter Ten

Kesta: Kingdom of Elden.

Rosa finished pinning her hair and Kesta sprang to her feet and looked out of the window to the Raven Tower. The birds seemed subdued this morning, three out on the roof but none in the air. There was a hint of a glow through Jorrun's window so he either had a fire lit or was burning candles even though the sun was coming up. A shadow moved behind the glass, arms moving as though gesticulating speech.

'I think he has someone in there with him!'

Rosa stepped to her side and leaned forward to peer across. 'You have better eyes than me, I can't see anyone.'

She frowned. 'It looks like he's talking to someone.'

Rosa sighed. 'What dress do you intend to wear for the king?'

Kesta waved a hand disinterestedly so Rosa picked out the green day dress. Jorrun's shadow moved out of sight and movement below caught Kesta's eye. People were back out working in the ward. She dressed and went down for breakfast; Catya was already at the table.

'Catya, does anyone live in the tower with Jorrun?' Kesta asked as she sat down.

'No, lady.' Catya shook her head.

'You're certain?'

'I only take enough food for one and often that gets left.'

'You go in the tower?' Kesta sprang to her feet and Catya shrank back.

'No, lady! I'm allowed just inside the door to leave and take the tray; that's all!'

'I didn't mean to startle you, Catya, I'm sorry.' She sat back down. 'And my name is Kesta, not lady.'

'What are you going to do today?' Rosa asked.

'I guess I can't go digging up herb beds when we don't know what time the king will arrive, but we should at least have a walk around to encourage everyone and see how it's going.'

'That would be appropriate.' Rosa gave a wry smile.

Kesta poked her tongue out at her which made Catya giggle.

***

They walked around the ward first, stopping to talk to the workers, including Adrin who was charming and friendly. As they walked away Kesta heard some of his warriors teasing him about her. It made her feel as though a centipede walked down her spine and mild nausea settled in her stomach. They went down to the boat yard to say hello and then walked the circuit of the clearing around the stronghold. Already a dozen trees had been felled and trimmed. As they came back to the stronghold, Tantony came out to meet them and for a moment Kesta feared that the king had arrived already.

'Nerim's boy, Nip, just came by from the stables,' Tantony said. 'Did you know that a horse arrived for you yesterday? They said you hadn't been in and apologised that they hadn't thought to send word.'

'No. They did tell me that a horse would be coming for me, but I didn't know when.' She hurried off at once towards the stables with Catya at her heels. Rosa and Tantony smiled shyly at each other and followed at a more sedate pace.

As Kesta rounded the keep approaching the stables she came face to face with Adrin. Despite the fact it was overcast he'd taken off his shirt to work. Kesta was so startled she stopped abruptly and Catya walked into her. Adrin put his hands on his hips and flexed his muscles with a grin. Kesta's skin flushed, and she gritted her teeth, wanting to put him in his place but momentarily stumped for anything smart to say. She narrowed her eyes and walked away. Behind her she heard Tantony growl, 'Put your clothes on! We have ladies at the hold now!'

She reached the stables feeling rather warm and spotted Nip at once.

'Lady!' he came scampering over. 'Sorry we—'

'No need to apologise. You did tell me a horse would be coming, and I didn't take the time to visit.'

'I reckon you haven't had much time for visiting.' Nerim came out from a stall wiping his hands on an old cloth which he slung over his shoulder. 'Your work is coming on fast.'

'Yes, I have had a lot of help.' Kesta smiled.

'You come to see the beast?'

'I have.'

'He's up here, though I'm not sure he is the best purchase the Thane has ever made. Lovely looking horse but a bit on the temperamental side.'

Kesta approached the stall slowly and drew up her *knowing*. At once she felt a spark of recognition and the horse trotted forward, ears up and blowing excitedly.

'You!' She opened the stall door and ignoring Nerim's shout of alarm went in and threw her arms around the horse's neck and shoulders. The horse tried to nibble at her hair and snuffled down her back.

'You know the beast?' Nerim asked in surprise.

'This is the horse I rode after my wedding.' She stepped back to look into her own reflection in its black eyes, revelling in the horse's excitement and happiness. 'Jorrun … Jorrun knew I liked him.'

'Well, he seems to like you too. He tried to kick me twice, and I thought I was good with horses.'

'He is an intelligent fellow who's been neglected, he'll be fine with a bit of patience.'

'So, you know your horses as well as your herbs,' Nerim said approvingly.

'Lady Kesta!' Tantony called out. 'The scouts have sighted the king's ship!'

Moments later a horn was blown. Kesta stroked the horse's nose. 'I'll be back when I can.'

She hurried toward the keep as Tantony headed out toward the small dock. Only moments later Jorrun stepped out of the Raven Tower and made his way toward her with purpose and poise.

'Thank you for Griffon,' she said.

'Griffon?'

'My horse.'

'You seemed well suited.'

She glanced at him but caught no expression on his face, neither frown nor smile. 'You're not as heartless as you pretend.' Without thinking, she touched his arm and, for the briefest of moments, the cold wind that always seemed to surround Jorrun paused and she drew in a sharp breath as grief struck her like a kick to her stomach. She bit her lower lip and looked up at him, but his attention was elsewhere. The king walked through the gates to the hold and Jorrun strode forward to clasp his wrist and bow. Kesta sank into a curtsy, her heart still racing.

'Your Majesty, we are honoured,' Jorrun said.

'Yes, I'm sure you are,' Bractius replied dryly. 'What's all this work I see? We passed a supply ship heading this way.'

Jorrun turned to Tantony, and the Merkis hurried off toward the dock with a nod of his head.

'The work needed doing,' Jorrun replied. 'Do you have any more news?'

'Silene Arrus and our warriors set sail from Taurmouth yesterday.' Bractius turned from Jorrun and approached Kesta. 'And how are you settling in? Does the Raven Tower have an heir yet?'

Kesta's mouth fell open, and she flushed at the king's bluntness. Jorrun glared at his friend, his own cheeks reddening, and the muscles of his jaw moved as he clenched his teeth. Bractius laughed at them and put his arm around Jorrun's shoulder.

'Come on, let's talk somewhere more private.'

They headed into the great hall and toward the south-west tower of the keep. The few warriors that were within scrambled to their feet to bow and Bractius waved a hand at them dismissively. Kesta turned to Rosa.

'Could you arrange for refreshment to be brought to the guest tower?'

Rosa curtseyed and hurried off.

Jorrun opened the tower door and Bractius led them up the stairs and to the receiving room. It was the first time Kesta had ventured into the south-west tower. It was furnished with burgundy and gold fabrics and dark wooden furniture. In the centre was a large round table on which several scrolls and a large open map were strewn; but the king headed for some comfortable looking chairs set close to the fireplace. There were four of them and the two men chose the seats closest to the fire and opposite each other. She wasn't sure why, but Kesta felt a need to support her unwanted husband and sat in the seat beside him.

'The ships you saw, tell me everything.' The king came straight to the point.

Kesta stared into the unlit fireplace and described every detail she could recall as she'd been taught to do as a *walker*. 'The salt seemed to be significant,' she mused. 'It was as though the Fire was making sure I saw it. It is not unknown for the fire-spirit to make its sentience known to a *walker* but it's very rare. Mostly we just *walk* the flame and see into one source and out of another like a conduit. We ... I ... surmised that the long boxes contained bodies that were to be preserved for a long voyage.'

'I can see your logic there.' Bractius nodded and turned to Jorrun. 'But why not just send living warriors? Why these ... 'undead?''

'There are practical reasons.' Jorrun shifted in his seat. 'They do not need to be fed for a start. It also saves your own warriors. The Borrows have just been conquered, and that means a large supply of bodies. Also, there is the fear factor; it's very hard to kill a man who is already dead.'

'I guess the more people you kill, the more warriors you gain.' Bractius chewed at his thumbnail. 'The odds against you get worse and worse.'

'There is a limit to how many a necromancer can control,' Jorrun said.

'Well, thank the Gods for that at least!' Bractius exclaimed.

'How are they controlled?' Kesta asked.

Jorrun glanced at the king. 'It is blood magic,' he told her. 'A scroll stone is placed within the body and it can be imbued with a simple command, such as "attack the living", or controlled more completely; like a possession. The more powerful the necromancer the more he can control.'

'Then it's not the spirit of the dead that's raised and enslaved?'

Jorrun shook his head. 'It is thought … some think that the soul of the dead person might be aware; that if they have not moved on but remained attached to their body, they become trapped. It's only supposition; no one knows for sure.'

'But the best way to defeat them would be to take out the necromancers,' Kesta surmised.

'Ha!' Bractius thumped the side of his chair. 'I like your thinking, woman.'

'It would be.' Jorrun nodded. 'But the necromancers are powerful and can control the dead from a distance.'

'How big a distance?' she demanded.

Jorrun glanced at the king again. 'The books suggest that it can be many miles, limitless even, with a simple command from a blood scroll. For a full possession they would need to be close.'

'And—' the king stopped speaking as they heard the door go below and several footsteps coming up the steps.

Rosa came in and directed the woman and three children with her to clear space on the table and set out the food and drink they'd bought.

'Will there be anything else?' Rosa asked.

Kesta hesitated; she didn't want to dismiss Rosa from the room like a servant, but she doubted that Jorrun or the king would want her to remain.

'No, thank you, Rosa; you may go.'

Rosa curtseyed and left.

The king went straight to the table. He picked up a meat pastry and took a large bite from it. 'You think they're heading straight here now rather than taking the Fulmers first?'

Jorrun turned to speak over his shoulder. 'I can't be certain of that. We know their plans for the Fulmers are long-term and not urgent.'

'But it's still an easier target for a strategic base than Mantu.'

'Actually no—'

'Hang on a minute!' Kesta spun in her chair to look from Bractius to Jorrun. 'I'm only getting half a story here! What plans for the Fulmers? What do you know?'

The king and Jorrun looked at each other. Kesta sprang to her feet.

'What?'

'We suspected, and the Icante's last message confirmed it,' Bractius said, 'they want the Fulmer's magic.'

'But that isn't something you can just steal. You might be able to learn how to use it but unless you're chosen by the fire to be a *walker* ...' She stopped, looking at their expressions and calling up her *knowing*. From Jorrun there was nothing; from the king impatience and secrecy.

'I've told you a little about Chem,' Jorrun said, although it was the king he looked at as he spoke rather than her. 'I—'

The king held up his hand to stop him and Kesta almost snarled.

'Her mother has worked it out, Kesta should know,' Jorrun said.

Kesta felt the king's annoyance with her *knowing*, but he nodded.

'Sit, please,' Jorrun invited.

She did so and waited patiently for him to find the words. 'The Dunhams and their allies came to power slowly and subtly over years by increasing their power. Like *fire-walkers* the magic of Chem is inherited. Women in Chem can carry the blood of sorcerers but are not allowed to learn to use it; women in Chem are seen as little more than slaves or possessions. They are bought and sold, and wars have even started to steal those of strong blood.'

Kesta's body tensed and her breathing came faster and deeper. She clamped her teeth together and bid him continue with a small nod.

'It is usual practice to breed better blood lines, to increase the magical ability of a family. This has included buying or steeling Fulmer captives from the Borrows. A … a Fulmer woman, especially a *walker*, is incredibly valuable in Chem.'

Kesta managed to loosen her jaw muscles long enough to speak. 'I see.'

Jorrun opened his mouth to go on, but the king handed Kesta a goblet of wine and said loudly, 'So you see, the capture of the Fulmers would be more a long-term aim of the Coven of Arkoom. If Dunham is already set for war, then it will be a case of which island gives him the best strategic advantage on his attack of Elden.'

'Why are they even attacking Elden? You have no magic here, not for many years.' Kesta followed the king with her eyes as he returned to the table to pick through the food.

'There is magic still here in Elden,' Jorrun said before the king could stop him. 'But it's inert. Use of magic was made a crime punishable by death long, long ago, before your ancestors arrived by sea to settle the Fulmers. People forgot how to use it. But I doubt that's the reason behind their attack. It is more likely greed. Greed for land to rule, greed for resources, greed for power.'

'Too many sorcerers all vying with each other for position and not enough Seats to fill.' The king nodded. 'So, how do we discover their plans? If we split our forces too much between the Fulmers and Mantu it will leave both vulnerable.'

'Not to mention you'll be leaving the coast open to attack.' Kesta swirled her wine in her goblet. 'There is every chance if they want to be cunning, they will sail wide of Elden and attack from the south or the east ... anywhere.'

'You will have to put more pressure on Osun,' Bractius told Jorrun. 'I'm afraid at this point we have no choice but for him to risk his life and push harder for information. He has not proved as useful as we'd hoped.'

'But he has given much for our service—'

'That is my order,' Bractius said softly.

Kesta froze and dared not meet Jorrun's eyes.

The muscles of Jorrun's jaw moved, but he said nothing.

'For goodness's sake, eat something!' Bractius laughed, clapping Jorrun on the back. 'I bet he hasn't been looking after himself, has he?' He grinned at Kesta and she forced a smile back. In truth she knew nothing of Jorrun's welfare.

Jorrun got up slowly and went to the table, he stood looking at the food but didn't touch it. 'I still think our best option is for me—'

'Jorrun.' The king shook his head. '*You* are not expendable.'

'There are things *I* can do,' Kesta offered. 'I can keep *walking* and hope either I or the fire can find something. I can also try to enlist more help from the creatures of the air and sea to watch for us although I would need to travel to the coast.'

'The Icante and the other *fire-walkers* are already doing that; but by all means *walk* as often as it's safe for you to do so.' Bractius scratched at his beard. 'I think I'll have no choice but to deploy warriors to the holds on the coast and send most of the remaining fleet to patrol out of Mantu. We have a small advantage in that they don't know we know they are coming.'

'Where would you like my warriors to report?' Jorrun asked.

'Send half to Taurmouth, the rest should remain to defend Northold should any ships make it up the river.'

Jorrun nodded. 'I'll get them on their way tomorrow.'

'Good. Come, then, let's have a think about things and we'll discuss it again later. Kesta, I think it would be good if I ate with the warriors in the hall tonight, stir them up a bit ready to go off and defend the north. Jorrun, let's go feed those ravens of yours.'

Jorrun looked at her and she knew he was expecting her to protest at being left out, but she had so much to think about that she simply curtseyed and left the room. She hurried down the tower steps and paused with her hand on the door. So much was not as she'd supposed. Even with her *knowing* she'd got the relationship between the king and his Thane completely wrong. Bractius was very clearly in charge but why did they let it seem otherwise? She bit her lower lip, breathing rapidly. Was the powerful and dreaded Dark Man nothing more than an act?

She stepped out into the hall and found a bustle of activity. Tantony and Rosa were directing some men with crates and barrels. There were also two chests with some scrolls resting on the top. She saw Rosa pick up one scroll and blanch at what she saw.

'Lady Kesta, these are some of the things you requested for the kitchens and the hold.' Tantony drew her attention and she walked over to him. 'One of the chests is apparently for you, from Jorrun. The other contains Rosa's belongings that Queen Ayline has sent.'

'The king wishes to eat in the hall with the warriors tonight,' she told him as she frowned at the chest. 'Half of you are to be sent to the north coast tomorrow.'

'I suspected as much.' Tantony sighed. 'I'm afraid some of your plans will have to wait.'

'Of course.' She bent to pick up the chest but Tantony almost barged her aside.

'My lady, I'll have that taken up! Hest!' he gestured at one of the men. 'Take these chests up to the receiving room in the south-east tower.'

The man hurried over and Tantony bent to pick up the scrolls; all but the one Rosa clutched to her chest. 'I'll tell Reetha what's happening,' Tantony said.

'Thank you.' Kesta glanced around at the crowded and noisy room, her muscles relaxing a little as her gaze stopped at the doorway to her own quiet tower. As she headed toward it, the door to the south-west tower opened and the king and Jorrun strode through the hall toward the main entrance. Jorrun glanced at her and gave her the briefest of smiles but they didn't stop. She entered her own tower, holding the door open for Hest who staggered up in front of them. Catya was waiting in the receiving room; Kesta didn't blame her for staying out of the way. Rosa sat in a chair and looked down at the scroll in her hands before slowly opening it.

As soon as Hest left, Kesta threw open the chest. She lifted away a sheet of linin and found several dresses folded below, all in the simple style of her wedding dress but with flowers or vines embroidered in silver and gold across the bodice. At the bottom she found two pairs of trousers and two long-sleeved tunics. She grinned to herself as she lifted them up.

'Your doing?' Kesta asked Rosa.

The older woman shook her head. 'No, Jorrun asked me who had made your wedding dress and must have placed the order.'

Kesta noticed at once how distracted Rosa seemed.

'Bad news?' she nodded toward the scroll.

Rosa looked at her, biting her lower lip. 'The queen has asked me to stay on permanently here with you; or until she recalls me, or you dismiss me.'

'You don't want to stay?' Kesta's heart sank, she'd hoped that Rosa had begun to feel the same bonds of friendship that she did.

'Oh, I want to stay!' Rosa said earnestly. 'But …'

Kesta waited.

'The queen wants me to spy on you and report back to her.'

'Spy on me?' She shook her head incredulously and laughed. 'What on earth for?'

'To see if you're a threat to her power at court. She's heard of what you're doing here and … well, knowing her she is probably livid that she didn't think of doing something like that first. Her popularity is her influence and power, she will not want you to outshine her.'

'Outshine her? I'm not a jewel.'

'No, you're not; that's what worries her.'

'She is queen. No one can take that from her.'

'Hmm, it would certainly be rare if someone did, but not impossible. Don't be surprised if the queen produces an heir.'

Kesta shook her head in disbelief.

Rosa shrugged. 'Women in Elden are allowed little power; she will fight for what she has even against an imagined threat.'

'I suppose I can understand that.' Kesta sighed. 'By all means spy away, Rosa, but make sure she knows all I care about is protecting my people.'

'Does that mean us?' Catya asked quickly.

Kesta stood up and walked over to the girl, placing a hand on her thin shoulder. She bent to kiss the top of her head. 'Yes, Catya, that means you.

Now then; let's get ourselves ready for tonight's feast with the king. We will all look our absolute best in support of this stronghold. Rosa, as a lady you will be seated at the high table. Catya, you will attend us but I won't have you standing there hungry, go to the kitchens and get yourself something to eat up here before we go down.'

Catya beamed at her. Rosa looked at her in surprise.

'Well, let's get to it!'

**

Kesta chose a blue dress with silver embroidery and also wore the leaf necklace Jorrun had gifted her. Rosa wore a lighter blue and lent Catya a simple silver chain. Kesta paused at the door to the great hall, took in a deep breath and called up her *knowing*. She picked up on both her companions' excitement and pride and she amplified it to drown out any anxiety. Catya opened the door and Kesta strode through with Rosa a step behind her. They had been keeping watch out of the window, so they knew Jorrun had just arrived. He stood at the back of the hall talking to Tantony and both men stopped to look up as they approached. Kesta noticed that Tantony's eyes didn't leave Rosa.

'I thought you might wear the trousers,' Jorrun said with his face so expressionless most would have missed his humour.

'I work with the weapons I have to hand.' Her mouth stretched to a grin and for a moment Jorrun's composure slipped, and a smile lit his eyes.

'Do you need more weapons?'

'I need a good quality dagger for Rosa and Catya.'

'Are you training assassins now?'

'No, I am training more weapons.'

'I see. Have you decided who your enemy is?'

She hesitated, her eyes still fixed on his, her heart beating faster.

Rosa coughed; the king had entered the room with his young servant. Jorrun spun about to bow and Kesta dipped in a curtsy.

'Come now, let's eat.' Bractius clapped Jorrun on the back, all amiability.

The room had filled with warriors and their families and as soon as the king was seated, they fell upon the food. Older children and a few women rushed forward to pour wine and lay out more dishes. Jorrun indicated with his head that Kesta should take the chair to the king's right, while he himself took the seat to his left. Rosa moved around to sit on Jorrun's other side. Tantony moved down to the top of the lower table and Catya took a jug of wine from one of the children. The king piled his plate high with meat and tore the heel off a loaf. Jorrun had taken only a thin slice of venison and a few carrots.

'So; tell me more of your plans for the hold.' The king glanced at Jorrun and then turned to smile at Kesta. She outlined her intentions, and he nodded as he ate. 'It's been many years since we had raiders this far inland, but it wasn't unusual in my great-grandfather's time. It's good to see you so quickly making Elden your home.'

She started at his words; was that what she was doing? Blood rushed to her cheeks at the thought people might perceive her actions as her abandoning her own land and so readily accepting this one, rather than the truth that she'd been forced into it. She looked down, blinking rapidly and drawing her hands into her lap to clench her fists.

'It's in the nature of my people to make the best they can of even a bad situation,' she replied, and she saw his eyes harden to wariness. As tempted as she was to call up her *knowing* she didn't want Jorrun to know that she spied on the king too often. 'I'm enjoying the hard work and delighted to be of use to Elden,' she added more diplomatically. He clearly wasn't fooled.

'It's understandable that you'd be unhappy at being taken from your people and your expected life; but this was important. Very important.'

'It would help if I understood your reasons and your plans.'

He drank down his wine and then put a large sliver of meat in his mouth. 'I'm not used to discussing matters of war with women. We are working to save both Elden and the Fulmers,' he replied eventually.

She clenched her jaw and took in several slow breaths to calm her anger. 'Will you allow Jorrun to tell me everything?'

Out of the corner of her eye she saw Jorrun freeze.

Bractius sat back and looked at her. She held his gaze as he seemed to try to assess her, perhaps adding her worth against her faults.

She took a risk. 'He told me he was a slave.' She tried to put both insult and humour into the remark.

It worked; Bractius let out a bark of a laugh and leaned across to thump Jorrun hard on the back. 'A slave!'

Several of the warriors looked up, wondering what had so amused the king. He turned and spoke softly to Kesta, his breath tickling her ear he bent so close. 'He is no slave. I will think about what you asked.' Then he waved at one of the girls to bring more wine. 'This is good wine, Jorrun, not Cainridge?'

'No, from Woodwick,' Jorrun replied. 'Tantony recommended it, he seems to have a good palette for wine.'

'Not a bad trait for a Merkis.' Bractius raised his goblet toward Tantony.

Talk turned to safer topics, trade, food, and gossip from around Elden. Bractius did most of the talking but both Jorrun and Rosa politely added to the conversation. Although the king acted merry and had his share of wine, Kesta was not fooled, she could see in his eyes that he was more alert and soberer than he pretended. He reminded her of her uncle Worvig who could drink most warriors under the table but still leap up to fight at a moment's notice.

She was relieved when the king announced he was going to his bed. She waited a moment longer before apologising to Jorrun that she too was tired.

'I must get back to my work, anyway.' He stood and bowed. 'Thank you for your patience this evening.'

He left before she could puzzle out what he meant by that and she and Rosa retreated to the south-east tower. Catya joined them quickly, a look of relief on her face.

'I'm sorry that was such a long evening, Catya,' she apologised. Catya shrugged and was overtaken by a huge yawn.

'Get to bed!' Kesta shooed her with a laugh. 'And you, Rosa.'

Kesta went up to her own room and hopping up sat on the sill of the window facing east. Light flickered in the Raven Tower, but she could see no movement. Eventually sleepiness won over, and she blew out her candles and went to bed.

Chapter Eleven

Kesta; Kingdom of Elden

The following day the king departed early, just after dawn, and Kesta left the tower to find several women and children cleaning up the great hall. Rosa and Catya had still been sleeping, and she'd decided not to disturb them. It was the first time she'd wandered the hold alone. Few warriors had come finding breakfast, and she guessed the ones that were there had just finished a night watch on the gates and walls. Tantony wasn't in the steward's room and there was no sign of him out in the ward. She paid Griffon a visit and also checked on Nettle, both seemed content and settled although Griffon itched to run out and stretch his legs.

'Soon,' she promised.

She went back out into the ward and surveyed their progress. Most of the land had now been cleared, and she decided to mark out where she wished the barn and the vegetable and herb beds to be placed. The cart where they'd been storing their tools had been moved up against the wall of the keep; probably to make the place look tidier for the king's visit. She picked out a mallet and a saw but turning she almost walked into Adrin. She was so surprised she dropped the saw.

'I'm glad I caught you.' He smiled charmingly, stepping closer as she stepped back. Her hip brushed up against the cart. 'I'm off with my men later today at the king's command and I wanted to give you a proper goodbye.' He reached out his hand to clasp her hair and bent his head toward her, but she managed to move aside despite being almost pinned by the cart.

'No need to be shy.' He grinned, and he grabbed for her with both hands. Rather than avoid him she punched him hard in the nose.

Adrin cried out in anger and clutched at his face. A small trickle of blood tracked down to his lip. She felt his rage rise and knew she had to act fast before he retaliated and really hurt her. She drew up all of her confidence and pride, every ounce of command, and hurled it with her words.

'Jorrun is your Thane and I am his wife. How dare you presume to lay a hand on me! My friendship is not an invitation to take more! You will give me the respect I am owed!'

His fists loosened, and he spat blood.

'You will apologise.' She forced her breathing to slow and uncurled her own fingers, but she could still hear the rush of blood in her ears.

'My mistake.' He glared daggers at her. 'I was only having a little fun.'

Were it not for her *knowing* she might have believed that, but his resentment for Jorrun flowed from him like a hot wind. He genuinely was a good warrior, clever, and even brave, but he was overlooked while the Dark Man, who barely ever lifted a blade or got himself dirty, was given all the credit and glory for saving Elden. What he refused to understand or recognise was that he was not promoted due to his dangerous arrogance.

'You are a handsome man, Adrin, and you could be a great warrior. I wish you luck defending the coast; I am sure you will make Northold proud.' Despite the fact her heart was pounding she picked up the saw and walked past him around the keep. She closed down her *knowing* and allowed her fear and anger to come. Movement caught her eye, and she saw Jorrun run out of the Raven Tower. He froze on seeing her and her steps faltered. It seemed an eternity that they stood looking at each other across the ward, her heart beating loudly in her ears; then he turned and went back inside the tower. Realising that Adrin was still close by she made her legs move and went to their pile of felled saplings to select thin trunks and stout branches to make stakes.

What had Jorrun been doing? Had he known she'd been in trouble? Had he somehow seen from the Raven Tower that Adrin had confronted her? She looked around. No, there was no way he could have seen the cart from the tower. Just a coincidence then? She would have to ask him when he came to see her tonight. She wondered if she should speak to Tantony about the confrontation. She decided against it; she'd dealt with it herself after all. She hoped she'd done so without making an enemy of the warrior; she had a feeling Adrin could cause a lot of trouble if he wanted to.

***

Rosa came to find her shortly after with Catya, and the three of them staked out the areas that Kesta wanted to mark. A few others came out and helped them begin to dig the herb bed, but with the work the king's visit had created they didn't do much and Kesta dismissed them early. The warriors chosen to go north to Taurmouth and fortify the coast gathered and left with much fanfare. Kesta joined Tantony to wish them well. Adrin didn't so much as look at her; his nose looked swollen, but his eyes had not blacked. She wondered what story he'd told the other men.

After they departed Kesta and Rosa went for a ride along the shore of the lake; exploring as far as the bridge across the river. Kesta could tell that Rosa was nervous, so she kept to a walk although it left Griffon impatient and frustrated. When they got back to the gates to the hold Kesta shouted back to Rosa, 'I'll see you at the stables!' Griffon needed no prompting but surged forward into a ground eating gallop. Kesta lay low against his neck and three times they circled the hold before he fell back into a walk and went without protest through the gates and back to his stable. Nip was there to take him from her and rub him down.

'How did he do?' the boy asked.

'He is a wonderful horse.' Kesta sent her feelings with the words toward Griffon. 'He is fast, but I didn't fear for a moment that he would let me fall.'

Nip grinned at her and patted Griffon's shoulder.

'You are a better horsewoman than me!' Rosa exclaimed.

Kesta didn't tell her it was only the second time she'd ever ridden a horse.

'Let's get cleaned up for dinner,' she suggested.

***

They finished their evening meal and sat in the chairs by the fire finishing their wine. Kesta had seated herself so she could watch the doorway; but Jorrun didn't come. Eventually she sent her yawning companions to bed, but she herself waited another hour before giving up and going up to her room. Was he angry with her for what had happened with Adrin? Or perhaps it was that she'd asked the king if he could give his permission for him to answer her questions? Then she felt a sick feeling in her stomach when she had recalled that she'd told the king Jorrun had said he was a slave. Had she betrayed a confidence? She'd spoken quietly so as not to be overheard but the king had blurted it out.

She went to the window and looked across. There was light, but it was soft and faint. With a sigh she went to the small fireplace and built it up. She felt strong enough to try *walking* the flame again tonight; but where should she try? She longed to see her home and feel some connection with it; but as ever the greater need was to know what the necromancers of Chem were doing. She looked deep into the flame and opened her mind to it, finding her connection with the life within. It was dangerous to daydream and allow yourself to be lost in the flame, it took great concentration and discipline to choose the path through which you wished to flow. She was not the first *walker* to be tempted to just let go and see where the flame took her; but did she dare?

No.

She set her thoughts toward Chem and pushed northward. It took little effort, and the flame seemed to pull her along easily until she found herself at the same docks she'd observed before. Except for three small fishing craft the docks were empty.

The dead army of Chem was on its way.

She came back to the room, her head pounding and her body chilled. She found the remainder of Jorrun's incense and threw it onto the glowing embers. She stood with a stagger and went to the window to close it. She froze; there was no light in the window of the Raven Tower opposite. Sharp pain pushed at her eyes and she stumbled to her bed and climbed gratefully in. Sleep quickly overtook her.

***

She woke with a start from a dream of being lost in the flame and unable to find her way back. Sitting up her gaze went at once to the window. Hadn't there always been a light in the window of the Raven Tower?

She got up and went to look. The tower appeared dark and empty. The ravens were cawing loudly and circling close to the tower.

Catya had left water out for her and she splashed it on her face, tied her hair back and dressed in her new trousers and tunic. She belted her dagger around her waist and went down to find the others. Rosa was going over the letters that Catya had drawn on her slate while the girl nibbled at some bread.

'Catya, when do you take Jorrun's food?' she asked.

Catya dropped the bread. 'Morning and evening.'

'Have you been this morning?'

Catya stood up, her eyes wide. 'I did, he hadn't etten anything.'

'Did it look like it had been touched at all?'

'What's wrong?' Rosa demanded.

'Probably nothing.' She shook her head but knew she was lying. Perhaps … perhaps she should have *walked* to the tower to see if she could see inside. Would Jorrun know if she did?

'I'm going to see Tantony.'

Rosa shot to her feet and both she and Catya followed her to Tantony's study.

'Good morning,' he said, looking up with wary resignation.

Kesta came straight to the point. 'When did you last see Jorrun?'

Tantony sat back in his chair. 'When he said goodbye to the king yesterday. It's usual for him to be holed up in that tower for days.'

Kesta nodded, but the frown didn't leave her face and the words didn't alleviate her concern. 'He hasn't visited for two nights,' she admitted. 'But he's probably just busy.'

'He was given a lot of work by the king.' Tantony watched her carefully.

Kesta nodded. 'And I had better get on with *my* work. I want to get the herb beds finished and planted today before the plants we were sent wither.'

'I'll be down later to help.' Tantony smiled, but his gaze turned toward Rosa.

Kesta forced a smile of her own and led her ladies back down to the hall and out into the ward. She started walking around to where she'd marked out the herb beds but stopped abruptly and turned back to face the Raven Tower. All the windows were dark, and the ravens were still unsettled. Gritting her teeth; she headed toward the tower.

'What are you doing?' Rosa demanded.

'I am going to get Catya to check his breakfast tray.'

'But you heard what Tantony said—'

'Catya.' Kesta turned to the girl. 'Is there always a light on in the Raven Tower?'

'Yes.'

'Are you worried?'

Catya hesitated. 'Yes.'

'You are making her worried!' Rosa said. 'You are making *me* worried!'

'Look, we'll just check.' Kesta stopped outside the heavy wooden door. 'Just look at the food tray you left,' she prompted Catya.

The girl walked gingerly to the door and grasping the large ringed handle, lifted the latch and pushed it open. Kesta noticed that she didn't use a key.

'It hasn't been touched either!' Catya darted back out.

'How unusual is that, honestly?'

Catya glanced at Rosa. 'He never eats much but he'll always take food up for the ravens.'

The ravens. Kesta stepped back to look up at the roof of the tower and called up her *knowing*. Birds were sometimes hard to pin down, but all the crow family had sharp little minds and often complex emotions; including humour. She felt their anxiety. She reached harder to see if any of the ravens would be willing to communicate and at once she was flooded with half a dozen responses. All showed her images of an empty window; two showed an arm on the carpet, palm up and fingers still.

'Get Tantony!' She turned to Rosa and then pushed past Catya into the tower. 'Neither of you follow me in!'

When the door closed behind her, she was plunged into darkness. After a moment, her eyes adjusted, and she could make out a wide room with no furniture but for a table on which stood the tray of untouched food. Opposite was the start of a stone stairway. She went to the foot of the stairs and drawing in a deep breath called up, 'Jorrun? Jorrun are you okay?'

She waited, her heart beating hard and her ears straining for any reply; all she could hear was the calling of the ravens.

She raised her voice further. 'Jorrun, if you don't reply I am going to come up the stairs!'

She listened again, trying not to let her fear grow for the consequences of entering the forbidden tower. Perhaps she should wait for Tantony, but then she would be getting the Merkis in trouble too. She bit her lip and stepped up onto the first stair.

'I'm coming up!'

Keeping a hand against the wall she ascended the steep stairway until she came to the first door. She knocked lightly, then louder, pressing her ear to the old wood to listen for a response. She tried the handle, and the door swung inward. There was no window in this room, but she could make out shelves full of books from floor to ceiling all around the curving walls. In the centre of the room were several wooden chests. As tempted as she was to look inside, she didn't dare and retreated out to the stairs. She went on to the next door and again knocked before going in. The room was similar to the first but for a small slit window that let in a shaft of light. Dust danced like glittering mayflies in the draft of the door opening. She closed the door at once and went on.

The next room was different. Again, it had only one slit window that left much in shadow, but the shelves were not full of books but with jars and bottles. There were also several cabinets with hundreds of small drawers set in them. There was a mixture of strong scents, both pleasant and acrid, and she found herself holding her breath. This must be where Jorrun kept the supplies he'd spoken of. She went back to the stairs and looked up; it was lighter, and she could feel a gentle breeze against her face. The sound of the ravens was louder.

'Jorrun? Jorrun!' She waited, hearing the pulsing of her blood in her ears. 'I'm going to come up!'

She had no idea what to expect in the last room of the tower, in the impermissible place that Jorrun spent all his hours. She crept forward, and the last door stood open. A shadow moved, and she blinked. Someone was there.

She drew her dagger and crouched as she reached the doorway and looked within.

A thin red carpet covered the floor and a large polished table took up much of the space. It was cluttered with books and scrolls as well as several statuettes of both wood and stone. To either side of the door and between the windows were more bookcases and a small bed rested beneath one open window. A candlestick stood empty on the windowsill, the wax frozen in drips that hung from stick to stone. The fireplace held nothing but cold ash. For a moment she thought the room was empty but then she saw the body between the table and the bed.

'Jorrun!' She sprang forward and rounded the table. She could see no blood but there was also no sign of his chest rising or falling. His eyes were closed and his skin paler than a man of Elden's. She knelt and felt for a pulse at his throat.

For a moment she thought there was nothing, but then the movement of blood tickled her fingertips. She let out the air she'd been holding in her lungs.

She heard footsteps in the stairway and Tantony's voice muttering, 'I'm going to be strung from the gallows for this. Jorrun? Kesta!'

'Here, Tantony! Help me!'

The scuffing steps turned to a run and Tantony appeared in the doorway. 'What's happened?'

'I don't know, I can't see any injuries.' She looked around. 'I thought someone else was here, but I must have been mistaken.'

'Let's get him up on the bed,' Tantony suggested.

Kesta nodded and took his legs. They lay him on the bed and Kesta took off his boots before covering him with a blanket. 'Can you get the fire going please? His skin is so cold.' She looked around and spotting a jug of water she poured some into a cup. She sat carefully on the bed, holding the cup between her knees and dipping her fingers into the water. She let the drips fall onto his lips, but he didn't respond. She carefully forced his mouth open and let the water drip onto his tongue. Eventually he swallowed but otherwise didn't stir.

'What do you think?' Tantony asked anxiously as he stood up from the fire.

Kesta frowned. 'He is cold rather than feverish, so I don't think it's an infection. There are no obvious wounds or injuries to his head otherwise I'd have suspected blood loss or concussion.' She pinched the skin below his eye. 'He is dehydrated but he could have been lying here a while and I get the impression he doesn't really look after himself. This could, of course, be related to his magic; I wouldn't know where to start with that.'

'What do we do?'

Kesta sighed. 'What we can, for now. We'll get him warm and see if we can get something nourishing inside him. Can you please ask Catya to go to the kitchens and have a broth made with plenty of garlic in it in case there is some infection? She should leave it on the table inside the door as usual. You and Rosa get well away from the tower; as far as we are concerned, you never set foot in here.'

'But—'

'No, Tantony, you mustn't take any blame for disobeying Jorrun's rule; I'll take full responsibility.'

Tantony shook his head but she could feel the mixture of relief and guilt pulsing from him.

'Tantony, he doesn't need to be dealing with both of us betraying him – even if we know we had to. Let him trust you still.'

'Although that is now ill-earned.'

'Not really. I don't think we have done anything wrong, but he will. Let's just say nothing more. I'll let you know when I can that he's awake.'

Tantony nodded reluctantly and went to give instruction to Rosa and Catya.

Kesta carefully placed her palm against his forehead; he was still cold but there was no clamminess. She touched his dark hair with the tips of her fingers. It was soft. She bit her lip, forcing herself to move her hand away and go back dripping water into his mouth. She took her time studying his face although her heart beat quickly with the fear that he might open his eyes and catch her doing so at any moment. Holding her breath, she touched his bottom lip with the tip of one finger. She jumped as the fire flared up; but it quickly settled, and she gave a snort of a laugh at her own foolishness. After a while she went down to get the food tray. There was bread there, cheese, nuts, and an apple. She ate the apple and put the rest on the windowsill. It wasn't long before the ravens arrived in twos and threes to eat it. She tried to impress on them all that if anything like this happened again, they must come and find her.

Jorrun stirred, and she hurried over to him, almost tripping over a wide, flat bowl that lay on the carpet. His eyes fluttered momentarily, but he didn't wake. She heard the door bang closed far below and went down to find that Catya had left another tray. As well as the broth she'd requested, the girl had also left her a small bladder of wine, some herbs for tea, some of her favourite thyme bread, goat cheese, and olives. She smiled to herself; Catya really was going to be a great student for her. If only the girl had been an apprentice *walker*.

Carefully balancing the tray, she made her way back up, and propping Jorrun's head up on a pillow and her lap, she began spoon feeding him a little of the broth. Each time she checked that he swallowed before trying a little more. His breathing had become more obvious, and she was pleased at how regular it seemed. She checked his pulse and then carefully moved off the bed and settled his head on the pillow. She sat cross-legged on the floor with her back to the bed and nibbled at her food. Eventually she dozed.

She woke with a start; she'd heard voices. She turned with her hand on her dagger and drew in a sharp breath when she saw Jorrun sitting up on the bed against the wall beneath the window. He was watching her. She scrambled to her feet and perched on the edge of the bed.

'Jorrun! How do you feel? Are you well?'

'I am. You disobeyed me.'

'You were in trouble. What was I supposed to do, leave you up here alone to die?'

He sighed. He looked exhausted. He had looked that way more often than not. In the dim light his eyes looked darker and less threatening, almost green.

'Who else has been in the Tower?' he asked.

'No one else,' she replied.

Faster than a hawk he grabbed her wrist and twisted her arm. 'Who?'

'No one!' she cried out, trying to pull free. He increased the pressure on her wrist and she stopped fighting and instead tried to push her pain back at him. Like her *knowing,* something in him seemed to block her transference magic. 'It was just me!'

'And Tantony.'

Had he been awake? Had he seen and heard them?

'It was just me,' she said again, crying out despite herself as the pain increased. 'You can trust Tantony.'

'But I can't trust you?'

'Of course, you can! You can trust me to do what is *right*.'

He let her go, and she stood up quickly to nurse her reddened wrist. She glared at him, breathing fast, her hands shaking. 'What happened to you?'

He pulled himself up straighter and the effort seemed to cost him. Despite how angry she was with him she picked up a cup and poured him some wine.

'You have your dagger with you,' he said as he took the wine. 'Why did you not defend yourself with it when your magic didn't work?'

'You were hurting me, not killing me.'

'You didn't look around the tower while you were here.'

'I didn't come here to see the tower, I came here to help you.'

'As did Tantony.'

She opened her mouth to protest but stopped at his sudden smile.

'I know Tantony was here.' His smile turned to a grimace as he sipped the sharp wine. 'I also know that you didn't pry but were only interested in helping me. I know I can trust the two of you and I'm glad you were willing to protect him. Still, it's not good that you entered the tower.'

'Don't worry, I won't bother again.'

'Not even if I invite you?'

She sat slowly on the very edge of the bed, her eyes fixed on his. 'Has the king said you can tell me everything?'

'He told me I could tell you what I *must*. Of course, that's open to some interpretation from me.' They watched each other for a moment before he went on. 'My ... illness ... was a result of me disobeying the king. I told you that I am a *dream-walker*; I hoped that I might find something in the minds of our enemies to tell me their plans. *Dream-walking* has similar dangers to *fire-walking*. You can become lost and exhausted; you can even be trapped.'

'You were trapped?'

'No; I was just a fool and underestimated how much power I had already used. I was … I hoped I might get us enough answers, so I didn't have to send Osun into the danger the king ordered. As you see, I failed.'

'I managed to *walk* and saw that the ships have left Chem; I know that doesn't help much.'

'It helps.' He reached out and fleetingly touched her hand. 'Would you excuse me please, Kesta, I really need to sleep.'

'Of course.' She jumped up. 'I'll come back later with some proper food for you—'

'No! Don't come back into the tower unless I've invited you. Leave the tray downstairs please.'

'You are in no state to be going up and down those stairs,' she said sternly. 'I'll fetch the food straight away and bring it up. After that I'll abide by your rules. If you want me to come up leave a lantern or candle in the window opposite mine. When there is no candle lit, I won't come up unless the ravens tell me it's an emergency.'

'The ravens?'

'Yes, the ravens.'

'Very well.' He sighed. 'I suppose that's acceptable.'

'Right; I'll be back shortly.'

'Kesta.' He stopped her. 'Do me a small favour and replace the candle there on the windowsill.' He smiled, and she found herself returning a grin. She picked up a fresh candle, lit it with a taper she found above the fireplace, and placed it in the holder on the sill. Jorrun had already lain back down on the bed and closed his eyes before she left.

Chapter Twelve

Osun: Covenet of Chem

Osun looked both ways before stepping out of the narrow ally and heading back toward the main street and the temple. His morning had yielded frustratingly little, both in terms of profit and information. Taxes had indeed been set high in the market, and the trade monitors patrolled it with seemingly gleeful malice, demanding to see the books of anyone they took a dislike to. He'd decided against setting up a stall and instead had chosen a few small, but valuable items to sell. He'd been stopped twice to have them inspected. He was glad to have found buyers early and had been able to get away in plenty of time to meet Farkle. Lunch had been pleasant enough, but Osun couldn't help being distracted. He was already regretting staying at the Sunset Inn, if he moved to another inn it would look he didn't have the money which would hurt his pride, but he was already resenting the loss of his savings. He could, of course, go on his way and head to Arkoom, but the idea terrified him. He needed to find another way to get the information his master needed, here, in Margith.

He found himself standing opposite the palace of Margith Coven, looking at the hard iron gates. Red-armoured guards stood motionless glowering out at the black paved street. If he was a braver man, he could have tried to ingratiate himself somehow with Adelphy Dunham and find out everything he needed. His hand went unconsciously to his jaw. Would Adelphy recognise him as the boy he'd kicked in the face all those years ago? Probably not, but it was possible he would see the Dunham features stamped in his bones.

He realised he'd been staring for some time and with a start turned toward the temple. He quelled the desire to hurry. There was a source of information he hadn't tried yet, it would have to be handled carefully, but it was considerably less dangerous than trying to speak to a Dunham. There was a geranna house near the market and the barracks where the city guards drank. It was rowdy, dirty, and not the sort of place an affluent merchant would frequent but Osun had always taken care to cultivate civility, if not friendship, with the city guards. It was time to see if it would pay off.

He stopped in the temple to leave a coin with Doranna's priest and then safely stowed most of his day's earnings in his wagon in the locked room of the inn. He considered changing his clothing; but decided to be himself rather than risk tripping himself up with too many lies. The market was still busy, and he wove his way through the buyers toward the long street that led to the city barracks. The geranna house was easy to spot from some distance away. Wooden planks over barrels made up tables and benches and off duty guardsmen spilled out across the black cobbles. The sign was painted with the images of a jug and fruit, proclaiming its main produce. Several of the guardsmen paused in their conversation to watch him as he approached. There were a few civilians – probably residents of the street – but not many. The door was ill fitting but swung in easily and Osun lost his composure momentarily in a coughing fit as the smoke hit him.

A man close to the door laughed at him and spat at the floor.

'You lost, master?' someone asked in the gloom and more laughter followed.

'Nah, just looking for a decent drink somewhere they don't dare water it down or charge exorbitant prices.' Osun tried to grin while blinking at his watering eyes.

'Ha ha, well this is the place.'

There were a few chuckles, and the room seemed to settle. He made his way around the tables to the bar and squeezed into a space to catch the barman's attention.

'Spiced or plain?' The barman was a retired guardsman with a pronounced limp, a crooked nose, and a scar on his chin.

Osun didn't particularly like either option; but asking for ale in a geranna house would seem odd. At least the spice would cut through some of the sweetness of the fruit-and-sugar spirit.

'Spiced.' He nodded.

The barman filled a long, narrow, horn cup and handed it to Osun. Osun placed a coin on his hand and made a slicing motion with his fingers to indicate he didn't want the change. The barman raised an eyebrow and dropped the coin straight into the pouch at his waist.

Osun spent four days visiting the geranna house, sipping as much of the spirit he could stomach and still keep some of his wits about him. The barman also served a simple selection of food that clung to the ribs. He picked up bits and pieces of conversation from the guards and from a few warriors and mercenaries that drifted through. The conquering of the Borrows had apparently been brutal. They had taken the largest settlement first, sparing no one but young women with potential bloodlines. A necromancer then animated every viable body with the simple command to obey him and kill all Borrowmen. They went from settlement to settlement, island to island until the Borrows were totally decimated. Had the separate chieftains and tribes come together they might have stood some kind of chance, but they fought only for themselves.

It was estimated that a few hundred might have escaped by sea, but the Seat of Arkoom didn't care about them. They had a huge supply of undead warriors and an armada to carry them across the sea.

From two warriors who had headed up from the coast to escort prisoners he heard something very interesting indeed. They seemed to believe that the first Chemman attack on the Fulmers had been unsanctioned. Argen Dunham had heard that Relta had been trusted with the task of attacking the Icante's stronghold and conquering it if possible; or at the least taking as many *walker* prisoners as he could. Seeing an opportunity to strengthen his own Seat and power, Argen had set off to beat him to the Fulmers. News that there was division and rivalry within the Dunhams – even though Argen himself was now dead – would be very useful to Osun's master indeed.

'Is that you, Oswan?'

He looked up from his musing and saw one of the guards who regularly had gate duty making his way across to the bar.

'Hello, yes.' Osun straightened up in his seat.

'What brings you to this hole?'

Osun lifted his geranna horn. 'Want one?'

'Nah, reckon it must be my round.' The guard pulled up a stool and waved at the barman. He was younger than Osun had assumed, most of his face hidden within a dark-blonde beard. 'You don't normally stay in Margith this long.'

Panic rushed through Osun, but he tried to keep a calm smile on his face. He hadn't realised that the gate guards had paid him and his comings and goings such close attention.

'Contemplating where to go next.' Osun sighed. 'Trade taxes are up here; trade taxes are up everywhere. I could head to the far north but it's too early and most of the roads will still be under snow. I normally head east to Rangun after Margith but I'm thinking it might be worth trying something new for a change.'

The guard swallowed his geranna and his eyes grew distant as he thought over Osun's dilemma. 'Well.' He scratched at his head. 'Did you already try the coastal cities?'

'I spend the worst months of winter on the coast but have been inland about a month.'

'My cousin just came up from Navere, he was part of the raid on the Borrows. He says there's a strange mix of shortage and treasure to be found in the city at the moment. Most of the spoils of the Borrows came through there; most of it's been claimed by the lords of course and sent onto their palaces or to Arkoom. Many warriors picked up trinkets though and sold them first chance they got in Navere. On the other hand, though, there's a shortage of foods and good drink due to the huge influx of warriors and slaves.'

'Do you mean the captives from the Borrows? I saw some outside the palace a few days ago.'

'Oh no.' The guard leaned forward, looking scared. He lowered his voice. 'My cousin said that the only captives taken were women with potential blood. All the warriors were slaughtered and ...'

'And?'

The guard's voice dropped lower. 'My cousin doesn't sleep nights anymore. Not without waking up sweating and shouting. He said the necromancers awakened the Borrows' dead and commanded them to fight for them. He wouldn't talk much about them, but he turned pale as the moon just at the thought of them. No, the ones at the city are the warriors and slaves set to tend and guard the necromancers' dead army. There are opportunities for trade in Navere all right, but I'm not sure I'd dare go.'

'Sounds like it would take a brave man to take up such an opportunity.' Osun held out a coin toward the barman and gestured to his and the guard's horns. 'Seems strange though that they're keeping all these dead men when the Borrows are conquered. It would be surely easier just to … dispose of them somehow.'

'I hadn't thought of that.' The guard nodded in thanks as the barman refilled his horn. 'Maybe they can't die now they have been … woken.'

Osun gave a shudder. 'That's not a cheerful thought.'

'No.' The guard winced. 'Part of me is morbidly curious to see such creatures for myself.'

'We might start seeing such things all over Chem now that blood magic is prevalent and no longer something hidden away,' Osun confided.

'Gods forbid!' The younger man shuddered. 'If I were you, master, having thought about it, I'd head the other way and follow the spoils and treasure to Arkoom.'

'But the prices will be high and the taxes higher there.' Osun swirled his geranna around in the horn. 'You have given me a lot to think about, brother, thank you.'

The guard grinned at being acknowledged as an equal and clicked his horn against Osun's.

***

Osun's head was swirling for more reasons than one as he left the geranna house later than planned and staggered toward the empty market. There was obviously a lot happening in Navere and it might prove a bounteous source of information. But there were two reasons – well, at least two reasons – not to go; Navere was in the opposite direction to Arkoom and it was also the seat of his father, Dryn Dunham.

Now he knew for a fact that Dryn wasn't in Navere, his father was busy ruling the covens from the comfort of forbidding Arkoom, but it was the city in which he'd spent his childhood. It was the place from where he and his master had escaped. It was where his master's beautiful and worshipful mother had died to save them. He had only been twelve, but twelve had been old enough for him to have his heart broken. His Dunham features would be as recognisable there as in Arkoom, even if no one remembered him for the bloodless slave that he was. But it was safer than Arkoom; anywhere was safer than that city of temptation, tantalising distortion, and moral corruption. It was both the heaven of the Gods and the hell of the Godless.

He headed back to the Sunset Inn and to his wagon. The inn's guard knew him now and unlocked the door without asking to see his key. Trying his best to be discreet despite the amount of geranna he'd drunk, he poured the old water from the jug into his scrying bowl and added three drops of blood.

He'd nearly nodded off when his master finally responded. His normally startling blue eyes looked red and bloodshot.

'Osun, have you found me anything?'

'Yes, master, I have.' Osun quickly related what he'd learnt.

'I've been warned of the undead at Navere, the fleet have set sail already and I think you will find the city now empty. Argen, though, that's very useful, any division in the Seats we can use against them.'

'Master ...' Osun hesitated, not sure of what to say and afraid of getting it wrong. 'Perhaps I could travel to Navere instead of Arkoom. There could be knowledge and news there of what the fleet have planned that I can discover more easily than in Arkoom?' He held his breath; as always, his master showed no emotion.

'My brother, trust me when I say that I do not want you to go anywhere where you might be harmed. Our king has commanded it though.'

Osun's chest muscles tightened. His master's hands rose in the still water to cover his face and draw down across his skin as though he were trying to pull away exhaustion.

'Osun, I will try myself to get information from Arkoom. For our mothers' sake, even for our king, I will not force you there. Go to Navere, see if you can uncover any of the plans of what the undead fleet intend or where they head. See if there's talk of Mantu, the Fulmers, or Elden. Hurry, brother; if Chem strikes before I have news for Bractius, then my life here may be forfeit.'

'I won't fail you, master,' he replied, and meant it with all his soul. 'For our mothers I will do my best to find you what you need.'

'I know it, brother. Watch your back and I will watch also as best I can. Safe travels.'

The water went dark and became just water. For a moment Osun remained as he was, his head bowed over the scrying bowl. Then he poured the water back into the jug and locked the bowl away. He made his way back up to his room, feeling suddenly much too sober. Milaiya was sitting in a chair at the table and clearly startled from sleep when he opened the door. A single lamp was lit, and he blew it out and felt his way to the bed. A moment later he felt the bed give as Milaiya quietly slipped under the blanket. A huge part of him longed to put his arms around her and feel her warm arms wrap around him. But she was just a slave; he was a spy, and she probably hated him. He lay alone in the expensive bed and the blankets were as cold as snow.

***

As soon as he woke, he gave Milaiya a shove.

'We're leaving today. Get everything packed.'

She roused slowly and sleepily; then gathering herself soon fell into her efficient bustle.

'We're going to go south,' he said, finding the silence uncomfortable. 'Back to the coast. I've had information that there are spoils to be had and possibly interesting items from the Borrows. We'll stop at Cheff on the way and pick up some spices; apparently there is a shortage of quality food stuffs in Navere.'

'Is it worth diverting a little to Poyin, master, for their good cheese?' she tied closed his travel bag and glanced up.

It was a great idea, except that it would take them more than a day out of their way. He silently both cursed and thanked her intelligence. He could think of no valid excuse on the spur of the moment for them to be hurrying to Navere with all speed. He would have to hope the extra day wouldn't cost his master too dearly.

'Thank you, Milaiya, that's a good suggestion. I'll let you pick a cheese to keep for yourself; let's get going.'

He blanched when he was handed the bill for the inn and scrutinised every item before handing over his gold. The bulls had obviously enjoyed their stay in the stables of the inn as they were awkward and belligerent when Milaiya tried to get them into harness. Osun watched impatiently but couldn't help but be impressed by his slave's ability to persuade the animals into position. Osun looked to see who was manning the gate as he passed through, but it wasn't his chatty friend. He had never even asked the man's name.

***

The slush and snow had already thawed as they made their way back south, but the ground was boggy and heavy going. It took eight days to reach Navere and the closer they got the more warriors they passed heading back inland. Most ignored him, but a few attempted to trade their loot for gold or basic food supplies. He'd gained an interesting silver torc and several small iron daggers with carved bone handles before he even saw the coast. Despite the harsh laws of the coven, he'd felt nervous of the large groups of heavily armed men. The punishment for theft was to be blinded, have both hands removed, both legs broken, and then be tossed out of a wagon onto the roads. Only a very few people with a devoted family ever survived such punishment. Even so, had these men chosen to take his wagon and slave by force there would have been little Osun could do. Had he been an ordinary trader he could have hired guards; but it was risky enough that Milaiya might catch him one day speaking into his scrying bowl. The more people he associated with, the higher the chance of him being found out. Also travelling with a single wagon and slave made him appear a poor target and belied the fortune he carried in his wagon.

His spirits lifted as soon as he scented the sea, even Milaiya smiled as he began to hum and then sing to himself.

'You have a good voice, master,' she said unexpectedly.

He was so taken aback he stopped abruptly. 'Thank you, Milaiya. Do you sing?'

He heard the rustle of her veil as she shook her head vigorously. 'No, master.'

A flock of gulls wheeled over, several diving low to investigate them and see if they had anything to steal. Feeling a little self-conscious, he lifted his voice again, this time in a humorous ballad; Milaiya didn't laugh.

***

Navere was very different to Margith; the walls were made of granite covered in yellow lichen and the white of guano. The gates were thrown open wide with a stream of wagons, riders, and walkers pouring in and out. The smell of fish was strong, and smoke rose in dark plumes from the fragrant smokehouses. Most of the buildings were made from small blocks of stone with slate rooves; but here and there a wooden building with thatch huddled between the larger houses. The temple and palace here were built into the narrow cliffside and accessed by steps chiselled into the rock. A maze of wharves stretched out into the sea with a multitude of boats tied up in dock. It was loud. Seabirds squabbled and shrieked above the sounds of sawing and hammering, rigging clanging, men shouting, laughing, and arguing. However, as they approached the market quarter, the atmosphere changed abruptly. Voices became subdued, fewer people walked the narrow, cobbled streets, and even the birds didn't seem to want to come here.

'I wouldn't head down there, brother,' one well-dressed man muttered as he hurried past.

Osun had a strong urge to pull up the bulls. He could try to turn them about and head to one of the more affluent inns; but he'd already spent too much in Margith and besides, he was here to investigate. Milaiya tightened her veil, shifting in her seat and glancing around.

'Get inside the wagon,' he told her.

She turned in the seat and opening up the canvas crawled through the small space into the wagon. The bulls came to a halt, snorting and rolling their eyes. One of them tried to back up into the wagon. Osun flicked his whip, but the bulls refused to move.

'Master?' Milaiya called anxiously from inside the wagon.

'Stay there!' he commanded, getting angry and embarrassed as the few people around glanced in his direction.

He jumped down and after threading a rope through the nose rings of the bulls, pulled hard and forced them to follow him. One of them gave a miserable and forlorn low.

As he rounded the corner of the street into the market he halted abruptly, the bulls almost knocking him off his feet.

The smell was unbearable.

It was the smell of death, of decomposing flesh.

The market was empty of stalls; but was not empty. It was crowded with the shapes of men. They were mostly men of the Borrows, dressed in ragged sealskin and flax linen, with their curly brown hair as wild as their islands. Here and there a warrior of Chem stood among them in tarnished unkempt armour. None moved their limbs, but they slowly swayed, their staring eyes showed despair, anger, intense hatred, or glazed over with emptiness.

The ground swam away beneath him and he clutched at the bull's curly fur to stay on his feet. He forced himself to breathe in through his mouth; but gagged as he tasted the contaminated air. He saw movement and turned to see that a slave, outside what should have been a busy market inn, had seen him and called his master. Hope lit the tall, smartly attired, man's face and when Osun didn't turn tail and run, he hurried over himself.

'Master, from your face I assume you've just arrived in the city? Let me get you a good brandy, master. Come and sit inside out of the way.' He gestured for his slave to come over and he did so cautiously, staying as far from the slave pens as he could. Osun realised there were several live guards circling the marketplace, all eyeing him with a mixture of wariness and curiosity. He wondered how many merchants they'd seen turn tail and run.

'Yes, yes, a brandy would be good.' He managed to find his voice. 'I was looking for somewhere to stay and do some trading.' His eyes followed the dead men as the innkeeper ushered him past. Behind them the slave struggled to get the bulls to follow. 'But—'

'I have lots of lovely rooms, master.' The innkeeper tried desperately. 'I can see you're a brave man and won't be scared away by these ... people. I'll give you a big discount, yes?'

'What's going on here?' Osun allowed himself to be dragged along.

'Let me get you that brandy and something nice and hot to eat.' The innkeeper sensed that he might be winning. 'I'll tell you everything once you're safely settled indoors.'

Osun found it hard not to smile. A big discount and a ready source of information. But his skin crawled and his stomach churned at the thought of what would be waiting outside the inn doors.

The inn was called The Narwhale and although clean and richly decorated didn't have anywhere near the size and grandeur of the Sun Inn in Margith. The stabling was behind a high, secure, wooden gate off the street but there was nowhere to lock away the wagon.

'I promise, nothing will be touched.' The innkeeper bustled about, ordering servants and slaves. 'Your wagon is safe.' He visibly jumped when Milaiya peeped out from between the canvas.

'Come out, Milaiya.' Osun beckoned. 'My slave will go to my room; make sure she is fed well.'

'You will stay, master?' the innkeeper asked in delighted surprise.

'Is your best room available for that discount you promised?'

'Well, of course you must have the best room!' he enthused, although his smile slipped a little.

When everything had been settled Osun found himself seated alone in a small dining room that was obviously used for the more discerning guests. The main dining room had been eerily empty. The innkeeper poured Osun a glass of brandy and placed the crystal carafe on the table. A large, steaming, swordfish steak was placed before him with some fried potato slices and carrots.

'Sit with me.' Osun invited the innkeeper, his mouth watering. 'What's your name and what news do you have?' Without waiting further, he cut off a slice of fish.

The innkeeper sat politely at the next table but turned his chair toward Osun. 'I'm Gulden, master, and you're the first person who has taken a room here since those ... creatures arrived. A few of my guests tried to tough it out, but ...' He shrugged. 'They were unsettling even before they started to smell so bad. There must have been near two thousand to start with. The city guards were ordered to clear out the traders to make room. Some stalls have been squeezed in along the wharves and some set up outside the city, but most travelling merchants have just chosen to take their trade elsewhere.'

'Where have the other creatures gone? How come some are left here?' Osun took a sip of the brandy; it was good, and warmth spread out from his belly and throat.

'Well, most of them have been taken off to fight in the war. I watched some of them being placed in boxes of salt and loaded on myself.' He gave a shudder. 'They just climbed in the boxes on demand and lay there unmoving as the salt was poured over them.'

Osun's appetite left him, and he put down his fork. 'Got another glass? You look like you need one yourself.'

'It wouldn't be very professional,' Gulden said, eyeing the carafe and looking a little green.

'Who is going to complain?' Osun indicated the empty room.

'Good point,' he beckoned one of the slaves over to get him a glass.

'You said they were off to fight in the war,' Osun said carefully. 'When I was up in Margith, we were celebrating that the Borrows had been conquered.'

'The Borrows, yes.' He poured himself a generous measure of brandy and topped up Osun's glass. 'But the Dunhams have set their sights on a bigger prize. Apparently the Borrows was a raid to gather the resources to mount an attack on the heathens of Elden.'

'By "resources" I assume you mean ...' Osun gestured toward the front of the inn with his head.

'Yes.' Gulden's nose wrinkled in distaste. 'And the ships. Those heathens won't know what's hit them.'

'They are certainly in for a shock. How come they didn't send all of those ... things?'

'I asked the guards that very question myself! We weren't best pleased to hear they were being left here that's for sure! Apparently, it's to do with how many of them a lord can control and who made them. This lot belong to Lord Adelphy Dunham. He's making his way up to Arkoom to take credit for the conquering of the Borrows and enjoy his moment of glory. The guards say he's coming back for this lot and sailing with the second fleet.'

'Second fleet?' Osun couldn't hide his shock, but Gulden didn't see anything untoward in his reaction.

'Yes; you didn't visit Parsiphay this winter then?'

Osun shook his head.

'They've been building war ships there. The first attack on Elden is to secure the coast. The second will be to invade and conquer. Adelphy gets the honour of leading the second attack.'

Osun cursed himself for not having discovered what was happening in Parsiphay; the town was several miles east of his usual trading route and one of the furthest points away from Elden on the south coast of Chem. 'So, who led out the first fleet? Lord Dryn? Relta?'

'Ha! No!' Gulden slapped the table. 'Lord Dryn won't leave the Seats unguarded for someone to slip in behind his back. As for Relta, rumour has it he never came back from his attack on the Fulmers.'

'He attacked the Fulmers?' Osun feigned surprise.

'Yes, and they gave us a bloody nose by all accounts.'

'Gods, I bet the Seats didn't take that well! I'm surprised they haven't sent both fleets straight back out there to smash those spirit worshippers into the next world!'

'You would think.' Gulden nodded, taking another gulp of brandy. 'But I haven't heard that's so. Mind you, I'm just an innkeeper. It's Karinna Dunham leading the first attack.'

Osun clenched his teeth and felt the temperature of his blood rise at mention of that name.

'Saw him myself parading down to the wharves,' Gulden went on. 'It was an inspiring sight, watching our warriors sail out. Just wish they'd hurry up and take the rest of these dead men with them.'

'Any idea how much longer you'll have to endure them?'

Gulden shook his head and swigged back the rest of his brandy. 'Nah, guards just tell me to clear off every time I ask them.'

'I don't envy them their job.' Osun shuddered. 'I imagine they need a brandy or two at the end of their shift themselves. Actually ... that gives me an idea. Since your inn is empty, perhaps you could offer them a small discount for a drink or two; maybe the odd free brandy for doing a good job – if you know what I mean. Get them onside and one might let slip to you when you expect to have them gone.'

'I can see you're a shrewd man, master Osun.' Gulden raised his empty glass toward him. 'Ordinarily I wouldn't want their sort in here, but times are hard. If you don't mind them, then I'll think about it.'

'Hey, you might even help me out. Looks like I'll struggle to set up a stall anywhere, but I have things to trade. Local guardsmen might be able to point me in the right direction or make a bit of space for me somewhere.'

'That's good thinking.' Gulden nodded.

'And if I get a stall, I'll be sure to let people know how safe and comfortable it is here in the Narwhale.'

'Well, that's very good of you, master.' He poured Osun another brandy.

***

Gods, that's not good! Osun thought to himself as he finished his meal and followed a young servant up to his room. He had some great information, that was true, but the fact that he'd not known of a fleet of warships being built all winter would not go down well with his master. He was relieved to find that the room he'd been given was at the back of the inn and didn't look out over the marketplace. Milaiya jumped as he opened the door. He could hardly blame her.

'You looked outside?' he asked her.

'Yes, master.' She hung her head so that he couldn't see her eyes. 'I was curious.'

'That is a bad trait in a slave.' Osun chastised. 'You're all right?'

She looked up in surprise. 'Yes, master.'

'Good. I'm going to take a walk about the city and see if I can find anywhere to trade and what the situation regarding stalls is. I'll send someone up to collect my laundry; I think you had best stay in here.'

'Yes, master.'

***

The smell of the undead warriors had pervaded the inn, but it hit Osun anew as he opened the door to the stable area. He gagged and put his sleeve over his face. He needed to stay in the city, so he could let his master know when Adelphy showed up, but he didn't think he would be able to stomach staying here much longer. There might be somewhere on the harbour where he could watch for ships. He could hear the bulls grumbling and shifting miserably and couldn't help feeling a little sympathy.

Only one man was present in the stable area, a paid servant who at once offered his assistance.

'I'm just going to check over my inventory, then I'm off to see if there is anywhere to trade. My bulls have been fed and watered?'

'Yes, master.' The man bowed.

Osun flicked his fingers toward him in dismissal and the man went back to his stool in the corner, holding a piece of ineffective cloth over his face.

Osun fetched some fresh water from the pump and, checking that the servant had not moved, took out his scrying bowl. He tried to call his master, but there was no response. He waited for half an hour and then gave up, feeling concerned but trying to dismiss it as nothing.

The smell of the market seemed to follow him at first as he made his way through the city, but as he neared the wharves, the smell of seaweed and briny water was blown toward him on an icy wind. He took in several, deep, welcome breaths. As the innkeeper had warned him, a few stalls had set up along the narrow wharves, but there was little room among the fishermen, net menders and permanent waterfront traders. He asked at a few of the waterfront inns, but all of those with any good repute were booked up. Reluctantly he headed back to the marketplace. The pen of silent dead men was even more unnerving as the light faded. How could the guards stand it? He headed straight for his wagon and called his master. He waited. Outside the wagon the darkness thickened. He could hear the restless bulls and the click of a gate as the servant went about his business. He waited. His master didn't answer.

Chapter Thirteen

Kesta: Kingdom of Elden

Kesta pushed the earth around the stem of a small rosemary bush and standing up brushed the dirt from the knees of her trousers. She looked around at the herb bed; Catya and Rosa were just finishing watering everything they'd planted. The sun was low and her shadow long across the ground. Tantony had left them some time ago to get on with his own work and most of the other women had gone in to see to the evening meal. Ricer and Kine, along with three warriors, were constructing a fence around the herb beds.

'Well, that's everything.' Rosa put down her water bucket and stretched with both hands pressed to the small of her back.

'Let's finish for today and start drawing water for a bath,' Kesta suggested.

Catya groaned.

'It will be worth hauling the water when you're soaking in it,' Kesta said. She looked up at the Raven Tower. The birds were settled and from where she stood she couldn't see the window that faced toward her own tower. The candle had been removed soon after she'd taken up Jorrun's food. He hadn't stirred, so she'd placed the small cauldron of stew before the fire and left him in peace.

They went up to their rooms and after their baths changed for dinner. Kesta checked again before going down to eat and the candle was still absent, although warm light pressed against the glass of the window.

'Did you take the food tray?' she asked Catya as she joined the other women at their table.

The young girl nodded. 'And he'd left the empty stew pot, so I think he's been eating.'

'Will you go back into the Tower?' Rosa asked.

Kesta itched to do so. 'No, I'll wait until he asks me.'

'You think he will?'

Kesta shrugged and selected some food to move onto her plate. 'I'll have to wait and see. So; tomorrow we plant what vegetables we have. It is a little late for most seeds, but we'll do what we can.'

'Can we do some more lessons?' Catya asked.

'I don't imagine you mean learning your letters!' Rosa laughed.

Catya pursed her lips and dipped her head to hide behind her hair. 'No, not letters, I mean daggers and useful stuff.'

Kesta had to bite her tongue as Rosa admonished, 'Letters *are* useful stuff!'

'We'll find time for you to learn a few more things tomorrow.' Kesta smiled. They'd talked of the uses of each herb they'd planted, and the young girl had taken in the information hungrily.

They heard the door close below.

'Surely that can't be the Thane,' Rosa said as they all paused to listen.

Kesta called up her *knowing* and the absence of any presence told her at once who it was. She sprang up and went to the stairs.

'What on earth are you doing climbing up and down towers?' she called down.

'Last I heard I was Thane and could go where I wanted on my own lands.' He stepped around the curve of the wall.

'Have you eaten?'

'Have I married a nag?'

He smiled to belie the insult and continued up to join her. She was startled when Catya ran past her to fling her arms around Jorrun in a hug. Jorrun put one arm about the girl, his face colouring slightly.

'I am well, Catya, don't fret.'

Catya stepped back, looking embarrassed and glancing at both Kesta and Rosa as if expecting a scolding.

'Would you like to join us?' Kesta asked.

Jorrun's eyes widened, and he looked from her to the stairway, and then at the receiving room. He swallowed but didn't speak. She decided for him.

'Catya could you please take the wine and that tray of pastries up to my room.' She didn't insult him by asking if he could even make it up three more flights of stairs.

Catya hurried to obey, Kesta and Jorrun followed more slowly.

'Are you well?' she asked quietly.

'Well enough,' he replied.

'I could have come to you.'

They waited until Catya had left and then sat in their usual seats at the table. 'I've come to invite both you and Tantony to meet me in the Tower tomorrow.'

For a moment, the thought crossed her mind that they were being invited to the Tower to be disposed of or punished for breaking the Dark

Man's rules. His face was once again composed and hard to read but for the shadows beneath his eyes. He looked down at the table, his long fingers playing with the stem of the wine glass that Catya had set there. 'Bractius and his father are the only ones I've ever spoken to of what I do and who I am. I … I will, to an extent, be defying my king and my friend; but I've realised I can't do this alone anymore.' He looked up, and she swallowed as his stunning eyes met hers. 'This battle will be fought with warriors, but it's controlled by sorcerers. I am alone. I need the Fulmers and I need you.'

'Well, you could have just asked for our help rather than marry me and be all secretive.' She sat back in her chair and took a sip of wine, biting back her annoyance. Despite her anger her heart pulsed rapidly with excitement.

'We didn't know we could trust you and we weren't fully aware of the gravity of the situation back then. Osun had regrettably not been privy to the plans to conquer the Borrows nor the intention to strike further at us. It was only your warning that showed us how bad things were and the political alliance made sense. We had to keep our need for your magic quiet and with the Fulmers having little trade benefit a marriage was the most obvious way to cement diplomatic ties so we could justify aid.'

She gave a quick shake of her head and scowled. 'Stop making excuses for Bractius. We could have just helped each other.'

'To keep ahead of the Seats of Arkoom, we need to be as secretive as possible and act quickly. They know now I exist, but they don't know what I can do.'

'Neither do I.' She looked up at him from under her lashes.

'And I will correct that; tomorrow. What I will tell you, you must not even tell Rosa or your family. I hope to speak to your mother as soon as I can persuade Bractius to allow it as there is information she really must know. It will change everything for *Walkers*.'

Kesta narrowed her eyes; this clearly affected her people deeply, so she was reluctant to make any promises that might betray them.

'Trust me just a little longer; please.'

'You assume that I trust you at all!'

'Even without your *knowing* you're very astute at judging people, Kesta. I had thought that perhaps Adrin had won you over as he seems very skilled at doing so; but you saw through him.'

Had he been jealous? Surely not, more likely concerned at how it would reflect on him or at the very best maybe a little worried for her welfare.

'I hated you when I met you.'

'No, you hated me before you met me based on the tales that are told of Elden. There is a good reason for those tales.'

She gritted her teeth in annoyance; she couldn't deny it.

'If you will excuse me, I must get back to my work.'

'Work! You're not working! You are barely on your feet! The only thing you should be doing tonight is sleeping.'

'I can't afford to miss anything—'

'For one night you can! Or do you want me to find you on the floor again tomorrow? Don't be a stubborn fool, you'll be no use dead. Please just rest tonight.' She touched the back of his hand and instinctively used her *knowing* to push her concern and growing affection toward him. His eyes widened, and he looked at her for a long time before his shoulders sagged in defeat.

'Very well, just for tonight. Come with Tantony tomorrow morning after you have eaten.' He finished the wine and with a forced, polite smile, went to the door. 'Good night, Kesta; thank you.'

She waited for a while after he left before going to the window. She watched as he walked across to the tower, his stride strong and purposeful. Nerim came over to meet him and they spoke for a few minutes before shaking hands. The stable master walked back toward the stables and Jorrun went inside the tower. There was already light in the window, but the candle remained unlit. As much as her mind wanted to wander, she saw no point in wasting her night speculating and worrying. Even so it was some time until she was able to get to sleep.

***

The first thing she did when she awoke was go to the window. Despite the early morning light striking against the glass of the Tower she could still make out the glow of the candle. She dressed quickly, automatically choosing her trousers and tunic and brushing her dark hair to a gleam. She went down to the receiving room and found Catya setting out the table.

'Tell Rosa that I am going to the Tower! You'll have to practise your letters or sewing until I get back.'

Catya groaned and almost banged her tray down on the table.

'All right,' Kesta waved a hand and grabbed up a thick slice of cheese. 'You can start work on the vegetable beds if you and Rosa think you know a pea from a carrot!'

Catya grinned at her.

'No knives without me though,' she warned as she went down the stairs.

She looked for Tantony in the great hall, but he wasn't there; she found him up in his study. As always, his eyebrows lowered, and his eyes narrowed when he saw her. He picked up a pen, put it down again and with a shake of his head stood up with a sigh. 'Well, I suppose we should to go.'

'He isn't angry,' she reassured him.

'No, he said as much last night.'

'What did he say?' she asked curiously.

'He said that you were a hard person to say no to.' He ushered her from the room and locked it behind them with a small iron key.

'Really?' she smiled to herself.

'I'm not sure it was a compliment,' Tantony mumbled.

She chose to ignore him.

***

The sun was still low, and the Raven Tower cast a long shadow across the ward and its protective wall. Some of the ravens were exploring the recently turned earth and two circled high above. The clouds looked like a ploughed field and held a rosy-red light. She reached out a hand to push open the door, but hesitated, biting her bottom lip and drawing in a deep breath. Ignoring her racing heart, she gave it a shove. Tantony went ahead of her to the stairs; the fingers of his right hand moving as though they longed to be gripping his sword. The old warrior hesitated for only a moment before striding up without looking around at her. Taking in a deep breath, she followed.

As they came close to the top of the tower, Kesta called up, 'Jorrun? We are here!'

'Come on up!'

His quick reply made her jump, and she laughed at herself.

The room had been tidied, and the table was almost clear. Steam curled upward from the spout of a clay teapot and wood cracked in the fireplace.

Jorrun stood waiting with his back rigidly straight and the joints of his fingers white where he gripped the back of a chair. He pulled it out from the table for Kesta and offered them tea.

'How are you feeling?' Kesta asked him to break the silence.

'Better, thank you.' He sat down and looked at them both. 'Tantony, I'm sorry to drag you into this but you also deserve the truth. You've had to endure my secrecy and take on the burden of work that should have been mine and have done so with loyalty and faith.' He paused and looked down at the table. Neither of them dared to interrupt. 'It is common knowledge that I am from Chem and that I was a baby when I was washed ashore alone in a boat. It is not entirely true.

'I was eight years old when I escaped from Chem. With me was a twelve-year-old boy called Osun who was the son of the woman my mother loved. Osun had no power despite the fact that his mother had been bred from a strong line of sorcerers. Most children born without power into a sorcerous clan are killed if they show no magical ability by puberty. Osun's time had almost run out. It was only the fact that he was a useful slave that had bought him so much time from an impatient master. I, on the other hand, had shown power almost from birth. I was a triumph for the leaders of my coven and especially for my father. My mother.' He glanced at Kesta. 'My mother was the daughter of a captured woman of the Fulmers; a *fire-walker*.'

Kesta drew in a sharp breath, feeling her outrage rise; but she clamped her teeth together and let him speak.

'I never knew my grandmother, she died in childbirth when my mother was eleven, but lived long enough to pass on some of her knowledge as a *Walker* to my mother – and her to me. My mother told me that all my grandmother's skin was tattooed with runes using ink made from blood which prevented her actually using her power. My mother's life was an unbearable one.' He stopped, swallowing and taking in a few breaths before going on. 'She was forced to have me so that my father could build a powerful coven. Her only consolation was the friendship and love she found with another slave; Matyla, Osun's mother. My father discovered it and gave Matyla away to one of his family. Within a month she'd been beaten to death.'

Kesta looked clenching her jaw and wrapping her arms about herself. When she looked up into his eyes again, Jorrun continued.

'At eight years old a boy is taken away from the women to begin his training as a sorcerer and a warrior. Long before then he has obedience and blind loyalty to the coven brutalised into him. Unfortunately for my father, even without my mother's influence, I could see the truth clearly and had ... I had too much empathy for life to survive in Chem. My mother came up with a plan to save both myself and Osun. She gave her life to ensure that we got away, and that I had some protection.'

Kesta blinked rapidly against the pressure building behind her eyes and the sting in her nostrils. She folded her hands together in her lap and drew in a deep breath through her mouth. Jorrun went on without looking up.

'We were at sea for some time with little in the way of supplies. It was only luck that steered us through the Borrows unseen. We were found by fishermen near Mantu and taken to the local Thane and from there to the king; Dregden. Only to he did Osun and I tell our full tale. The king decided our fate and as children in a strange land we had no choice but to obey. Osun was to train as a spy and return to Chem as a merchant. I ... I was to become the king's sorcerer.'

Tantony cleared his throat. 'Why all the secrecy?'

Jorrun leaned forwards and looked at him earnestly. 'Because if my family had known that I lived and was in Elden they would have attacked long ago either to win me back or to ensure my death. Others of Chem would also have sought for me for an alliance against my family; or to make sure I never re-joined them. There are also people aplenty in Elden who would have gladly had me killed and needed little encouragement or reason. I needed time to gather information, to learn and strengthen my power.'

Kesta slowed her rapid breathing and drew herself up straight. She looked him in the eyes and asked, 'Who are you Jorrun?'

'I am the son of a slave. I am also the son of Dryn Dunham. I am supposedly the strongest sorcerer that Chem has bred.'

Tantony stood up. 'You are Jorrun *Dunham*? As in the necromancers that rule Chem?'

'I am.'

Kesta waved a hand toward the Merkis, her eyes not leaving Jorrun's face. 'Sit down, Tantony.' Without her *knowing* it was like looking at a painting; yet there was still so much to read there. She'd once thought his pale eyes cold, but she could see now how hard he tried to hide behind them. The muscles of his face were relaxed and expressionless, but he hadn't managed to fight the tension in his back and shoulders. Tantony sat down and Jorrun moved to a cabinet to take out a decanter. Tantony's eyes didn't leave his Thane's hands as he brought over the brandy to pour a little into each of their tea. Kesta wondered if Tantony noticed that Jorrun's hands were shaking.

'So.' Kesta breathed out. 'You have an excellent understanding of our enemy and are powerful. How much of a chance does that give us?'

Only two rapid blinks and the widening of his eyes gave away Jorrun's relief at her calm response. 'Not much.' He sat down heavily. 'I am one against many.'

'How many?' Tantony reached for his tea.

'Of truly strong sorcerers? Maybe thirty. But of those with some magical ability we are talking over a hundred.'

'Hundred!' Tantony spat tea across the table and Kesta jumped out of her seat in disgust.

Jorrun looked around, then spotting a cloth, grabbed it and handed it to Kesta. 'But I'm not quite alone. We have allies that have long been unknown; allies that aid the *Walkers* although they do not know it.' He turned toward the fireplace. 'Azrael, come out please.'

The fire flared, and a flame seemed to lift from it and moved toward them. Kesta dropped the cloth and backed away. Tantony stood again, tipping back his chair. The flame shifted and curled, metamorphosing into a man-like form with an elongated neck and legs that melted into a long whip of a tail.

'Demon!' Tantony made a sign against evil.

'Not a demon; Azrael is a fire-spirit.'

Kesta could barely breathe as the raven-sized creature stopped before her. She could feel its heat as from a normal flame. Fear made her skin cold; but she drew in a deeper breath to speak. 'The Spirits have not had dealings with humans since before my people came to the Fulmers.'

'You have been dealing with them all your life,' Jorrun replied. 'Azra,' he called gently, and the fire-man drew away from Kesta. 'When you ask the flame to carry you to what you wish to see, it's the fire-spirits who take you. When it's important enough, they will take you from your chosen path to warn you of danger. It was a fire-spirit – or drake – who burnt the ship that came to conquer the Icante's stronghold.'

The fire drake spat, hissed, and crackled but Kesta made out a word, a name; *Doroquael.*

'Why are they helping us?' Kesta asked.

'Because of Necromancy. Blood magic goes against the order of nature and of the Spirits; it's the magic of men.'

'Can the Spirits kill the necromancers for us then?'

Jorrun shook his head and Kesta's heart sank. 'The Spirits are powerful but limited. There are ways to defeat them, ways to trap them. They are few in number and no drake has been born in many, many years. Their numbers have dwindled and some of the Dunham clan are powerful enough to kill them.'

'You haven't trapped Azrael, have you?' She demanded, her hands clenching to fists.

Jorrun's face broke into a smile and the fire drake brightened. 'Kesssta!' It seemed to laugh her name.

'I haven't trapped him,' he reassured her. 'He is my friend.'

'That's all right then.' She managed to relax a little and studied the drake, aware that Tantony was waiting to take his cue from her response. Jorrun was also watching her avidly. 'Can you spy on Chem?'

'Yessss – and no,' Azrael breathed.

'The Spirits can be detected and warded against,' Jorrun explained. 'As I said they can also be trapped and killed. It's as dangerous for them to spy as it is for Osun.'

'Yet if what you say is true, they have helped me to do so.'

'They will risk much to help a *walker*, especially one they like and whose intention they approve.'

'Why?'

'Your ancestors and the drakes have a friendship going back centuries although the tale is lost now in history.' Jorrun looked around at Tantony. The Merkis was almost pressed against the wall, one hand on his sword, his eyes wide. He sighed and glanced at Kesta before saying, 'This has been a lot to take in. Tantony, I ask nothing more of you than you do for me already; other than you keep what you have seen and heard here to yourself. You need time to think; please feel free to go and we will talk later.'

'Yes, Thane,' he replied rather stiffly, but he hesitated to leave.

'Kesta, I will visit you tonight if you will allow it? We need to start talking about magic.'

She folded her arms across her chest, not happy at being dismissed when she still had so many questions. Then she noticed that Jorrun was leaning on the table and remembered he was still recovering. 'Tonight will be fine,' she replied and turned to the drake. 'I'll speak with you again soon, I hope, Azrael.'

'Assszra.'

She nodded. 'It is nice to meet you Azra. Jorrun; rest!'

He rubbed at his face to hide his smile and Azrael pulsed brighter.

With a last glance at Jorrun, Kesta grabbed Tantony's hand and pulled him toward the stairs. The old warrior didn't speak until they'd left the tower and she'd closed the door behind her.

'Well,' he exhaled, looking at Kesta guardedly. She called her *knowing* and wasn't surprised to find that the man was both wary of her and hoping at the same time that she was someone he could trust.

'It sounds like we have a tough fight ahead,' she said slowly. 'We need to think about what we can best do to aid Jorrun and the king.'

'Right.' Tantony straightened up. 'We've lost a portion of our warriors to defend the coast, but we should still attempt to finish your works as rapidly as possible and throw some more resources into it; a siege this far inland is not improbable. We'll increase the warriors training time too.'

'And the women's.'

'What?'

'How many of your women can use a bow?'

'Well, there will be a few I suppos—'

'It should be all.' Kesta slapped his arm and strode toward the keep. 'If every woman and strong child can shoot a bow, then you more than double the defences of the keep.'

'Well, that makes some sense but—'

'And we should of course begin collecting stores of weapons and food. We should take a look at the woods too; plan out spots for traps and ambushes. Do you have look out posts for advance warning?'

'Well, no; we would rely on messages sent by bird from the coast.'

'Yes, well, I wouldn't rely on that!' Kesta raised an eyebrow. She chewed at the tip of her thumb. 'The bridge over the river. It might be an idea to make that an outpost and have men there to protect it or destroy it if necessary. We might also want to plan some ways to stop enemy ships coming up the river to the lake if that isn't something you have already. Nets that can be pulled up, fire archers, that kind of thing. We should think about it and meet up this afternoon. I need to see what Rosa and Catya are up to; I'll see you later.'

Tantony halted as she strode away. He swore under his breath.

She found her two ladies working hard on the vegetable beds. Catya was digging furiously at the earth while Rosa carefully placed seeds and covered them up.

'We should dig a small pond and get ourselves some geese or everything will be eaten by slugs and snails in no time,' Kesta mused aloud.

'Won't the water just sink away here?' Rosa asked.

'We can pack it with clay and waxed cloth.' Kesta knelt and took some seeds from Rosa.

'How did it go with Jorrun?' Rosa asked cautiously.

'Well.' Kesta stopped to regard her friend. 'I can't tell you any details.'

'Because Ayline asked me to spy on you?'

'No, because Jorrun asked me to tell no one.'

Rosa nodded. 'Then I won't ask more.'

'Thank you.'

Some of the stronghold's other women came and went, helping them with their work. Ricer and Kine finished the fencing and went out with their father to cut more trees for the barn. Kesta marked out the area for the duck pond and then went to find Tantony. He was drilling some of the warriors and she paused to watch him. He was encouraging to those who tried hard; but clouted one man round the back of the head with his training sword when he stopped paying attention. He jumped in often himself to liven up a fight that became too slow or too predictable. His knee hampered him, but he compensated well by forcing his opponents to come to him; he was faster and stronger than most and seemed to read every move before it happened. With a twinge of her chest muscles she realised how much his injury must have cost this warrior and the patience he must have to live with his fate.

He spotted her, and his shoulders sagged as he stepped away from his men. She regretted more than ever the way she'd spoken to him in the past.

'Tantony.' She smiled and pushed as much warmth toward him as she could. 'I've interrupted you at a bad time, I can come back later.'

'No, now is fine.' He sighed.

'I wanted to dig a pond to keep some geese.'

'For eggs and meat? Wouldn't chickens be easier?'

She shook her head. 'I'll see to building the pond, but could you please get me some clay and wax cloth to line it?'

'You'll have arms like a blacksmith's if you dig a pond of any size.' He frowned. 'I'll give you a hand tomorrow and I have some lads who could do with building up. Listen, I've been thinking about your plans and agree. I have a warrior here who deserves more responsibility and reward for his service; I'll put him in charge of setting up a camp at the bridge and seeing to the river's defences. He's a clever chap and I think we can trust him to be inventive.'

'Sounds good.'

'We have some good hunters who know the forest inside out; I'll put them in charge of sorting lookout posts in the forest. If ... if you think of anything else, my Lady, let me know. I'm sure you will, anyway.'

'You can always trust me to give my opinion, Tantony, even when you don't want it!' She grinned and Tantony caught it, he laughed, and she felt relieved.

'Yes, indeed.' He lowered his voice. 'So, you will speak to the Thane again tonight?'

'I will, if he does visit me.'

The old warrior seemed to struggle internally before saying, 'Be careful.'

She nodded. 'I will.'

Chapter Fourteen

Kesta: Kingdom of Elden

'Are you going to turn all the women in my hold into savages?'

The three of them spun about to see Jorrun leaning in the doorway. Catya's face split with a wide toothy grin, Rosa looked mortified; Kesta merely smiled and lowered her dagger to tuck it into her belt.

'Just the best ones,' she replied to Catya's delight. 'Would you like a lesson?'

'Not really my weapon.' He unfolded his arms and stood up straight. 'Shall we talk about magic?'

Catya gasped, her eyes growing wide.

'After you,' Kesta indicated.

She followed him up the stairs and smiled to herself when he paused momentarily on the threshold of her room. She'd placed tea, cups, and a selection of food on the table in preparation. She went to the fireplace and swung the small kettle over the fire and then pushed at the logs with a poker to get the flames going. With a grin she called on her magic to send a flow of air toward the fire so that it flared upward.

'Show off.'

She turned to see that Jorrun had seated himself at the table and was watching her over his steepled fingers.

'Other than *walking* I haven't used my magic much since coming here,' she admitted as she joined him. 'I didn't want to frighten anyone or get myself burnt at the stake! I know there's no magic here and they think we of the Fulmers are witches.'

'The law, in theory, still stands regarding magic; although it has been many years since anyone was burnt for a witch.' Jorrun sat back, placing his arms flat on the table before him. He seemed much less tense than she'd ever seen him, and she felt her own muscles relax in response. 'But then until I arrived here no magic has been practiced in Elden in a very long time.'

'What happened to Elden's magic?'

Jorrun's face lit up briefly. 'Be careful asking me about history, I've done a lot of studying and love the subject.'

'Go on, I really want to know.'

He sat back, crossing one long leg over the other and resting his left wrist on his knee. 'Elden's magic was in the earth; it was in herbs and healing and manipulation of the mind. They used water to scry and could see through the eyes of birds and beasts. They could also *dream-walk*. There were those who used their gifts for ill, but most were healers and midwives. It is said that one king, many, many years ago, fell in love with a witch. She didn't return his love and rejected him, but he was obsessed and would not let her be. The queen was angry, hurt and jealous and declared that the witch must have be-spelled the king. The king, spurned and embarrassed, agreed that it must be the case and ordered the witch hanged. Afterward the king, in despair, turned to drink and was killed by a boar in a hunting accident. Of course, the queen believed the boar to be another witch. A decree was sent out that all witches be captured and executed for crimes against the throne and people began to believe the lies about the evil of magic. Eventually all those with magic were either slaughtered or hid and stopped using their magic. The magic of Elden died.'

Kesta blinked, realising with annoyance that she was leaning forward and had somehow fallen into the Dark Man's eyes again. She stood up to hide her discomfort and fetched the kettle to pour water in to the pot.

'Nettle and chamomile,' she informed him.

He nodded.

She placed the kettle before the fireplace and sat back down. 'Does that mean there is no magic in Elden?'

He shook his head and uncrossing his legs leaned forward. 'There is magic in Elden but is unused, untrained. There are some who perform small feats of magic without knowing they are doing so. Healers; mothers.'

'So, it's women's magic like that of the Fulmers?'

'No. The women tend to be much stronger, but men can develop magical ability too. They tended more toward scrying and *dream-walking* though.'

'And the magic of Chem is man's magic?'

Jorrun took in a breath and bit his lower lip. 'I don't think so. I think it's a magic that both men and women can use but women are not allowed to learn to use it. I have considered ...' He hesitated, looking down at his hands.

'Go on.' She shifted her chair closer to the table, for some reason butterflies were dancing in her stomach.

'I have wondered; if there were some way to train all the women with strong magical bloodlines, they could break free from slavery and overthrow the Dunham dynasty.'

'That would be brilliant!' Kesta leapt up. 'But how could we do it? It would have to be done in secret somehow or no doubt the women would just be killed. I could perhaps allow myself to be captured—'

Jorrun stood up so quickly his chair almost tipped. He grabbed her hand, his fingers soft but strong. 'No Kesta; never! The things you would have to endure …' He shook his head and realising he had her hand quickly dropped it; his composure didn't quite return. 'It's not an option. Believe me I've thought over that plan for nights on end. My mother and grandmother both tried but the women of Chem were too afraid to even consider it; even those that were close and trusted them. We will have to find another way.'

We. She looked up but couldn't meet his earnest gaze.

'You saw the books in the tower?'

She nodded.

'I've spent many years collecting and studying them. They are books on history and magic, also on herb lore and any other subject I thought might be useful. If I can trust you to go no further than the library without invitation, you're welcome to go in and read any time you like. Just please don't allow anyone else access to the books.'

Her eyes widened, and her throat grew tight; swiftly followed by the gritting of her teeth and a rush of her blood. Why should she feel grateful to this man who had stolen her life? Even so she managed to thank him politely.

'I would love to look at your books.'

They both sat back down and sipped at their tea in uncomfortable silence.

'I should go,' Jorrun said.

'Oh no, you don't have to,' she said to her own surprise. Was she really starting to like his company and enjoy his conversation? 'Finish your tea.'

He cocked his head. 'Is that an order? I'm starting to understand how poor Tantony feels.'

A blush rose to her cheeks. 'A request that you're not allowed to refuse!' She was relieved to see a sparkle of amusement in his eyes. 'Catya is doing very well; I like her a lot.'

'I'm glad.'

'Tantony and I have come up with some plans for the defence of the hold.'

'He told me.'

They both sipped at their tea. Kesta played with her cup.

Jorrun laughed, a loud delightful sound that came from his chest and Kesta stared at him in shock.

'Kesta, we are neither of us any good at polite small talk. I must get back to the tower anyway; Bractius is not happy that I have no news for him of the Chem fleet. Are you strong enough to try a *walk* for me sometime soon?'

'Yes, yes of course.' She stood with him. 'I'll do it tonight.'

'I'll let Azra know; he'll watch over you. He may even be able to alert one of his brothers, so you can see further. I'll see you tomorrow.'

'Yes, see you tomorrow.'

He hesitated just a moment too long, making them both feel awkward, before heading out the door without another word.

'Spirits!' She cursed aloud. She'd somehow not managed to ask him about his own magic and what he could do.

She put some cushions down on the floor before the fire and settling comfortably she pushed thoughts of the Dark Man from her mind and focused on the flames. A familiar presence infused her with a warm feeling of welcome.

'Kessta!'

'Azra? I need to try to find the Chem fleet.'

'Ssssss. Drakes cannot travel through water and not far over it, kessta. We do not ssee the Chemmen from the land. Jorrun knows thiss.'

'But he asked me to try.'

'Yess. The king of this land demands answers and if he does not find another way Jorrun must ssend his brother to an evil place.'

'His brother?'

'Ossun Dunham. I am going to pass you to brother Ssiveraell, he is on Mantu and the furthest out of the Elden Drakes. He will take you as far out asss he can, but do not let him search too long lest he fall into the ssea! Here, I give you to him.'

There was a subtle change to the temperature and vibration of the flame and Kesta felt herself pulled through the bright, gyring, fire. Without warning she was spat out over the midnight-blue sea, the stars like static fireflies up above. They turned about together scanning the horizon; Mantu a distant shadow with an Elden warship between them.

'Siveraell?'

'I am here.'

'Where should we go?'

'Drakess are not of thiss realm, Kessta, we cannot go far or stay long without being linked to a spirit of thiss place. Thiss is already farther than I have gone alone from Mantu. We should head towards Shem a little more and then we choose either easst or wesst.'

'That's as good a plan as any, friend Siveraell. Let's go.'

It was disconcerting *walking* the flame knowing now that she was inside the head of a living thing; a revered spirit. She dared not think in case it read her thoughts and she somehow came up short or caused offense.

'Ssss, Kessta, do not freeze! We must move!'

'I'm sorry, I didn't mean to hold us back!'

She forced herself to relax and pushed forward toward the northern horizon; more fearful of the fire-spirit's limits than her own. When Mantu was far over the horizon behind them they stopped to scan the sea again. Little light remained in the sky, but the sea was strangely luminescent.

'Easst, or wesst?'

Kesta considered. West would take them to the quickest route from Chem and the Borrows to Elden and the Fulmers; but Chem would want their attack to be a surprise. What would she do? Circle about the east and attack from the south, perhaps? A ship of mostly dead men would mean they didn't have to worry about supplies on the ships so a longer journey without setting down would be possible.

'We will go east.' She pushed them both that way as she spoke. 'Let me know when you need to turn back for Mantu.'

Siveraell didn't reply but took them rapidly east, the flame vortex forming around Kesta's mind. Several times they stopped and scanned the constant waves only to see a vast emptiness from horizon to horizon. Kesta was filled with a sudden feeling of vulnerability and fear; as much the spirit's as her own.

'Come on, Siveraell, let's go back.'

'We have not found them!'

'No, not yet, but we will look again. We need to get you safely to land.'

The fire-spirit felt somehow heavier as she turned about, and they pushed back the way they'd come. She could more than sympathise with its reluctance to return without the information they'd hoped for. Then the tunnel of flame began to dissipate, and panic came from the fire-spirit.

'Siveraell?'

The drake didn't reply but came to a halt over the sea. Kesta looked around, but it was so dark now she could see nothing but the stars. With growing fear, she realised she wasn't even sure which way it was back to Mantu. She thought she could draw back to her own body but that would mean abandoning Siveraell.

'Do you know the way? Can you make it?'

'I feel the land and the call of my brothers. I am tired, Kessta, but I cannot cross to my realm through the sea.'

'Oh, spirit! Why did you not turn back sooner?' Even away from her body she felt the tensing of anger at the spirit's foolishness as well as a deep sinking sensation of dread at its predicament. She refused to let herself panic, there must be something she could do. 'Start heading back,' she commanded. 'Would it help or make things worse if I left?'

'Worse!'

'Then I stay.' Was there any way she could give him strength, deepen his connection to his realm of fire? Would her magic be of use or even work? There was only one way to know. 'Stop a moment!'

It was a risk delaying the spirit, but she needed to try. Calling up her magic she agitated the air, stilling it in one place to chill it, stirring it to a rapid speed to heat it in another and then adjusting the balance to whip up a strong wind. Siveraell gave a crackle and hiss that seemed to express excitement and then with a strangely human 'whoop' he flew into the wind. Kesta concentrated hard on increasing the wind and she felt the fire-spirit latch onto her more tightly as her own grip on the flame began to falter. Like most *walkers* she could only normally sustain small bursts of strong wind, but somehow over the sea and linked to the spirit she was able to build up a wind greater than she had before. It was exhilarating.

'We are here. Thank you, Kessta.'

She was pushed and then snatched into another funnel of fire, this one strong and fierce.

'Azra?'

'Yess.'

'We failed to find anything. Why did Siveraell take such a foolish risk and chance his life for nothing?'

'You are angry, Kessta!' Azra seemed amused which made her the more furious.

'Of course, I am! We nearly lost a precious spirit for no reason.'

'Precious. Thank you, Kessta. Like you, Siveraell did not want to fail and come back with nothing. Our brother is being held captive, and he is afraid and dessperate. Even spirits can be foolish.'

'That's not comforting.'

Azrael chuckled and spat, 'You are home now, Kessta. Sleep now.'

***

She became aware of her pounding head before she woke completely. Something damp and cold lay across her forehead and she reached up to touch a wet cloth at the same time as realising she was in bed. She sat up and was shocked to see Jorrun sitting at her table with a map and books spread before him. She checked quickly and was relieved to find that she was fully clothed.

'What are you doing here?' she demanded.

'Returning a favour,' he replied without looking up. 'Azra said that you were able to manipulate air while your spirit was attached to Sivaraell's. I didn't know that *walkers* could do that.'

'*I* didn't know we could do that.' She sat up and drew in a sharp breath as a needle of pain shot through her skull. Gritting her teeth, she stood and went over to the table. 'I think I may have been using Sivaraell's form to manipulate the air. My mother is excellent with wind and storms. She has wrecked raiding ships before now.'

'Then the king had better watch out.' He pushed his book aside and picked up a tiny message cylinder. 'I just received this from Bractius; apparently the Icante has made her feelings very clear about his stealing a *walker* and first choice for future Icante. Bractius has in turn made his feelings very clear to *me* that I am to get you to tell your mother that you are happy, or the alliance is off.' He sighed and rubbed at the bridge of his nose.

Kesta's hand went to her stomach as a heavy, sick feeling settled there. She looked toward the fireplace, eyes wide and stinging with tiredness. She desperately wanted to go home. But she didn't want to leave Rosa or Catya or …

She bit her lower lip and glanced at Jorrun. He'd placed the cylinder down and pulled the map out to lay on top of everything else.

'Azra thinks this is the area you and Siveraell searched last night.' He ran his finger over a long section from the north of Mantu out toward the eastern edge of Elden.

She studied his still face and called up her *knowing* to try to get a hint of what he was feeling. As always her *knowing* was brushed aside. She pulled out a chair and moved it closer to him so that she could study the map from the same angle as him; but she couldn't think about the map.

'You're not going to *make* me tell my mother I'm happy, are you?'

He froze, his eyes fixed on the map. 'I wouldn't ask you to lie.'

'If you don't want to make me do anything why in the name of the spirits did you force me to marry you?' She clenched her fists so tightly her nails dug in to her palms.

He looked at her, then back away at the map. 'Bractius—'

'I'm not asking about Bractius, I'm asking about you!'

For a moment he looked like a cornered animal before he regained his poise. A part of her felt some admiration that he didn't make excuses to run. 'I had to agree that the king's idea made sense; to link our two countries and add to our magical strength. It would be a firmer bond than trade deals and promises and it had to be someone of importance here because of your status so that it wouldn't seem an insult. That's the way things are done in this land and I think your mother's letter has only just made Bractius realise exactly what he has done to the Fulmers. He won't retract or apologise for it though.'

She stood up and went to the window, looking across to the Raven Tower and gripping the ledge so tightly her finger joints turned white. She hoped he could feel her anger through whatever defence he had against her *knowing.*

'For myself; I didn't know at first when Bractius was outlaying his plan that he meant the other half of the marriage bargain to be me. I mean no insult to you when I tell you I refused and argued against it. He pointed out to me that he'd *allowed* me to avoid a political marriage up until now, but that I owed it to him and to Elden. I rarely disobey an order; but that night he had to threaten me.' He looked up, his eyes distant. 'It wasn't that I objected to you as a person; in fact, I greatly admired your strength, courage, and honesty. I also ... you are beautiful and of my mother's people.' He said it quickly as though to avoid her hearing it, but her heart gave an involuntary leap. 'I will keep no living thing captive against its will. Osun and Azra are bad enough. If you stay here long enough to help me defend our people against Chem, I will not stop you going back to the Fulmers no matter what Bractius threatens.'

She spun around. 'You mean it?'

He held her gaze and nodded.

She sucked in a sharp breath and turned quickly back to the window. She swallowed, aware of her racing heart. Looking down at the ward she recalled its wild state, the animals roaming free, the almost empty stables, and realisation hit her like a punch to the gut. Suddenly her ordered fences and gates didn't feel like such a victory. Rainbows blurred her vision, and she blinked rapidly.

'Should I leave?' Jorrun asked. 'We can finish this later.'

'No.' She wiped her face with her hands and forcing a smile went back to her seat at the table. 'Show me again where you think we searched.' Her heart still pounded, and she felt light headed as though she'd awoken from a fever, but she tried to concentrate on the map.

'Here,' Jorrun said. 'Why eastward?'

'I assumed they will be sneaky rather than go for a direct attack on your north coast.' She leaned forward to better see the detail. Her father and Uncle Worvig would love to have a copy of this map. She became uncomfortably aware of the scent of the soap Jorrun used; jasmine, bergamot, and cinnamon. She cleared her throat and concentrated on the map. 'From their attacks on Fulmer Isle they seem to favour the tactic of trying to attack and hold a major target. I think they'll look for somewhere defensive to make into a base and it will either be somewhere they think we don't expect – like the south or east – or ...'

'Or somewhere we think they wouldn't dare take that's of huge strategic importance.'

'Yes.' She sat back. 'I think they will go for the Fulmers again, Mantu, or as I said circle round to your least protected coast.'

'And you would suggest?'

'On the Fulmers during the raiding season we have signal fires set up all around the coastline. Older children man them. It allows both for quick communication and for *walkers* to watch the length of the coast. I would suggest a network of beacons here in Elden and as many messenger birds as you have sent out to key points.'

'We have messenger birds set up already, but the beacons are a good idea. What else?'

She worried at her bottom lip with her teeth. What would her mother do? What would her father and Worvig put in place?

'Let's think about it for a bit.' Jorrun sat back and turned to face her. 'Azra gave me more news about the drakes. Apparently, one has been captured by a necromancer hiding on Fulmer Island.'

'There is a Chemman on Fulmer Isle?'

He lightly touched the back of her wrist with the tips of three warm fingers. 'Your family are safe and a strong drake, Doroquael, is helping them.

Azra has suggested that tomorrow night he link with Doroquael and you can speak with your mother through the drakes—'

'Tomorrow!' Kesta turned her hand to grab his. 'Can we do it today?'

He smiled but pulled his hand away. 'No. Your mother is busy as are Doroquael and Azra, not to mention the fact you're still in pain from your long *walk* last night.'

She scowled at him but couldn't disagree.

'Tomorrow night, after dinner, come up to the tower and Azra will take you to your mother.'

Kesta's heart lifted and without thinking she leaned forwards to kiss Jorrun's bearded cheek. She recoiled at once, biting her lower lip and feeling her cheeks burn. 'Thank you,' she murmured, although she gritted her teeth after the words. She still felt that she owed this man nothing but her anger.

Jorrun himself looked as though he'd been turned to stone, as if he did not dare to react or allow himself to feel anything. He quickly gathered up his map and books, all but one that he left for Kesta, and headed for the door. 'Follow your own advice and get some rest,' he said without looking back. 'I'll see you tomorrow.'

The door closed with a click behind him.

***

Catya came up to her room frequently during that afternoon and evening, at first out of concern and then out of impatience as the girl wanted to be out doing things. Rosa tried to distract them both and keep the peace but Kesta was as restless as the girl.

Jorrun had promised her freedom.

The next morning, she suggested they go riding, and she looked at her two friends as they readied Nettle and Griffon. She'd grown very fond of them in such a short time; would they come with her to the Fulmers if she asked? Would it be fair of her to even ask them?

She noticed that Catya had gone very quiet. The girl was eyeing Griffon with trepidation and she realised the horse would look huge to a girl who had never ridden.

'Did you know I can talk to horses?' Kesta said. 'It's part of my magic.'

'Can you really do magic?' Catya asked. 'The women say you're a witch, but you don't seem evil to me.'

Rosa put her hand over her mouth to hide a laugh.

'No, I'm not a witch.' Kesta smiled. 'That's what they used to call the women of Elden that could use magic; but even they were not evil. I'm what is called a *fire-walker*.'

'A fire-walker?'

Kesta raised her hands, and fire danced across her fingertips. Rosa gave a small gasp of surprise, Catya shrieked and then laughed at herself.

'That's amazing!' Catya stared wide-eyed at the stick.

Kesta let the flames go out. 'So, you see, I really have magic and can really talk to Griffon. He is a clever horse but a bit naughty – just like you! He won't hurt you though.'

Catya reached up to touch Griffon's neck, and the horse blew into her hair. Kesta got up on his back and Rosa helped Catya up to sit on Griffon's saddle in front of her before mounting the much-improved Nettle. It was wonderful to get out of the hold for a while and its enclosing stone walls. Still, she couldn't quite shake off the shadow of her fear for the Fulmers and even for Elden. She told herself that her impatience to see Jorrun again was purely down to her need to be doing something and getting things done. The improvements to the hold were going well now, without much need for her supervision, and Tantony had reported that his warriors were settling in with enthusiasm at the bridge.

'Can you teach me to be a *walker*?' Catya asked.

Kesta took in a deep breath. 'I'm so sorry, you have to be born a *walker*; you cannot be made one.'

The girl slumped in her lap. 'Then I will be a warrior like you, perhaps even a queen!'

Kesta laughed. 'I imagine that's something you can certainly achieve, Catya. I'll tell you what; in the Fulmers every Icante has female bodyguards – the best of the best. My mother has two twins, Heara and Shaherra, who guard her. Until we find you a kingdom to rule would you like to train to be my bodyguard?'

'Oh, yes!' Catya sat up excitedly. 'Will Rosa be your other one?'

Rosa snorted and gave a shake of her head.

Kesta bent down to speak softly in to the girl's ear. 'Rosa is wiser than both of us put together; we should remember that.'

Catya nodded against her chest.

***

Kesta almost ran up the long steps of the Raven Tower, pausing at the last door to compose herself and give a light knock.

'Come on in!' Jorrun called out.

She pushed the door open and found Jorrun clearing space on the table, his sleeves rolled back past his elbows. He pointed to an ornate bronze bowl. 'Do you scry?'

'No.' She shook her head, spotting Azra hovering near the fireplace. '*Walkers* only see through the flame, never water. You?'

'Yes, I scry. Also,' he winced. 'You will not like it but there is a certain blood magic that allows me to speak to specific people.'

'You use blood magic?'

He held her gaze. 'I use what I have to, to protect those I care about. If it makes any difference to you, that's the only blood magic I utilise; although I've studied it to understand our enemy.'

'It's not my place to judge what I don't know.' She moved closer to look into her reflection in the bowl, at her mismatched green eyes. The thought of blood magic did make her shudder. It was something that the *walkers* whispered of as evil, as the very opposite of what they believed in and stood for.

'The magic of the Fulmers and of Elden are about working with the spirits, the elements and with life,' he said softly. 'It is about respecting and keeping a balance. Blood magic is about commanding, dominating, and destroying.'

'Well, we can't allow that so we had better make sure we win.' She turned around to find him standing uncomfortably close. Her pulse quickened. 'Why does my *knowing* not work on you?' she demanded.

His hand went to his chest just below his throat; there was something beneath his shirt. 'Because the coven lords enslave *walkers* and those with their blood, they came up with a way to protect themselves from a walker's *knowing*. It also deflects some other magics.'

'May I see it?' Holding his eyes, she reached for the button of his shirt and his hand dropped to his side. She undid two buttons and looked down to see a wooden amulet covered in runes with a single red gem set in the centre. His chest stilled as he held his breath.

'Doroquael is ready.'

Both Kesta and Jorrun jumped as the fire-spirit spoke; Kesta took a hasty step back. Jorrun re-buttoned his shirt. 'Can you use the fire, or would a candle be better?'

'The fireplace is fine,' she replied, looking around and grabbing a cushion off a chair.

'No,' Azrael dipped lower and flew in front of the fireplace. 'Focuss on me!'

Kesta glanced at Jorrun, then placed her cushion on the threadbare carpet. 'I'll try.'

It was harder to get her focus to begin with, knowing that she was looking in to a living being rather than just the conduit of a flame; but once she convinced her mind, it was no different, she triggered her *walking* trance and found herself within the fire vortex. Azrael didn't speak, but she felt his familiar presence and then that of another drake as they linked. Barely a heartbeat passed before a voice that hurt her heart called out through the conflagration.

Kesta?

'*Mother!*'

Are you hurt? Are you well? Have they mistreated you?

'I am well! Wait a moment and I'll tell you!' Kesta hesitated, recalling that the fire-spirits could hear everything and wondering if they might speak to Jorrun of everything they said. 'I'm not happy about this marriage but Jorrun seems to be a good man; he won't hurt me and will let me go home once we are safe from Chem. I have friends here, good friends, and you'd be proud of how much I've done! Mother, I am learning a lot; but we can't find the Chem fleet. I saw ships readying to sail but we don't know where they have gone!'

I'm glad you're safe. So glad. But I am surprised you are so calm! We have seen no ships, but a necromancer survived the last attack on the Fulmers. He ... he is killing and turning families into his undead warriors. He has also captured a fire-spirit. We are hunting him. Kesta, it is important that you understand their way of fighting. They take hold, then spread their evil increasing their army. Don't let them get a foothold on Elden.

'I don't intend to. Oh, be careful. I should be there—'

It sounds like you are where you are needed, fire-child.

'I miss you. Is father okay? Tell him he did the right thing. And Uncle Worvig?'

Your father will be better for knowing you're okay. Worvig is good.

'The necromancers wear amulets that prevent us feeling them with our knowing.'

Ah, that explains it. I have found that I can reach and affect them when I touch them.

'That's good to know. Mother, we can use our magic while being carried by a fire-spirit; Siveraell and I created wind together!'

Kesta felt her mother's approval.

Kesta; to come through to our realm and stay, fire-spirits must take the place of a human spirit. Siphenna gave her life for Doroquael to come here and fight for us.

'Siphenna!' Kesta's shock sent the flame vortex spinning and spitting. 'I'm so sorry!'

She made the bargain willingly. I must go, my darling fire-child; I hope we can speak again soon.

'I love you.'

Kesta felt the drakes break their connection. She hoped that her mother had heard her last words.

Slowly she became aware of the room again and Azrael moved toward Jorrun. Jorrun placed a bowl of black oil on the table and the drake rushed at it, drinking quickly.

'I didn't know that they drank.'

'When they come over permanently to this realm, they need fuel to sustain themselves. They love oil and coal.' He offered her a cup of steaming nettle tea and she took it, carefully avoiding his fingers. Her mother had said that Chemmen could be affected by *knowing* through touch; did that mean Jorrun could be too? She tried to recall the few times she'd felt something from him, had she been touching him then?

She looked up and saw he was watching her. 'My mother gave me some useful information. She told me that a *walker*, Siphenna, had given her life so that Doroquael could come through permanently to this realm.' She glanced at Azrael. 'Does that mean Azra had to do the same?'

Jorrun sat down heavily. For a moment she didn't think he would speak. 'Yes. My mother made a bargain with Azra; her life for his protection of me.'

'Oh.' She looked down at her hands, her stomach muscles tightening.

'I'll send a message to Bractius with everything we've learnt. I'm glad you got to speak to your mother.'

For once Kesta felt lost for words as she looked up at his blue eyes.

'Tantony tells me that your work on the hold is coming on well?'

'Nice change of subject.' She smiled and got to her feet. On impulse she touched his hand, calling her *knowing* as she did so. She froze as she felt a tumult of emotion from him despite his amulet. She withdrew quickly.

'Are you all right?' Jorrun frowned. His fingers moved unconsciously toward the hand she'd touched.

She forced herself to breathe slowly but couldn't meet his eyes. 'Yes, it was just … a lot to take in, speaking with my mother. I have a lot to think about. Please excuse me, Jorrun, Azra; let me know if you need me for anything. Goodnight.'

Jorrun nodded, and she left quickly, heading back to the safety of her own Ivy Tower.

***

She spent the next two days looking through the library of the Raven Tower, setting a few books aside that she wanted to read on the table beneath the small, slit window. Most of them were about Chem and one on the history of the magic of Elden. There was only one book in the whole library about the magic of the Fulmers and it was speculative and humorously inaccurate. She found several pieces of paper folded within its pages on which corrections had been written. She recognised Jorrun's hurried and almost illegible writing, at odds with the precision of his maps. She saw nothing of Jorrun himself, but he did leave a note on his food tray for Catya to bring her, apologising that he wouldn't have time to visit. She watched the window of his tower, but no candle was lit.

As much as she wanted to immerse herself in the library and the books, she made sure not to neglect her friends and the hold. They made a tour each day to speak to as many people as they could, check on the progress of the works on the hold, and lend a hand here and there. They were out talking with Aven and her daughter when a warrior came running out of the gate, looking flushed and worried.

'Lady!' he called spotting her. He paused to catch his breath. 'You are needed urgently!'

'What's happened?' She nodded toward the two women to excuse herself, then hurried toward the warrior.

Rosa grabbed Catya's hand, and they followed after.

'I'm not sure, exactly.' The warrior indicated that they should follow and set off at once back into the hold. 'Two ravens arrived with messages, one after the other. The Thane came straight out of his tower to fetch Tantony and asked me to find you at once.' His eyes widened. 'You are to meet them in the Raven Tower.'

Kesta nodded, glancing back at Rosa and Catya, then surprising them all by breaking into a sprint. The door to the tower was ajar, and she barely slowed, taking the steps two at a time.

'Jorrun?' she called up as she went.

Above the tower she could hear the uproar of the unsettled ravens.

She heard Tantony's anxious voice before she pushed into the room.

'What's happened?' she panted.

Both men turned to stare at her, Tantony's mouth fell open.

'Have you never seen a woman run before?' she scowled, blushing and trying to get her breathing under control.

'Actually—'

Jorrun elbowed Tantony in the ribs to shut him up.

'We've had news from Bractius. Three ships have been sighted off the coast of Elden to the east.' Jorrun pointed the small town out to her on the map. 'They lit their beacon and a messenger bird was sent at once from one of the larger towns.'

'Three ships?' Kesta looked up.

Jorrun nodded, holding her gaze.

'That's not right.' She shook her head. 'They have more than three ships.'

'We were just discussing why they might split their force.'

'Does Bractius have any ships in pursuit?'

'There is only one ship close enough to engage and it won't do so on its own,' Jorrun replied. 'It will hold back from a distance until they come to shore and then join our land forces. He has sent orders for some of the Mantu fleet to head east—'

'No!' Kesta sat down heavily. 'No, it's a diversion. Just three ships.'

'We can't be sure of that,' Tantony said. 'The rest of the fleet could be further out beyond sight of land.'

'The Chemman aren't such poor sailors that they would let three ships drift within sight and give themselves away. Surely if they were looking for somewhere to attack it would be the whole fleet?'

'I've already sent word to Bractius that I think it's a feint.' Jorrun smiled grimly. 'I think he already considered that himself, but he can't take the risk that it isn't an attack and send no one. He thinks Chem wouldn't dare take Mantu. He doesn't know Dryn Dunham.'

'It could also be the Fulmers.' Kesta looked down at her hands and saw they were shaking.

Jorrun stepped closer and placed a hand on her shoulder. 'I've sent a raven with a message straight to Burneton and they will send it on to your mother.'

He removed his hand before she had a chance to call up her *knowing*.

'The drakes will also pass the information on, they're quicker than birds,' Jorrun continued, and he glanced toward Azrael who had remained discreetly away from Tantony and just within the fireplace. 'One thing is for sure; I think an attack is imminent and if it happens without warning, Bractius will hold me responsible.'

Both Kesta and Tantony protested at once.

'He just wants to protect his people,' Jorrun defended his friend.

Kesta turned to Azra. 'Are there any drakes near the three ships who can take me out to look?'

'Yesss, Kesta. Riguille is near.'

'Let's go then.' Kesta picked up her chair and placed it closer to the fireplace.

'You're going to do magic?' Tantony asked in alarm.

'Sit back here with me and keep very quiet,' Jorrun ordered him.

Kesta gave a nod of thanks and then settled, fixing her gaze on the inner blue of Azrael's eyes.

She tumbled into the vortex, feeling the fire-spirit catch and steady her. They travelled rapidly, pausing a moment before they connected with the other fire-spirit.

'Riguille iss more cautious than Siverael, Kessta,' Azrael reassured her. 'But lesss friendly to humans. I will be waiting for you here.'

She didn't have time to thank him before she felt herself pushed toward the other spirit. Unlike the other two she'd now met, this one seemed to emanate no warmth or concern, as though she were a task that must be endured.

'It is nice to meet you, Riguille,' she tried.

The drake didn't reply but formed its whirling portal to speed out over the sea. Kesta saw no point in being offended but let it take her where she needed to go.

286

The vortex dissipated, leaving them high above the sea. She could see the three ships, all of them captured from the Borrows by the build and colours. On board were a small crew, barely enough to sail them. The oars were drawn in and the sails almost lazily set. Wherever they were heading, they were not in a hurry. She gently nudged the fire-spirit into looking around. In the far distance she could see a fourth, larger ship, trailing the three; an Elden ship. There was nothing else from horizon to shore.

'Can we go out a little further to see if anything is staying just beyond sight of shore?'

The spirit seemed annoyed, but it formed its fire channel and they moved outward, stopping abruptly. When she looked around, they were a long way out with the shore no longer in sight but the three ships still visible.

'And parallel, but back toward the Elden ship?'

The drake hissed and spat but did as she asked. Again, when they stopped, she looked around but saw nothing but what she'd already observed.

Feeling downhearted, but not surprised, she asked the fire-spirit to take her back to Azrael.

He didn't need to ask her how she'd done, feeling her disappointment and mirroring it.

She came back to herself slowly, her vision blurred before her eyes focused on the room and she readjusted to her own familiar body.

'Kesta?' Jorrun knelt down by her side and placed a hand over hers. Her *knowing* was still open, and she pulled her hand back to her chest in shock; he cared about her, he *really* cared about her.

'I'm sorry.' He stood up quickly. 'I didn't mean to startle you.'

She looked up and saw hurt in his face.

'It's okay,' she murmured, her breathing fast and her heart galloping. 'You just surprised me.'

'Did you find anything?' She heard Tantony stand up behind her and move closer.

'It is as we thought.' She glanced up at Jorrun. Her whole body seemed to tingle with embarrassment at what she'd felt from him and … and what? Excitement? No! she clenched her fists and her teeth.

'Kesta?' Jorrun prompted in concern.

She told them everything she'd observed without looking up, finally bringing herself to turn about in her chair to look toward Tantony as she finished speaking. 'I definitely think the ships are a decoy.'

'I should have sent Osun to Arkoom.' Jorrun sighed, looking down at the carpet.

'Your brother,' Kesta said softly.

'My half-brother.' He looked up and captured her eyes. 'But yes, he is.'

Kesta looked from his eyes to his mouth, her blood seemed to rush to her own lips and burn there. She looked back up at his eyes and her breath caught, she felt a wave of dizziness.

Tantony coughed. 'So, what do we do?'

Without turning away from Kesta, Jorrun replied, 'Send a warning to Bractius at once. He will reply just as swiftly to demand we find where the rest of the fleet is.'

Kesta cleared her throat. 'Have you tried scrying?' She broke eye contact, feeling a blush rise, feeling her anger rise, and feeling every muscle grow weak. She touched the bronze bowl, gripping the edge hard between thumb and finger to wake herself up.

'Yes, it's an inaccurate and unpredictable tool at best.' He sounded frustrated. 'There is one thing left for me to try. I would imagine the attack will at least include, if not be led by, someone of my blood.'

'Blood magic?' Kesta let go of the bowl as though it had burnt her and spun to face him.

'Ssss Kessta!' Azrael came to Jorrun's defence.

Jorrun raised a hand. 'Not quite. I'll use the magic of Elden, but a blood link makes things easier.' He paused and then fetching another chair placed it in front of Kesta and sat facing her. Tantony looked on awkwardly. 'There is a way of communicating directly through water by scrying. If you add a drop of the blood of the person you wish to speak to into the water and they possess an amulet that contains your blood, you can speak to them as though looking through a window.'

He watched her carefully, and she tried her best not to react emotionally.

'Go on.'

He nodded. 'Without them having an amulet of your blood you can watch them, but not speak to each other. I have no blood of the Dunham's, other than Osun's, and he has mine. I cannot accurately spy on my family by scrying. I might be able to find one of them by *dream-walking* if he is a close enough blood relative.'

'Dream-walking?' It was Tantony's turn to be shocked. 'Isn't that a myth?'

'Not a myth, an old magic.' He looked up at his Merkis and Kesta's muscles relaxed as his intense gaze turned away from her. 'If they are close enough and I can get into the dreams of one of our attackers, I will be able to learn a lot.'

'How close is close?' Tantony asked.

'We are talking many miles.' Jorrun waved a hand. 'Like with *fire-walking* distance, in *dream-walking*, is relative.'

'Is it dangerous?' Kesta demanded.

Jorrun turned to look at Azrael. 'Like a fire-spirit coming through into this realm, my spirit could be captured in another's dream. But they would have to know what I was doing, how to capture me, and be strong enough to hold me.'

'Don't do it!' Kesta sprang up, placing both her hands against his chest, the fabric of his shirt warm beneath her fingers. 'Don't.'

He swallowed, looking past her at Tantony rather than at her. 'It's the only option left. I have to keep trying it.'

Kesta turned to Tantony; the Merkis nodded and her heart sank.

'I have to.' Jorrun placed a hand over hers and then stood and moved away.

'Not many are as sstrong as Jorrun, Kessta,' Azrael tried to reassure her.

'Is there anything we can do?' she asked. 'Anything to help?'

He shook his head. 'Look after the hold for me.'

Both Kesta and Tantony were ushered from the room reluctantly and stopped just outside the Raven Tower.

'Are you all right?' she asked him carefully.

Tantony took in a deep breath. 'This is all way above my head; I'm just a warrior.'

'You are not *just* anything, Tantony,' she said sternly. 'Do you want to come up and eat with us this evening? I have a feeling it's going to be a long night.'

She could see the emotions play across his face as he considered his answer.

'No, I'd better not. Let me know as soon as you hear anything though.'

'Of course; you too.'

Tantony nodded and then strode away with his slightly awkward gait.

**

Kesta found herself unable to eat but pushed her food around on her plate. Rosa and Catya did their best to distract her, but she couldn't bury her concern, or her hope.

'What's worrying you?' Rosa asked gently. 'Are you allowed to say?'

Kesta looked at Catya and then at her, shaking her head. 'Jorrun is putting himself in danger tonight to try to save us.'

Catya sat up straight.

'You are concerned for him?' Rosa tried to hide her surprise. 'I know that you have begun to change your opinion of him—'

'I would be concerned for anyone.' Kesta closed her eyes and winced. 'I'm sorry, Rosa, I didn't mean to snap.' She looked up at the older woman. 'My opinion of him has changed very much.'

'Oh.' Rosa looked down at the table and then back up. 'That's good.'

Was it? Kesta took a sip of wine to avoid answering. She didn't want to like him, that was the truth of it, what she wanted was to go home.

'I'm going to bed.' She stood up and forced a smile. 'I'm sorry to be such miserable company.'

'Not at all.' Rosa frowned.

'Do you need anything?' Catya looked almost tearful.

'No, thank you, Catya.' She bent down to give the girl a hug. 'It will all be fine.'

But would it? She went straight to the window as soon as she reached her room and looked across to the Raven Tower. Light flickered behind the glass pane, but no beckoning candle invited her over. She sat on the window ledge as the light faded and stars began to appear beyond the slow-moving clouds. When her back became too stiff, she paced her room and stretched her muscles, returning to sit and watch the light across the ward. She was just beginning to nod off when a movement caught her eye. She sat up and looking across to the window saw a bright light dart swiftly past the window several times. Then it winked out, and she jumped to her feet.

Seconds later the low fire in her room burst upward, sparks flying across the carpet as Azrael came flying out.

'They have him! Kessta! They have him!'

Chapter Fifteen

Dia: Fulmer Isle

Dia looked up at the dying sun and wrapped her arms tightly about herself. They would be burying Siphenna now at Otter Hold, returning her body to the earth. She stood up and brushed the dirt from her trousers.

'Well?' Arrus demanded.

Doroquael hovered before them.

Four days they'd been tracking the necromancer, enough time to circle Fulmer Island more than once, yet he eluded them. Still, Doroquael had allowed her to speak to her daughter and her words had brought her comfort and new determination.

'Kesta is well,' she reassured her husband. 'The Dark Man hasn't harmed her, and she believes he'll let her come home in time.'

Arrus's eyes darkened with a frown. 'We have no reason to trust him.'

'And yet no reason not to. Kesta has given me some useful information. The necromancers wear talismans that hide them from the *knowing* of *walkers*, yet they are vulnerable to it if we touch them.'

'As you discovered,' he cut in proudly.

'But that doesn't help us find him.'

'No.' Arrus looked around at their camp. Heara was out scouting and Shaherra was taking a moment to rest and get some sleep. They had twelve warriors with them from both Fulmer and Otter holds as well as the *walkers*

Larissa and Everlyn. Merkis Vilnue had insisted on coming with them with two of his men; Arrus eyed him warily.

'We should get some sleep.' Dia nudged him.

He looked at her and gave a snort of a laugh. 'You mean pretend to sleep. I'll get no rest until that sorcerer is dead and I know you won't.'

He knew her too well for her to deny it. Even so she lay down on her blanket and he settled beside her, lending her his warmth. Despite her anxiety she did eventually drift off. She dreamt of Siphenna, lost in a landscape of fire. She dreamt of her daughter in a tower so high the stairs went on forever.

She awoke not long before dawn as urgent voices intruded into her dreams. Moving Arrus's arm she sat up and saw that Heara had returned and was kneeling beside her twin. The two of them noticed that Dia was awake and beckoned her over.

'I have some tracks at last.' Heara spoke quietly. 'This sorcerer knows what he's doing. He's been following the streams and river to hide his tracks but last night he struck twice to increase his dead warriors and supply himself with food. He'll not be able to hide now. He has a head start on us, but I'd say that he's heading south for Eagle Hold.'

A sharp stab of fear went through Dia. She reached out to call to her gulls that had been following and acting as scouts. Two came down to land on the edges of the camp.

'I'll warn them,' she said. 'Who ... who did we lose?'

Heara closed her eyes and drew in a breath. 'Cygnet farm and the smallholding at River Fork.'

'There were at least four families there!' Shaherra said in horror.

'Survivors?' Dia forced herself to ask.

Heara shook her head.

Dia shot to her feet, her teeth clenched. 'Up! Everyone up! Our enemy is sighted. We move in five minutes.'

No one spoke as Heara led them toward the stream. She didn't follow it but took them swiftly south-east toward where she'd last left their enemies' tracks. Dia felt a coward for her relief that she wouldn't have to see the places in which her people had been slaughtered. The responsibility was hers and she would have to live with the guilt of her failure. When the sun rose, to her it seemed to bring little colour, the song of the birds held no joy. The wind was cold, and the emotions of her companions were like sharp needles.

She shivered and closed down her *knowing*.

Larissa and Everlyn stepped up beside her, each woman placing a hand on her shoulder. They said nothing but Dia let her eyes water, drawing in a deep breath and letting it out very slowly. She nodded her thanks. Grief and despair had their place, but it would not serve them now.

They had been travelling nearly two hours when Heara asked them to stop and gestured for her twin to come and look with her. Dia waited impatiently while the two scouts examined the ground. They didn't look happy with what they'd found.

'They're at least half a day ahead of us,' Heara called back. 'We'll have to pick up our pace if we're to catch them before they get to Eagle Hold.'

'Would they take on a hold with so few of them, some of them ...' Merkis Vilnue looked around at the faces of the people of the Fulmers. 'Some of them just children?'

'He can increase the size of his force still, as he goes,' Arrus growled. 'Word has gone out but not everyone will have been reached or have heeded.'

'Let *me* go ahead!' Doroquael bobbed into the space between Dia and the twins. 'I am fasster! If I get ahead of the necromansser I can send as many as I can ssouth to Eagle Hold.'

'They'd be terrified, a spirit appearing!' Larissa warned.

'But they would flee.' Dia felt some hope return. 'Yes, Doroquael, warn as many as you can; but don't go near the necromancer!'

The drake turned blue and then bright yellow. 'No! No trap for Doroquael!' Then he was away faster than a swift.

'Come on, this isn't making time.' Dia started walking, not waiting to see if the others were ready to follow. She caught up with the twins and they set off ahead at a jog, stopping to study the ground now and again.

They rested briefly only four times before the day began to slip away toward evening; disappointment and frustration growing as they seemed to gain very little ground. The first home they came to had shown signs of slaughter, no bodies remaining but for two goats that had been ripped apart. The other homes they came to were empty, the animals turned loose or taken with the fleeing people. Dia silently thanked the fire-spirit.

Shortly before night fell one of her gulls found them, shrieking down at them before landing clumsily on Dia's shoulder. Arrus automatically dug in his bag to find food for it. Dia called up her *knowing* and reached up a hand to touch its chest.

'Show me.'

Her breath caught in her throat and her eyes flew open wide as the gull pushed images toward her of an abhorrent group erratically moving across meadowland. She counted the dead creatures in the bird's memory. She retched when she saw that the smallest of them couldn't have been more than four years old. The gull flapped and squawked before she gave it a push off her shoulder, concerned it would accidentally catch her in the eye. She leaned forward with her hands on her knees, sucking in clean, cold air.

'Dia?' Arrus threw the food and put a hand on her hip. 'What is it?'

'They are moving out in the open.' She straightened up but took hold of Arrus' arm to steady herself, shaking her head to try to displace the image the gull had given her. 'They are twenty-nine in total. Twenty-eight of our people murdered and turned into monsters.'

'Did you see where?' Heara asked.

'Meadowland.' She looked up at her friend. 'They are still north of the forest that surrounds Eagle Hold.'

'We go on.' Arrus turned to address the others. 'They probably won't stop, and neither will we. We can catch them yet!'

With renewed energy they left the central forest of Fulmer Isle just as the world turned them away from the touch of the sun. Dia was aware she was letting her body run on adrenaline and forced herself to eat on the move and give herself some real fuel. She spotted a light in the distance and at first thought it was a lantern in a window, it grew larger and larger, its brightness almost blinding.

Several warriors drew swords but Dia waved a hand at them. 'It's Doroquael.'

The fire-spirit darted around them all twice as though to reassure himself they were all still there and safe, then stopped to hover before Dia and Arrus.

'You are two miless from *him*! He has stopped to resst and called on poor Tyrenell to demand information about your hold.'

'Spirit I told you not to go near him.' Dia admonished.

'Doroquael knowsss!' He dipped in shame. 'But Tyrenell took a moment to call out for help while he wass out of the trap! Relta iss the name of our enemy. He thinkss he will gather more dead in the homes outsside the hold. He doessn't know that Dia and Doroquael have warned them and the homes are empty.'

'Blessed spirit.' Dia reached out a hand to touch it, then recoiled, realising her foolish error. She turned to the others. 'You heard him, we're gaining, and he'll find himself trapped between the hold and us.'

She didn't miss the ripple of uncertainty. Nineteen of them and a fire-spirit against a necromancer and twenty-eight abominations. 'We can do this,' she hissed, showing her teeth. She threw her courage and determination into her *knowing* and Larissa and Everlyn echoed it.

Arrus let out a roar, and he set out into the black night with his sword drawn, the others close in his heels.

***

As night set in and no moon showed its face, they were forced to slow their pace to avoid any foolish falls. Doroquael kept his light as dark a blue as he could although Dia sensed that to do so used a huge amount of energy. They found the necromancer's abandoned camp, and the twins guessed that they'd gained an hour on them. She felt every touch of the earth as her feet hit it, as her heart beat, eating up the distance between her and her foe. Her breathing became the rhythm of the Fulmers, those that ran beside her the guardian spirits of the islands; even the strangers from Elden. They reached the forest and weaved through it as though the trees had opened up the way. Earth, air, fire, water, and spirit; she sensed them reaching out to her to lend their strength against this sorcerer of blood.

'Hold!' Heara stopped abruptly. The scout didn't so much as breathe as she searched with ears and eyes. Dia saw her friend's nostrils flare. She made a quick motion with her hand, demanding that they all stay where they were. Shaherra stepped up to take her sister's place as the scout disappeared.

They waited breathlessly. Doroquael made himself small. Dia could feel Arrus shifting his feet at her side.

Heara was beside them so suddenly Dia gasped.

'They're just ahead.' The scout spoke close to Dia's ear so that the others had to strain to hear. 'They've taken up position in an abandoned village. The dead stand completely still out on the road.'

Dia felt dizzy with both anxiety and excitement. They had him. Could they defeat him?

'Icante?' Arrus prompted.

She spun around to address them all. 'We know the dead can be destroyed by fire. They can also be incapacitated by taking out their legs. I need you all to cut me a path to the necromancer. Larissa, Everlyn, Heara, Shaherra, stay close to me. Doroquael, burn as many as you can. The undead may be people that you knew, but it's no longer them. Don't think of them as human, they are monsters now, you will be doing them a mercy to end them.' She took in a breath and drew her dagger, looking everyone in the eye, Arrus last of all. 'For the stolen lives of Fulmer.'

The twins both drew a short sword and dagger and with a nod from their Icante led the last creeping distance toward the village. The smell hit them before the first unnatural shapes resolved themselves in to the gently swaying forms of the dead islanders. Doroquael was the first to reach them, increasing in size to engulf one of the creatures. The twins leapt, both hitting one full in the chest and severing the heads with sword and dagger. Arrus smashed a knee with his sword and then also took off a head, spattering those behind him with gore. Dia called up wind, blowing in the door to the cottage in which the necromancer had taken shelter. An answering blast of air sent the windows and the door hurtling outward in shards and Dia raised her arm to shield her face. Heara managed to roll behind her falling undead to use it as a shield. Shaherra cried out as wooden splinters speared her left arm and side. Doroquael sent up a wall of flame that protected most of the others but Dia and the other *walkers* were thrown to the ground.

The undead awoke from their stupor and the speed with which they turned to attack was shocking. Heara screamed as the body she lay beneath grabbed her and began to squeeze the air from her lungs, she heard the crack of a rib. It was Vilnue that hacked through its shoulder, barely missing the scout's face. He ripped off its arm and pulled Heara out from beneath it.

Shaherra had run to the *walkers* and despite her injuries lifted Dia to her feet. Dia was in time to see Doroquael set two more undead alight before darting down through the chimney of the cottage. She called flame to her hands and ducking below the window stopped with her arm against the edge of the door. Bile rose to her throat, and a horrified groan left her as she saw Arrus chop the tiny dead child from shoulder to hip, it continued to try to bite and claw at him until he smashed its skull. Tearing her eyes away she took in a deep breath and spun into the cottage, blasting fire out from her hands as she did so. She went to her knees and the two other *walkers* sent a second wave of fire blazing over her head. Smoke and heat made her eyes water, but she blinked away the tears and saw a table had been tipped in front of the far wall, blistered, smouldering red and black. Cupping her hands together she formed a whirling vortex of air and she threw the table to smash it against the ceiling. The necromancer wasn't there.

'You missed.'

The women didn't have time to turn before the beams above them gave way. Instinctively all three *walkers* called upon the wind to shield them. Shaherra ran at the necromancer, slashing with her dagger and then following with her short sword. With a gesture of his hand, he sent a broken beam shooting toward her to impale her through the chest against the wall where she hung, the light going from her eyes.

Dia's insides seemed to turn molten and collapse downward while her feet froze her to the floor. She couldn't blink, couldn't loosen her larynx to scream her friend's name.

Stones from the chimney erupted outward and Dia was knocked to the floor again as Larissa covered her with her own body. Doroquael flew out, furious at having found himself trapped by a blocked fireplace. Sparks bristled and danced around him while he burnt such a fierce blue he could barely be seen. With a feral grin the necromancer took a small box from his pocket and placed his fingers on the catch to open it.

Dia pushed herself to her feet and used her magic to tear the box from his grasp. He barely shielded in time as Doroquael, Larissa, and Everlyn all blasted him with scorching heat. Surrounding herself with a shield of air Dia ran through the conflagration straight at the Chemman, he didn't see her through the fire until her dagger plunged into his heart. She snarled against his cheek as he slipped to the ground.

'Dia, come on!' Larissa urged as the remainder of the roof creaked and slipped a little.

She turned to look at Shaherra, at her muscles gone slack and her eyes grown empty. A ball of pain flared larger in her chest.

'Tyranell!' Doroquael almost wailed.

Dia dropped to her knees, behind her Larissa gave a grunt as she strained to keep the roof up. She felt something large and hard within the folds of the man's coat and fumbling for the pocket pulled out a second small box.

'That'sss it! Come on!'

They ran for the door, Everlyn bumping into Heara and Merkis Vilnue. The scout looked at their faces and froze.

Behind them Arrus and the warriors were standing catching their breath, gazing about themselves at the fallen undead.

'Shaherra?' Heara's voice came out in a choked whisper.

Dia threw her arms around her friend.

* * *

Dia cradled the open box in her lap, staring without seeing the strange runes within. They were dark brown in colour and she guessed that they'd been written in blood. She tossed it into the fire. The process of contacting the families of the dead and arranging burials had been taken over by Larissa; the thought crossed her mind that the younger woman might be a good choice to succeed her as Icante.

'Kesta *is* coming home,' she told the fireplace.

As reluctant as she was to leave the room and face taking up her mantle of Icante, it was Heara that she had to admit she was avoiding. She couldn't bear to see and feel her best friend in so much pain. She was being a coward, and she knew it. They'd beaten back the necromancers of Chem again, but she couldn't help but think that the price had been too high. And

302

just to make matters worse they'd managed it so far without the help of the Eldemen. If they'd put Kesta through the ordeal of marriage to that sorcerer for nothing it would be too bitter to take.

She called out to the empty room. 'Doroquael?'

The fire stirred and sparked.

'Icante?'

'Come on out.' She sighed. 'Your friend, Tyranell, he is all right?'

'Yesss. Thank you for freeing him.'

Dia shook her head. 'You saved many of my people yesterday. Siphenna ... Siphenna would have believed that worth her sacrifice. Is there any word from the other spirits?'

'They search sstill for the main Shem fleet.'

She sighed. 'I should go and see Heara.'

'You sshould,' Doroquael buzzed. 'Family and friends are presscious.'

'They are, spirit.'

She stood up and, leaving the sanctuary of her room, went to find Heara. She knocked at the door of the room she'd been given and was startled when Merkis Vilnue opened the door. She was about to apologise when he smiled and murmured, 'I'll leave you both too it.'

She watched him leave and then closing the door behind her went to sit beside her friend on the bed. 'I should have been here sooner,' she apologised.

Heara shook her head. 'You had your own grieving to do.'

Dia stopped fighting against herself and let go, she held her friend and let her cry into her shoulder as her own tears pushed up from her tightening chest. Heara was such a seemingly indestructible woman her shaking body and loud sobs were incredibly hard to bear. Her fingers clutched desperately at Dia with bruising force and her wordless keening hurt her soul. She felt hot and exhausted, her heart labouring as though she had a fever.

Heara sniffed loudly, wiping at her nose. 'How do I go on without half of myself?'

Dia swallowed, her throat painfully constricted. 'You go on *for* her. You go on because you deserve to live still. You go on because there are people here who love you and need you. You go on because you have purpose yet to discover.'

'Why her? She was so strong, so full of life.'

'You know that death has no sense of fairness, my darling.' She stroked Heara's long hair.

'I wish that I had been the one to kill the necromancer.'

'I fear you might get the chance to kill one yet.'

Heara sat up. 'There are more on the Islands?'

'No, I hope to the Spirits not. There is a fleet of Chemmen still out there somewhere though. We'll see to our dead tomorrow and then head back to Fulmer Hold to plan what to do next.'

'Can we take Shaherra back to our hold?'

'Of course.' Dia let go of her friend and moved to the edge of the bed. 'I've neglected my duties and should go and face the hold. You'll be all right?'

'I don't think I will ever feel all right again,' Heara admitted. 'But I will survive it, no matter how much it hurts.'

Dia nodded. 'Oh! And what's this with Merkis Vilnue?'

Heara gave a low chuckle. 'He gave me the comfort I needed.'

'Don't forget Eldemen have different ways than our island men,' she warned.

'He is still a man,' Heara grinned. 'And Larissa has such beautiful red hair. Perhaps I could have a red-haired daughter.'

'Heara!' Dia punched her friend in the arm. Then she kissed her cheek. As long as it helped her friend then there was no harm. 'The day after tomorrow we go back to Fulmer Hold.'

* * *

Worvig had done a good job of settling the Eldemen in her absence and both of their warships were out patrolling the sea around the islands. The loss of the seemingly indestructible Shaherra hit the hold hard and the celebrations of their victory were somewhat subdued. Dia did her best to keep a smile on her face but she had to leave it to Arrus and Worvig to stir their spirits.

'Dia!'

She started, unsure if she'd really heard the whisper. She looked around, but no one seemed to be looking at her or trying to attract her attention.

'Icante!'

Her eyes widened as she recognised the sibilant voice and moved closer to the fire in the centre of the hall over which their feast was being cooked.

'Arrus!' she commanded, straightening and hurrying to her own room. She used her magic to light a candle and Doroquael sprang out of it at the same time as Arrus stumbled through the doorway behind her.

'Newss from Elden!' The spirit darted about their heads. 'Mantu was attacked lasst night. The Shem fleet is there, and they are overrun. Thane Jorrun is captured in his dreamss. Elden iss in trouble!'

Dia's first thought was relief that the Chemman fleet had not come to the Fulmers after all. Then the magnitude of the fire-spirit's words sank in and she sat down on the edge of the table.

'What do we do?' Arrus's fists were clenched.

Dia regarded him and the fire-spirit. 'Call Merkis Vilnue in here, he must hear the news. We will send a letter at once to King Bractius and tell him we're returning his ships and men to him. We will also offer to meet with him in Taurmaline to discuss the possibility of sending him more *walkers* to fight the necromancers.'

Arrus opened his mouth to protest, but she stopped him with a glare. 'If Elden is overrun, then there'll be nothing we can do to stop the Chemmen taking the islands. We cannot stay out of this fight. Not if we want to survive.'

Chapter Sixteen

Jorrun: Kingdom of Elden

He leaned against the window, his forehead pressed to the cold glass and his smile grew. The weight that had been pressing hard against his lungs lifted and pins and needles prickled at his heart as it was freed momentarily from his fears. It was so good seeing Catya so carefree and actually having fun; the change in the girl since Kesta had arrived was amazing. His smile faded a little as he watched the Fulmer woman working in the ward, laughing, and totally unselfconscious of her appearance in her trousers and tunic. The light caught her hair and it glistened like a raven's feather. He closed his eyes, stepping back from the window as his heart was clenched once again in fear's cold fingers. *I am* not *falling in love with her. I can't. It's just a foolish infatuation born from... from the need for someone.*

'She needs to go home.'

'Jorrun?' Azrael asked in concern, hovering closer.

'Nothing.' He glanced at the drake and forced his lips into a thin smile. 'Anything from the others?' He could feel his pulse still fast against his ribs.

Azrael made himself small, the fire-spirit's equivalent of a negative. 'But there iss another messsage from the king.'

Jorrun's shoulders dropped as he turned around and looked at one of the other windows. A raven peered in through the glass, perched on the wide sill. It tapped twice with its beak, getting impatient. He grabbed a slice of meat and opened the window. He had learned long ago to take the message cylinder before giving the raven any food, they were crafty birds and would keep flying off and coming back for more otherwise. At the rate Bractius was sending them he would have to catch a few and ship them off to Taurmaline sooner than usual.

He was tempted not to read it.

Clenching his jaw, he broke the seal and tipped out the tiny scroll.

Yes, I know it's probably a ruse. Any news from Osun? I need answers. I expect them when I arrive at the hold tomorrow.

He dropped the scroll with annoyance. The last thing he needed was Bractius under his feet. He went back to the north window and was disappointed that Kesta had gone in; then scolded himself for having even looked.

'Not good?' Azrael prompted.

'He is visiting tomorrow.' Jorrun gave a shake of his head. 'I don't know why he thinks his being here will somehow make me able to see that fleet!'

'He thinks a lot of things sshould happen becausse he says so. That's kingss.'

'Know a lot of kings, do you?' Jorrun's mouth twitched upward in a half smile.

'More than you!' The spirit retorted.

'Come on, let's get things ready.'

'Are you ssure about thiss?' Azrael drifted higher so that he was eye level.

'Not really,' he bent to pick some books up off the floor and flung a discarded shirt onto the bed. 'I really should tidy this place up.'

'Huh!' Azrael spat.

He chose to ignore the drake. He'd never been a particularly tidy person, there were always so many other things to be doing.

Azrael buzzed softly. 'I don't like thisss Jorrun!'

'I know.' He turned to look at the anxious drake. 'But Kesta has risked herself to try, you drakes have all been risking yourselves, and my brother puts his life at risk every day because of the misguided belief that I and Bractius are his masters.'

'Ossun needs the sstability of someone to follow because of his childhood.'

Jorrun waved a hand dismissively as he cleared a space on the floor. It was an old argument and there was no time to go over it yet again. He gathered together five candlesticks, hesitating at the one that sat at the window opposite Kesta's.

'You don't have to pretend with her, you know.' Azrael's words were as hypnotic as paper curling at the edges of a fire.

'Yes, I do,' he replied stubbornly, although he looked across to the Ivy Tower, anyway. 'I am the dreaded Dark Man, unbending, vengeful, loyal to the king—'

'Ssoft-hearted, addle-brained …'

He scowled but couldn't help but laugh. 'Pest!'

Azrael crackled and snapped, then became serious. 'Your guise has kept you and Elden ssafe for many years; but that time hass gone. I've hated watching you being sso lonely here.'

Jorrun shook his head, not wanting to think about it, fighting against the sick, empty feeling in his chest. 'I'm happy enough, spirit; anyway, how can I be lonely with you here to annoy me?'

'How indeed?'

He knew Azrael did not miss his automatic glance toward the Ivy Tower. 'Stop being a nuisance and let me finish preparing, bug.'

Azrael hissed at the old insult. 'Human!'

It was so tempting to stick out his tongue, but he kept his dignity and refrained. He set out the five candles and the five objects that would represent the five realms; water, fire, earth, air, and spirit. Were he a necromancer, he would have slaughtered some poor animal and splattered the place in blood. He felt bad enough eating meat; but as the son of a slave he'd learnt to eat whatever was put in front of him. His thoughts turned back to Kesta. *Walkers* ate no meat, his mother had been forced to, to survive.

'Jorrun?'

Azrael brought him back to the room, and he picked up a small bowl off the table.

'Your head isss not here,' the drake scolded. 'Don't roll your eyesss!'

'I wasn't going to!' He made his way down the steps to his supply room and carefully measured out what he needed for his dream trance. He checked that the drake hadn't followed and then both rolled his eyes and stuck out his tongue. He knew it was childish, but he felt better. When he returned to his tower room, he checked everything over and set down the bowl. He was ready. He looked up at the still bright sky, his eyebrows drawn in tight over his eyes. He tapped his fingers on a book that balanced on the edge of a table and let out a heavy sigh. There was no point trying until he thought his enemy might be asleep.

'You should eat sssomething.'

'You should mind your own business.'

'You are my busssiness.'

'You're my pain in the—'

'Eat!' Azrael flared up to three times his size.

'Okay!' Jorrun raised his hands. He went down the tower steps, stomping as loudly as he could for dramatic effect. His tray of food was waiting. Catya always arranged it so neatly, the care she took shouted loudly of how much he meant to her. He ran one finger along the side of the tray, swallowing and then clenching his jaw. The girl deserved better than he could give her. She needed a real father not someone who neglected her and pretended coldness. At least perhaps ... he swallowed again as pressure built behind his eyes and stung his nostrils. She had Kesta now, and he knew that she would protect and even love his little Catya.

He cleared his throat and taking in a deep breath stomped his way back up to his room.

He could tell that Azrael was unamused by the spirit's stillness and dark, almost blue, colour. The drake was the only being with whom he could truly be himself and the spirit knew when he was putting on an act. He could fool himself, but never Azrael. He looked down at the food and his stomach tightened further. It somehow didn't look real, like it was carved from wood and not actually something to eat. He didn't want to admit to himself that it was fear he was feeling. All he wanted to do was go to the Ivy Tower and drown himself in those mismatched green eyes and that oh so fiery soft skin.

'Jorrun Dunham, if you don't ssstop daydreaming I will burn you!'

He started. He dropped the plate on the table and sat down, throwing a glare in Azrael's direction.

'What hasss got in to you?' Azrael asked more gently. 'You don't have to do thiss you know? Bractius would not want you to risk yourself—'

'Yes, he would!' He grabbed up a fork and stabbed it into a crooked carrot. 'He may be my friend, but he is ruthless when it comes to his throne and protecting it, you know that.'

Azrael didn't disagree. 'I am worried for you.'

'I know.'

'You are sstrong, but you have not had the training of a Dunham; only your books.'

'Books bring us the world.'

'In theory, in your head, not out in real life.'

Jorrun put his fork down. 'What would you have me do?'

'Take Kesta home to the Fulmers and be her Silene.'

'What?' He sat back in his chair, holding his breath, his wide blue eyes turned unblinkingly toward the drake.

'It is not an imposssssible choice.'

Jorrun shook his head, pushing the painful hope down deep to crush it. He pushed his plate away. 'I owe Elden, I owe Bractius.'

'You owe yoursself; you owe me and your mother.'

He stood up, knocking his chair over. 'I'm doing this. It's the right thing to do. Anyway ... anyway she hates me.'

'Idiot.' Azrael stole a piece of coal and shot off up the chimney.

Jorrun glared after him. When he didn't come back, he made himself some tea and gnawed at a carrot to try to stop the churning in his belly. *I have to do this.*

He growled at himself as his eyes strayed towards the window to the Ivy Tower.

***

Azrael came back shortly after the sun set and twilight sank into darkness. They politely ignored each other for a while, neither one of them wanting to back down.

With a sigh Jorrun got up, picked up his bowl of herbs and walked over to the fireplace. Azrael moved closer, his flame turning to a gentler yellow; his way of apologising and pleading.

'I have to,' Jorrun whispered, glancing at the fire-spirit and casting the herbs onto the small blaze in the fireplace. At once a blue-black smoke rose and the herbs popped with sparks of different colours. Jorrun closed his eyes and took in a deep breath of the sharp and sweet scents. He lit the candles, following the direction of the sun and then sat himself in the centre of his star. He looked up at Azrael.

'Be careful!' The spirit bobbed, changing colour to red and blue.

'I will.'

He lay down, folding his hands over his chest and taking in long, deep breaths. The smoky air tickled his throat, but the powerful perfume of the herbs soon overcame him, and he drifted toward sleep. Slowly he began to chant, reaching out with his mind for dreams. He glanced across the familiar feel of those in the hold and cast further out.

Blood to blood, soul to soul, dream to dream.

Blood to blood, soul to soul, dream to dream.

Blood to Blood, soul to soul, dream to dream.

He found himself in an icy land, the wind hitting him so hard it was difficult to catch his breath. The colours were subdued; grey and blue with the whites as sharp as glass. He could feel the undertones of the dream, anger edged with fear. There were fine crystals of snow in the air and they built up in mounds against his legs with unnatural speed. He tried not to react, to not feel the fear, but instead to quest toward the mind of the dreamer.

Where are we?

A city seemed to form before his eyes. The walls were black and jagged like rotten teeth forced up through bleeding gums. He could hear distant music throbbing, enticing, repulsive. The dreamer felt both physically excited and terrified; Jorrun struggled to remain calm and impassive and not react. Gently, subtly, he turned the hiss of the icy wind in to the shush of a gentle sea.

They were rocking. The waves were incessant but not rough. Jorrun suggested stars and let the dreamer fill them in. They were random; whoever the dreamer was, he was not a navigator.

The ship creaked, and the dreamer's fear returned. Images of dead men in crates came to mind. The fear was not of the dead, but that the dreamer could not wake enough of them.

They are awake, you can control them all. Where will we send them?

Greed for victory, greed for power and recognition flowed through the dreamer. Jorrun fed it. There was jealousy, sneaking, bitter jealousy; he was better than his son.

Yes. You are better than …

Adelphy. Posturing brat. He was strong but not half as clever as he thought he was; and to think he would step over his own father who gave him everything! Dryn would see; they needed no second wave. He, Karinna, could take the whole of Elden with ease.

What of the Dark Man, what if he is at …

Mantu. So what? Some weak Elden conjurer? They had all heard the tales that it was some brat washed up from Chem or from the Gods. Elden magic was dead and even if it was some get of Chem, the Dunhams were too strong to beat; himself among the best.

What of the Fulmers?

Breeding stock; spirit worshipping whores with no purpose but to strengthen the magic of Chem …

Jorrun's anger flared. He couldn't help it. The colours of the dream changed toward brown and red like dried blood.

Got you!

Too late, Jorrun realised that the dreamer was cognitive. He tried to pull back, tried to flee back to his own body, but he was held fast. He fought back his panic, he *had* to stay in control.

Who are you, little nosey noser? Karinna demanded. *Dryn told us to watch out for dream spies. Did you think we wouldn't feel you poking about these past months or know how to deal with you? Well?*

Jorrun froze. The feel of Karinna Dunham trying to rifle through his thoughts, pawing at the edges of his mind, made him nauseous. Years of playing the 'Dark Man' had given him mastery over his own thoughts and emotions and he forced his mind to blankness. He was stronger; just.

No matter. I set a dreamer's trap every time I close my eyes. We all do now. Enjoy your eternity in hell!

Jorrun felt the presence withdraw, but he didn't believe it was gone. He carefully tried to feel for the edges of the trap, fear creeping in like heat when he could find no weakness. He tried to struggle against the trap, subtly at first and then with growing desperation. If he'd been within his body, he would have been breathing hard. It was getting more difficult not to think, not to give in to his dread at what would happen if he failed, if he didn't get back to … He tried to suppress it, not wanting to give anything away that could be used against him. Not thinking was too hard, so he thought of something neutral. Clouds. Birds flying in the clouds above.

Who is Kesta?

Anger and panic rose to engulf him, and he fought and clawed his way through it to draw on safe images and lead Karinna away from her. He thought of fire, he thought of the sea, he thought of ravens. He thought of her hair, of her eyes, of her mouth.

A Fulmer whore? We'll take her with the rest and breed an undefeatable coven. I'll have that one myself—

Fury blinded him and snatching for Karinna's mind he tried to force his way in, but the Chemman fought back, keeping control where he did not. The Chemman ripped through his bleeding mind, worming into his heart, and fouling his soul. Pain tore through Jorrun as the Chemman drew forth image after image, gloating, feeding off his fear like a bloated tick. Karinna found his mother.

I know this woman. This was Dryn's Walker. *She bore Dinari and …*

Jorrun.

Joryn. Joryn? Karinna laughed. The sound shattered Jorrun into a thousand pieces. *Are you my cousin's boy? Your mother's lover bled to death in my bed and I sent her worthless carcass back to her. Matyla never could produce a child worth spit.*

Red light exploded in his mind and he fought against his anger and fear with every atom of his being. He recalled his mother's strength and nobility. He recalled the love that flowed between her and Matyla. He thought of Azrael's faith, of Bractius's courage and devotion to his people. He thought of …

Kesta.

Kesta.

Raven hair, eyes green as the forest, skin golden as the earth, heart of fire.

Jorrun seized control of the dream and threw them back into the snow, dragged them toward the black city of pain and desire. He called down the music that pulsed with the rhythms of the heart and the blood to try to drown Karinna in his own fears. He threw up images of his father, Dryn Dunham, his face angry and vengeful. He showed Karinna his perfect son, Adelphy; favourite of the Overlord of the Covens.

For a moment Jorrun thought he'd won. Karinna's grip loosened, and he tried to flee back; back toward his body and the Raven Tower. Back toward Kesta.

But blackness snapped down tightly around him.

He could feel the ice wind cutting at his skin although he was blind.

Nice try, Joryn Dunham. You are better than we thought. I'll tell you what; I'll come visit you when I have your whore in my bed!

Black anger pulsed in bright flashes and Jorrun flew at the bounds of the trap that held him. He reached out for Azrael, he reached within for his own power, he battered at the cage within which he was trapped.

Karinna!

Karinna!

The necromancer didn't reply. Ice prickled at his lungs and the snow mounted up against his body.

Kesta, he breathed. *They won't touch a hair on your head! I'll kill them all!*

I'll kill them all.

Chapter Seventeen

Kesta: Kingdom of Elden

Kesta threw open the window so Azrael could fly straight out and grabbed her trousers and tunic. She didn't even pause for shoes before racing down the stairs and banging on Catya's door. She pushed it open.

'Catya! Wake Rosa and tell her to go to the Raven Tower and wait just inside the door, and then go to Tantony and tell him to meet me there urgently. Catya!'

'Coming!' she groaned, throwing off her blanket.

Kesta turned back to the stairs and took the remainder as swiftly as she dared. She checked the great hall was empty and sprinted across to the doors. She had to throw her shoulder against the heavy wood to get it moving. The grass was cold and wet with dew, but she barely noticed it or registered the bruising stones as she raced to the tower. She turned the metal ring and Azrael was at her shoulder as she entered.

'What's happened?' she asked the spirit, breathing hard as they ascended the stairs.

'Whoever's dream Jorrun entered detected him and trapped him!' The spirit's flight was erratic. 'We need to ssave him, Kessta!'

Kesta's heart palpitated rapidly, she had no idea how to save him; she could only hope that the drake did. She reached his room and saw Jorrun lying on the floor. In the flickering candlelight his skin seemed to hold colour still, but his chest barely rose.

'Can I enter the circle?'

'Star,' Azrael corrected. 'Yes, you are ssafe.' He darted across himself to hover above Jorrun's head.

She got onto her hands and knees and, holding her breath, reached out tentatively to check the pulse at his throat.

'So cold, already.' She grabbed a blanket off the bed and threw a log onto the fire on her way past. Tantony came rushing into the room as she tucked the blanket around Jorrun.

'What's happening?' he demanded.

Kesta rocked back onto her heels. She swallowed, and her voice caught in her throat as she replied. 'Someone caught him spying on their dream. Azrael says he is trapped.'

'Can we get him out?'

Kesta turned to the fire-spirit who seemed to shrink and turned red and blue. 'To rescue him the trap musst be broken or the one that casst the trap must be killed.'

'How do we break the trap?' She got to her feet and moved around the table.

Azrael buzzed and spat. 'Smassh it, Kessta!'

'So, it's a physical thing?'

'A box enchanted.' Azrael bobbed with agitation.

'And we would find it where?'

'With the dreamer.'

Kesta and Tantony looked at each other.

'There is no other way? Nothing we can do here? Anything we can do to help Jorrun save himself?' She waited, watching the fire-spirit with wide eyes.

Azrael shot up and back and made himself small again. 'Nothing but try to keep his body alive.'

Kesta sat heavily on the chair, feeling sick. 'His body will die?'

'He cannot eat. His organss will sshut down.'

She turned back to Tantony whose Adam's apple bobbed as he swallowed. 'Is there any way to know where the trap is or the person who cast the trap?'

'Ssomeone close, ssomeone strong.'

'Could it be the necromancer on the Fulmers?'

'Possibly. I will have Doroquael contacted at once.' Without warning he darted into the fireplace.

'We should tell the king,' Tantony suggested. He turned to the table where Jorrun's ink and quill stood. He almost fell backward as Azrael came bursting back out.

'Mantu iss under attack. Ssiveraell iss calling all the drakes!'

'Mantu.' Kesta stood and grabbed Tantony's arm. 'Send a raven at once.' She ran out to the top of the stairs and bellowed down for Rosa.

'What are you thinking?' Tantony glanced at her as he wrote as carefully and swiftly as he could.

'That the dreamer was at or near Mantu. I'll have to ride out as soon as dawn breaks—'

'Wait, what?' Tantony almost dropped his quill.

'The attack on Mantu might fail, but it might not. If we win the dreamer might be killed; great for Jorrun. If he flees we may never see him again or, if the Chemmen win …'

'His body dies.' Tantony looked down at his Thane.

'I have to find that trap or make sure the dreamer dies.'

'You'll go to Mantu? With a whole army of necromancers there?'

Kesta took in a breath, lifting her chin to hold his gaze.

'What's happening? Oh!' Rosa halted in the doorway, Catya tried to push past her into the room. Rosa's eyes widened when she saw Azrael, but the Elden lady-in-waiting didn't turn and run.

'Okay, you all need to listen.' Kesta looked around at them all. 'Jorrun is caught in a magical trap; we don't have many days in which to get him out. To do so I have to go to Mantu. Rosa, I need you to take care of Jorrun as best you can. Keep him warm, see if he can swallow and take water.' Catya was crying, but she remained quiet, holding tight to Rosa's hand. 'Azrael, I'll need you to come with me. Tantony, you'll have to deal with the king—'

'No!' The warrior crossed his arms, his face reddening. 'No. This is stupid but if it's the only way then I'll be going to Mantu with you. I know the island.'

Kesta bit her lip, she regarded the Merkis, taking a moment to slow and steady her breathing. 'All right.'

'And me!' Catya cried out. 'I'm your bodyguard!'

She crossed the room to the young girl and placed a hand on her shoulder. 'No, I need you to guard Jorrun and help Rosa. With me and Tantony gone Rosa will be in charge of the hold.'

'What? Me?' Rosa turned pale.

'Yes,' Kesta replied firmly. 'With whichever chieftain Tantony chooses to command the warriors. You know my plans, you know how to defend the hold.'

Rosa straightened her shoulders and nodded.

'We should prepare for our journey straight away,' she continued, turning back to Tantony. 'I want to be gone before Bractius tries to stop us.'

'We'll be fastest by ship.' He rolled the parchment and placed it inside a cylinder. 'Straight down the river and then out to sea. We'd be able to eat and sleep without stopping or worrying about changing horses.'

'Arrange it.'

Tantony gave a single nod and hurried from the room.

Kesta looked down at Jorrun and moving to kneel beside him she placed a hand on the side of his face. There was still no warmth to his skin and she gently drew her fingers along his bearded jaw and called up her *knowing*. She could feel nothing from him, but as she leaned further forward to touch her forehead to his she pushed all her heart and soul toward him.

'Leave that candle burning in the window, Jorrun. I'm coming.'

***

It took her only moments to shove a couple of changes of clothes into a bag, strap her dagger to her waist, and pull on her long boots. She looked around quickly for anything else that might be of use, grabbed some bread and fruit from the table, and then returned to the Raven Tower. The sun was just beginning to spread its fingers through the clouds.

Rosa had managed to get Jorrun up into the bed with help from the others and had propped him up with cushions. Azrael kept a discreet distance but was peeping out from the chimney. Catya seemed more enthralled than afraid of the little fire-man.

'He has his swallow reflexes,' Rosa said.

Relief swept through her. 'That's something.'

Kesta looked through the disorder on the large table and found a letter opener. She tested its edge and found it was sharp enough for what she needed. Picking up a message tube she sat beside Jorrun and lifted his arm, placing it in her lap. She pierced the soft skin below his wrist, drawing blood.

'What are you doing?' Rosa asked in alarm.

'This is part of his magic.' Kesta glanced up at her friend, catching the slow flow of blood in the cylinder. She held his hand to her cheek, closing her eyes briefly before letting it drop. Her face and neck burnt with a mixture of anger and fear. It terrified her that the person they were all hoping could save them from Chem had so easily been beaten and, yet again, someone she was relying on had been reckless with their own life for something they could have managed without. Her jaw clenched. She hated Bractius for his manipulation of both herself and Jorrun. She could hardly believe that both she and her father had thought Jorrun the ruthless schemer, and the king thoughtful and kind!

She drew in a breath and looked up at Rosa. 'Would you bandage this for me?'

Rosa frowned but did so while Kesta sealed the message tube with wax and then tied string about it before securing it around her neck. She stabbed the paperknife into her own arm, flinching at the pain, and collected her blood into another tube which she gave to Rosa.

'If ... when he wakes, give him this, he will know what to do with it.'

'I will.' Rosa took it tentatively with a frown on her face.

Kesta added some coal and a jar of oil to her bag. She hugged the older woman tightly and then Catya, who dug her fingers into her back but refused to speak or look at her.

'Look after each other and protect our home.' She looked from one to the other, her heart muscles clenching as she memorised the details of their faces.

'We will.' Rosa's voice was tight.

With a nod Kesta went to the door, but she turned to look at them again.

'Order bows and arrows to be bought or made; Tantony probably didn't do it. Get all the women learning archery and make sure you both practice every day. If you don't become brilliant at it by the time I come back, I'll be very angry.'

Rosa laughed, Catya burst in to tears.

'Just come back,' Rosa said.

***

Tantony was waiting for her at the small dock, giving his last instructions to two warriors who she recognised but couldn't name. Kurghan was waiting for them on a small boat with a single mast; it seemed the carpenter had offered to take them. His wife and sister were up and about and talking quietly together.

Tantony saw her approaching. 'You're ready?'

She nodded.

'You're sure you want to do this?'

She scowled at him and jumped light-footed into the boat. Settling in the seat at the back she placed a lantern beside her and used her magic to light it. At once Azrael sprang out, staying within the glass out of sight of the others.

The boat rocked as Tantony untied the mooring rope and clambered in. Kurghan used an oar to push them out and then adjusted the sail to catch the wind. Kesta closed her eyes and calling on her magic agitated the air. A strong wind arose, snapping the canvas and pushing them out onto the lake. As the boat turned, she caught a last glance of the Raven Tower through the trees.

It took them a day and most of a night to sail down the river Taur, even with Kesta using her magic to help whenever she could. If Kurghan noticed anything unnatural about the winds, he was too polite to say. Kesta barely slept, watching the shore unfold before her, changing from forest to farmland, passing through large towns and small. She worried about Rosa and Catya, she prayed that her family and people on the Fulmers were okay; she hoped that Bractius wouldn't do anything stupid when he saw what had become of Jorrun. She pulled her blanket more tightly around herself as twilight deepened.

'Kessta!'

'All will be well,' she whispered, more to herself, than to the spirit.

The smell of Taurmouth reached her first, rolling with the briny breeze up the estuary. Lights pierced the night and sound followed as the river swept them swiftly on.

'What's your plan from here?' Kurghan asked.

Tantony looked around at Kesta, his grey eyes bright. 'Some of the Northold warriors may still be here, depending on how quickly they've received orders and been deployed to Mantu. We should see if we can travel with them; if not...'

'If not, we cross the sea in this,' Kesta said. 'My magic will get us there quicker than any warship.'

Tantony and Kurghan glanced at each other but said nothing.

Kesta's anger stirred at their distrust, but she bit her tongue.

***

They tied up at a dock and Tantony threw a coin to the harbour master. Azrael withdrew inside the lamp and Kesta carried it with her as they clambered ashore. She had to take a moment to stretch her muscles before they would let her move properly.

'I'll make enquiries,' Tantony said. 'You two go and get some hot food. The crab and oyster there are good; just save me something.'

Kesta was anxious to get going and reluctant to go to where the docks were crowded; but it made sense for Tantony to update them on what was happening. Kurghan seemed to sense her unease and suggested she sit out on the harbour wall while he went in to get them some food. She perched on the rough stone with the lantern beside her, pulling the hood of her coat up over her long hair. She called up her *knowing* to alert her of any potential threat. It reminded her of how vulnerable she'd felt when she'd first come to Elden, how shocked she'd been by the unguarded thoughts directed toward her by Eldemen.

She was relieved at how quickly Kurghan reappeared, balancing several dishes and three mugs of ale on a tray.

'They didn't have much without meat,' he apologised. 'Just bread, cheese, and some boiled vegetables.'

'It's kind of you to remember.' She swung about to place her feet back on the street. She helped him set the food out on the wall.

They ate for a while in uncomfortable silence.

'This must seem odd to you,' she said after a while.

Kurghan shrugged. 'When your Thane is a sorcerer, I suppose you shouldn't be surprised by anything. That fire demon of yours did give me a fright though.'

'He's just a spirit.' She looked around at the lamp.

Both of them jumped as Tantony came striding up with his hitched gait.

'Well, we missed the others. The warriors sailed out yesterday afternoon to reinforce the garrison and fleet on Mantu. We'll have to make our own way.' He grabbed up a heel of bread, slapped some meat on it, and bit into it hungrily.

Kesta looked at the two men. 'I should go on my own from here.'

'No!' Kurghan said.

Tantony almost choked on his food. 'Absolutely not!'

'Do you have any money?' she demanded of Tantony.

He reluctantly nodded.

'Give it to Kurghan. Kurghan, I want you to get a room here on the docks and wait for us.'

'Don't you need me to sail the ship?'

Kesta shook her head. 'Like I said, I can get us there quickly using magic. Tantony, if you're sure you want to come, then I want to get going as soon as you've eaten.'

He swallowed down the food he was chewing. 'Of course, I'm coming!'

She nodded, picking up the lantern and returning to the boat.

She didn't have to wait long until Tantony joined her. He undid the mooring rope without a word and pushed them away from the wooden piling with his foot.

'Get us out to sea and then I'll do the rest,' she said. 'Thank you, Tantony.'

He grunted in reply.

***

When the lights of the busy harbour shrank beyond the edge of the horizon, Kesta leaned out over the black sea and plunged her hand beneath its cold skin. Calling up her *knowing* she reached out to the intelligent creatures of the deeps, pleading with them for their help. It wasn't long before a family of dolphins breached the surface, circling the boat and chattering in their own clicking tongue. One came close enough for Kesta to touch and she placed her fingers against its warm, smooth skin. She showed it images of Jorrun lying motionless amid the candles and let flow all the emotions it evoked in her. She showed it images of the map, of Mantu, of the dead men she'd seen being loaded onto ships. She conveyed her desire to defeat them.

The dolphin fell back into the sea and its family followed. The boat bobbed idly under the infinite sky.

'What now?' Tantony whispered.

A dolphin leapt up, spraying them in salty droplets that caught the myriad stars within them. One by one the dolphin family broke the surface just beyond the prow.

'Help me tie some ropes to the ship and the throw the ends out over the water,' she instructed.

They tied three lines and as soon as they were thrown out dolphins snatched up the ends and began racing out toward the north-east. They took off so quickly that Tantony fell off his seat backwards and Kesta had to grab the lamp to stop it smashing.

328

They slept fitfully, Azrael the most anxious of the three of them, far from land and locked away from his natural element. He nibbled on coal and Kesta kept the lamp fed with oil. By unspoken agreement they took turns keeping watch, the daylight hours as nerve-racking as the night. Through a night and a day and a night, the dolphin family pulled them across the ocean. As midnight passed. and they drew closer to morning, several dolphins came up to the surface to chatter at Kesta.

She sat up to see a horizon red with flames.

Mantu was burning.

The dolphins surfaced briefly and then left them.

'Tantony.' Kesta cleared her throat and tried to make herself sound more confident. 'Merkis, where should we steer for?'

'If you don't mind climbing there's a small rocky cove on the west side of the island. It can only be reached by sea or by climbing the cliff, but it was a great spot for fishing and finding a moment's peace. It's about a mile from the northern port of Promise.'

'Sounds good. Azra, I'll need to cover the lantern – and you.'

Azrael made himself small and vanished at once into the lantern's flame. She placed it carefully beneath the seat and wedged it in as securely as she could. She realised she was chewing at her lower lip and she fought down her anxiety. She took several swallows of water to try to quell the churning of her stomach. It was too late to turn back; not that she could. Sharp blue eyes and a face that gave nothing away seemed to plague her every thought no matter how hard she tried to turn her mind away. It was like an addiction she couldn't conquer.

She put down the water jug and dug her nails into her palms to wake herself up from her daydreaming. 'Let's take down the sail and row in closer.'

The sounds of battle began to drift toward them and several times they bumped up against the wreckage of a much larger vessel. As quietly as they could they rowed toward the island, Tantony indicating silently when they needed to correct a course. She kept her *knowing* open to warn them of the approach of anything living. She caught Tantony watching her with a deep frown on his face, he gave a slight shake of his head before looking away.

They drew closer to the jagged cliffs and her nerves finally began to get the better of her. She closed down her *knowing* to take a few slow, deep breaths and get herself under control before she infected Tantony with her emotions.

'It's somewhere here,' Tantony whispered. 'But it's too dark for me to be sure.'

The sea surged between hidden rocks and Kesta had to fight her oar to keep them from being dragged against the cliffs.

'We'll have to risk some light; hold on a moment!'

She pulled in her oar and grabbed the lantern out from under the seat. The boat lurched and bucked, Tantony grunting as he tried to control the boat alone.

'Azra, can you guide us in?'

The drake emerged hesitantly from the lantern flame, hissing and spitting at the sea spray. He passed close by the struggling Tantony's shoulder and hovered at the narrow prow.

'You need to head north a bit more.' The spirit flickered.

Kesta clambered back to her seat and grabbed her oar. By the time they'd forced the boat into the tiny cove her hands were blistered, and her arms and back were on fire.

Tantony jumped out into the shallows and hauled them part way up the shingle. Kesta climbed out more carefully, every muscle shaking. She looked up at the dark cliff and the stars between the clouds so far above. She felt a moment of exhaustion and despair.

'The stairs are just here to the left,' Tantony whispered a little breathlessly.

'Stairs,' she said with relief. 'Azra, while we climb can you try to speak with the other drakes? Get us a heads up of what we are facing. Also see if they know the locations of the strongest necromancers.'

Azrael rocketed up the cliff face at once and vanished over the top.

'Wish I could do that.' Tantony adjusted his sword belt and turned to look at her. 'The steps are pretty steep, but you can find them by touch. We should take it slow.'

'You'll get no argument from me!'

He surprised her with a grin and then headed for the foot of the stairs.

He set a steady pace, both of them using hands, feet, and knees to crawl and pull their way up. Twice they stopped to catch their breath.

'I'm getting old,' Tantony groaned.

'Nonsense,' she whispered back, wondering how much this was hurting his knee. 'How much further?'

Instead of replying, Tantony got up and continued his crawling climb. With a sigh she followed.

When Tantony reached the top, he perched with one leg over the edge and reached down to clasp Kesta's wrist and help pull her up. She sat down heavily, her back against his arm.

'*I'm* getting old too,' she said, her throat raw. 'We'll wait for Azra's report.'

He didn't reply but she could feel his chest rising and falling. She almost laughed at how pathetic a rescue party they must look, battered before they even met an enemy.

It was nearly half an hour before Azra found them. He was burning a dark blue and hard to see.

'Promise harbour iss taken. Sseven ships of our enemy are anchored there, our own ssunk. There are many fires in the town. Dead men roam the island; mosst are attacking the southern port, Haven. Our warriors sstill defend there with Ssiveraell. Live warriors of Shem are taking up defensse of Promisse; we think the necromancers work from there.'

'The island isn't lost yet.' Tantony sagged in relief.

'If we take out at least some of the necromancers, then those dead men will lessen and give our warriors a chance.' She scrambled to her feet.

'Can you really beat them?' Tantony regarded her, eyes narrowed. 'Or are you biting off more than you can chew, like Jorrun?'

'My mother has killed at least two. If I can sneak into that town and catch any of them alone, I should be able to deal with them.'

'And if you don't catch them alone?'

'I'd be stupid to try to take on more than one. I should be able to get us past the Chemman warriors using my magic, but I'll have to rely on the two of you to help watch out for dead men. The necromancers might also be invisible to me if they wear amulets like the one Jorrun has. Tantony, where do you think the best place would be to get into the harbour and where are they likely to have set up their base?'

Tantony scratched at his cheek. 'The town itself is walled; the harbour would have been the easiest way to slip in.'

They looked at each other, both knowing they probably should have remained down with the boat until Azrael had reported.

'But the wall is scalable if we can go unseen,' he went on. 'As for where, I imagine they will have taken the fort.'

'No, no!' Azrael said excitedly. 'The fort itself is sstill being held againsst them! Some warriorss have managed to barricade themselves in there.'

'Well, let's get ourselves in and we'll go from there,' Kesta suggested.

Azrael guided them along the cliff path like a bright will-o'-the-wisp, the sky to their right stained with flame and distorted by smoke. After about a quarter of a mile Tantony suggested they cut inland and avoid the main paths. It was mostly rugged pasture, but gorse and bare-branched apple trees allowed them some cover. Kesta noticed movement and calling up her *knowing* was chilled to find that she felt nothing.

'I think one of the dead men is just up ahead, maybe more than one,' she whispered. 'I don't know how much the necromancers can see through them and we should try to keep our approach undetected.'

Tantony growled, glancing at Azrael who intensified his flame to blue. 'It's a shame not to take a chance to kill them, though.'

Kesta didn't disagree but continued toward the glowing harbour. A fox came running toward them, stopped to sniff at them, glanced back over its shoulder and then ran on. Kesta felt its sharp fear. She gestured to the other two to go on, while she slipped away into some trees to their right, moving quickly and as quietly as she could.

Tantony gave a cry of alarm as a large shape lumbered toward him out of the darkness. He drew his sword and stood on guard, knees bent and ready to move. Even in the darkness Kesta could see the shock and fear on the warrior's face. As the creature swung a heavy fist, in which it grasped a studded mace, Kesta darted in behind it. Tantony caught the blow with his sword and staggered back. Ducking low Kesta cut hard and deep across the back of its legs, severing its tendons. The creature collapsed, arms still flailing, Tantony took off a hand and its head in one swing.

He stood panting, unable to take his eyes off the still moving dead man; until the awful smell of it registered through his fear and he stumbled around it to Kesta.

'Shouldn't the spirit burn it?' He looked around for Azrael.

She shook her head, setting off again at once. 'The less the necromancers see of me and Azrael the more chance we have of getting to one of them.'

Tantony grunted and increased his pace to match hers.

The wind brought smoke to them in choking snatches that stung their eyes. Now and again a male voice would sound out, the words indistinguishable. Azrael came hurtling toward them, his trajectory erratic.

'Kessta! I've found some of the necromanssers! There is a tall building collapssed that has breached the wall. There are sstill flames, but we can go that way!'

Kesta nodded, saving her breath. She cast out her *knowing*, trying not to let Tantony's anxiety become her own. She could feel the mood of the conquered town; it was feral. Bloodlust, aggression, jubilation; she could almost smell the testosterone. Underneath it was the terror, pain, despair ... the conquered who were still in the town, hiding, if they were lucky. She

334

pulled her arms in tight around herself, feeling sick, feeling chilled to the bone; not wanting to think of those women who were not so lucky. There was only one thing she could do to help them now.

Azrael flew ahead, camouflaging himself among the small fires that still burnt in the ruin of what might have been an Elden church. Wooden beams and sections of stone had collapsed across the wall, smashing it, and tumbling beyond to create a jagged uneven stair. Figures moved on the wall; it wasn't unguarded.

'They'll shoot us down before we get a yard up that wall.' Tantony put his hand on his sword hilt.

Kesta shook her head, biting her lip. 'I'll try to move them.'

She drew up her magic, sending wind toward where the fires danced close to the Chemmen warriors. Azrael caught her intent, and he threw his own power into the flames so that they burst upward in a conflagration of sparks and smoke. The warriors cried out in alarm, beaten back by the sudden intensity and heat. Kesta grabbed Tantony's arm and ran for the rubble. They only had a small window until the fire died down and the warrior's night vision returned. They scrambled up it, pausing to help each other and almost blindly jumping over the wider gaps. The heat was at times barely tolerable and several times Kesta burnt her skin on stone that was still deceptively hot.

Relief surged through her as her feet touched ground. A scream pierced their ears and even Tantony shuddered.

Azrael squeezed up from between two blocks of stone. 'Thiss way.'

Steeling herself, Kesta called up her *knowing* again, although this time she didn't cast it out so wide. Several times she sensed the approach of warriors and they were able to duck off the street before they were seen.

Then their luck ran out. Four warriors came bursting out of a house further ahead, laughing and staggering; one still swigging from a jug. Tantony tried the nearest door, but it was firmly barred. They rushed to the next one.

'Hey!'

Kesta froze. She turned to face the oncoming men, placing one hand on Tantony's arm. She switched off her *knowing* quickly, not wanting to know what was in the hearts of these Chemmen warriors.

'Stay where you are!'

One of the men gave a long, low laugh. He dropped his jug.

Tantony and Kesta instinctively moved apart to give themselves room, and the men recognised them as warriors, sobering at once. Two of them drew swords.

'Look at her eyes,' one of them hissed.

Kesta drew her dagger and sprang at them. She ducked under a sword, kicked out at his knee, and then leapt to put her whole weight behind the foot that landed in his groin. As he doubled over her dagger lashed out and blood sprayed from his throat. Tantony had engaged the other man with the sword; the remaining two, realising this wasn't going the way they'd expected, also drew their weapons. They went for Kesta. She turned and ran, but instead of fleeing she grabbed a post and vaulting around it planted both feet in the face of one of the men. Azrael came at the second, engulfing him in a blaze so violent he had no time to scream. Kesta had landed another kick, breaking the man's jaw before finishing him with a stab to the side of his neck. She ran back to Tantony as he slashed his opponent across the stomach and chest.

'You okay?' he panted.

'Yes, let's get out of here.'

'Who taught you to fight like *that*?'

'Uncle Worvig.' She grinned. 'He says there is no point fighting fair if someone wants to kill you.'

'I'd like to meet this Uncle Worvig.'

They got off the main street and, once Tantony gained his bearings, they headed toward the docks. Several times they had to change their route because of fires and larger groups of warriors.

'Sss.' Azrael came close. 'There are several necromanssers in the biggest inn! One of uss has been peeping, but they have lain trapss for drakes!'

'Sounds like Promise Inn.' Tantony wiped the soot and sweat from his face. 'It's certainly the most luxurious place to stay on Mantu although not particularly fortified. If they are cocky enough to think the town and harbour are theirs despite not taking the fort, then I can see why they might set up there.'

'I imagine it will be heavily guarded and not by drunks.' She tried to ignore the ache in her bones and the tiredness of her muscles. Her throat was still tight from smoke and her lungs heavy. 'Do you know the inn; can we get inside?'

'There is a way in. The barrels are delivered into a yard at the back where there's a hatch down into the cellar. There's a porch above the cellar right up against the fence. You can climb straight from the street onto the porch roof and from there into the window of one of the rooms.'

'How do you know that?' she asked.

'I was a young man once.' He smiled wistfully. 'I imagine the yard will be guarded, maybe the street too.'

'I'll look,' Azrael offered.

'What of the traps?' Kesta frowned. 'I don't want you to get caught.'

'I'll be very careful, Kessta.'

He shot off before she could argue further.

'Come on,' Tantony urged. 'It isn't much further, but we'll come very close to the docks.'

Several times as they approached the inn Kesta's resolve almost faltered. This was stupid, she knew it was. The three of them against an army of Chem. The town's desperation battered at her *knowing* and she thought of Rosa and little Catya back at the hold. If the necromancers weren't stopped, they would share the same fate as the women here. If she didn't break the trap ... she drew in a sharp breath at the intensity of feeling blue eyes and a shy smile brought to her soul. It was crazy, she still barely knew him.

No more than lust for a handsome man, she told herself.

But she wanted to know him with every fibre of her being.

Clenching her fists, she moved closer to Tantony. He was checking the way ahead was clear, pressed up against the edge of a building. She could smell the brine of the sea with the ammonia tang of sewage. She forced aside her doubts and pressed courage toward the Elden warrior as much for herself as for him.

'Okay.' He turned, and she could feel his breath against her cheek. 'The way to the inn is mostly clear.'

'Mostly?'

'There are two warriors guarding the alley. They are at the far end watching the main street and looking bored. We have to assume there are more in the yard. If ...'

She felt his concern. Concern for her.

'Tantony, I am a *walker*, I can take care of myself.'

His face softened, and she had to look away. 'That doesn't mean I wouldn't blame myself if anything happened to you. I *am* trying to forget that you're a woman and treat you like a warrior. I am. But I can't forget that you mean something to ... um ... Northold and the Thane. Anyway, Rosa would kill me if I came back without you.'

'She'd kill *me* if I came back without *you!*' She grinned. 'Enough of this soppy nonsense, get on with your plan!'

Tantony scowled. 'Okay then. I'll lift you up so you can get up onto that roof, then I'll go take out those two guards. You'll have to get into the window of the inn without being seen. When I can I'll follow, and we'll go from there. We may end up on our own. If that's the case, then we should both try to get back to the boat and wait there for the other.'

Kesta swallowed. 'I agree.' She looked around, Azrael had disappeared again for the moment. 'Let's get this done.'

Tantony took a last look and then ran out into the alley. He stopped at the fence and crouching he twinned his fingers together to make a step for Kesta. She leapt, letting his strength increase her momentum as her foot landed in his palms. She grabbed for the top of the fence and dragged herself up; below her the Chemman warriors gave a shout of alarm and Tantony drew his sword. Not allowing herself to look, she lay flat to the roof. There were four warriors in the yard. One of them sat snoring in a chair, two were just below her talking softly, the fourth stood with his back to the yard gate, glowering with his arms folded. She thanked the spirits that the distressing sounds from the harbour seemed to drown out Tantony's fight just beyond the fence.

As quietly as she could she inched her way up the sloping roof to the window. It was dark and reflected the flickering fires of the ravaged town.

She edged her fingers along the length of the window frame; it seemed to be locked. Drawing her dagger, she looked for where the latch lay, glancing to check the position of the guards. The latch was down, she would have to smash it.

Her eyes widened as light flared in the room and then subsided to a deep blue. The latch moved upward, and she pulled the window open. Without speaking she gestured for Azrael to go down and help Tantony. The spirit fluttered its concern but went anyway. Not daring to breathe, Kesta put a leg over the windowsill and then another. Looking around the room she saw a man sleeping in the bed. He seemed to be in his late twenties with dark red hair and a beard cut tight to his chin. She could see the fine links of a gold chain around his neck and the edges of an amulet.

A necromancer.

Biting hard at her lower lip she placed a foot on the carpet and put her weight on it. The floorboards gave a long creak. The man didn't stir. Setting down her other foot she padded across to the bed. *This is no time to have a conscience* she told herself. *No time to play fair.* She plunged her dagger down into his heart. His eyes opened wide to stare at her and his hands grabbed for the dagger. She held his gaze as the light faded from his eyes.

Was he the one? Was Jorrun free? She touched the message cylinder beneath her tunic; there was no way for her to know.

She would have to kill more.

She went to the door and opened it a crack. She could hear several voices, some muffled in other rooms, most coming from a room down below. Her heart sank at the enormity of her task. She would have to try to take out every necromancer here until they were all dead, or she was. She dared to open the door a little more and saw that the room opened out onto a landing that was open to the main room of the inn below. Almost at once her eyes found a man with dark hair and blue-grey eyes. He was older than Jorrun with grey in his hair and a wider face; but the resemblance was still there.

He was the one she wanted. She knew it.

A crash from the room next door made her flinch, and she drew back; a woman's sobbing was drowned out by the angry shouting of a man. A light scuffling behind her told her that Tantony was on his way.

'Azra?'

'Here, Kessta.' the spirit bobbed in through the window.

'Can you get into the room on the right and make sure the door is unlocked so I can get in?'

'Yess.'

'I'll be a moment!' She opened the door again and checking the hall was clear darted to the next room. She tried the door and found it *was* open. She stepped confidently in and shut it behind her at the same time as Azrael materialised from a candle making himself ten times his normal size. The woman screamed, throwing herself into the corner and covering her head with her arms. The man tensed, calling up power. Kesta threw her dagger, but the man deflected it aside with his magic. Azrael tried to engulf him but was held back by a fierce wind that swirled in through the window. Kesta lunged, grabbing for the man's arm. He snatched at her wrist to subdue and control her, the skin on skin contact was enough. Kesta poured her fear into him, every doubt, every moment of despair. The man curled up like a dying spider, his grip so tight that she cried out. She pushed the pain of her wrist to his heart and his eyes bulged. He released her and, panting, she ran for her dagger. He struggled to his feet, gripping his chest. She stabbed her dagger through his hand and between his ribs.

They both crumpled. Tears tickled their way down Kesta's hot cheeks. She shuddered at the sticky blood on her hand and wiped it on the bed.

'Kessta!' Azrael bobbed anxiously.

'I'm all right.' She took in a sharp breath and got unsteadily to her feet, swallowing against the nausea. She took a blanket from the bed and draped it around the naked women whose skin was black and red with bruises. 'Hey there, little one, brave one,' she crooned as she pushed calm and love through her *knowing*. 'You are safe now, we're here to save you.'

The young woman could not relax nor untangle her limbs, not for all Kesta's gentle magic.

'I need you to help me, beautiful girl. The man who is in charge, the dark-haired one.' The girl shuddered under her hands. 'Which is his room?'

Kesta's heart made several rapid beats before the girl stirred. 'On the next level. At the end.'

'Thank you.' Kesta kissed the top of her hair. 'Now get dressed. Go to the room next door and you can escape through the window and down the alley. You are stronger than you know. They can't break you.'

Kesta filled her with as much courage and strength as she could muster, knowing that it would never be enough to heal what had been done.

Closing off her *knowing* so that the woman couldn't feel it, Kesta let her rage build and consume her. These people would never, ever, conquer the Fulmers or Elden, not as long as she breathed.

Pushing the woman before her she went back to the first room to find a startled Tantony there. Without a word the battered woman crawled out of the window.

'I know who has Jorrun and where his room is.' Kesta grabbed Tantony's bloodied hand. 'We need to go there and wait.'

'Could we just find this trap and get out of here?'

Azrael hissed.

Kesta wrapped her hatred around herself to build a shield. 'No. He dies.'

They waited until they were sure the hallway was clear again and then hurried for the stairs. One Chemman opened a door as they passed and Tantony stabbed him through the belly, pushing him back in his room and closing the door. The room at the end was locked, but Azrael slipped a flaming arm into the lock and manipulated the tumblers. They were in. Kesta's heart pounded in her ears.

The room was neat and looked unused, making Kesta's hopes plummet; but then she saw a chest placed at the end of the bed with a robe draped over it.

'So, what would this trap look like?' Tantony asked.

'A box,' Azrael crackled.

Kesta went straight to the chest and flipped it open. It contained nothing but clothes and a short sword. Kesta buckled it to her belt with a shrug at Tantony. They checked under the bed and in the one chest of drawers; nothing.

'So, we wait.' Kesta sighed.

'They'll find those dead bodies sooner or later,' Tantony warned her.

She scowled at him and sat herself on the bed. With a sigh Tantony positioned himself to one side of the door.

***

It was only about half an hour until they heard movement in the hallway. Tantony straightened up and Azrael withdrew into the fireplace. The door swung open and a dark shape moved into the room. With a splutter and hiss the fireplace burst into flame and the man stood looking at Kesta in the flickering light. He laughed, making her skin crawl.

'Well, well; I thought I'd have to search Elden and the Fulmers to find the woman he dreams of. How good of you to come to me.'

Her eyes widened at his words and her stomach turned in disgust, this man shared Jorrun's features and yet was so much not him. She didn't bother with her *knowing*, didn't let her eyes leave his face and give away Tantony who took a tiny step forward.

'Where is the trap?' she growled.

'Straight to the point.' He grinned 'Such a shame you're wasted on the wrong master—'

'I have no master!' She showed her teeth as she leapt from the bed, dagger in hand. Tantony lunged with his sword, only to go flying across the room and smash against the wall with a wave of the necromancer's hand. Azrael burst from the fireplace but was pushed back at once by a strong gale that made his flame gutter. The necromancer caught Kesta's wrist with viper speed and twisted the dagger from her hand. He threw her to the bed and pinned her down with his weight. Terror made her muscles go to water, but she fought it to try to call something useful to her *knowing*.

'I'm going to enjoy showing Joryn this,' he said into her hair. His breath smelt of spicy meat.

With a roar she pushed up with all her strength, gaining enough room to get her teeth to his neck and bite as hard as she could. He locked a hand around her throat and ripped his flesh from her grip. He punched her hard in the face with his free hand while she gasped and choked for air. Bright light flared behind her eyes and her consciousness swam away and back.

Azrael shrieked, the curtains and the edge of the bed caught fire as he battled against the necromancer's wind. Tantony gave a groggy shake of his head and tried to drag himself up against the wall.

Kesta brought her knee up but there was no strength behind her attack. She tried to feed her fear to him, but she couldn't focus.

'I won't kill you, don't worry about that.' The necromancer's grinning face was just above her own. 'You are much too valuable. You'll be tattooed with forbidding runes to restrain your power.'

She called the wind. The window blew inward showering them all in glass. She called on the earth. Hundreds of rats in every cellar, in every sewer, pricked up their ears and heard the call to come; come and fight. She called fire. His clothes began to smoulder, and he leapt up to counter her magic with his own. As soon as his weight lifted, she drew the short sword and plunged it up under his ribs. His weight dragged her down to her knees as he collapsed to the floor.

'Kesta!' Tantony crawled toward her, trying to get to his feet.

She couldn't find her voice, couldn't bring herself to move.

Tantony grabbed her arm and pulled her to her feet. 'Azrael ... Azrael, we have to get out!'

The drake blew the door to the room open and Tantony dragged Kesta out into the hall. He grabbed her by the chin and looked into her eyes. 'Don't you dare go weak on me now, lady!'

Kesta shook herself, her ears ringing. She squeezed his arm, and they raced along the hall to the stairs and down. From below came shouts of alarm and squeals of fear.

'The rats.' Kesta grinned.

'What? Come on!' Tantony led them back to the room they'd first entered. Another cry went up within the inn.

'Fire! Fire!'

'Ow!' Kesta's hand went to her chest as something burnt her. She fumbled at the message cylinder and pulled it out from under her tunic. It was glowing and scorching to touch.

'Kessta!' Azrael darted about joyfully. 'He is back'

'What?'

'You did it, Kessta! Jorrun iss back! You must find water, quick! Quick!'

She looked about the room and saw a jug and washing bowl. She poured the water in.

'Do we have time for this?' Tantony demanded through gritted teeth.

'The blood! Three drops!' Azrael said urgently.

Kesta fumbled at the cylinder and after opening it, let three drops fall into the water. She drew in a sharp breath as Jorrun's image appeared before her, distorted by the ripples of the blood as they settled and stilled.

'Jorrun!'

'Where are you?' he demanded. His face was pale, his eyes bloodshot.

'We are in Promise. We killed—'

'Get out of there,' he said angrily. 'Get out of there now!'

'There are people here still fighting, we can't abandon them.'

'You can't take on the whole God's damned Chem army!' He hit the water with his fist, causing Kesta to step back. 'Get yourselves back to Taurmouth!'

'You're in no position to lecture me about taking stupid risks.'

'I'm not arguing with you, Kesta, meet me at Taurmouth.'

The water went dark. Kesta threw the bowl across the room. 'Of all the arrogant—'

'Kesta, the inn is on fire!' Tantony frantically indicated the window.

She let out a cry of frustration but followed Azrael out through the window and across the roof to the alley. Dawn was just beginning to seep past the burning horizon.

He was alive. She swallowed, landing in the alley and wrapping one arm tightly around her body. Jorrun was alive.

Chapter Eighteen

Osun: Covenet of Chem

Osun chewed at his nails, staring into the water and following the familiar lines of the runes in the bowl. It was the fourth night in a row that he'd tried and failed to contact his master. Anxiety gnawed at his stomach as well as the traitorous thought that perhaps he was free. If his master was unable to contact him, then the Elden King would never be able to find him; he could finally have his own life.

But his master was also the only person in the entire world who his life meant anything to.

With a growl he stood up and tipped the water back into the jug. He placed the scrying bowl back in its chest and he paused to regard the vials of his master's blood. They had dwindled hugely over the years. It had always been intended that he return to Elden before it ran out. He wondered if he would ever set foot in that heathen land again.

He jumped down from the wagon and tied the canvas shut. He thought he might have got used to the awful smell by now, but it still churned his stomach. He was sure his clothes must stink of rotting flesh by now.

Inside the inn a few guardsmen sat around a table, two of them gave Osun a friendly nod.

'Master Osun!' The innkeeper, Gulden, came hurrying toward him. 'Some good news at last! These fellows here tell me that word has come from Lord Adelphy that he'll be here tomorrow! The Overlord of the Covens has opened up his house for him by all accounts.' He scowled. 'It's a shame he didn't make some amends for my loss of trade by staying here.'

'Your inn is certainly worthy of accommodating a coven lord.' Osun commiserated. Silently he cursed his luck. He'd hoped to get close to the necromancer but there was no way he could gain access to the palace. Even if he did, it would be suicide; there would be servants and slaves there who might recognise him. He touched his long beard. He had worn the soft face of a child when he'd fled with his master.

'Still, we should be rid of those things soon.' Gulden gestured toward the door. 'And not a moment too soon.'

'You think they'll be heading out to finish our conquest of Elden soon? It must be going well then.'

Gulden shrugged and looked at the guardsmen.

'We don't get told anything.' One of them spat on the floor and Gulden gave a horrified gasp.

Osun tried to hide his own disgust. 'Will you have to go on the ships with the dead?'

He winced as the guardsman went to spit again but the man caught Gulden's expression and thought better of it. 'Nah, thank Monaris. It's home for us when this lot are shipped out.'

'Well, all the best to you.' Osun politely took his leave and went up to his room. Milaiya had already gone to bed; he didn't blame her. For the first time, he wondered if she got bored being trapped in the room while he went out around the city. He told himself that it wasn't his concern and that it didn't matter.

***

He got up early the next morning and, going down to the wagon, picked out some of the new items he'd acquired that had been looted from the Borrows. He added some cloths and metal polish to the crate and took them back up to his room. Milaiya was standing by the table using his left-over water to wash. She quickly covered herself.

He dumped the crate on the bed and without looking at her said, 'Give these a good clean.'

'Yes, master.'

With a glance at her he went back down for his breakfast, as always, he struggled to eat much with the God's cursed smell from the creatures outside. Several of the things had fallen over since he'd come to the inn and lay unmoving where they'd collapsed. It occurred to him that he'd never seen any flies despite the stench and the slow rot. He went outside and watched them for a while, confirming his observation. By rights they should have been crawling with maggots – his breakfast nearly came up at the thought – but there wasn't even the buzz of a single fly. Just like the birds and the rats, no living thing wanted to be near.

He shuddered.

So, where would he most likely get a glimpse of Adelphy Dunham? The man liked to be worshipped so there was no doubt he'd make a show of his arrival in Navere. The main gate would get him a view but probably little chance of any information. Would he come to the marketplace to inspect his creatures? Very likely, but he wasn't going to discuss his business with the guardsmen or with Gulden. For all his bluster he doubted the innkeeper would dare approach the coven lord, let alone ask him when he'd be on his way to Elden.

Where else might he go where he might ask questions or be questioned? The last two ships had arrived from Parsiphay two days ago; surely Adelphy would want to check them over and see if they were ready for his use? He'd watched them being loaded with supplies, including long coffin-like crates. He'd seen no fresh goods taken aboard as yet.

Did he dare simply follow Adelphy? Would his warriors notice one merchant in the crowd trailing them and think it odd? They might.

It occurred to him that with his master missing he might even be doing all this for nothing. Concern crawled through his intestines. What had happened to Jorrun? As much as he dreamt and plotted his freedom he'd never been without a master. First his own father, Dryn Dunham – although it had been Jorrun's mother, Naderra, who had secretly commanded his love and loyalty – and then his half-brother. Even as a small child Jorrun's magic had been astounding. They'd hidden it as much as they could, afraid that Dryn would take him away much earlier than the traditional eight years old.

There had been rumours from time to time that after they'd escaped Dryn had sired another child of exceptional skill on a woman with Elden magic in her blood. Quinari was the name that was whispered. If it was true, it was not someone Osun had ever seen, and the boy had been hidden away from the common people.

Looking up, he realised he'd made his way toward the palace. He stared up at the place where he'd been born. He should have died there too; the child of a coven lord with no magic in his blood was worthless. A waste of resources not to mention a possible threat.

He jumped as someone barged past him, scowling as though it was Osun who had been at fault. He would go to the docks, he decided, and turned to stride off in that direction.

***

He slowly made his way along the stalls and browsed the shops that lined the wharves. The smell of fish was actually a relief from the smell of the marketplace. He'd already traded away all his fresh goods and purchased the few objects he thought he could make a profit from. He found himself standing outside a flesh house. Two women stood in the window, one of them fully veiled to show that they carried virgin stock. The other was stunningly beautiful with hair that was almost silver, and grey eyes. Her eyes looked as dead as the creatures in the market place.

Not for the first time that day ice prickled Osun's skin.

A buzz of excitement stirred the wharves and Osun quickly purchased a fish pastry from one of the stalls and hurried toward the ships. His morning of observation had given him the opportunity to establish who seemed to be in charge of the two warships. He found a spot opposite the main gangplank and leaning up against the front of a shop began to slowly nibble at his pastry. A small crowd surged from the main street onto the wharves, swaggering warriors yelling for them to move. At the centre of it all Adelphy Dunham strode with an air of disinterest. His eyes fell on the ships and a covetous smile grew on his face, showing just a gleam of teeth.

A huge man with wild mousey hair hurried down the gangplank and reached out to clasp Adelphy's wrist. 'Welcome back, Lord Dunham. Please, follow me.'

Osun cursed as the necromancer followed the captain up the gangplank. He should have realised they would never stand about in the open discussing their plans. Perhaps it was just as well his master had vanished, he'd have little to tell him. With a jolt he wondered if that were it; he'd failed to provide warning of the attack on Mantu. Would King Bractius have harmed Jorrun for *his* failure?

He forced himself to breathe and pushed away from the shopfront to wander along the dock, weaving through the curious men who had come to curry favour with one of the most powerful sorcerers of the Coven Seats. He was considering giving up and returning to the marketplace when he heard voices above him. He halted and held his breath.

'She is a good ship, it's only fitting that she conquers Elden on her maiden voyage.'

'When can you be ready to sail?' Adelphy's voice made the hairs stand up on the back of Osun's neck and a growl came to his throat.

'Oh, we are almost loaded. We can take on fresh water and food as soon as you command it and be on our way within hours.'

'Well, I command it! I want to be on my way early tomorrow. We'll get my chattel on-board tonight and the warriors first thing.'

There was a pause. Osun could imagine the ship's captain contemplating having the necromancer's dead 'chattel' aboard.

'You father's attack on Mantu goes well then?'

The captain's voice faded as they moved away from the ship's rail and although Osun strained his ears, he couldn't hear Adelphy's reply.

'Oi, you there! What are you doing?'

Osun jumped up from the crate he'd inadvertently sat on. 'Trying to eat in peace.' He glared at the warrior who had sauntered over and shoved the rest of the pastry into his mouth. He folded his arms and continued to hold the man's gaze while he chewed angrily. The warrior gave him a derisive sneer, not impressed by him at all; but he didn't move closer. Osun swallowed, giving the man another angry stare, before striding off toward the market. The further he got, the easier he breathed.

***

It was two hours before one of the guardsmen rushed into the inn, hissing at his fellows to get out quick as the master was on his way. Osun swallowed down his brandy, trying to drown the instant fear that rose up to weaken his muscles.

'Perhaps the Lord would appreciate some refreshments?' Osun suggested to Gulden as he went over to the window that overlooked the market square.

The innkeeper yelled to one of his servants, 'Get Keppa to warm up some of his best pastries! Fetch some fresh geranna cakes and the best brandy!' He glanced at Osun with a wince, realising he'd given away the fact he hadn't been giving his guest the best.

Osun pretended not to notice. His hand went to his beard. Would Adelphy see through his scruffy appearance, long curling hair, and broken nose to the Dunham features below? Did he dare? A huge part of him wanted to prove his strength and courage by looking the man in the eye; the man who had beaten him as a child. The man whose father had killed his mother.

He wanted to look him in the eye and stab him in the heart.

The guardsmen were all standing to attention for the first time since Osun had come to the marketplace. Adelphy's warriors fanned out around the edge of the space before the coven lord himself showed his face. Gulden was flapping about his servants, rearranging the cakes and checking his crystal cut glasses were spotless. Satisfied, he opened his doors wide and bustled out. Osun automatically put his hand over his nose as the powerful stench wafted in.

'My Lord Dunham.' Gulden beamed, giving a low, sweeping bow. 'Welcome back to Navere. May I offer you some refreshments?'

Adelphy's face wrinkled in disgust. 'How could anyone eat here?'

Gulden's smile crumpled as Adelphy snatched a glass of brandy and swigged it down.

Osun's hatred got the better of his fear and he jumped up and strode out to stand beside Gulden. He gave a begrudging bow, saying as he did so, 'Lord Dunham, it's an honour to meet you.'

Adelphy looked down his nose at him, his lip twitching in distaste. 'And you are?'

'Osun, master.' Oh, how that word choked him inside. He had only one master, a man worth ten of Adelphy. A man who was missing. 'Just a humble merchant. I came to admire your great work of magic.' He pointed to the undead.

Adelphy laughed, making Osun's bones crawl out of his skin. He became very aware of the dagger on his belt, heavy against his hip.

'Oh, this is nothing.' Adelphy's hazel eyes glinted and the already tall man seemed to grow even taller. '*This* is magic!'

He raised his hands dramatically to head height and a glow seemed to form about his fingers. At once all the terrible, pitiful, creatures in the market place began to stir. No life came to their dead eyes, no sound came from their rotting mouths, but they twitched and moved; the fallen ones getting to their feet.

Gulden gave a shriek and ran for his inn which seemed to delight Adelphy. Osun refused to budge and Adelphy's eyes narrowed. He regarded Osun more closely.

'Alas, that my blood is so poor.' Osun sighed, dropping his eyes. 'That is amazing.'

Adelphy seemed satisfied. 'We could have conquered Elden long ago had the old covens not been so afraid of necromancy,' he complained.

'I wish you luck on your conquest, not that you need luck. I ... I imagine that once you have taken Elden there will be many great opportunities for those willing to put themselves forward.'

'There would be indeed.' He looked Osun up and down. 'Come and see me when I am sitting on the Elden throne. I like a man with ambition – just not too much ambition. The bloodless have their place.'

'Indeed, master. You honour me.'

'Yes, I do.' With a sniff Adelphy turned to concentrate on his creatures, bidding them to head toward the dock. The warriors and guardsmen hurried to follow them although they needed no herding. Without a glance at Osun, Adelphy Dunham walked casually away, cutting straight through the undead without flinching.

Osun let the air out of his lungs and clutched at his stomach, bending forward as though he'd been punched. His muscles loosened and tingled with pins and needles and his vision blurred a little. Then he drew himself up straight, and a smile grew into a wide, almost manic grin. He hurried back inside the inn to throw himself into a chair.

I faced down Adelphy!

I faced down Adelphy.

'You all right, master?' Gulden asked. The innkeeper still looked shaken.

'I could do with another brandy, brother. It doesn't need to be your best, just strong.'

Gulden nodded.

***

Four times Osun tried to scry to his master before he gave up and went to bed. He lay wakeful and eventually got up and went to the window. The smell of the creatures was beginning to subside. He couldn't help but contemplate Adelphy's offer. As much as he hated the man an opportunity to get out of Chem and set up with some influence and power in Elden was tempting. But then what would be the point of going to Elden if it was to become another Chem? That thought was chilling.

He gasped as he felt heat against his skin.

It couldn't be!

He fumbled for the amulet that held a small vial of his master's blood. It was warm!

Elation lent him speed as he threw on a shirt and dragged up his trousers, taking the stairs two at a time. He paused to check no one was around before heading to his wagon and pouring water into the scrying bowl with shaking hands.

'Master?' He leaned low over the water, willing the image to form, to see those startling eyes.

'Osun! You are safe?'

'Yes, master!' His relief was overwhelming. His master didn't look well though, his eyes were bloodshot. 'What happened to you? I have been trying to speak to you.'

His master closed his eyes briefly. 'I was captured, brother, held in a dream by Karinna.'

Osun ground his teeth together.

'Brother, Karinna is dead.'

Osun sat down hard; missing the crate to land on the floor and bruise his coccyx. He almost knocked over the scrying bowl and he grabbed it quickly, barely daring to look back within.

'He is really dead? You killed him?'

The hint of a smile played about his master's mouth. 'No, my wife killed him.'

Osun stared at him incredulously. A woman had killed Karinna? The justice of that felt so perfect. He pulled himself together. 'You have a wife?'

His master laughed, and Osun's own mouth stretched upward in a smile, his heart tingling with warmth.

'Yes, I have a wife. But Osun, Mantu is overrun. They fight still and with Karinna dead they have a chance to turn things around—'

'Master!' Osun interrupted quickly. 'Adelphy sails today. He has only a few hundred of his dead creatures, but he brings all the warriors of Chem! It is to be a full-on assault with … with new warships.'

He held his breath while his master put his hands together and tapped at his lip with his forefingers. 'Osun, this gives me an opportunity that I think I must take. Are you still in Navere?'

'Yes, master.' He saw Jorrun wince at that title, but he couldn't help using it.

'Stay there. I think I will be coming to join you.'

'You're coming to Chem?'

'Yes. Yes, I think so. I think it's about time someone succeeded in killing our father.'

Osun's mouth opened in shock.

'Brother, I have to go ...'

Chapter Nineteen

Jorrun: Kingdom of Elden

Jorrun cursed as he heard voices and the heavy tread on the stair that could only be the king.

'I'll speak to you soon, brother, look after yourself.' He drew his hand across the water and staggered across to the bed only moments before Bractius came bursting in.

'Jorrun!' He looked his friend up and down. 'You escaped?'

He shook his head. He couldn't believe how exhausted he felt considering he hadn't moved in days, almost a week. His body still trembled. He hid his face in his hands, trying to stop the pounding in his head. His skin felt as though it were burning, his eyes stinging and dry. It had been a living hell, forced to face his worst fears over and over while Karinna prodded and poked at his mind. There was no reprieve, no sleeping, no break from the horror and heightened emotions. He pressed the heels of his hands into his eyes to stop the tears and looked up to face his king.

'You defeated the necromancer?' Bractius demanded again, pulling a chair around to sit close.

'No.' Jorrun sighed, looking up. 'Kesta killed him.'

'Kesta!' Bractius barked a laugh. Just as quickly his expression clouded. 'How did you let yourself be captured? I thought you were stronger than the other sorcerers of Chem?'

He tried to sit up straighter but had no strength in his muscles; he really didn't need this now. He needed his friend, not the king. 'Strength isn't the problem.' He gestured around the room. 'Knowledge is. All I know is the little my mother taught me and what I've read in books—'

'Well, thank goodness the witch knows what she's doing.' Bractius stood up and went to the table, picking up a book and then throwing it down again. Jorrun winced. 'And we've had an offer from the Icante to come here and discuss her fighting the necromancers for us. I have of course accepted. It's embarrassing that our great country has had to accept aid from the people who a few weeks ago were begging us for help! Especially when we boast the strongest sorcerer of our three nations.'

'I'm sorry—'

'The Icante also said she has killed the necromancer hiding out on the Fulmers. Name was Relta.'

'Dryn's oldest son, my half-brother,' he whispered.

'His son?' Bractius looked shocked. 'Well, I don't imagine Dunham will let that pass.'

'Actually, Dryn was never that fond of Relta. He always favoured his cousin's boy, Adelphy, more.'

'I need to get back to Taurmaline and start preparations to receive the Fulmer delegation. Ayline has announced she is pregnant, so she is too busy fussing about to concentrate on her duties properly.'

'Congratulations—'

'And I need to keep up to date on what is happening on Mantu. There's at least half a day's delay in messages getting to me here!'

'Your majesty.'

Jorrun's use of his title in private annoyed him enough that he paused to look at him.

'Kesta killed two other necromancers so the undead army is reduced. She told me they are still holding off the Chemmen on Mantu; the island isn't lost yet.'

'Is she still on the island?'

'No, she's on her way back to Taurmouth.' He hoped she was. He prayed she'd listened to him. He swallowed, trying again to sit up.

'Shame,' Bractius grumbled. 'She sounds like she is more use there than my whole damned army. It's a pity you didn't breed me a few more sorcerers before now.'

Jorrun froze, his eyes widening as he clenched his hands into fists and the heat of his skin increased with his heart rate. He watched Bractius pace back and forth, making the tower room feel far too small.

Jorrun cleared his throat. 'There is something else.'

'Well spit it out!' Bractius spun around to glare at him.

'I've spoken to Osun. Adelphy Dunham is on his way with the entire Chem army. They leave today.'

'Gods, Jorrun! Anything else I should know?'

He shook his head, realising he was breathing hard. 'Only … I think I should go to Chem.'

'What?' Bractius was incredulous. 'The whole Chem army is coming here with this Adelphy and you want to go to Chem? Isn't Adelphy their strongest sorcerer next to Dunham himself?'

'Allegedly so,' he replied slowly. 'But think about it. With his strongest allies out fighting this war for him it would be the ideal opportunity for me to get to Arkoom and … and kill my father.'

Bractius sat on the edge of the table, frowning heavily.

'Kill Dryn Dunham and the whole of Chem falls into disarray. There'll be a scramble for the Seats. Adelphy and the others will have to rush back to Chem or risk losing everything. Dryn is the key but none of the Covens dare stand against him. We *should* dare while we have this chance.'

Bractius shook his head. 'He won't have left himself completely unprotected.'

'Of course not. He might be looking for plots and rebellion from the other Covens, but he wouldn't expect Elden to attack him in his own home.'

'You really think you could take on Dryn? After your recent failure against Karinna?'

Shame burnt the skin of Jorrun's neck. 'We could end this war with one stroke. At least let me head to Taurmouth. If you decide against me going to Chem I'll be in position to meet Adelphy wherever his army sets down.'

Bractius let out a long, loud breath. 'I'll think about it.' He got up and went to the door. 'Jorrun, I'm glad that you're okay.'

Jorrun's shoulders sagged as Bractius's footsteps moved away down the stairwell. Moments later a very light knock was followed by Rosa's anxious face.

'May I come in?'

He forced a smile and nodded.

'You won't turn me into a raven or anything?' she asked as she made her way over to the fireplace.

The reminder of Azrael's absence stung, but he laughed anyway. 'No, Rosa, I won't.' With a groan he lay down.

'How do you feel?' She swung the kettle over the flames and then kneeling beside the bed, tentatively took his wrist to feel for his pulse.

'Not good.' He grinned, closing his eyes.

'Catya has been demanding to see you.'

'Not yet!' He placed his free hand over Rosa's. His nightmares nipped at the edges of his mind. 'Not yet.'

Rosa nodded and got up to make him some tea, adding what he guessed to be willow bark. 'Do you think you could eat?'

He grimaced. 'I'm not hungry.'

'Would you try?'

He sighed. 'I suppose I should.'

'I …' Rosa approached him slowly, carrying the tea. He opened his aching eyes to see the worry and fear on her face. He couldn't help but think that Bractius would be pleased; everyone was supposed to be afraid of the Dark Man.

'It's okay, Rosa.'

She glanced at him and then sat in the chair the king had recently vacated.

'I didn't mean to pry, but I heard you mention that you had spoken with Kesta?'

He realised that she must have been waiting outside the door and had heard everything that had passed; he turned away, placing a hand over his eyes. 'Yes. Her blood in that cylinder allowed me to speak to her.'

'She is safe?'

He wanted to say yes, but in truth he didn't know. 'I hope so, Rosa. I commanded her to get to safety in Taurmouth.'

'You *commanded* her?' Amusement lit her soft brown eyes.

Jorrun chuckled. 'Yes.'

Rosa stood and placed the tea down on the chair. 'Please try to drink this, you're very dehydrated. I'll go and make you some soup and be back shortly. If you're going to go and meet Kesta you'll need to get your strength back.'

He nodded but couldn't find the energy to reply.

Kesta. Raven hair, forest eyes. Kesta.

***

He awoke to find light streaming into the tower. Above, the ravens were scratching about on their perches and glancing up he saw that two of them were eyeing him from the open window.

'I threw food out for them, but they seem intent on watching you.'

'Rosa.' He turned over in the bed to face her. 'How long have I been asleep? Is it still today?'

'Just a few hours.' She crept closer to peer at him. 'You're still very dehydrated. How's your head?'

'Unfortunately, still on my shoulders. Ow!' He clutched at his stomach.

'Cramps?'

'That or I swallowed a live raven and that's why they're glaring at me.'

She snorted at him, trying to remain serious and not laugh. 'Raven or no, I need you to try to eat some more.'

'And I thought Kesta was the nag.'

'Kesta cares about you.'

He couldn't reply to that. Kesta and Tantony had gone racing across Elden to face the Chem army alone to save him. She was supposed to hate him. She *had* to go back to the Fulmers.

'Thane?' Rosa needled gently. 'Eat something?'

He looked around himself and, realising his dilemma, Rosa spotted a shirt and handed it to him. It was wonderfully clean and smelt of his favourite jasmine and cinnamon. As he slipped the shirt on, he paid attention to his room for the first time, realising that Rosa had carefully cleaned it, preserving all of his things in their places as much as she could. He didn't deserve such kindness.

'Is the king still here?'

Rosa scowled as she handed him a bowl and spoon, a cloth beneath it to protect him from the heat. 'Yes, he is still here.'

Of course, she'd seen a side to Bractius that he rarely showed in public. 'He is just worried about his people; he was right to be angry with me.'

She didn't reply, diplomatically keeping her thoughts to herself.

'Would you do something for me?' he asked. 'I need to take a ship to Taurmouth; tomorrow if possible. Did Kesta and Tantony take my ship?'

'No, Kurghan took them.'

'Really?'

'Oh!' She stood up so suddenly he thought she'd burnt herself. Reaching into a pocket in her skirt she pulled out a tiny scroll. 'Kurghan sent a message addressed to me. Um, Kesta left me in charge. Kurghan wrote to say he is staying at the Green Inn and hopes that Kesta and Tantony will rejoin him there.'

'Nothing else?'

She shook her head.

'All right. Thank you. Get my ship ready with a small crew and I'll eat this soup. Would you let Catya know I would love to see her this evening?'

'Of course.' Rosa gave a small curtsy as she took her dismissal. She looked at the bowl.

'I'm eating it!' He laughed, putting the spoon in his mouth.

She smiled back and quietly left the room.

***

His stomach seemed to settle after he ate the soup and he soon found that he was ravenous. He heated up another bowlful while selecting a few things to put into a travel bag. He picked up two books, one on dream-walking and the other on necromancy, and put them in his bag. When he finished the soup, he took them back out again and sat looking at them. There was every chance they would become lost or damaged if he took them to Chem. He laughed at his own foolishness; he would risk his own life but not his precious books! He put them back in the bag. He could always leave them in the cabin of his ship when he'd finished studying them again.

He managed to get a little more sleep before the light creak of the floorboards woke him. It was quite jarring to have all the coming and going in his once private tower. However, when he saw who it was, he couldn't help but smile.

'Catya!'

'Jorrun!' She ran over and threw her arms around him in a hug.

Physical contact was such a rare thing for him, the Dark Man of the Raven Tower. Like the invasion of his rooms, it was both disturbing and comforting.

'I thought you would die!'

The girl was crying.

'No, Catya, I was just in a deep sleep.' The muscles of his chest squeezed inward and dark images whispered at the edges of his mind. He stroked Catya's hair and swallowed against the tightening of his throat.

'Rosa said you were trapped in bad dreams.'

He tucked a strand of her long brown hair behind her ear and took a moment to compose his reply. Nightmares were something Catya could definitely relate to. It had taken him months to turn her dreams to more pleasant things. It had been her dreams as a tiny child that had warned him of what her uncle was doing to her.

'Yes, I was trapped in bad dreams, but we know how to beat them.'

She nodded. Oh, how he wished it had been true. Would he ever have the courage to *dream-walk* again? His heart pounded even at the thought of it.

'Rosa says you're leaving tomorrow.'

He nodded. 'I'm going to find Kesta and Merkis Tantony.'

'I should come, then; I'm Kesta's bodyguard.'

'Hmmm.' He tried not to smile, not wanting to seem to mock or doubt her in any way. 'Well, the problem is, I need someone to protect Rosa and help her look after the hold while I'm gone. And there are the ravens. Someone needs to feed them and look after messages. Only you and Rosa are allowed in the tower.' He watched her as she thought it over.

'I want to go and help you and Kesta.'

'I know. But it would be a huge help to me to know the ravens are being looked after and that I don't need to worry about the hold.'

'All right.' Her shoulders rose in a sigh. 'I'll guard the tower.'

'Thank you. There's one other thing I need you to help me with. Will you help me eat all that food you brought up, so Rosa doesn't tell me off?'

She laughed. 'Okay!'

***

Bractius came up just before darkness set in. Catya scampered out of the room, her face hidden under her hair. The king looked somewhat contrite, although Jorrun didn't believe it for a moment.

'You look better.' He went to stand by the window, looking out rather than at Jorrun. 'I thought about what you proposed. With the Icante and her *walkers* coming here I think I can spare you for your reckless plan. One more magic user here probably won't make much difference; but if you take out Dunham it certainly will. Head to Taurmouth. If there are no different instructions from me waiting for you when you get there, go on with your plan.' He turned around to regard Jorrun. 'Do you need me to leave someone here to take charge of Northold?'

'No, Merkis Tantony and Kesta will come back to do so.'

'You intend to go to Chem alone?'

'With Azrael. If he can bear to cross the sea.'

Bractius grunted. 'Well.' He crossed the room and offered his hand to Jorrun who took it quickly. 'Be careful.'

Jorrun nodded.

'I'll be leaving for Taurmaline in just a moment.' Genuine concern seemed to crinkle the corners of his eyes for a moment as he looked Jorrun over. 'I hope that I'll see you again.'

Jorrun took in a breath. 'I will do my best.'

***

As much as he didn't want to say goodbye to Catya, he knew it would be unforgiveable of him to sneak away without doing so; especially as he might never come back. He was proud of how composed she was as he hugged her and then walked away up the small wharf to his ship. His own self-control was another matter and he excused himself that it was his recent captivity and torture that had left him feeling so emotional. Even so, he managed to throw a wave toward Catya and Rosa before ducking down into the safety of his cabin.

He pulled a book out of his bag but couldn't muster the concentration to read the words on the pages. Before he realised it, he was back on his feet and heading for the deck. They had already moved out onto the lake and were steering for the river that bled from it. Looking back across the forest he could see the top of the Raven Tower, a single bird lazily circled it. It looked dark despite the dawn light touching its windows.

He went back into the cabin and found a candle and calling a small flame to the tip of his finger he lit it.

He set the candle in the window.

Chapter Twenty

Kesta: Mantu, Kingdom of Elden

Kesta jumped down into the alley behind Tantony only moments before warriors from the inn burst out of the gate in front of them. All of them froze; except Azrael who expanded at an amazing velocity to ten times his size, pulling the most frightening face he could muster. The guardsmen fled.

'Come on!' Tantony grabbed Kesta's arm and pulled her out into the street.

'We can't just leave! What about all the people?'

'Jorrun's right, we need to get out of here while we can. We may have pushed our luck too far as it is.' He shoved her into a doorway as a large group of men came running toward the inn.

'It doesn't feel right,' she whispered.

'I know.' Tantony looked her in the eye. 'But you've given them a chance. Besides, how many times have you been angry at Jorrun for risking himself unnecessarily? How do you think he would feel if you got yourself killed?'

'He'd probably be relieved,' she muttered. 'But point taken. The way feels clear.' She leaned out to check with her eyes. If anyone still lived on this street they were staying well out of the way.

Azrael appeared before them. 'Thiss way.'

He led them down a narrow side road, pausing at the end before darting out into a wider street and then down another narrow alley that divided the backs of several small yards. The sounds from the inn grew steadily further away as the dawn light grew stronger.

'Maybe we should hole up until tonight,' Tantony suggested anxiously.

Kesta hesitated. Staying in the town might also give her another chance to kill some more necromancers.

'No, come on.' Azrael darted about like a crazy moth. 'We are nearly at the hole in the wall.'

With a glance at Tantony, Kesta pushed away from the wooden fence to follow after the spirit. It took them only five minutes to reach the collapsed church. Most of the fires were out, but the rubble looked treacherous. They checked the walls but could see no warriors.

'All gone to fight the assassinss at the inn.' Azrael crowed. 'Quick now!'

They scrambled up and over. Twice Kesta slipped and was only saved from hurting herself by Tantony's quick reactions and strength. She'd never felt so battered and exhausted in her life and with a sinking heart, she recalled the hike to the west coast and the descent down the stairs still ahead of them. Tantony was limping quite noticeably as they ran for the cover of the nearest trees.

'We need to rest,' Kesta panted, looking at the fire-spirit appealingly.

'Not ssafe yet. And Azra needs fuel.'

Kesta cursed. She'd left everything for Azrael back in their boat. 'Spirit, go back to the boat and get the coal and oil there. We'll be with you as soon as we can.'

'No, I can't leave you.'

'Yes, you can.' Kesta told him. 'And you can make sure our escape route isn't cut off.'

The drake flickered and spluttered.

'Go on,' Tantony urged. 'We'll be right behind you.'

The fire-spirit moved away slowly and then shot off like a shooting star. Was that what the outside of a *walker's* fire vortex looked like?

Without a word Tantony set off at a jog.

***

They stopped to rest for an hour beside a small stream once they'd cleared the open meadowland. They'd only spotted one dead warrior still moving but had come across several collapsed on the ground and buzzing with flies. Kesta caught Tantony regarding her anxiously.

'What?' she demanded.

'That looks pretty sore.' He pointed to her cheek and then looked down at her throat.

She raised a hand self-consciously. 'Just bruising.'

'I'm sorry that ... I should have stopped him.'

She felt her eyes begin to sting and drew in a long, steadying breath. When she swallowed, it hurt. 'He was a sorcerer, Tantony. You couldn't have stopped him.'

'I'd never have forgiven myself if—'

'It's okay.' She slapped his arm. 'We're both okay. Come on, let's get down those spirit forsaken steps before I lose the will to face them.'

He grinned, pulling his twisted knee around with a groan so he could stand up.

***

They found Azrael peeping over the edge of the cliff waiting for them. He flew up as soon as he saw them and Kesta was pleased to see he looked brighter and more fiercely blue toward his centre. She stared down the long steps with a feeling close to despair.

'I'll go first,' Tantony offered. 'It would be better for you to slip and fall on me than the other way around.'

She snorted a laugh. 'At least we'd get down quicker.'

Tantony set a slow, steady pace. Despite the fact they'd not seen anyone for a while Kesta couldn't help but keep looking over her shoulder expecting them to be discovered at any moment. When they finally reached the bottom, she let herself sag onto the shingle.

'I never want to see another step again.'

'That will please the Thane, his wife staying out of his tower.'

She was too tired to do anything but pull a face at him. 'Thank the spirits the boat is still here.'

Tantony rubbed at his forehead and looked out to sea. They couldn't see far out past the high cliffs of the cove. 'I'm not sure what's going to be worse, setting out in a small boat in broad daylight where anyone can see us, or waiting here until nightfall.'

Kesta stood up, sliding and crunching across the shingle to join him. 'Would they bother with a small boat? Surely they would assume we are just refugees fleeing the island and prefer to concentrate on winning here?'

'You're probably right.' Tantony frowned. 'Come on, let's get it in the water. Any chance of calling your fish friends?'

'Dolphins,' she corrected with a frown. 'We'll have to get out a bit first, but I'll try.'

They pushed the boat down into the surf, jumping in as soon as the sea took its weight. Kesta grabbed her spare shirt and shredded it with her dagger, wrapping strips around her hands.

'Need any?' she asked the warrior.

He glanced down at his own rough hands. 'Wouldn't hurt.'

She threw him the cloth, fighting hard to keep them from being pushed back up onto the beach until he was ready. She shook her head. Yet again their planning had been poor, but she hoped they might still get away with it. Despite the fact the tide was against them it didn't take them long to get out beyond the shelter of the cove. In daylight, the sight of the wreckage they'd passed in darkness was shocking. Gulls screeched and squabbled over the bloated bodies that floated among blackened barrels and beams. It seemed as though the ship had gone down in flames and then been smashed to pieces against the rocks. They set the sail and Kesta used her waning strength to call a wind to push them away from the coastline. They could see plumes of black smoke rising from the south of the island.

'Haven,' Tantony said, his eyes distant.

Kesta couldn't let herself think about the people still fighting there, the guilt it brought was too huge. Instead, she leaned over the edge of the boat to touch the water, sending out a call for help. She gasped, slipping back into the boat and curling up in a ball as a blinding headache hit her, making her stomach heave.

'Kesta?' The boat rocked and Tantony's large hand settled on her shoulder.

She felt ashamed at the whimper that escaped her lips and curled up tighter against the pain.

***

She awoke to a deep, dark-blue sky with strands of wispy white cloud. Stars were beginning to blossom and for a moment she gazed at them, allowing a feeling of peace to seep into her battered body. She realised they were moving far quicker than they should be and sat up. Tantony was sitting at the rudder and looked up when he saw her move.

'They came.' He smiled. 'Your dolphins.'

She stood with trepidation, getting a feel for the movement of the boat before stepping over a seat and taking Tantony's offered hand. She sat beside him and then searched around the boat with her eyes.

Tantony pointed beneath him. 'Azrael is in the lantern,' he reassured her.

She settled in her seat, smiling as she watched the pod of dolphins swimming alongside them, three of them holding ropes in their long mouths. Up ahead a towering mountain of rock loomed, growing steadily closer, crowned with shaggy seagrass and a few battered shrubs.

'What's that?'

'That is the first of the two pillars,' Tantony told her. 'They're almost as big around as Lake Taur, but so high and inaccessible that no one lives on them. It means we are about a third of the way to Taurmouth.'

She slumped a little in her seat, slowing her breathing and scouring the horizon. 'Have you slept?'

'Not yet,' he admitted. 'But I'll try now if you don't mind?'

'Of course!' She moved aside to let him pass, holding to the side as the boat tipped a little. He made himself comfortable between the seats and mast, stretching out his bad knee.

Night deepened as they reached the passage through the middle of the rugged natural monoliths. The dolphins stopped, dropping the ropes and carrying their heads out of the water to peer at her with their intelligent eyes.

'You have to go,' she understood. She pushed her gratitude and affection toward them with her *knowing*. They chattered at her in their own complicated tongue and then with several leaps and splashes headed back out to sea. Trying not to wake Tantony she unfurled the sail, setting it as best she could to catch the wind and head them toward Taurmouth; it was south-west from their position from what she recalled of maps. Her skin prickled with cold and she drew the lantern out from under the seat and put on her coat. Azrael had made himself tiny, no bigger than a candle flame.

'Are you all right in there?'

Azrael made a mewling sound. 'I hate being over the ssea!'

'Even for us humans it can be disconcerting. Keep me company for a while?'

Azrael flashed his agreement. They watched as the stars multiplied, and the pillars grew slowly smaller behind them.

***

'There!' The relief and joy were evident in Tantony's face as he pointed to a busy looking town just a few miles further along the coast. 'Taurmouth!'

Kesta tried to stretch her cramped muscles. Her throat and cheek still throbbed. She couldn't help herself; she called up more wind to speed them toward the harbour.

'There are still ships here.' Tantony frowned. 'They haven't been sent to help Mantu.'

Kesta glanced about with trepidation. Warriors lined the harbour walls and ran drills on the three largest warships. The people of the town seemed subdued, fearful even.

'Something is happening.' Her voice came out quietly.

'Let's get to the inn and see if Kurghan has any news.'

They tied the boat up and paid the harbourmaster. The ground felt odd under her feet, and her legs didn't quite seem to want to work the way she wanted them to, as though she were drunk.

They asked after Kurghan at the inn and were told he'd gone out and hadn't yet returned. 'He's kept a room for you and your husband, my lady,' the innkeeper said. 'Your friend received a message here just this morning that the Thane was on his way.'

Kesta's heart leapt and then continued to beat rapidly.

'Shall I show you up?' He looked with puzzlement at Kesta's lamp. Although it was heading toward evening, it was far from dark. 'Will you be taking one of the other beds in your friend's room?' he asked Tantony.

'Yes, that's fine. I think we'd both like a bath and something hot to eat,' Tantony replied.

Kesta enthusiastically nodded. 'No meat for me, though.'

'Ah, of course.' He regarded her mismatched eyes and flushed when he realised he was being rude. 'Follow me.'

Kurghan returned shortly after they'd settled in Kesta's room to eat. He looked as though he'd been running. 'You're alive!' He closed his eyes and shook his head at the tactlessness of his outburst. 'I saw my boat in the harbour and came straight back here. What news?'

Tantony stood to clasp his wrist.

'They were still fighting on Mantu when we left,' Tantony told him. 'But Kesta killed their leader.'

Kurghan turned to look at her, he hesitated only a moment before moving to clasp her wrist with a grin. 'I knew you'd done something as I received word from the Thane. He should be here by tomorrow afternoon.'

'What did he say?' Kesta asked, trying not to show any emotion as excitement rushed through her blood.

'Just that he was on his way.' Kurghan shrugged. 'There's more news though. Apparently, there is a huge fleet on its way from Chem carrying thousands of warriors. We're expecting to be invaded and soon.'

Kesta's emotions changed so suddenly it was as though someone had opened a pit beneath her for her to fall through. She looked at Tantony.

'That will explain why Mantu has been left to struggle alone.' Tantony clenched his jaw. 'It sounds as though we may have been lucky to get back here without running into them.'

'A lot of people have started to leave the coast.' Kurghan winced. 'Can't say I blame them.'

Kesta looked down at her food. Was Jorrun coming here just to take them back to Northold? She doubted it. It was more likely he was coming here to fight.

***

The day was dragging with frustrating slowness. After a night of fitful sleep and startling dreams, she'd got up early to walk to the harbour and back. Tantony and Kurghan had gone off to the marketplace and Azrael was skulking in the fireplace, having only come out to grab a piece of coal. Her nervousness was grating on her own nerves. Her anger at Jorrun had long faded and instead had been replaced with a ridiculous desire to see him that clawed at her belly and made her feel almost light headed. She hadn't felt this obsessed with someone since she'd been a foolish teenager.

She sat at the window and watched the people pass to and from the harbour. There were noticeably fewer than the day before and the majority of boats seemed to be heading up the river. She wondered how many refugees Rosa might be asked to take in.

She caught her breath. An unmistakable figure was making his way toward the inn with the confidence and assuredness of a cat. Dark clothes, dark hair, but oh so piercing eyes.

She leapt up and ran down the stairs to the front of the inn, stopping when she reached him with her heart pounding. She hesitated only a moment before putting her arms around him, she bit her lower lip, feeling his warmth. One of his hands tangled in her hair.

'You're here.' He breathed.

She pulled back a little to look up at him and was shocked when he leaned down to kiss her, tentatively at first and then with such passion she could barely breathe.

'Let's get off the street.' He grabbed her hand and led her inside the inn. He paused at the stairs and she didn't allow herself time to think or even look at him before guiding him up them and into her room.

She turned to face him, her heart thrumming loudly in her ears, and he reached up to touch the side of her jaw carefully with two fingers. 'Who did this?'

'Karinna.'

His eyes narrowed, but he nodded.

Shyness that had never been hers crept over her, but she stepped closer, holding his gaze. She realised she was trembling. She rose up onto the tips of her toes and placed her hands on his shoulders to kiss him again. His arms went around her, his fingers digging into her shoulder and hip and she closed her eyes, losing herself in the feel of him. She stepped toward the bed but instead of moving with her he grabbed her by the arms and pushed her away from him.

She stared at him in shock, lightheaded from the fast flow of her blood.

His face had reddened. He looked ... angry.

'Kesta, there is something you should know.' He searched her eyes, still holding tightly to her arms.

She swallowed, unable to speak, unable to look away.

'Bractius ...' she could see the muscles of his jaw moving as he clenched and unclenched his teeth. 'Bractius came up with an awful plan some years ago, before his father had even died, that I should ... that I should have children, in the hope that they would also be sorcerers, so that Elden would have more protectors against the rising danger from Chem. I told him that I found the idea reprehensible, disgusting even; that he would be turning Elden into Chem. The idea never left him though. He talked of marrying my children into the royal line to create powerful kings and loyal magic users. I always tried to laugh it off as he never pushed me. One time, when he was drunk, he even suggested that I get Ayline pregnant so that he could have a magical heir. I told him he was an idiot.' He paused, looking away and then back at her.

He let go of her, but she still couldn't move.

'You should have seen her face. She was there when he said it, Ayline. I thought he'd forgotten all about it until you and your father arrived at Taurmaline. He saw it as his chance to tie us to a country in a way that would be mutually beneficial against Chem ... as well as to advance his plan to bring magic back to Elden. As I told you, we argued, and he threatened me. Things have been ... strained between us ever since.

'I won't do it to you, Kesta. I won't do this to myself. I'm not a Chemman.' He looked away again, taking in several breaths. 'You need to go back to the Fulmers.'

She opened her mouth, but no words came out. Every beat of her heart seemed to shake her. She blinked, her vision blurring although her eyes were dry.

Without another glance he turned and fled the room.

Kesta stared after him, feeling cold, feeing hot. She was trembling, her body still aching for him even as shock drained the blood from her. Her feet wouldn't move so she sat down on the floor. She drew her knees up and bit hard on her thumb as pain welled up from deep inside her forcing release through her eyes.

He was protecting her from Bractius's awful plan, protecting himself from becoming something he hated. He was protecting any children he might one day have had. She was shocked by the horror of it; that his so-called friend would demand such a thing from him knowing his past. And it hurt her pride that he'd walked away.

Her hands were shaking almost violently, and she drew her arms in even tighter. Had she got it so wrong? How had she let her guard down and allowed herself to feel so much? She lowered her head onto her knees, squeezing her eyes shut, feeling sick.

But he did have strong feelings for her; she'd felt it through her *knowing*. He had kissed her first. And she ... yes, there was no doubt, she had strong feelings for him too. Part of her knew she was being foolish. She hardly knew him, not the real Jorrun. The fact he could make her body tingle from head to toe with just a look was one thing, but was what she was feeling for him, genuinely about *him*?

He kissed me first.

But what did this mean for them?

Because of Bractius, Jorrun would never allow any romantic or physical relationship between them.

She drew in one, sharp, desperate breath, as though surfacing from under the sea, and cried harder than she had in many years.

***

Someone knocked at the door and reluctantly she stood up. She'd washed her face and managed to calm herself, finally falling in to a groggy sleep. Her lungs still ached, and her throat burned. Poor Azrael had fluttered around her several times, unable to touch her and at a loss as to what to do. In the end he'd gone back to hiding in the chimney. She'd gone over everything in her mind so many times she felt dizzy.

She drew in a breath and opened the door. Tantony's eyes widened when he saw her red swollen eyes. 'Um, Kurghan and I just got back, and the innkeeper says Jorrun arrived. Apparently, he asked for another room.' He shuffled his feet awkwardly. 'Lady … if he has said something to upset you then I'll put him straight about what you did for him on Mantu.'

Kesta couldn't help but smile at the idea of the Merkis putting the Dark Man straight.

'It's okay, Tantony; if anything, I upset myself. I'm just really tired.'

He grimaced in sympathy. 'I know that feeling. The innkeeper has put aside a small room for us to talk in and have something to eat if you want to come down?'

'Yes, I'll come.' She quickly brushed through her hair and then called up the chimney for Azrael. The fire-spirit came out and found an unlit candle to settle on. Kesta picked it up and followed the Merkis down the stairs.

Kurghan was already waiting for them and Kesta caught him exchanging a glance with Tantony when he saw her face.

'I got the best wine I could,' Kurghan said quickly.

Azrael flared up on his perch on the candle. 'Three things Jorrun lovess! Wine, bookss and—'

'Bug!' Jorrun interrupted as he stepped into the room.

Azrael darted backward in mock startlement.

Jorrun didn't look at Kesta, going straight to Tantony to grasp his wrist and give him a brief hug. He turned to shake hands with Kurghan and then sat down, pouring them all some wine.

Kesta watched him with her eyes narrowed, she gritted her teeth and her nostrils flared. She couldn't believe he was pretending nothing was wrong and that nothing had happened between them. She felt her anger rising. There was a momentary flicker of emotion on his face as he caught her eyes when he passed her a glass. He avoided her fingers.

'Azrael has told me what happened in Mantu,' he said quietly, swirling the wine in his glass. 'Thank you all for freeing me.'

'It was mostly Kesta.' Tantony shifted in his chair. 'Has there been any news from Mantu?'

'The latest is that they are still fighting. Elden still holds Haven. It might become a matter of who has the most supplies unless we can get ships out to them, and with Adelphy on his way we have none to spare.'

'Do we have a plan?' Kurghan asked.

Jorrun drew in a breath and dared to regard Kesta. She didn't look away as his eyes flickered over the bruises on her cheek and throat. 'The Icante is coming to Elden. She's meeting with Bractius and they'll plan our defence. The *walkers* will be key to defeating Adelphy.'

Kesta almost ground her teeth at the thought of her mother meeting the Elden King. Dia didn't know what he was really like, didn't know what he'd done to Jorrun; and to her.

'Kesta, you will of course go back with Tantony and Kurghan to Northold. It is between you and the Icante as to what part you will play in defending our lands. Perhaps you should go back to the Fulmers if she is here?'

'And what are you doing?' she demanded.

He looked down at his glass and she saw him swallow. 'I am going to Chem.'

'What?' She sat up straight. He'd spoken so quietly she thought she must have misheard.

He steeled himself to hold her angry gaze. 'I am going to Chem to kill my father.'

'Not without me you're not!'

'Kesta, there is no way I would let you anywhere near that place.'

'Then I'll go back to Mantu and finish what I started there.'

'Kesta!' He leapt up, his eyes blazed, and his cheeks burning red.

Tantony and Kurghan flinched. Had they ever seen their Thane lose his temper before?

She stood, leaning forward over the table, her own anger a cold knot in her belly. 'I am going with you, or I am going to Mantu.'

'Kesta, I really don't need this from you now.'

'Actually, you do!' She gripped the edge of the table so hard it hurt the joints of her fingers. 'You know if you go to Chem alone you're never coming back. But then you would rather just throw your life away than dare to care about anyone else and risk losing them!'

He took a step back, blinking twice but not looking away.

Tantony cleared his throat.

The anger faded from Jorrun's blue eyes and they softened in a way that made Kesta swallow. 'You don't understand what might happen to you if you go to Chem.'

'Yes, I do.' She pointed to her throat. 'But if you don't succeed, then Elden might become Chem, as will the Fulmers. Will my being here make that much difference to the defence of Elden? Possibly, but most likely not. Will it make a difference to your chances of defeating your father? You know it will!'

'I can vouch for that.' Tantony dared to speak up. 'I don't particularly want either of you going to Chem, for what my opinion's worth, but I'd rest easier and have more hope if you went together.'

Kesta tore her eyes away from Jorrun and sat down.

Jorrun also sat and steepled his fingers as he silently regarded his Merkis.

'At least think about it,' Tantony suggested. 'Let me get some more wine, I have a feeling we all need it.'

Jorrun nodded.

'What about me?' Azrael detached himself from the lantern on the wall in which he'd hidden and came to hover above the middle of the table. 'I sshould definitely go with you, Jorrun. For your mother'ss sake.'

'You hate being over the sea, Azra,' he said gently.

'But I do it, don't I, Kessta? Sometimes you have to endure thingss you hate, to do what iss right; even if it hurts.' The drake turned himself a dark fierce blue. 'Don't you, Jorrun?'

They all watched the Thane as he contemplated Azrael's words. He turned to Kesta. 'Very well, you may both come.'

She almost retorted that she wasn't waiting for his permission, but she bit her tongue. Jorrun stood up to leave, but Tantony put a hand on his shoulder. 'Stay. I'll go get that wine.'

'How was the work on the hold coming on when you left?' Kurghan steered them toward a safe topic.

Kesta studied Jorrun as the five of them quietly talked of the hold and of their fears for Elden late into the night. He rarely looked toward her and avoided catching her gaze, but when he did his ice eyes were far from empty.

***

The next morning, they said farewell to Kurghan and Tantony, the two of them heading back to Northold. Kesta squeezed Tantony tightly.

'Thank you for coming with me to Mantu. You'll look after Rosa and Catya for me?'

'Of course,' he replied gruffly.

They clambered into Kurghan's boat and Jorrun untied it from the dock. They watched them for a while, the dock itself almost empty.

'I have a few things to arrange before we go,' Jorrun said. 'I'll see you back at the inn.'

She nodded but sat by the waterside for a while watching the river flow by. She was nervous about going to Chem but was she quite scared enough? It wouldn't be the first time her over-confidence left her flat on her face. A mistake in Chem though was likely to be fatal. It was the right thing to do, of that she was sure, and not just because of Jorrun. She still felt shame at fleeing Mantu and leaving the people there to their unknown fate.

When she returned to the inn, she looked over her small supply of now battered clothing. She set about washing everything and trying her best to patch it up. She didn't have any money, and she wasn't about to ask Jorrun for any. She and Azrael were messing about drying her things with wind and flame when a loud double knock startled them. Reaching out her *knowing* she felt no one there and immediately tensed.

'Jorrun,' she mouthed to Azrael. The drake moved out of sight but didn't vanish when she opened the door.

He came straight to the point. 'I have everything arranged. We leave this afternoon. Is there anything you need me to get for you?'

She glanced back at her things. 'No, I think I have all that I need. Oh! Unless I would be able to take a bow?'

'You couldn't carry a bow in Chem; even I couldn't. But it wouldn't hurt to have one on the boat. I'll get you one.' He stood there awkwardly for a moment. Kesta resisted her urge to invite him in. 'Get something to eat and then meet me at the ship in a couple of hours.'

He left without waiting for her agreement.

***

When she got to the boat, she found Jorrun stowing some things in the cargo hold. She handed him the lantern in which Azrael hid and then jumped across, managing to keep her balance. Jorrun looked from the small bag she carried to her, but said nothing.

'Where are your crew?' she asked, realising they were alone.

'I bought them passage on another ship back to Northold.'

She nodded. The ship was small enough to be managed by the two of them; one if necessary.

'Will you tell me your plan?'

In answer he gestured with his head for her to follow him into the cabin. She'd never entered it before, having stubbornly remained on the deck with Rosa on their wedding day. Had that really been less than a month ago?

Jorrun put the lamp down. She looked around the room. There were three windows which were presently all shuttered. A table stood at the far end and took up most of the room. It was covered in writing implements, books and odd artefacts. It reminded her at once of his room in the Raven Tower. A single narrow bed was pressed up against the wall to the left.

'I'll sleep on the deck,' he said, following her gaze.

She shrugged, choosing for once not to argue. He reached over to pick a sea chart up off the table and unrolled it for her to see. 'The Chem fleet are sailing from Navere, they have no reason to do anything but come straight south toward Taurmouth now that they're mounting an all-out attack. We will aim to avoid them by heading here, through the Borrows.' She watched his finger as he slid it across the parchment. 'We'll leave the ship at the Borrows and go on with the boat we are towing. Osun is to find us a safe place to land. From there we go with his wagon to Arkoom.'

'Won't the Borrows be guarded?'

He shook his head. 'From what Osun told me they were decimated, then abandoned.'

Kesta sat down hard on the chair, looking up at him with her eyes wide. The Borrows had always been the enemy of the Fulmers, but the deaths of all those people and the destruction of a society didn't bear thinking about. Blood drained from her fingers and lips.

He moved so that he could look her directly in the eye. 'Are you sure you have to do this, Kesta? You're not just doing this because—'

'I'm doing this for lots of reasons,' she broke in, saving them both from treading on difficult ground. 'All of them right.'

'Did you remember my coal?' Azrael popped out of the lantern, making them both jump.

'And your oil, bug.' Jorrun smiled. Then said seriously, 'Shall we go?'

Kesta nodded.

***

Their journey was awkward at first. Although she had more experience of sailing, Kesta swallowed her pride to accept that this was his boat and therefore he was the captain. Whenever he asked her to do something she did so at once. She didn't push him into conversation either; she wanted him to feel safe being himself again and come out from behind his shield of the Dark Man. She was treating him like a wounded animal; she didn't imagine he would be pleased at such a comparison.

She caught herself watching him too often and determined to keep her attention on the horizon and any potential danger.

She sensed it when he called up wind. It felt different from when a *walker* used their magic. The wind he stirred up was strong but lacked control and direction, missing the subtlety of a practiced *walker*.

'May I ...' She bit her lower lip.

'What?' He lost concentration, and the wind whipped away from the sail and out across the sea.

'Could I show you how *I* summon the wind and maintain it?'

A slight scowl settled on his face, but he nodded. 'Go on.'

She agitated the air with one hand and stilled it with the other, subtly adjusting the intensity of each until wind swirled around her in a gyre.

Steadying its direction, she filled the sail, finding and maintaining a perfect balance.

'Did you feel the difference?' she asked, still concentrating.

'I think so.' He let go of the rudder to move closer, watching her hands.

'You *are* very strong,' she said without turning. 'I think you could probably learn to call storms like my mother. The way you use wind is great if you want to blast someone across a room, but for sailing you need to be subtler and you have to measure your endurance. Do you want to try?'

'Maybe later.'

She realised that he was embarrassed at the idea of failing in front of her.

'How does your mother call storms?' he asked.

She ceased her magic and turned to face him, her wind slowly dissipated. 'You need to generate heat where there is moisture and create a large rain cloud; really large. I could never quite manage it.'

'I can do fog.'

'Fog?' she asked excitedly. 'I don't know anyone who can call fog, how does that work?' She adjusted the sail to catch the natural wind and sat down.

He still seemed wary, as though expecting some kind of trap from her; she supposed she couldn't blame him.

'Dew is good, or the ground just after rain,' he said slowly, looking out to sea. 'Rivers are too tricky, and the sea is difficult, but a lake works well. You heat the water gently, like a warm summer sun, and then you pass a cold wind slowly over it.'

'Who taught you that?'

'An Elden witch. In a book.' The slightest of smiles played at the edges of his mouth and Kesta's muscles relaxed a little. She smiled in return.

'I shall have to spend more time in your library.'

A shadow fell across his face and she cursed herself for saying the wrong thing.

'There are some books in the cabin, you're welcome to read them.'

Before she could even think of saying thank you, he'd moved away to take up the rudder again.

***

They took turns that night keeping watch and keeping the ship on course. They also ended up taking turns using the bed in the cabin. When Kesta got into it, it was still warm and smelt of Jorrun. Vindictively she hoped he'd found the same from her and that it tormented him just as much. Unable to get to sleep she got up to look at the books.

'Are you all right in there, Azra?' she asked the lantern.

'I don't feel good,' Azrael replied, the lamp growing dimmer.

'Would you like some coal?'

'No.'

'Do you want me to get Jorrun?'

'No! He will jusst say that he told me sso!'

She snorted. 'Yes, he probably would. Is there anything I can do?'

'Would you read to me, Kessta?'

'If you turn that lamp up a bit so I can see.' She ran her fingers over some of the books. 'Do you want *The Witch Trials of Elden*, *Herblore of Chem*, or *A History of Elden Magic*?'

'*Elden Magic*, please!'

Kesta settled on the bed and opened the book while Azrael crept out of the lamp.

***

They settled into a still somewhat uneasy routine over the next two days, one of them steering while the other kept watch. Jorrun had got better at summoning wind to the sail and she guessed he'd been practising while she slept.

On their third night out from Taurmouth Jorrun came into the cabin to wake her.

'My turn?' She stretched like a cat.

'We've reached the Borrows. Can you take over for a moment while I speak to Osun?'

'Of course.' Her stomach tightened into a knot. They were at the Borrows already? She laughed at how quickly Jorrun darted out of the room when she sat up to grab her tunic.

'We're close to land now, Azra.' She tried to reassure the drake.

Jorrun was waiting just outside the door, his cheeks still slightly flushed. 'Would you use your *knowing* to feel for anyone nearby?'

She nodded, clambering past him to check the sail and take the rudder. The stars were mostly hidden from view and it took a moment for her eyes to adjust. She reached out her *knowing*, feeling the cold rejection of Jorrun's amulet and the slippery spark of Azrael's alien mind. She could feel nothing else but vast emptiness. Slowly a dark shape formed before her, not a single light showing along the length of the Borrow island.

She started as Jorrun came out of the cabin.

'Osun has found us a place three miles west of Navere,' he almost whispered. 'We'll approach it at night, of course, but we will have to leave the Borrows before nightfall tomorrow to be able to reach Chem before dawn. I've been thinking that if we work together, we might be able to create a fog bank to follow us out to sea.'

'We could try it.' She shivered.

'I'll get you a coat.'

'It's not the cold.' She shook her head. 'It's the lack of life on the islands. I should feel something.'

Jorrun's face grew paler. 'Blood magic. Animals hate it. The necromancer's have left its stain upon the land. Not just the humans have fled the Borrows.'

'But it's spring,' she said in shock. 'What of all the nests, the seal pups?'

He put his hand on her shoulder for just a few seconds but said nothing.

She clenched her teeth and snarled. 'The sooner we get this done the better!'

'I'm going up the front; let me know if you feel anything.'

She nodded, even though he couldn't see her.

***

They passed midway between two of the islands and Jorrun came back to take the rudder and steer them around the north side of the westward one. At last Kesta felt the touch of life, a flock of horned sheep; their heightened level of fear was heart-breaking.

'Are you all right?' Jorrun asked.

She forced a smile. The newly rising sun had given his skin a golden tint, making his Fulmer heritage more evident. 'There are some domestic animals on this island. They have no way to escape the unnatural feel of the land. It … is hard for me to feel, but I'm okay.'

He took a step toward her and lifted a hand but stopped abruptly and let it fall back to his side. 'It will fade. Blood magic leaves a stain, but nature heals it in time.'

'Will Mantu feel like this if they win?'

He hesitated but decided on the truth. 'It could. It depends on what spells are cast and … and on the amount of blood that's used. Let's put in here, we should be hidden unless anyone sails in from the same direction.'

They set down the anchor and as always took turns to rest and keep watch; although they both read rather than slept. Jorrun brought some food out for her at midday and sat with her on the deck while he ate his. They didn't speak, but their silence no longer felt uncomfortable. Azrael even dared to come out of the cabin and join them for a while.

Jorrun transferred everything he wished to take with them into the smaller boat and Kesta added her bag. As shadows lengthened Jorrun became restless, and she guessed that anxiety at what they were about to attempt was setting in. It didn't help her own nerves, and she didn't dare try to comfort him in case he withdrew from her again.

'We need to go,' he said finally. 'For sea fog we need to warm the sea and then run a cold wind over it. We'll then need to keep it with us with as long as we can.'

'Well, I should probably balance the wind while you steer us.'

'Agreed.'

He fetched Azrael in his lantern house and stowed him carefully. The boat they'd been towing was somewhat smaller than Kurghan's fishing boat, but it had canvas stretched over the front of it to form a small shelter. Jorrun rowed them to the edge of the cove before they unfurled the sail. Leaning over the side he called up heat to warm the shallows of the sea.

When he felt it was ready, Kesta began to summon a cold breeze from the air. She was delighted when fog began to form and thicken.

It took all of her concentration to keep the fog rising and moving while Jorrun himself created more. She almost missed the brush of emotion somewhere close by. She could feel at least four differing personalities, ranging from fearful to predatory. She touched Jorrun's shoulder and pointed through the fog. They could see nothing, but a male voice came to them, its meaning deadened by the water in the air.

Kesta hardly dared to breathe.

Slowly the presence of the men moved away, and she fought to regain her concentration on the wind. A headache was beginning to creep in and she feared she was coming toward the end of her magical endurance. Jorrun seemed to sense it and he moved up to sit beside her.

'Take the rudder,' he said. 'I'll try to manage the fog from here if you can carry on with just your *knowing*?'

'Thank you.' She almost put a hand on his shoulder to balance herself as she stood, but she stopped herself at the last moment. With her *knowing* open she would have felt what he was feeling. He seemed to realise what she'd done, and his eyes followed her until she sat down again and turned his way.

Night seemed to fall painfully slowly and Jorrun's shoulders were hunched with fatigue long before he let the fog fall away. Kesta insisted he take the first turn at sleeping. He curled up under the canvas, speaking softly to Azrael for a few minutes before his breathing told her he was asleep. She shifted in her seat to relieve the ache in her muscles, rubbing at the bridge of her nose to try to push away the headache. It was a risk, but she switched to using her *knowing* in much shorter bursts and relied more on her eyes to warn her if anything approached. She'd almost drifted off at the rudder when Jorrun stirred and slowly crawled up onto a seat. He stretched and cracked his joints before making his way around the sail to her.

'Your turn. Have you seen anything?'

'Nothing,' she replied.

There was no room beneath the canvas to do anything other than curl up. She snuggled into Jorrun's blanket and used her own arm as a pillow.

***

The shush and hiss of surf woke her with a start. Her head hit the canvas as she tried to sit up and she blinked at the grey light of pre-dawn. She'd slept more than half the night.

She scrambled quickly out and stood to see Jorrun watching her with an amused expression on his face.

'You let me sleep.'

He put a finger to his lips and she spun about to see a low cliff line with jagged rocky feet. The cliffs themselves held a reddish colour, and she spotted a light not far away, set in an alcove so that it could only be seen from the sea. A lantern. He gestured to the rudder, and she took it while he rolled up and tied back the sail. He pulled out the oars but shooed her away when she tried to take one. She sat glaring at him with her arms folded, but he ignored her, a spark of humour in his eyes.

A wave lifted them, and they hit the narrow beach hard, were dragged back out for a moment and then lifted again. A man appeared from behind the rocks, but far from being alarmed, Jorrun jumped out to help him drag the boat out of the water. He was just a little shorter than Jorrun, with wild black hair and a thick beard. His face didn't have the severity of Jorrun's, but the nose and the forehead were the same. His eyes were also blue, but darker; his paler skin held no touch of Fulmer blood.

Jorrun held out a hand to help her out of the boat.

'Kesta, this is Osun.'

Chapter Twenty-One

Kesta: Covenet of Chem

Osun stared at her, taking in her eyes, her clothing, her uncovered face.

'She is my wife, Osun, from the Fulmers,' Jorrun said warningly.

'Of course.' The Chemman visibly shook himself and took a step forward to bow in her direction. 'My lady.' He spun quickly back to face Jorrun. 'It is good to see you, master.'

Kesta tilted her head, Osun's accent was captivating, soft with rolling 'r's.

Jorrun winced. 'It is good to see you, *brother*.'

Kesta studied the two of them, the way Jorrun took a small step forward suggested his wish to hug his half-brother, but Osun stood unmoving and tense.

'Master, we should get up to the wagon,' Osun said.

'For goodness' sake, Osun, my name is Jorrun!'

Osun gave a slow shake of his head. 'Not here, master, not if you're adamant you must reach Arkoom.' He turned to look Kesta up and down again. It made her want to growl.

'Yes, we'd better start looking the part as soon as possible.' Jorrun went to the boat and taking out Azrael's lantern he handed it to Kesta along with her small bag. He buckled his sword belt around his waist, handed a bag to

Osun, and then slung another over his shoulder. 'Did you manage to get everything I asked for?'

'Yes, master.' Osun smiled for the first time, like Jorrun, it completely changed his face.

They made their way along the beach and then up a narrow path that clung to the side of the cliff. It was already starting to get light and as she reached the top she was greeted by the sight of a long valley between high hills on her left and the beginning of a mountain range to her right. Smoke drifted lazily from the flat summit of one of the peaks. It was incredibly green. A wide river shone silver and red where the sunlight caught it in sharp beams that felt their way between the mountains.

She heard Jorrun draw in a breath and she followed his gaze. He was looking at a large settlement at the river mouth.

'Is that Navere?' she asked.

Osun looked at her in shock, then closed his mouth quickly with a glance at Jorrun.

'Yes, it's Navere,' Jorrun replied softly. 'It was the seat of my father. Our father. Where we were born.'

'Do you wish to go there?' Osun asked.

Jorrun shook his head. 'No. No there is nothing there I wish to see.'

'This way,' Osun indicated, his shoulders and jaw seemed to loosen.

Kesta instinctively reached out her *knowing* to check the area around them. Osun was experiencing a tumultuous mixture of joy and fear. Ahead she could feel the peaceful presence of two bovines, the flightier feel of two horses, and the gentle aura of a woman. They found her seated outside a small tent beside a large wagon, rocking gently as she hummed to herself. She was wearing a long green dress with a hood up over her hair and a veil that covered the tip of her nose and her mouth. On seeing them she stood, her eyes widened as she regarded Kesta and she took several panicked steps backward, almost falling into the tent.

'Milaiya!' Osun said in annoyance. 'This is my master. The woman he has brought from the Fulmers. Fetch her the clothing I bought yesterday.'

With a bow, her eyes not leaving Kesta, the woman climbed into the wagon.

'What clothing?' Kesta turned to Jorrun, her eyes narrowed.

'Clothing that will keep you safer than any armour,' he replied calmly. 'In Chem only woman who are available for the use of any man go without any face covering. Women who have not been touched by a man go fully veiled, including their eyes. No one will be able to touch you without my permission, to do so carries a harsh sentence. It's the best way to protect you here and will also hide what you are.' He looked at her mismatched eyes.

'Your permission?' she growled.

'Yes.' He couldn't help himself, he grinned. 'You have to do what I tell you here.'

She punched him in the arm, furious at the same time as trying hard not to laugh with him.

'Master!' Osun gasped in shock.

Jorrun indicated Osun to make his point, his smile not yet leaving. 'See.'

'I think you're enjoying the idea of our disguises a bit too much.' She scowled at him.

His smile faded, and he became serious. 'Our lives will depend on our blending in and playing our roles.'

She nodded. 'I understand.'

The woman, Milaiya, came back out of the wagon and cautiously handed Kesta a cloth bundle. It was soft, a dark blue colour.

'For appearances' sake my lady should sleep in the wagon,' Osun said. He hesitated before going on. 'As your servant I should sleep under the wagon and Milaiya with you in the tent.'

Jorrun, Kesta, and even Milaiya all protested at once.

'Is there room for both Kesta and Milaiya in the wagon?' Jorrun asked.

'If we move things about a bit. I can sell some stock on our way and not purchase more,' Osun thought aloud.

Milaiya and Jorrun both looked equally relieved and Kesta felt her own twinge of jealousy subside.

'Good,' Jorrun said. 'Is it safe for us to stay here and sleep?'

'Well, yes,' Osun said. 'But shouldn't we be on our way?'

'It was not an easy journey here, brother, I think we both only ever slept with one eye open. You are probably right though. Perhaps we could just sleep in the wagon for a while.'

Osun nodded. 'Milaiya, pack the tent away, we'll move on at once. Would you like something to eat and drink?' He offered Jorrun.

'Yes, please.' Jorrun put his bag down and sat beside it on the ground. Osun went to the wagon, completely ignoring Milaiya who struggled with the tent.

'Take that angry look off your face,' Jorrun said with amusement.

With a snort she sat beside him. 'On the Fulmers we help each other.'

'This isn't the Fulmers.'

'Don't I know it already.'

'Kesta.' The seriousness of his voice made her turn, his intense gaze made her heart catch. 'While we are here, I may have to play a role that will not seem very pleasant, but it isn't me.'

'Like the Dark Man.'

He didn't reply but looked quickly away.

Osun brought them both a cup of apple juice and a bowl of dried fruit. Kesta nibbled at hers while Milaiya packed up the camp and harnessed the bulls. Osun tied his newly acquired horses to the back of the wagon and shifted a few things inside to make room.

'We're ready,' he announced.

Jorrun climbed up into the back of the wagon, turning to take Azrael's lamp and then reaching down a hand to help Kesta up. He placed the lantern on a box on a low shelf and then picking up two blankets shook them out and lay them in the narrow space on the floor. Kesta took a staggered step back as the wagon jolted into movement. Jorrun sat on the floor.

'Come on,' he said, lying down, and folding his arms across his chest before closing his eyes.

She crawled into the space beside him, lying awkwardly on her back with her arms pulled in tightly so they didn't touch. *This is stupid, and uncomfortable!* She rolled over to lay her head on his chest and slid her hand across to his shoulder. Almost at once he moved his arm to let her snuggle closer and lay it tentatively across her back.

They fell asleep to the rocking and jolting of the wagon.

***

Kesta waited until Jorrun had left and then slipped on her Chemman clothing. The long dress was a good fit, and she wondered if Jorrun had given his half-brother measurements. She looked at the head covering and veil. There was a panel of blue gauze to go over her eyes and allow her to see. She gripped the fabric and clenched her jaw hard, telling herself that it was necessary. If she and Jorrun didn't succeed, then every woman on the Fulmers would have to wear something like this.

Taking in a breath and sighing it out, she put it on and left the wagon.

They had stopped outside a small town and Osun was bartering away a set of bone handled daggers under the shade of some trees. Milaiya was watering the bulls and Jorrun had climbed up to sit in the driver's seat of the wagon. He'd changed into some baggy trousers and a sheepskin coat.

'Where are we?' she asked.

Jorrun turned to look her up and down. 'In Chem, women are not allowed to speak until spoken to.'

'What?' She clenched her fists and glared at him. To make it worse he laughed. 'I'll get my own back, Thane Jorrun,' she promised, secretly relishing his playfulness.

She made her way around the two long-furred bulls, stroking one and reaching out with her *knowing*.

'They like you,' she told Milaiya.

The woman regarded her with absolute horror, looking up at Jorrun as though expecting him to attack her there and then.

'Oh, for spirits' sake!' Kesta cursed, putting her hands on her hips. 'What now?'

'They don't curse by the spirits here for a start.' Jorrun's face became serious. 'Come on, let's take a walk and I'll explain better how things are here before you get us all in trouble.'

'You should have told me in the first place rather than having fun at my expense.' She sulked.

'Probably,' he replied with no sign of remorse. When they'd moved out of sight and hearing of the others, Jorrun stopped and turned to face her. 'I told you a little of my mother's life. All women here are slaves, Kesta; all. They are treated the same as cattle – as property. They have no rights and no protection except for the laws against theft and damage. I warned you this is an awful place, there is a reason I wanted to keep you away. Chem will break your heart, Kesta.'

She watched his face. Chem had broken his heart, and he'd only been a child. She wanted so badly to put her arms around him. He looked away and took a step back.

She swallowed. 'What rules do I need to follow?'

He drew in a breath. 'Women obey without question. They do not speak – even to other women – in the presence of a man, without permission or being spoken to first. You are allowed to call to me for help if someone tries to touch or take you without my permission. You can only talk freely when there are no men around.'

She folded her arms and reluctantly nodded. 'I can manage that. But only here!' She raised a finger and added quickly. 'And only because I don't want us to get caught.'

'Think of Milaiya also.' He stepped closer, appealing to her gently. 'This is her culture; all she has known. Your behaviour will seem shocking, even dangerous to her. I certainly have no problem with you showing her how things should be; but don't give her false hope or put her at risk. Osun has been to Elden, but she never has.'

'I understand.' She sighed. 'I'll tread carefully. We have enough to deal with here already without me attempting a revolution for women.'

'Thank you. But you'll find it easier said than done; as will I. You know I hope to find a way to change things. Destroying the Dunham's grip on Chem might allow more moderate leaders to step in.'

She nodded. 'I'll trust you in this.'

'Only in this?'

She looked away. She wanted to tease him, to be playful, but it would lead to nothing but frustration and hurt. Because of Bractius. Because of what they were.

'Kesta?'

'We'd best get back to the others,' she said.

***

When they stopped for the evening Kesta took care of the horses while Milaiya unhitched the bulls. Jorrun and Osun sat talking quietly together while Milaiya began to set a fire and bring out food for cooking. When she was sure that no one was watching, Kesta placed the lantern on the step of the wagon and Azrael quickly flew out and away.

She joined the others at the fire, her stomach turning when she saw the array of meat in the pan. She looked up at Jorrun, hoping to catch his attention and wondering how long she could endure this before she gave in and opened her mouth.

He realised quickly something was wrong and saw what Milaiya was doing.

'Milaiya, would you make me and Kesta something without meat?'

She looked surprised, then worried.

Jorrun smiled to show he wasn't angry with her, but didn't explain himself, going back to talking with Osun.

Kesta wanted to offer to help but wasn't sure how to without speaking or startling the woman. She felt guilty at having made more work for her.

When they'd finished eating, Milaiya set up the tent for Jorrun, and Kesta managed to help her clear away the cooking things without getting too much in her way. Osun dismissed Milaiya and the young woman went straight to the wagon. With nothing else to do, Kesta followed. As she climbed up into the wagon, she looked around to see Jorrun watching her, he quickly turned back to Osun.

Milaiya had removed her hood to reveal long, curly, copper hair.

'Hello,' Kesta called up her *knowing* to best assess how to approach her. She felt mostly fear and suspicion. 'I'm sorry if I startled you today. I've never been to Chem before and your ways are very different. I'm from the Fulmers.'

The woman nodded, shaking out a blanket, she hesitated, then handed it to Kesta.

'Thank you.' She tried pushing calm and warmth toward Milaiya, but she just took down another blanket and lay down in the narrow space on her side.

Kesta sighed. This was going to be a long journey.

***

Kesta managed only four days until she broke. Four days with no one to talk to except brief exchanges in the wagon with Azrael. Four days of not being able to ask anything or be a part of any planning. Four days of Jorrun treating her almost as though she wasn't there. She'd never felt so isolated and alone in her life. If anything, the four animals gave her more company than any of the humans. She began to sympathise more with Milaiya and understand her bond with the bulls even as she was annoyed by her prickly refusal of any friendship.

Then it struck her that friendships between women in Chem probably brought their own pain. They could be separated at the whim of a master and they would have to endure watching each other's suffering. She recalled what Jorrun had told her of his mother; that she and Osun's mother had been lovers.

She bit her lip, but she couldn't bear to be silent any longer. 'Would you tell me more about your mother?'

Kesta felt a small amount of evil satisfaction when Milaiya gasped and dropped the spoon with which she was stirring their meal. Both men turned to look at Kesta who lifted her chin and met their eyes. Jorrun gave a loud sigh, and she wasn't sure if the spark in his eyes was amusement or anger. She was surprised when it was Osun who eventually spoke.

'Naderra was very young still when we fled Navere.' He looked down into the fire. Jorrun became very still. 'Not much more than a child herself when she had Jorrun. Her hair was long and black and curled a little at the ends, her skin was paler than yours but darker than Jorrun's. One of her eyes was the colour of mead, the other the colour of a new oak leaf. She was always so full of life, no matter what she suffered. She was always giving us hope, even when there was none. She shone; and our father was both fascinated and terrified by it. And she could do magic!' His eyes lit up, and he smiled at the memory. Milaiya ceased her stirring to stare at him. 'Only ever in front of my mother and us, but she could talk to the animals, light a candle by touching it, and she could give you courage when yours had gone.'

Jorrun got up and walked away from the fire. Kesta moved to follow him but he turned and said forcefully, 'No Kesta.'

She sat back down, watching him with her heart aching.

'You killed the man who killed my mother,' Osun said.

'Karinna?'

He nodded. 'I wish I could have done it, but I'm glad he's dead.' The next words came to him awkwardly. 'Thank you.'

'Trust me, it was a pleasure.'

He snorted and smiled. He was quite handsome when he wasn't glowering.

'I'm, er.' He glanced at Milaiya. 'It is a long while since I was in Elden.'

She realised he was attempting to apologise at his awkwardness.

'It's okay. I should keep trying to obey the rules.' She sighed. 'It's just been, well, lonely and horrible not being able to speak my mind or talk when I need to.'

'I know that feeling.' Osun bit at his thumbnail.

That surprised her, she'd never considered how much the culture of Chem isolated men as well as women. She looked in the direction Jorrun had gone.

'If it's any consolation,' Osun went on. 'Naderra never could bring herself to obey, despite the fact she was born in Chem, neither could Jorrun when he was here. They both suffered for it though. Me, on the other hand, I learnt how to keep out of trouble.'

'Maybe you could teach me to do that.'

'Maybe I could.' He smiled shyly.

***

When she climbed in to the wagon later Milaiya seemed to take longer than usual to get undressed and shake out her blanket. Kesta carefully quested toward her with her *knowing* and felt that, although still afraid, the woman was also burning with curiosity. She set out her own blanket and managed to catch Milaiya's eyes long enough to smile.

'The master … the master said *your* master's mother could do magic.'

Kesta sat down on the edge of a trunk, only glancing at her so as not to be threatening. 'Yes, she could. Jorrun's grandmother was from the Fulmers, like me.'

'You …' Milaiya cautiously sat at her feet. 'You said that the bulls like me. Do you speak with the animals like your master's mother?'

'I do.'

'I didn't know that women could do magic.'

Kesta looked at her frightened, but hopeful, brown eyes. She wasn't going to lie, but Jorrun was right, she should be careful. 'Here, as you know, it's forbidden. In my land, the Fulmers, it's very different.'

They sat until the stars had spun past middle-night, Azrael moving close to the glass of his lantern. Kesta described first the islands, and then the people that she loved there. Her mother, her father, her beloved Uncle Worvig and his dubious exploits. Milaiya sat enraptured by her description of her mother's protectors, Heara and Shaherra. They lay back to back, Kesta could feel the other woman's lungs empty and fill.

'But … these are just stories? Not real?' Kesta felt her hold her breath.

'It's real,' she whispered. 'When you ask me to, I'll show you some magic.'

Milaiya gasped, but she didn't ask.

***

The next day brought their first taste of trouble. Jorrun and Osun rode ahead while Kesta sat beside Milaiya on the wagon and their road took them close to a large town. At the fork in the road that led off toward the town stood a wooden building with a turf roof. A sign depicting a sword and shield swung from the porch and a man, who had been sprawled in a chair, stood on seeing them. He called out and four other men came out to join them.

'Get inside the wagon!' Milaiya whispered to Kesta urgently.

'What's wrong?'

'Guardsmen. A woman of your value wouldn't stay out to be seen by such men.'

With a scowl of annoyance, she opened the canvas behind her and awkwardly clambered through, leaving it open enough that she could see past Milaiya. She reached out her *knowing*; these men were bored and hoping to cause some trouble for their own entertainment.

'Halt, there!' Their leader called out.

Osun stopped at once, but Jorrun walked his horse slowly around his brother to glare down at the men. They grew uneasy.

'Just doing our job,' one of them mumbled.

'Do we look like thieves or bandits?' Osun demanded.

The leader bristled. 'No, but we'll take a look in the wagon, anyway.'

Kesta felt fear from Milaiya and concern from Osun.

Osun got down from his horse, some of the men put their hands on their weapons. 'Come and look then.' Osun sighed, gesturing for them to follow.

Two of the men were whispering to each other and Kesta felt recognition in them and growing tension. They had perceived Jorrun and Osun's Dunham features. 'Ur, Captain!' one of them called out nervously.

'Not now!' he snapped in annoyance, stomping behind Osun toward the wagon. Jorrun continued to glower at the guardsmen while Kesta quickly sat herself down on a chest, checking that Azrael was out of sight. Osun pulled back the canvas and Kesta sat completely still, not allowing herself to look up; much as she wanted to.

'Surprised you don't have guards, carrying valuable cargo.' There was suspicion in his voice.

'Does my master look like someone who needs guards?' Osun snapped. 'Have you finished?'

'Not yet.' The captain climbed up into the wagon just to make a point. He poked at a few things, taking his time. Kesta didn't move.

Eventually he got out and jumped down. 'All right, I'll just speak to your master.'

'Your funeral,' Osun murmured, just loud enough for the man to hear. As they moved past the bulls, Kesta got back up to watch through the canvas. One of the other guardsmen hurried to their captain and whispered in his ear. The man's eyes widened, and his posture altered completely. He marched over to Jorrun and gave a bow.

'Master! I must humbly apologise! I didn't know who you were!'

Kesta snorted; he still didn't.

Jorrun narrowed his eyes at the man and without speaking turned his horse and headed back onto the road. Milaiya clicked at the bulls and followed at once as Osun got back on his horse and pushed it to a trot to catch up. Kesta crawled back out to sit with Milaiya.

Jorrun cursed. 'Are they likely to talk about that to anyone?'

'Sadly, yes,' Osun replied. 'But with most of the covens away fighting hopefully the news won't get to anyone who would wonder who you are. I'll try to keep us away from any other guard posts, but we might still meet the odd patrol, especially as we get closer to Arkoom.'

Jorrun nodded. She wished she could see his face.

***

At night, Kesta continued to tell Milaiya tales of the Fulmers and the little she knew about Elden; knowing that poor Azrael, who was more confined than she was, enjoyed listening too. She was careful not to talk of Jorrun or give away anything of who he was.

'What of you, Milaiya? Tell me of your life,' she said in the darkness.

She felt the woman shrug. 'My mother was just a general slave, like me. She belonged to a master who had a big house in Margith, he was a coven lord but not strong, I think. Not a Dunham. I was trained as a general slave too. I was lucky, my mother had poor blood lines as did the man who lay with her. She said he'd been a visiting trader and my master had allowed him to have her while he stayed.'

Kesta clenched her teeth to hold back her anger and managed to remain silent.

'I was not pretty enough or valuable enough to be a breeder or a skin slave. I was lucky. When I was twelve, things changed. My master was in some kind of trouble with the Seats. He sold lots of us to make money and left Margith. I don't know where my mother went. I was sold to a travelling merchant and learnt how to care for animals. It gave me some happiness. My new master had a breeder, so he left me alone.

'When his breeder's oldest child was of an age to take over my tasks, he sold me to Osun.' She hesitated. 'You will not tell him anything I say?'

'Of course not.' Kesta turned to her.

'He is … he is in some ways a better master than I've had before. He lets me speak to him when we are alone. He has never hit me, not once. He will sometimes buy me things, things just for me, like a cheese that I love. But …'

'But?' Kesta's stomach tightened. She almost didn't want to hear it. She'd started to like Osun, despite his sometimes-sulky nature.

'But he lies with me. I hate it.'

Kesta gasped and sat up. 'He rapes you?'

'What? I don't know that word.' Milaiya was confused.

No, I bet you don't! Her fury grew so that her head pounded, and she could hardly see. *I bet the women here are never allowed to even contemplate the idea of free will.* She got up, flinging her blanket aside and untying the canvas with clumsy fingers. As she jumped out, she recalled that Osun slept under the wagon. She wondered if he had heard their conversation; she hoped he had. She went straight to Jorrun's tent and without hesitation crawled in.

'Did you know your brother forces Milaiya to sleep with him?'

'What?' he rubbed at his face and propped himself up on his elbows.

'You heard!' she snapped, her heart thundering in her ears.

He closed his eyes and breathed in and out slowly three times before opening them again to study her face. 'Kesta, this is Chem. He is a master; she is a slave.'

She stared at him in shock, her cheeks burned as blood rushed there. Had he really said that? She drew in a breath and held it, not blinking, her muscles frozen. 'You are excusing him? You?'

'No.' He sat up and reached toward her, then thinking better of it pulled his hand back. 'No, I am explaining it. It doesn't make it right; but in this land, in this culture, what he has done isn't wrong.'

414

She shook her head, sitting back on her heels and pressing her nails into her palms. She felt sick. Rage was clawing its way up from her stomach to her throat. Tears spilled from her eyes and she furiously wiped them away with her fingers. 'I want to kill him!'

His voice was so gentle when he replied it hurt to hear it. 'I understand. I hope you don't kill him. He is my brother and we need him. We can't change what has been, nor what is, but we can influence what will be.'

'For too many people it will be too late.'

'Yes, and that's hard to endure.'

She looked at him, his eyes darker than usual within the tent. She wanted so much to feel his arms around her at the same time as having an overwhelming desire to scratch his beautiful eyes out. Why did he have to be so reasonable? She growled at him and turned away to wipe her face again. She forced words out through her constricted throat. 'I'll try not to kill him. But I can't not hate him.'

He nodded, his eyes searching her face.

She held his gaze for a long time. With another exasperated growl, she crawled back out of the tent. She couldn't face Milaiya, couldn't deal with what had been done to her. For nearly an hour she paced up and down the camp, one moment swearing she would kill Osun, the next losing her resolve and re-sheathing her dagger. The skin around her eyes was sore and her throat raw by the time she returned to the wagon, getting in and tying the canvas shut behind her.

'Are you all right?' Milaiya whispered.

'No, not really.' Kesta wrapped her blanket around herself and reaching out she found Milaiya's hand and squeezed it. Her heart still raced, and she had to force herself to calm down and breathe slowly. Logically, she knew that Jorrun hadn't betrayed her, but her heart felt as though he had.

***

They met three patrols the following day, despite approaching Arkoom along less travelled roads. Kesta had mostly remained either in the wagon or with Milaiya on the driving seat. She'd completely avoided Osun; if he had noticed he hadn't shown it. She'd observed Jorrun frequently watching her. Without her *knowing* she wasn't sure if it was because he was worried about her or scared that she really would attack his half-brother. She still wasn't sure how she felt about his calm and reasonable reaction; he was right but *so* wrong at the same time in her opinion. Hadn't he killed a man for hurting Catya?

The patrols had mostly ignored them although they received some curious looks and occasionally someone seemed to startle as they saw resemblance to the Dunhams in Jorrun's face.

That night, as they camped, Kesta tried to put aside her anger and disgust and came cautiously to the camp fire, sitting as far away as she could from Osun. He smiled at her, but she couldn't bring herself to return it. Her *knowing* brought her his hurt, his own anger, and his unwanted shame. She quickly shut it off.

'Tomorrow we will reach Arkoom,' Osun said.

'We cannot go on as we are.' Jorrun threw some of the food he'd been eating into the fire. 'I'm too recognisable as a Dunham. Perhaps if I dressed as a servant rather than a master?'

'That might be an idea.' Osun nodded.

'And at least you would stop calling me master at last.'

Osun grinned at him. Kesta had to look away.

416

'What should we expect in Arkoom?' she asked.

'I've never been,' Jorrun replied.

'Nor I,' Milaiya spoke up. No one chastised her.

'It ...' Osun frowned, searching for the right words. 'It is the centre of Chem, as though the very best and worst of what we are is squeezed in to one great city. It is both captivatingly beautiful and hideously ugly. The markets are overwhelming, even for a trader, if there is anything in the world you want to buy you can find it there. Anything. And the temple district in the inner ring, it's a dangerous place, you can almost feel the Gods walking with you; but sometimes they are not Gods but demons.' He glanced up at Kesta and she quickly turned away. 'I dread to go there not least because I long to go there. For the weak, for the lost, for the hopeless, and the hedonistic, it's an addictive place.'

She frowned, wondering if Osun meant to describe himself.

'Do you have any ideas about how to get into the palace?' Jorrun asked. 'Do you have any contacts there?'

'One.' Osun seemed reluctant to consider him. 'In the temple district. He is not a nice man.'

Neither are you! Kesta thought spitefully.

***

As they cleared up their camp for the night and checked on the animals, she couldn't help but allow a little anxiety to come creeping in. This would be their last night out in the stunning countryside of Chem. How soon might they have to face Dryn Dunham or any of the other coven lords? She took off her head covering and was about to get ready to sleep; she hesitated. She knew it was just an excuse to see him, but she took Azrael's lantern out to Jorrun who still sat by their dwindling fire. 'I thought you might like some company tonight; I know Azrael would.'

'Thank you.'

The way he studied her uncovered face, as though wanting to drink in every detail, made her flush.

'How will we get Azrael into the palace?'

'He will have to try to find his own way from whatever inn we stay at.'

She tried to think of something else to say, something to delay her having to go back to the wagon. Her heart was a painful knot that only his presence seemed to ease.

He smiled. 'We will never be any good at small talk, Kesta.'

She grinned back at him.

Osun walked slowly over to them, her heart sank as her hackles rose and she gritted her teeth. 'Goodnight.' She turned and headed to the wagon.

She was glad when she found Milaiya had already wrapped herself in her blanket and closed her eyes; she didn't feel much up to telling tales tonight. Selfishly, she didn't think she could deal with hearing more about life in Chem either. She got annoyed with herself when her thoughts immediately began to drift toward Jorrun. Her feelings had most definitely not changed, and she was sure his hadn't either, including his resolve that they never act on them. This was hardly the place or the right circumstances for them to get to know each other though.

'Kesta?'

'I'm awake.'

'Would you show me some magic?'

She sat up. 'Are you sure? I don't want to frighten you.'

'Is ... is your magic bad then?'

'No, Milaiya, no it isn't. I suppose it could be used for bad things, but us *fire-walkers* live under a strict code. We're allowed to defend ourselves and our people, but we try to do no harm. We don't use blood magic like the necromancers here.' Even as she said it, her hand went to her chest where the small message cylinder containing Jorrun's blood still hung. She'd used blood magic.

'Would you show me something then?'

In reply Kesta felt in the dark for a candle. Agitating the air to create heat, she lit it.

Milaiya gasped, shuffling forward to look at the flame. 'Can you teach me to do that?'

Kesta's heart clenched as she looked at the slave. 'I'm so sorry, Milaiya. There has to be something in you, in your blood, for you to be able to perform magic. You said that you were considered here of having poor blood. I imagine that means you would have no magical ability.'

Hope faded from the woman's eyes, but she watched the steady flame burn. Kesta opened her mouth to speak but stopped herself, Jorrun's warning still fresh in her mind. She wanted to promise Milaiya that she would get her out of here, but it was a promise she didn't know if she could keep.

***

When she left the wagon the next morning, she found Jorrun and Osun attempting to disguise themselves for their entry to Arkoom. Osun had trimmed his beard, tied his wild hair back in a neat queue, and put on some expensive looking and well-fitted clothing. She grudgingly admitted that it changed his appearance for the better, although it made him more obviously Dunham. She realised with a jolt that Osun was deliberately taking attention to himself and putting his own safety on the line for Jorrun.

Jorrun himself had dressed in some undyed linin trousers and had just finished buttoning up a shirt. He paused at the top button, shaking his head with his back to her.

'No, this is still too fine. Do you have anything plainer?'

'Just this.' Osun lifted a couple of shirts that hung over his arm and pulled out a white cotton one.

Jorrun pulled the shirt he was wearing up over his head. A rush of warmth flowed through Kesta's muscles and she bit her lower lip; then gasped. His back was covered in scars. Very old and small, but they criss-crossed like the lash of a whip. She held onto the wagon, feeling light headed. He had only been eight when he'd left Chem, hadn't he? Surely, they would not have beaten such a young child and one who was the son of a coven Lord? Or had he received those scars in Elden?

She jumped as Milaiya climbed down from the wagon. The men heard her and turned toward them, Jorrun quickly pulling the white shirt over his head. With a smile beneath her veil, Milaiya went off to see to her bulls. Kesta quickly put her own head covering on and went to help with the morning chores. Kesta caught Milaiya looking at Jorrun with a dubious look in her brown eyes.

'What is it?'

Milaiya appeared embarrassed. 'He still looks like a master.'

Kesta followed her gaze. She was right. 'Come on.' She placed a hand on the reluctant woman's back. 'Jorrun, your disguise doesn't work. Milaiya?'

Jorrun looked at the Chemman slave and she blushed scarlet, but she found her courage and spoke her thoughts. 'Master, you do not move or look like a servant. It is in your eyes. Your eyes tell that you have power. You move like you have power. A slave is born already broken.' She hesitated and looked at Kesta for support. 'They learn not to hope. A servant still hopes, they covet what little power they have and guard it, but they have a little. Do I make sense?'

'Yes.' Kesta couldn't bear the look in his eyes. He knew exactly what she meant. 'I understand. Thank you, Milaiya,'

She gave a bow. 'Master.'

***

They met their first patrol after only an hour on the road. Jorrun had gone from riding beside Osun to riding behind the wagon. The patrol's captain stopped to speak to Osun, but the trader was easily able to convince him that they were harmless. They passed several lone men and were overtaken by one riding swiftly as though his life depended on it. They caught up to a larger caravan of traders who politely gave way to let them by.

As they reached the summit of a hill Kesta caught her first sight of Arkoom. Mountains stood as its dramatic backdrop, still crowned with snow, the highest peaks above the low-lying cloud. It stood upon a hill, two rivers coming about its feet to merge and cut a wide valley through the soft bedrock. An evergreen forest spread between them and the city and smoke rose above it despite the hour and the warmth of spring. It was the largest settlement Kesta had ever seen and could have swallowed Taurmaline. Jorrun pulled up alongside the wagon and despite her full veil, he found her eyes.

The road plunged downward and wove through the shadows of the tall pines. Another patrol overtook them, heading towards the city, not giving them much more than a glance. Kesta felt her courage begin to falter and excusing herself she crawled back into the wagon. What in the spirit's name was she doing? She liked to think that she was clever and strong, but the reality was she'd fought in few real battles. Borrow raiders were one thing, but this was a whole city full of men who would kill her as soon as look at her, and not just the sorcerers. She tried to pull herself together.

'Azra, how are you doing?'

'Kessta! Azra wishes he hadn't come. But Azra will be needed. Sssoon the other drakes will come, and we will fight the blood magic. You are scared?'

'Yes.'

'Me too! We have to try though! For the spiritss, for the *walkers*, for Jorrun.'

She clasped her hands under her chin and leaned forward, elbows on her legs. 'And for Milaiya.'

It was evening when they reached the gates of the city. They were huge, whole tree trunks bound together by strips of iron. Kesta counted thirty guardsmen before she slipped back inside the wagon. Azrael was nervously circling his lantern, making himself as small as he could. She found herself searching for her dagger. She slipped it into the long boots she still wore under her Chemman dress. The wagon moved forward, and she caught her breath. They were entering the city. She wished she could hold Azrael's hand.

It felt like an eternity until they came to a stop at an inn. She barely breathed until Jorrun opened the canvas to indicate that she should step out.

'Do you require a safe cell?' A servant of the inn regarded her and Milaiya.

'No need.' Osun gave a flick of his fingers. 'I require a suite with a servant's cot.'

'Yes, master.' The servant bowed. 'Follow me.'

They were taken up to the top floor, and the servant gave Osun a quick tour while the rest of them waited just inside the doorway.

'Yes, this is adequate,' Osun said in a bored tone. 'Send up some food and then leave me in peace.'

The servant bowed and backed out of the room. Whatever else he was, Kesta had to admit that Osun was a brilliant actor.

As soon as the door closed, they all drooped in relief.

'We should eat and then go on to the temples,' Osun said to Jorrun.

Jorrun glanced at Kesta before nodding.

Kesta could feel that something was wrong. 'What?' she demanded, looking from Osun to Jorrun. 'What are you up to?'

Jorrun's eyes were sad as he regarded her, she didn't like the farewell in them. It was Osun who was brave enough to reply.

'We have to go into the temple district to get to the palace. The ... the only reason to take a woman into the temple district is to sell them or ... or to gift them to the Gods.' She was shocked when Osun knelt on one knee in front of her. 'Lady, I know you hate me. I don't want to, but I will have to sell Milaiya before we go through the temples.'

Her mouth fell open, and she stared at him in shock, glancing up at Jorrun.

'No, mistress!' Milaiya threw herself to the floor, grabbing Kesta's arm. Osun scrambled back, turning to Jorrun.

Mistress. Never had such a word been used in Chem, not for hundreds of years.

Kesta's breathing became more rapid as Osun pleaded with his dark-blue eyes for her to understand. 'I am just trying to do what is best for her. If I leave her here and something happens to both me and Jorrun, then what will be done to her will be a hundred times worse than anything … than anything I might have done. I cannot leave her to the temples and the Gods know I don't want you to see what is there. If I sell her in the market, I can at least try to find her someone who won't hurt her.'

Kesta held Jorrun's eyes as she shook her head in denial, her anger and grief choking her. No.

'No!' She shook Milaiya off and drew herself up straight, although forcing the word hurt her throat. 'No.' She stepped forward to stand nose to nose with Jorrun, her fists clenched. 'Not one more. Not one while I live and breathe and can do something about it!' She spun around to face Milaiya. 'We are going to try to get into the palace to kill Dryn Dunham. We will probably die. If you want to live, then … then you must let Osun sell you. We could just let you go, or wait here, but as Osun said, we might not come back. It is your choice.'

'My choice?' Milaiya stared at her wide-eyed. 'My choice?'

'Yes,' Osun said so quietly it was less than a whisper. 'You are owed at least that much.'

Jorrun closed his eyes and turned away.

Milaiya stood and took slow steps toward Kesta. 'My choice is that I go with you, fire-mistress. My choice is that I give myself hope. I think I know that my mistress will go to fight the Dunham lord. I am not afraid to go to the temple district if you're there. I would rather die trying to do something meaningful, than be sold again like I am nothing.'

Kesta sucked in a sharp breath, overwhelmed despite having closed off her *knowing*. She didn't see the tear that tracked down Jorrun's face. She nodded, struggling to find her voice.

'That is your choice.' She bowed. 'We will all go to the temples.'

Jorrun didn't speak to her as they picked at their food and then prepared themselves to leave the inn. Osun handed Milaiya a full headdress and Kesta realised, that just as Jorrun had done for her, Osun was offering Milaiya the only protection he could give her. She still couldn't bring herself to forgive him, to her what he'd done was beyond redemption.

Osun led them down through the inn, Jorrun bringing up the rear. They left the market district and followed several long, winding roads, through houses that varied from those barely standing to opulent mansions. By the time they came to the high wall that separated the temple district from the rest of the city Kesta's feet ached.

At the gate the guards demanded their business. Osun simply nodded toward the two women.

'On your way, then,' the guard growled.

They were through.

The first thing that hit her were the sounds, a cacophony of voices and cries both eerie and ecstatic. It was mostly men she heard but the laughter of a woman cut through her nerves like a saw, so alien in this land. The smell of incense was intense and cloying, the cooking meats made her feel nauseous, too close to the smell of burning human flesh. Bright colours assailed her even through the veil, and lanterns blazed below every eave.

Foolishly she called up her *knowing*, and she recoiled, clutching at her stomach and chest as though hit by a giant fist. It was too much! Despair bled into desire, hunger into hatred, love into jealousy. She could barely draw in breath at the power of the unbridled emotions, her blood roared in her ears.

Vaguely she was aware of Jorrun's voice, but he sounded so far away, under water. He was standing painfully close, unable to touch her because here, they were both slaves. She wanted him to touch her with every inch of her being, but she couldn't move. Osun stood staring with his mouth open, useless, scared, confused.

It was Milaiya who put an arm around her with an angry look at the men. With the same gentle coaxing that she used with the bulls she got her to take a step forward.

'Turn off your *knowing*, Kesta,' Jorrun hissed at her.

With a gasp she drew in air and managed to switch off her magic. She staggered, but Milaiya held her up.

'Come on,' Osun commanded, playing his role as they drew unwanted attention. 'Or do I have to whip you?'

Even through the veil she couldn't bear to look up into Jorrun's eyes. Osun had been right; this place was hell.

Chapter Twenty-Two

Rosa: Kingdom of Elden

'Kurghan's ship has been sighted.'

Nip, the young stable boy, came running up to their improvised archery range. Rosa's muscles relaxed, but she took in a deep breath and clenched her fists. She hadn't really taken Kesta's command that she take over running the hold seriously, instead leaving most of it to Tantony's chieftain. There were some members of the hold, however, that had insisted on looking to her. The artisans, craftsmen, and women in particular seemed to have taken Kesta's wish as sacrosanct.

'Thank you, Nip, you best let your dad know.' She saw a warrior hurrying toward the keep, no doubt taking the same news to the chieftain. 'Come on, Catya.'

They dropped their bows and left the ward, Rosa keeping to a dignified fast walk toward the small dock. She'd tried hard not to worry since Kesta had left, but there had been a part of her that thought she would never see her friend again. She didn't want to go back to Taurmaline and the pettiness of the young court, she wanted the freedom and excitement that her outlandish foreign mistress brought. Most of all she wanted the company of someone who respected and valued her.

As the fishing boat came across the lake toward them, she could see only two people aboard that she recognised, Kurghan himself and Merkis

Tantony. There was a woman and two children as well. Happiness flooded through her at the sight of Tantony, at the same time as dread at the absence of Kesta and Jorrun. Could they be returning together in the Thane's ship? She hoped so.

'I don't see Kesta.' Catya fretted at her side.

'Let's not worry until we're sure.'

Tantony spotted her and a smile instantly lit his face. Her own face flushed with heat.

You're a bit old for blushes, Rosa, she chastised herself.

The boat bumped up against the narrow landing, Kurghan jumping out at once to tie up. Tantony stopped to help their passengers out before ushering them toward Rosa.

'Refugees from Taurmouth,' he told her.

Startled she demanded, 'Refugees?'

Tantony opened his mouth, looked away and then taking in a breath turned to say, 'Although Mantu hasn't fallen, thanks to Kesta, there is apparently a large invasion force on its way to Elden.' He glanced down at Catya. 'How are your preparations going?'

'I think they are going okay.' Rosa cringed. 'I'm not a Fulmer woman!'

'Thank goodness.' A smile crinkled the corners of his eyes.

'Where's Kesta?' Catya demanded. 'And Jorrun?'

'Well.' Tantony looked up and Rosa followed his gaze to see his chieftain striding toward them. 'Let me catch up with Evin and I'll meet you just inside the Raven Tower.'

'But they are alive?' Rosa pleaded.

'I think so,' Tantony replied. 'But I don't know.'

***

Rosa sat on the bottom step of the Raven Tower, her fingers played with the fabric of her skirt and she kept looking from the closed door to the darkness of the stairway up above. She clenched her teeth and breathed out loudly through her nose as Catya dragged her feet in another circuit of the small entrance hall. She stood quickly on hearing the rattle of the door handle and Tantony stepped in, red faced and breathing fast as though he'd run there.

'What happened?' She demanded at once.

'This must be kept quiet; the tower is the most private place I could think of to talk. The Thane and Kesta have gone to Chem to try to kill the coven's Overlord.'

Rosa's knees weakened and Tantony grabbed her arm. 'My lady?'

'I'm all right.' It was hard to catch her breath. 'It was just a shock. They have really gone to Chem? Not just the two of them, surely?'

'He wanted to go alone, but she insisted on going with him. It would make it easier on all of us if they just admitted how they felt about each other.' He caught her eye, and they both looked away, their cheeks reddening.

'I should have gone with them.' Catya scowled. 'I'd have killed a few Chemman.'

'You're far too bloodthirsty!' Rosa shook her head but couldn't help a smile.

'You'll probably get a chance to kill plenty of them here.' Tantony looked seriously down at the girl before turning back to Rosa. 'The invasion fleet won't be too far behind us, I fear. I asked Evin how Kesta's plans were going but the idiot seems to have dismissed them because she is a woman. Please tell me we are ready to defend ourselves?'

Rosa drew herself up. 'We have supplies in for a siege, the women and stronger children have all been practising their archery. The bondsmen and craftsmen have been working on repairing and improving the walls. Your man out at the bridge reported he has strong nets ready to pull up across the river and fire arrows aplenty.'

Tantony smiled at her and she felt her pride grow.

'That's the best news I've heard in a while,' he said. 'Would you ... shall we ... will you walk around the hold with me, so we can speak to everyone and see what else needs doing?'

'Of course, if you'll tell me what happened on Mantu?'

'Yes. How many necromancers did you kill?' Catya interrupted with much too much enthusiasm for Rosa's liking.

'Let's sit down in the great hall this evening for dinner and I'll tell you then,' Tantony suggested. 'I think the men need to hear what Kesta did for us. The Icante herself is apparently coming to Taurmaline and it would be well for people to know how much they should respect the Fulmers.'

***

Rosa felt incredibly self-conscious seated at the table beside Tantony in the great hall. They had decided not to use the high table both due to their low status and as a reminder of their Thane and Lady's absence. All Tantony revealed to the hold was that they'd left them at Taurmouth to face the Chemman. Catya's eyes shone, taking in every word from the Merkis as he recounted a second time how Kesta had defeated three necromancers. Rosa was sure he'd missed out many of the less pleasant details. A few of the warriors still remained dubious.

'Has there been any news from Mantu?' Rosa asked.

'Nothing yet although the king should have received my message by now. He's probably too busy to worry about a Merkis and a single hold.'

'Although we are the key to the lake,' she mused. 'I wonder if they will strike straight for Taurmaline up the river or try to take the land a mile at a time.'

He was grinning at her.

'What?' She placed her hand on her chest.

He gave a shake of his head. 'I thought I was in for a nightmare of a time when I first met you both; but I have to admit she is the best thing that could have happened to Jorrun and this hold. And you ...' He looked at her and then down at his food. He cleared his throat. 'I like having you around.'

'Oh.' She looked quickly away and swallowed. Was that all she could think of to say? She regarded him as discretely as she could. She'd always thought he had a kind face despite his roughness. She took in a deep breath. 'I like being here.'

Tantony poured her some more wine and gave her another of his shy smiles.

'Tantony, can you teach me some sword fighting?' Catya spoke up.

The Merkis almost choked on his wine. 'That woman is the very worst influence!'

'Or the very best.' Rosa smiled to herself.

***

The following morning Rosa was awoken by Catya urgently calling her name.

'What is it?' Only a little light showed through the shutters.

'A raven has come with a message!'

Rosa sat up. 'We had best take it to Tantony now he's back. Would you hand me my dress?' She took only a moment to brush and pin up her hair before slipping on her shoes and hurrying down the stairs after Catya. The girl handed her the message cylinder as she knocked on Tantony's door. They heard a muffled reply before Tantony opened the door a crack, only to slam it shut again. A moment later he came out, now fully dressed and rather red in the face.

'What is it?'

Rosa handed him the cylinder, and he cracked it open to unroll the small parchment. His complexion went at once from flushed to pale as death.

He drew in a breath. 'Chem struck Taurmouth last night. The warriors are holding out, but ships have landed further along the coast to drop off warriors both dead and alive. They are under siege and don't expect to last. It ... it says they are vastly outnumbered.'

Catya grabbed Rosa's hand with both of hers.

'We ...' Rosa found her jaw trembling, and she clenched her teeth tightly, drawing on her resolve and courage. 'We must send word at once to warn our men at the bridge and any of our hold folk who are not living within our walls.'

Tantony nodded. 'I'll get word out at once.' He scratched at his head. 'I think I'll send warriors to reinforce those at the bridge with the instructions they must withdraw back here as soon as it looks like the bridge will be passed.'

'We will have the women prepare.' Rosa nodded. 'I think it would be as well to have as many as possible move into the ward and fort.'

'Agreed.' Tantony took a deep breath. 'Let's get to it.'

***

The following day brought mixed news. Aven's daughter arrived back from Taurmaline having gone there with one of her cousins to trade. The carpenter came running to find Tantony.

'Good news! Mantu has taken back Promise harbour, and the island is ours!'

'You're sure?' Tantony stood up from behind his desk. Rosa's hand went to her mouth, and she stared hopefully from one to the other.

'It is all over the city! There is talk of some kind of fire demons helping.'

Tantony and Rosa smiled at each other.

'If I hadn't met Azrael for myself, I'd have thought it nonsense,' Kurghan went on.

'Anything from Taurmouth?' Tantony asked hopefully.

'Nothing new, nothing good.' Kurghan shook his head.

'Is it worth our celebrating Mantu's victory to keep our spirits up?' Rosa suggested.

'I don't know.' Tantony regarded her thoughtfully. 'I don't imagine we will have much to celebrate in the coming days. Let's spread the word, but we'll leave off celebrating until we know what's happening at Taurmouth.'

She nodded.

Later that evening she was glad he'd ignored her suggestion. A raven arrived from the king with news that made her cold. Taurmouth had fallen.

***

The hold was on edge, tension high, tempers frayed. Rosa wished with all her heart that Kesta were here, she would know what to do to calm everyone. Several refugees had fled up the river and news reached them that the Icante of the Fulmers was now at Taurmaline. Of Taurmouth there was no more news. People fleeing by horse and then on foot passed by the hold, only a handful of exhausted families begged to shelter with them. As concerned as he was that they might not themselves survive an attack or siege, Tantony could not bring himself to turn them away.

Two days later their scouts sighted the king's own royal ship sailing across the lake and down the river. No more ravens had returned, and speculation ran through Northold; surely the king hadn't himself gone to face the Chemmen on the river with only one ship? That evening a fierce wind came down from the north and thunder rolled across the wide river valley. Rain threatened to put out their watch fires and many of the hold crowded into the great hall. Rosa and Catya made a last dash through the rain to check on the ravens before night set in, in the hope that there was some news. They were both soaked to the skin as they lit a lantern and clambered up the stairs. Rosa climbed up into the bird loft and looked around at the ravens, the almost reptilian smell of them was strong in her nostrils. Their black eyes glinted in the firelight. None of them had a message cylinder tied to its leg. She came slowly back down with a sigh.

'It was worth a look.'

The sky lit up and thunder cracked and boomed. Rosa went to the north-facing window, her face so close to the glass it misted the pane. Catya joined her, linking her arm in hers and leaning against her.

'Where do you think they are?' the girl asked.

'Kesta and Jorrun?' Rosa drew in a deep breath and let it out slowly. 'They will be together, and they will be doing their best to keep us safe.'

'Rosa?'

'Yes?'

'Are you scared?'

Another flash lit up the trees and the tower itself seemed to tremble.

'Yes, I am. But being scared is not something to be ashamed of, it's something to defeat. We are both fighters in our different ways, Catya.'

She felt the girl nod.

She looked down at her. 'Come on, there is nothing more to be done here tonight. Let's get back to the hall; someone there must know a good tale to tell or a few songs to pass the time.'

***

They awoke to an almost eerie silence, the sky like a bruise; all purple and black. The water level in the lake had dropped several yards to reveal a bed of mud and weeds. Smoke rose from behind the trees from the direction of the river and bridge.

'I've never seen anything like that in my life!' Kurghan exclaimed. Rosa and Catya had come out to the small wharf with Tantony and the carpenter. Several of the warriors and the chieftain, Evin, had followed. The smell of silt and burnt wood came to them in bursts on the cold wind.

'What's that?' Catya's head went up, and she turned toward the north.

Rosa heard it too, hoofbeats, a moment before a horse burst out of the trees ridden by a young boy.

'They're coming,' he cried. 'We've abandoned the bridge, the Chemmen are coming!'

'Evin, send a message to the king immediately.' Tantony strode forward to grab the horse's halter. 'You are not the only survivor?'

'The others follow.' The boy was wide-eyed and breathing hard.

'Get yourself to the stable.' Tantony regarded his warriors. 'We'll form a rear-guard up the path there for our men from the bridge until they get into the hold. Rosa, have your archers man the inner walls.'

She was about to obey when she realised it wasn't the best plan. He was probably just trying to get them out of the way and keep them safe. She dared to speak up. 'Merkis, pardon me but we aren't actually very good. If we try to shoot from the inner wall, we would be just as likely to hit our own men. We should man the outer wall and shoot when you're clear.' A blush burned her cheeks.

Tantony studied her as he thought over her words, weighing necessity against the lives of the women and children. Rosa didn't envy him. 'Very well. Get them up on the outer wall but stay low and hidden. Let's draw those Chemmen in close and make them think we are poorly defended. Uzra here will keep watch and signal when you should stand and fire, so make sure everyone is watching him. The moment myself, Evin, or Uzra tell you to fall back, you all go to the inner walls, no argument.'

Rosa gave a curtsy. 'Yes, Merkis.' She lifted the hem of her dress and ran for the hold, her heart thundering in her ears. Catya ran ahead of her, her face determined with not a trace of fear. Rosa hesitated as they reached the doors of the fort, uncertain how to take command. A pigeon flew out and up from the Merkis' study window.

She was shocked, and a little in awe, when the previously silent Catya went straight into the great hall and bellowed, 'Rosa's archers! Get your weapons!

Rosa snapped her mouth shut and drew in a breath to straighten her spine. The old queen had never taught this kind of thing to her ladies-in-waiting, perhaps she should have! She couldn't help but feel proud and impressed as the women and children scrambled to be ready in just a few minutes. Catya brought her bow and quiver, handing them over almost reverentially.

'Okay.' Rosa cleared her throat to try again, forcing more volume and feigning confidence. She gave them Tantony's instructions and, with no further speeches, led them out and up onto the ramparts. The few male archers they had gave way somewhat grudgingly. Uzra was already in place and gestured for them to get down and settle. Rosa and Catya joined him and she couldn't help but peep up over the wall past him to see what was happening below.

Their warriors were hurrying toward the trees even as ships appeared on the lake from the river, one of them still smoking where it had been fired. Rosa gasped at the number and size of the vessels. Then the sound of shouting came from within the trees and every muscle in her body tensed. Their men from the bridge came running out, many of them injured. They were ushered through their waiting warriors, Rosa spotted Tantony at their head and her pulse thundered in her ears. His warriors made a sudden surge forward and there was a clash of metal as the pursuing Chemmen fell upon them.

'Get down!' Uzra hissed at her. 'They're starting the retreat!'

Several of the male archers fired off shots, just enough to make the Chemmen pause and give their warriors the slightest of advantages. Rosa found her eyes glued to Uzra, watching his eyes, waiting for him to move. The warrior raised his arm.

'Archers!'

She sprang up, nocking an arrow as she turned to look over the wall. The Northold warriors were almost in but they were seriously overwhelmed in number, there must have been over a hundred Chemmen. Rosa fired, amazed at herself when her arrow struck one man in the shoulder. Arrows hummed and thudded home; the Chemmen retreated toward the woods and she heard the gate slam shut below her.

Tantony was quickly with them to assess their situation with Uzra. Rosa gripped her bow hard to stop her hands shaking. Beside her Catya wore a wild grin on her face.

'Do you think they'll go back to join their comrades?' Uzra asked.

Tantony shook his head. 'We can't count on that. They'll be more cautious now, spend some time checking us out.'

'Merkis!' One of the men shouted and pointed back toward the forest. Something moved in the shadows, it looked like a man, but its movement was all wrong. It swayed out from between the trees, arms hanging as though it didn't know what to do with them. Rosa let out a small cry and immediately felt embarrassed.

'Gods damn, it's one of our people!' Tantony swore, then remembered there were women present. 'Sorry.'

'No, don't apologise.' Rosa shook her head, her eyes wide as she watched the creature stagger closer.

'It means they have a necromancer,' Catya murmured.

Rosa and Tantony regarded each other in horror.

'The kid's right,' Tantony growled. 'Or at least they had one fighting against our people at the bridge, we can only pray they didn't hang about.'

'There's more!' Uzra pointed.

Sure enough, seven more came jerking out of the trees. As they came closer, they seemed to become more co-ordinated, faster, surer of their movement.

'We need fire,' Tantony turned to Uzra. 'Get the men to shoot them down with fire arrows!' He glanced at Rosa, 'No offense to the women.'

438

Rosa shrugged.

'They look wet.' Catya pulled herself up to see better over the wall.

'They do.' Rosa frowned. A brazier was lit, and several archers touched their specially prepared arrows to it. There was something not right about the water soaking the dead men, it looked too thick to her, somehow …

'Oil!' she cried. 'Stop, Tantony, they are covered in oil!'

'Hold!' he bellowed.

One arrow sailed up over the ramparts and struck an undead in the chest. At once flames billowed upward to engulf it. Instead of falling it began a staggered run toward them.

'Damn it, it's going to burn down the gate!' Tantony looked around for inspiration.

'Water!' Rosa shouted so loudly it strained her throat. 'Ladies! Buckets of water!'

'Not enough time!' Tantony shook his head. He pushed past her and went hurtling down the steps. 'Open the gate!' he commanded. His men looked at him as though he'd gone crazy. 'Let it in! Quickly! Save the gate!'

Understanding dawned, and they dragged the gates open as the creature reached a sprint to throw itself at the wood and iron. Tantony drew his sword and Rosa grabbed Catya by the shoulders as the Merkis swung it, charging at the flaming human torch. With a roar he took out its legs, rolling away as his clothes ignited. Two of the warriors fell upon him, beating at the flames with their own shirts, hastily removed. Others shouldered the gates to close them again while Uzra hurled a spear to pin the monstrosity to the ground.

'Tantony!' Rosa ran past the shocked warriors and down the stairs. Her aching lungs were too tight to draw in enough air and she felt a wave of dizziness.

The Merkis was getting slowly to his feet, she could see even before she reached him that his left forearm was red and blistered. 'I'm all right.' He waved them all aside. He took in a few breaths to steady himself while one of the women brought him a bucket of water to plunge his arm in to. He sucked air sharply into his lungs at the pain.

'What now?' Rosa's shoulders rose and fell as she drew in deep breaths of her own.

Tantony looked at her. 'No more fire arrows for a start. We wait. That's all we can do; that and pray we can hold them off.'

Chapter Twenty-Three

Dia Icante: Kingdom of Elden

Dia gazed up at the high walls of Taurmaline as they rode past lines of fleeing refugees all hoping to take shelter within. She felt incredibly small.

'Not an unwelcome sight.' Arrus grinned at Vilnue who rode at his side. 'Smells a bit, though.'

The Merkis laughed. 'Worse on the inside!'

One of the Elden warriors rode ahead, clearing a way through the gate. Dia's concern grew when she saw the amount of people already crowded within the city. If they were held under siege for long, starvation and disease would be a real problem. Merkis Vilnue guided them through the winding streets to the main keep. The king came out himself to meet them, clasping Arrus's wrist and taking Dia's hand to kiss her cheek.

'Icante, Silene, welcome, we are honoured that you would come.' His eyes glanced across those they'd brought with them. Heara, of course, along with five *walkers* and forty warriors. She'd left Larissa and Worvig to take charge of the Fulmers.

The king invited them in as servants led away the horses.

'Who would have thought things would change so quickly and you would be here to defend us?' He chatted amiably as they walked toward the throne room. Dia narrowed her eyes. She'd politely not called up her *knowing* but even so, her intuition prickled.

Servants were waiting with bowls of water and cloths for them to wash their hands. Food had been lain out on the tables at the edge of the room and both wine and beer were offered around. Dia's gaze fell on the throne and the stark black seat that stood a little to the left of it.

'Where is my daughter?' she asked.

'Ah.' The king smiled although it didn't reach his eyes. 'She and her husband set out some days ago to assassinate the Coven Overlord in Chem.'

'Chem!'

Several people turned around at her raised voice, including Arrus who almost choked on his beer and demanded, 'What did you say?'

'They've gone to kill Dryn Dunham and therefore end this conflict.'

Dia glanced at her husband, it was like Kesta to go charging off into danger, but with the Dark Man? 'How long ago? Have you heard anything?'

'This isn't the place,' Bractius said quietly. 'When we've finished putting on this show, we'll go and talk in a private chamber.' He turned to Vilnue. 'Merkis! How did you enjoy your visit to the Fulmers?'

Dia's anger boiled. Unlike her daughter's her temper was slow burning; however, her patience was not infinite. While she understood the need to hide some things for the sake of morale, this all felt far too false to her. She could see her husband's face darken and he went from laughing and drinking to carefully assessing the room.

A well-dressed servant with blue-green eyes and dark hair came over to them and bowed, trying hard not to look at her mismatched eyes. 'Icante, if you will please follow me, we have a room ready for you.'

She was reluctant to leave the other *walkers*.

'It's fine.' Arrus touched her arm.

She nodded, trusting her husband's judgement and experience of the Elden court.

442

They were taken up to the room that Arrus had used on his previous visit and the same young page hovered on their heels in case they needed anything. Arrus stalked across to the window.

'He is putting on an act, but I think he is terrified,' Dia said.

'He is right to be.' He rubbed at the back of his neck. 'Elden is a big land, and he spread his warriors too thinly to defend it.'

'But then, if he'd pulled them all back here, this Adelphy could have taken the coast and spread his undead army across the land as they did in the Borrows.' She sighed, perching on the edge of the table. 'These aren't Borrow raiders, they're not predictable.'

'I can't believe Kesta's gone to Chem.' He walked over and placed a hand on her shoulder, his fingers unconsciously digging into her muscles, kneading to ease her tension and his own.

'I can.' She snorted. 'Tell me again about Thane Jorrun, I wish I'd met him. Would you say he is a handsome man?'

Arrus scowled. 'How would I know? Are you thinking our sea urchin has had her head turned? She's far too sensible for that.'

Dia smiled to herself, more men had caught their daughter's eye than Arrus would like to admit, but he was right, Kesta had learned her lessons quickly and was careful of her heart. Anyway, it was harder to fool a *walker*, though not impossible. No, it was more likely Kesta had seen a chance to take it upon herself to save them all and taken it. As much as she trusted and respected her daughter, she couldn't help but be afraid for her alone in Chem but for the Dark Man.

Someone knocked loudly at their door and Arrus opened it to find a steward standing with their page.

'Your majesties, the king has asked to see you at once.'

Arrus grinned at the title and Dia couldn't help but enjoy his amusement. 'Lead the way.'

The steward took them to a small room away from the throne room. They found the king pacing there with two warriors they hadn't yet met. Merkis Vilnue reached the door only moments after they did, forcing a thin-lipped smile of greeting.

'Ah, come in! Close the door behind you, Vilnue.' Bractius pulled at his beard, his eyebrows drawn in tight towards his nose. He didn't meet their eyes until the door was shut. 'Taurmouth has fallen. The harbour was breached, and the town overrun. Their sorcerers set everything alight and from the level of destruction it seems unlikely they intend to make a base of it from which to strike. I've sent commands for all warriors to head for the river or for Taurmaline. It seems we must have one large and decisive battle rather than the skirmishes we are used to.'

'No matter what you did they would change their attack to match it.' Dia felt a little sympathy for him. 'Is there any account of how many sorcerers they might have?'

One of the men shook his head. 'There was not much detail in the message.'

'But from the damage done it sounds like there are several,' she mused aloud.

'Maps!' The king pointed at the table and his steward quickly placed down a scroll and unrolled it. 'I think we should avoid a siege if possible. I imagine these necromancers have no difficulty getting past gates and walls.' His eyes ran down the wide blue line that marked the river. 'Your daughter and the Thane have done some work to strengthen the defences at the bridge here. I should have married a Fulmer woman myself.'

Dia and Arrus caught each other's eyes but remained diplomatically silent.

Merkis Vilnue spoke up, addressing Dia and Arrus. 'Ordinarily it would take about two days and two nights for someone to sail up the river from Taurmouth to Taurmaline. If they use magic as you do—'

'I've witnessed a necromancer use elemental magic in a similar way to that which we do in the Fulmers.' Dia looked from the Merkis to the king. 'They could use wind and even water to speed their way here, although it would deplete their energy before they got here.'

'I'm all for them depleting their energy.' The corner of the king's mouth twitched upward. 'I've sent archers to harry the riverbank and warriors to meet them should they come ashore before the lake.'

'I could sail down river to meet them if you have a suitable ship.' Dia saw her husband open his mouth to protest, but she stilled him with a look. 'It would, of course, deplete *my* energy but I could do some serious damage to his ships.'

Bractius regarded her with his eyes narrowed. 'It's an option worth considering. The other *fire-walkers* would stay here?'

'I'd be wise to take one other with me.'

Bractius turned back to his map. 'Let's see how much damage we can do with traditional warfare first before risking you, Icante. If he gets more than halfway up the river with most of his ships and warriors intact, then you shall have my royal ship and the best crew I can give you.' He looked over his shoulder at Merkis Vilnue. 'Make sure everything is ready in case you have to sail at short notice.'

'Yes, Majesty.'

'That is all for now.'

The three Merkis bowed and left, Vilnue trying to indicate in as subtle a way as he could that the king had also dismissed her and Arrus.

Dia folded her arms and tilted her chin to regard the Elden King. 'What of our daughter?'

Bractius smiled politely, but it didn't reach his eyes. She noticed his left hand clench briefly. 'I've had no news of her or Jorrun since his Merkis arrived back at Northold. I'm afraid all I know is that Jorrun was meant to go alone. It was his idea; he believes that if we kill Dryn Dunham, the necromancers here will all go running back to fight over their Seats. I couldn't say why Kesta chose to go too.'

She quickly called up her *knowing*, she was in time to sense some confusion from the king. Part of him was pleased but there was also a bitter tang of annoyance.

'A dangerous, perhaps foolish, plan, but one that would indeed change things if they succeed,' Dia acknowledged.

The king stood looking at them with his eyebrows raised, Dia's nostrils flared and she stubbornly remained where she was.

'Um, perhaps we could let the *walkers* know what's happening?' Arrus shifted his feet.

Dia smiled without turning away from the king. 'Yes. Until later, your majesty.' She gave a slight nod of her head.

'Icante.' He nodded politely back.

Once outside, Arrus hissed under his breath, 'Is this really the best time and place to be contesting who has the biggest balls?'

She grinned up at him. 'You know that will always be me.'

He pursed his lips and shook his head but there was a spark of amusement in his eyes.

'Bractius needs to remember that I am his equal.' Her eyes narrowed. 'Not his to command or dismiss.'

***

Messages came by bird and by horse, several scouts risked their lives to send them news. It seemed that an army of some two hundred dead had been loosed on the streets of Taurmouth and they speculated that they were there to keep Adelphy's retreat open should he need it. It also meant he must be intending to leave at least one, if not more, necromancer at the harbour town. It was mid-afternoon on their third day at Taurmaline that they received a summons to attend the king's private audience room. Adelphy was on the move and had begun his journey up the Taur.

Reports came in throughout the rest of the day and on through the night. Archers had been thwarted by unnatural winds, fires had sprung up in riverside villages pushing back their warriors. The Chemmen progressed steadily closer and for the most part unopposed.

'They are using up their power though.' Dia tried to give them some small amount of encouragement. 'I wonder, though ...'

'What?' Bractius waved a hand at her.

'They are expending magical power rather than wasting warriors. It makes me wonder if they know that Thane Jorrun isn't here.'

'You think that Jorrun may have been captured? Or even killed?' Bractius bit briefly at his thumbnail. He stood up, his eyes glancing over his maps. 'It suggests they don't know you're here.'

'Or perhaps they no longer fear Jorrun since Karinna captured him *dream-walking*,' Dia suggested. 'As for *walkers*, despite the fact we have killed several of them, I think they're too arrogant and misogynistic to fear a woman still.'

'I think we are going to have to teach them to fear *you*.' Bractius looked her in the eyes.

She nodded.

'I'll ready the ship.' Merkis Vilnue straightened up and headed for the door.

***

'I should come,' Arrus growled.

She reached up to put a hand to his bearded cheek. 'You should stay, I need someone here I know will protect the other *walkers* from Bractius as well as Adelphy.' She turned away to slide a dagger into her boot. 'Heara has my back.'

'Just return to me,' he mumbled.

She kissed him quickly and slapped his rear. 'Stay out of trouble!'

Heara stood in the door grinning and she blew a kiss to Arrus as they hurried from the room.

'Fetch Everlyn,' she asked Heara. 'She has the most battle experience of the other *walkers*. Meet me at the ship.'

Heara nodded and ran off with her swift but energy conserving lope. Dia herself went to where their warriors were being housed and pointed at five of them to accompany her. They made their way down through the city to the wharves and she recognised the ship that was the king's at once. She'd expected something showy, all gilt and polish, but this ship was a sturdy warship built for speed.

'Icante!' Merkis Vilnue spotted her and waved at her to come aboard. 'We'll be on our way within the hour.'

She hurried up the gangplank to join him.

'I'll show you your quarters.'

'I don't need quarters.' She looked past him and then made her way to the prow. Stretching out her *knowing* she got a feel for the ship. Although it was not alive, such a vessel often took on the feel of the crew and its captain through the once living wood. There was determination. Courage.

Good.

'I need room here for myself, Everlyn, Heara, and two of my archers,' she told Vilnue without looking around. 'Tell your men to expect storms, bad storms. Keep us from running aground, be prepared to fend off boarders. When any of my people tell you to, you must get your rowers to take us back up river as quickly as they can. I don't see the point in getting us all killed if we can prevent it.'

'Yes, Icante.'

'Oh, and if you hurt Heara, you'll have me to deal with.'

'I think it far more likely she will rip *my* heart out, Icante. Probably eat it too.'

She turned to stare at him and then laughed as his serious face turned in to a grin. 'Yes, most likely,' she conceded. She turned back to look across the lake and her resolve faltered. Adelphy was by all accounts a very powerful man. She wished that Doroquael had been able to cross the sea to come with her, the spirit gave her courage. It was not unusual for *walkers* to fight in battles but rarely had they ever competed against other magic users. They sometimes trained together and always worked with an apprentice; this was something new though.

'Icante?' Vilnue took a step toward her.

'Be ready to sail,' she replied firmly.

***

Heara, Everlyn, and two of the Fulmer warriors joined her as they set the sails and headed out across the lake; the other three Fulmer warriors standing guard. Dia gripped the railing and watched the shoreline pass. Lake Taur was almost half the size of Fulmer Isle. In the distance she spotted the top of a tower rearing up beyond the trees. Merkis Vilnue saw the direction of her gaze and placed a hand near hers on the railing.

'That's the Raven Tower. Northold, where your daughter is now the lady.'

Her muscles tightened, and she struggled to keep the resentment and anger from her face. She had no way of knowing if her daughter was even still alive.

As they approached the bridge, she saw that archery towers had been recently constructed from poles and planks. Men hurried forward to man the winches and two sections of the bridge began to lift upward to allow their tall masts to pass through.

'Vilnue, warn those men to get to high ground and beware of the river.' Dia regarded the faces of the warriors as they drew closer. Men she would probably never know or meet but whom she was here to fight beside. But for their paler skin they could just as easily have been Fulmer men.

Night had set in when a rider came pounding down the tow path. He pulled up sharply and waved wildly at them. 'Hello, king's ship!' He hailed.

'We hear you, man!' Vilnue inflated his lungs to bellow back.

'Enemy ships half a mile downriver!'

Vilnue gave a wave of acknowledgement and the man kicked at the horse and was away at once.

Dia gripped the railing and took in a long breath before turning to address those around her. 'Vilnue, we need to move the ship to the side of the river, somewhere where it will not smash into trees when the river rises. Everlyn will do her best to protect us from the elements. Heara, you know what to do. I want you men to take any opportunity you can to shoot down the Chemmen necromancers.'

Merkis Vilnue strode away to shout out his orders. Dia didn't wait but closed her eyes to concentrate on heating the air. Very soon vapour formed and thickened, rising up to become a dark thunderhead above them. Light flickered and glowed deep within it and thunder growled like an angry cat.

She stopped the flow of the river, letting the water build up into a wall that battered against her wind shield while Everlyn formed a second shield to separate the ship from the huge wave that was forming. Fat, warm drops of rain began to splatter against the deck, stinging where it fell on skin. Several of the Eldemen cried out in alarm at the growing mountain of water that towered higher and higher above them. With a nod at Everlyn Dia let it all go. Water broke over them and Dia sent a swirl of wind upward to strengthen Everlyn's barrier and they found themselves in a black tunnel of water. No one chastised the men who threw themselves to the deck and covered their heads, sucking in air as though they feared suffocation.

As the water subsided and poured away from their invisible shield, Dia changed her magic to pull at the tide, increasing the speed and ferocity of the river's flow. A stab of pain sparked within her skull and she dropped to one knee. Heara was beside her at once and Everlyn faltered.

'Keep going,' Dia snarled through gritted teeth. She staggered up, Heara supporting her under her shoulders. She was breathing hard. The deck rocked and Vilnue almost skidded across the wooden planks toward them.

'Gods!' He gazed wide-eyed at Dia, his mouth open in a wild grin. 'That was impressive!'

'We'll see.' Dia turned to lean against the railing, trying to see through the gloom downriver. The storm still grumbled on, lightning forking downward toward the earth.

'There!' Heara pointed.

Something large moved, blacker against the darkness. First one ship and then another came fighting impossibly against the tide.

'If they had any sense, they'd just anchor up and come at us again in the morning,' Vilnue murmured.

'Arrogance.' Heara snorted. 'The man who leads them feels he has to prove himself the more powerful.'

'He might not be wrong.' Dia rubbed tiredly at her face. She counted seven ships of varying size, all of them showing signs of damage from broken rails to smashed masts and tangled sails.

She could feel the magic that flowed from the front three. So; three strong necromancers to face. Which ship contained Adelphy?

'Everlyn, do you have enough strength left to deflect fire if they send it back at us?'

The younger *walker* nodded, her face drawn.

Dia cupped her hands and drew flame from the air as Heara snatched up her bow and joined the two men at the rail. The foremost and central ship was the obvious target, but she picked the one on the right and sent two balls of fire toward it. Almost at once they were deflected away, Dia showed her teeth in a smile as she sent wind of her own to curl her fire balls around and smashed them into one of the unprotected smaller crafts. From all three of the larger ships a blast of flame came back at them and Everlyn cried out as she was battered back, Dia once again strengthened her barrier with one of her own. A sharp stab of pain split her skull in two and she felt something trickle from her nose. She wiped at it with the back of her hand Blood.

'I see one,' Heara hissed.

Dia nodded. 'Close your eyes.' She called up a blast of intense blue and then exploded it into bright white. Beside her Heara opened her eyes again and took her shot. She screamed in triumph as the Chemman necromancer dropped, an arrow through his belly. 'Shaherra! For Shaherra!'

Everlyn fell against the rail and one of the warriors hurried forward to grab her. Blood trickled faster from Dia's left nostril. Even so, she called flames to her hands in small bursts, faster and faster, spinning them toward the ship of the fallen sorcerer and behind to the unprotected ships. Some of them caught and smoke billowed up. When the Chemmen replied with strong blasts of their own, Dia was barely able to call upon her magic, all of them dropped to the deck as flames licked and cracked above their heads, setting their ship alight.

'Your archers,' Dia panted to Vilnue who had fallen beside her, red and black blurred her vision. 'Your archers then abandon ship!'

'Archers!' Vilnue bellowed. He scrambled to his feet, grabbing Heara by the back of her tunic and hoisting her to her feet. 'Volley!'

Heara stooped and lifting Dia threw her over her shoulder. While arrows were loosed, they ran for the side of the ship. A returning arrow struck Vilnue in the shoulder as he shielded Dia with his own body.

'Abandon ship!' He roared. 'All ashore!'

Heara dropped Dia to her feet and shook her to rouse her enough to respond. Heara saw the arrow protruding from Vilnue and with a brief glance into the Eldeman's brown eyes she reached around him to snap the shaft. He grunted at the pain but didn't hesitate in dropping over the side of the ship to cling to the ladder. He took most of Dia's weight between himself and the side of the ship as they made their slow way down. Already the king's own warship was engulfed in smoke and flame as its crew leapt the distance to shore or scrambled down the other rope ladders.

'Where do we go?' Heara demanded of the Merkis.

'Northold is the nearest place that might still be defensible,' Vilnue replied. 'The Raven Tower; but there will be enemies between us and them now.'

'We go there,' Dia said, her voice little more than a breath. 'The Raven Tower.'

Heara nodded at Vilnue, and then setting her shoulder to Dia's stomach, lifted the smaller woman over her shoulder again. 'Lead the way, Merkis.'

Chapter Twenty-Four

Jorrun: Covenet of Chem

He forced his muscles to relax and unclenched his fists, recalling Milaiya's warning that he didn't look like a servant. Every instinct was screaming at him to draw his sword. Was Azrael near? There was no way of knowing in this tumult of human activity. Men crowded the streets, laughing, brazen, stalking slowly, eyes darting to see who was watching. Geranna houses plied their sweet, sickly trade, and clean fronted eating establishments pretended refinement by offering wine. Skin houses predominated and Jorrun couldn't bring himself to look at the tortured women there, painfully aware of Kesta at his side. Some of the women that stood outside with beckoning hands and too naked flesh were empty eyed; others wore hazy smiles and glazed gazes, overcome by the drugs they took and the incense they smoked until they no longer cared.

Not just the women here took opiates and breathed in fumes to escape from a meaningless and cruel life. Men also sprawled on the cobbles and stumbled in and out of the open doors. The temples were worse. Priests yelled out their warnings and curses, red faced, frowning, gesturing wildly. Outside the temple of Domarra, two men were being flogged while the temple of Hacren had several undead men and women chained up outside. Every hair on Jorrun's body seemed to prickle and stand on end while his stomach cramped. From inside the darkness of the death God's temple came the sound of laughter, screaming, and a single voice cried out unintelligibly.

He swallowed back bile, picking his feet up as they faltered. Osun glanced over his shoulder at him, his lips pursed, and his eyes darkened by a frown.

Jorrun took in a breath through his mouth, regretting it instantly as a waft of incense scorched his throat. Beside him Kesta made a small sound, and she stopped. He followed the direction in which she seemed to be looking, her voice was tight as she forced words out. 'They sell men too.'

Several male slaves stood below the porch of a brightly lit shop wearing nothing but chains.

Jorrun's chest muscles tightened, his vision blurred for a moment and forgetting, he reached out to touch her arm. 'Everyone is for sale here. We need to go.'

'Mistress!' Milaiya pleaded, her eyes huge as they darted around.

Jorrun took a step forward and his muscles loosened a little as Kesta followed. Osun led them up some steps that ran between a geranna house and an incense shop. A group of five men showed more interest in Kesta's hidden form than Jorrun liked, his hand went to his sword hilt and he showed his teeth, they turned back to their business. They followed a narrow pathway that ran behind and above the main street and Osun came to a halt at a large, ornate door. He banged on it firmly with the side of his fist and moments later a servant opened it.

'I need to see Daviid.'

'And you are?' The servant raised an eyebrow.

'Master, is what *you* call me! Get him now.' He kicked the door open wider, and the servant scuttled back.

Jorrun strained his ears to listen, tightening and loosening his toes within his boots. His fingers twitched toward his sword hilt. Voices were followed by firm steps that took their time.

'Osun!' A tall man with blonde hair and blue eyes, set a little too widely apart, appeared in the doorway. 'Well, I didn't expect you! How long has it been? Five years?'

'Six.' Osun reached out to shake the man's hand. 'Listen, Daviid, I'm after a favour and I'm willing to cut you in on a deal that could set us both up for life. Can I come in?'

'I'm intrigued.' Daviid gestured for him to follow.

The hallway was narrow and dark, but the room he took them to was large and lit by several oil lamps on the walls. Books lined the shelves and Jorrun couldn't help but run his eyes over the spines. Account ledgers were set out on a table, but the glass of brandy and book beside the deeply cushioned chair suggested Daviid hadn't been working. 'Tell me,' the Chemmish merchant prompted.

'It would be easier to show you,' Osun smiled. 'Jorrun, take off her covering.'

He took the edge of Kesta's hood and snatched it off, she spun about to face him, eyes wide and mouth slightly open. Her mismatched green eyes were like daggers cutting into his soul as she stared at him unblinking. His breath caught painfully in his throat at the fear he saw in her face. Daviid stepped forward and reached up a hand to take hold of her chin. Jorrun caught the movement of her fingers as she clenched her fist and her muscles tensed. He darted forward and grabbed her wrist before she could throw a punch. She stamped down hard on his foot and tried to elbow him in the stomach, but he wrapped his left arm tight around her and stepped forward to press his body against her back.

Use your knowing! He silently willed her. *Kesta, feel what I'm feeling!* He wished he could rip off his amulet.

Her struggling stopped. Had she understood? He tried to feel calm, not knowing how to send his feelings the way a *walker* did. He turned his head slightly to hide his face from the others and breathed in the scent of her hair. He opened his heart, closing his eyes briefly at the pain. *I love you, do you feel that?*

He glanced up to see Milaiya glaring at him.

'As you can see, she is still quite wild,' Osun smiled smugly. 'A genuine *walker* from the Fulmers.' He clasped his hands together and raised them to his chin, watching Daviid's reaction.

The merchant looked Kesta up and down, lingering on her eyes and face. He licked his lips and Jorrun felt her tense against him again.

'Well, Daviid.' Osun slapped a hand on his thigh and grinned. 'Do you still sell to the Overlord? Think you can get me in to see Dryn Dunham?'

Daviid raised his eyebrows. 'For this, I should think so. When do you want to see him?'

'Sooner rather than later,' Osun nodded toward Kesta. 'It isn't easy to control.'

Kesta gave a low growl and Jorrun squeezed her wrist warningly.

'Well, wait here a moment and I'll see what I can arrange.' The blonde man gave a shake of his head, regarding Kesta again before smiling at Osun.

The moment the man left the room Jorrun let Kesta go. She whipped round to slap him hard across the face. 'You could have warned me of your plan!'

His ear rang, and he moved his jaw to loosen it, thinking he'd been lucky she hadn't thrown a punch. Osun spoke before he had a chance to make his excuses.

'No one stopped you joining us to make our plans.'

More heat rose to Jorrun's face, surely Osun hadn't done this on purpose to spite Kesta because she'd avoided him after finding out about him and Milaiya? He saw Kesta's hands curl into fists again and he quickly stepped between them. 'We can't fall out now. Kesta, Osun, I need you both.'

Osun shrugged and then folded his arms over his chest. Kesta narrowed her eyes at him and turned to Jorrun. Her eyes softened, and she studied his face in a way that made his pulse quicken. How much had she read with her *knowing*?

'So, what are the chances of us getting to see Dryn Dunham alone?' she asked eventually, her gaze only briefly flickering toward Osun.

'It won't be completely alone,' Osun replied. 'Especially, I'm afraid, as we are boasting a *walker* from the Fulmers. He'll take precautions in case you have power. Our advantage will be that he won't expect any of the rest of us to have any. I imagine he'll have some guards and at least one member of his coven with him.'

'Wouldn't we be better off trying to find our own way into his palace and catching him alone?' Kesta placed a hand on her hip.

'Know a way in do you?' Osun smiled.

Jorrun placed a hand on Kesta's shoulder as she took a step forward. He closed his eyes and clenched his jaw. 'This is the plan we have. We would be unlikely to be able to just sneak in and to do so would take days, weeks even, of staking the place out and hoping not to be caught. A direct approach like this will take them off guard.'

'You hope.' She knocked his hand aside and took a step back.

'When we get in there, we should defend against Dryn and take out those around him as quickly as possible before concentrating on him. I don't know where Azrael has got to, we'll have to hope he is able to join us.'

One of the lanterns sparked and he couldn't help the grin that grew rapidly on his face. The bruise on his cheek made the smile uncomfortable.

'I'm here, Jorrun, alwayss here.'

Some of his tension fell away, he hadn't realised how tightly he'd been holding himself together. 'Thank you, bug.' Milaiya caught his eyes, and he turned to look at the red-haired slave. She looked pale, fine lines creased the edges of her eyes, but her posture was straight and upright. 'Milaiya, if we start fighting you should just get out of the way and stay down. Or ... or perhaps we should see if we can leave you here with Daviid?'

She shook her head vigorously.

He took in a deep breath and regarded Kesta. A huge part of him regretted walking away that night in Taurmouth. They might die soon and there was too much unsaid and undone – especially on his part.

The door opened, and he started, all of them turning around guiltily as Daviid stepped back in. 'I've sent a message; we just have to wait for a reply.'

Jorrun was relieved when Kesta voluntarily put the covering back on over her head and face although her murderous looks did add credibility to their story. The two women moved into a corner and Jorrun placed himself between them and the rest of the room, head down. Kesta's arm brushed against him as she turned her back to them all to face the bookshelves. His limbs felt heavy and his stomach twisted itself in knots. Did she hate him? Did she regret coming here to fight with him?

Osun and Daviid talked of trade and of the Arkoom merchant's business. It became apparent very quickly that he traded in humans, Jorrun's nose wrinkled in distaste despite his efforts not to react. He could only imagine how Kesta was feeling. She was too still behind him, like a storm waiting to break. He knew Osun well enough to know he was acting, playing a part, and he was very good at it. Kesta wouldn't know that though.

Unlike himself, Osun had never been able to fit in and settle in Elden. Perhaps it was their four years difference. Chem had had more time to break and manipulate his half-brother. Osun had been dismissed as useless as he'd shown no sign of having inherited magical blood, the beatings he'd received had been far more brutal than anything Jorrun had endured. Osun had learned to survive by studying people, knowing what they wanted and needed, becoming good at anything he chose to do including the lowliest of tasks. He'd once been the most subservient of slaves and it broke Jorrun's heart that his brother could not seem to break free from the need of a master, even if an imagined one.

They heard someone knock at the door and the servant moved along the hall. Jorrun tensed, fighting against the urge to look up. Kesta placed three fingertips very lightly against his back. He didn't know if she was comforting herself or him, but he breathed easier.

The servant came to the room and bowed. 'A message, master.'

He held out a scroll, leaving as soon as Daviid took it. Jorrun tensed his toes inside his boots.

'He will see you.' Daviid grinned at Osun.

'When?'

'Now.'

***

Jorrun's head buzzed as his nerves momentarily got the better of him. Daviid walked just ahead with Osun and a guard of his own, leaving Jorrun to follow last behind the women. He took them up another set of steps away from the main street of the temple district, even so the disturbing smells and sounds seemed determined to bite at his senses. They reached a main road and proceeded to an iron gate. Daviid showed the guards his letter, and they opened the gate to let them through into a huge garden.

Night may have fallen but the way to the palace was brightly lit by lanterns hanging from iron posts. The garden was actually beautiful, and he found himself breathing more easily. Flagstone paths wound through clipped hedges and he could hear water falling gently somewhere close. The musky scent of roses was refreshing and somewhat heady after the cloying incense and distressing human smells. The only thing that jarred the calm of the gardens were the guards that patrolled it. Twice Daviid had to show his letter, and they were directed around to the side of the grey-stone palace.

The trade entrance was guarded by four men, one of whom was dressed in expensive clothing and adorned with jewellery depicting symbols of the death God. Jorrun surmised that he must be a necromancer and kept his head lowered and his face turned away as much as possible. Once again, Daviid showed his letter. Jorrun found himself holding his breath, and he took a step closer to Kesta. He could feel the blood pulsing in the main artery of his neck.

'Go on.' The necromancer nodded toward the door with his head. 'The man inside will show you the way.'

Jorrun tried to concentrate on his surroundings to stop the doubts that pushed at the edge of his thoughts. It was too late to turn back now either way, the Chemmen would never let Kesta walk out of here. If he didn't fight, if he didn't win, he was condemning her to a life beyond unbearable. Her strength was different than his mother's had been, his mother had endured by being subtle and infinitely patient, by finding hope in small things. Kesta would fight. She wouldn't stop fighting. And they wouldn't stop hurting her. It made him feel sick just to think of it.

He tripped over his own feet, putting out a hand to steady himself against the wall.

'Jorrun.' Osun glowered at him over his shoulder.

He bowed toward his 'master', his face feeling warm with the rush of blood that flowed there. Kesta had slowed her steps, and he found himself walking more beside her than behind. He took in a sharp breath as her little finger curled around his; the lightest of touches. He was not surprised to find that she had more courage than he.

He'd expected something grand and threatening but the room they were shown into was stark and cold. It was as large as Bractius's throne room but empty of anything save a table and a single, tall chair. The flagstone floor was the same colour as the walls and nothing adorned them except for six lanterns. He breathed out in relief at the sight of them, trusting Azrael to be there. He realised they had instinctively moved to stand together at the centre of the room and he purposefully stepped back to keep everyone, and the doors, in his sight. Milaiya was almost leaning on Kesta, he hoped the woman was stronger than she appeared for her own sake, and Kesta's.

All of them turned as a loud crack echoed about the chamber, the door in the far wall opened. Jorrun tensed and sucked in air through his mouth. He had to stop his hands calling up flame; his palms itched. Two guards in leather armour entered and looked them over.

'Your swords,' one demanded.

At once Osun, Jorrun, and Daviid's man handed their weapons over. Jorrun silently cursed. He should have expected that. The two men took up position either side of the doorway. They waited. He could hear Daviid's loud and rapid breathing. Osun glanced at him but Jorrun turned his eyes back to the floor. Kesta shifted her feet slightly. The door opened again, and a bald-headed man dressed in blood-red robes and dripping with gold walked in. Jorrun barely gave him a glance, his eyes finding the man that followed behind him. It was almost his own face he saw, older and beardless with grey in the long hair, but the eyes were his as were the jaw and nose. The man wore wide-legged black trousers and a dark-blue shirt, no weapon hung from his belt. The way this man walked proclaimed that he *was* the weapon. Jorrun felt his blood turn to ice.

'Master!' Osun dipped in a low bow and they all followed, all but Milaiya who threw herself to the floor, and Kesta who drew herself up and lifted her chin beneath her hood to face him.

Dryn Dunham.

His eyes, the colour of a stormy sky, searched all of their faces with painful slowness. Jorrun's breathing was shallow as he endured the gaze with his head lowered and his eyes on the hem of Kesta's dress. Dryn's voice, when he spoke, was deep and slow, reverberating in a pleasant way.

'Trader Daviid, I was intrigued by your note. My eldest son failed to secure me a *fire-walker* and yet here you are claiming your associate has one.'

'Lord.' There was a slight tremble to Osun's voice. Jorrun lifted his eyes a little to better see his brother. 'We have brought this woman not from the Fulmers, but from Elden. I can promise you she is a *walker*. May I?' He took hold of the edge of her hood.

He nodded. 'Please do.'

Jorrun had to stop himself stepping forward. Osun hesitated and flexed his fingers before taking hold of the cloth. He removed it clumsily, catching Kesta's long, dark hair so that it fell back partially obscuring her face.

Even so, the red-clothed necromancer sucked in air noisily, stepping forward and raking his teeth over his lower lip. Dryn's eyes widened ever so slightly. Jorrun clenched his teeth as the Overlord of Chem's eyes travelled over her.

'How do you control her?'

Jorrun realised he was breathing hard. His eyes went from his father to Kesta. As Dryn stalked closer her fingers curled up, her eyes narrowed, and her shoulders stiffened. He found his own hands closing into fists and he forced them to relax.

'She was sold to the king of Elden in return for his aid to the Fulmers against you, master,' Osun replied. 'She has been made to obey.'

Dryn's head shot round and he stared at Osun unblinking. 'Really?'

Osun's nostrils flared, but he otherwise held his ground. Jorrun felt the warmth of pride chasing away the chill of fear in his bones.

Dryn Dunham stepped back, glancing at the others in the room. He paused when he came to Jorrun, the slightest of smiles twitched at his mouth. 'Strip her, let me see what I'm buying.'

'No!' Jorrun sprang forward, putting himself between his father and Kesta. For the first time he looked his father straight in the eye.

The whole world seemed to pause and Jorrun's heart pounded in his ears.

Dryn Dunham threw back his head and laughed. The sound went through Jorrun like a jagged blade. Jorrun's fingers twitched, longing for the reassuring grip of his sword. His father found his eyes again and then moved over him with the same slow scrutiny with which he'd regarded Kesta. Jorrun didn't move, but his shoulders rose and fell noticeably with his breathing.

The guards had stepped forward, Milaiya curled into a tight ball with her hands over her head. Osun took a step toward where their swords had been placed and Daviid and his man backed away several feet. The bald-headed necromancer stared open-mouthed from Dryn to Jorrun.

Movement caught Jorrun's eye, and they all turned to stare as Kesta reached down to grab the hem of her skirt and pull it up over her head. Underneath she wore the trousers and tunic Jorrun had bought her and he saw the hilt of her dagger sticking out of her boot. The muscles of Jorrun's face surged upward into a smile.

Spirits, I love that woman!

Her posture changed, hips moving slightly as she secured her balance in a fighter's stance. There was a challenging gleam in her eyes.

Dryn's eyes barely flickered, his mouth curling into a grin higher on one side of his mouth than the other and showing the glint of a canine. He turned to Jorrun. 'Did you think I wouldn't know you, *son*?'

Jorrun's mouth went dry. For years he'd dreamt of confronting his father, taking vengeance for his mother, ending the dominance of the necromancers over Chem. He couldn't think of a single clever thing to say.

Osun replied for him. 'Your *sons*, although there is no pride in that fact.'

'Oh yes, the bloodless slave.' Dryn's lip curled in distaste. 'I remember that I gave your worthless mother away for free.'

Osun stiffened, his eyes darting toward the swords. Quickly Jorrun spoke. 'That you're our father is not even relevant—'

'Isn't it?' Dryn's pale eyes flashed as he turned back to Jorrun. 'So much potential and yet such a disappointment.' He looked Jorrun up and down. 'You could have been Overlord after me.' He circled like a predator around to Jorrun's other side. 'Not just of Chem, but of Elden and the Fulmers. You could have had fifty women all finer than this one.' He lifted his chin toward Kesta and grinned when he saw Jorrun react. 'They get under your skin, you know, *walkers*. You think you're safe with your amulet.' He pointed at Jorrun's chest. 'But they worm their way in, make you think you love them. Make you think that worthless slaves of no blood are worth keeping. And they give you disloyal and ungrateful sons!'

'Sounds like we give you what you deserve,' Kesta snorted.

Dryn hissed through his teeth. 'Oh, *you'll* get what you deserve!'

Sparks flared behind Jorrun's eyes and he called fire to the tips of his fingertips. He was shocked when Kesta laughed. Then she gritted her teeth. 'Coward! You have never faced a *walker* whose wings you hadn't clipped from birth!'

She leapt and spun, not toward Dryn but away, calling up a shield of air as she drew her dagger and sliced it through the throat of Daviid. Osun lunged for the swords, punching one of the guards in the stomach and face as he tried to stop him. The red necromancer drew flame to himself from one of the lanterns, his snarl turning to a scream of horror as the flame changed shape to become Azrael.

Neither Dryn nor Jorrun moved, facing each other and drawing their magic close. Jorrun called up a swirl of air that circled his feet and ankles and held fire in his right hand. Dryn summoned a huge blaze before him that changed his eyes to the orange of sunrise. He didn't even blink as his red necromancer was engulfed in Azrael's bright embrace. From the corner of his eye Jorrun saw Osun snatch up his sword, and he engaged the two guardsmen.

'Well,' Dryn said pleasantly. 'They said you would be strong, Joryn, shall we see?'

Dryn's wall of flame expanded rapidly toward him and he ducked instinctively as he pulled the shield of air upward to surround himself. The force of his father's magic sent him staggering backwards, and he had no chance to even contemplate striking back. The pressure relented as a second strong wind came from behind him and Dryn's flames were forced back to curl up the wall and across the ceiling. Kesta had taken out Daviid's man and came to stand at Jorrun's side, their shields of air combined. They heard Osun swear as one of the guards broke away from him to run to the door and shout for help. Osun stabbed the man through the back and then kicked him aside, he ran to tip the table and tried to drag it across to the door.

Dryn's fire died down and he looked from Jorrun to Kesta, a smile still playing around his lips. Nothing in his expression gave him away as he sent a sudden gale not at them but toward Osun, hurling the man across the room with the heavy table tumbling after him. It was Kesta who called up a fierce whirlwind of her own, sending it around the room to smash the table against the wall inches from Osun. As both of the winds died Azrael shot toward the door in time to face two necromancers who came running in. As he had done in Mantu, the fire-spirit made himself gigantic and distorted his features to look terrifying. One of the necromancers reached into his pocket for a box and Azrael recoiled, shrinking rapidly. With a quick nod at Jorrun, Kesta ran to the door. She set fire to the shards of the table before lifting them and hurling them toward the two necromancers. They shielded easily and sent flames broiling out toward her.

Jorrun gasped in air and almost lost his balance as the ground heaved beneath his feet. The flagstones cracked and several of them rose upward to form a crater as a jet of water ruptured, showering him with burning droplets. He sent a burst of fire toward his father even as he shielded, steam hissed like a host of angry demons, scorching his skin. The back of Jorrun's shirt clung to him and he wiped the sweat from his face with his hand. He was breathing hard. It seemed that Dryn had no qualms about pulling his palace down around them.

He strained to see through air thick with condensation, a shadow the only warning that his father had moved closer. He couldn't see Osun or Milaiya, but Kesta and Azrael had the necromancers retreating out of the doorway. He tried to rein in his fear, to slow his racing heart.

'What is it you want, Joryn?' His father's voice was compelling, hypnotic.

Jorrun clenched his jaw, backing slowly around, careful of each step as he tried to keep track of where Dryn Dunham was. It was hard not to listen to his voice, impossible not to let it touch every sensitive nerve.

'Revenge for your mother? Poor, little slave boy. That is what you chose to cling to instead of rising to be Overlord of three lands?'

He refused to answer although the words wormed in deep. Water flowed across the shattered flagstones. Summoning a little heat, he caused mist to rise.

'Or is that what you want? Do you have more ambition than I gave you credit for? Are you here to take my Seat for yourself?'

His father's grinning face was suddenly before him. Jorrun recoiled and shielded quickly as fire lashed out to engulf him again. At the same time the flagstones cracked under him and the walls gave a mournful groan. He fell back hard, his shoulder blades and elbow smashing into the stone. His shield faltered, and heat seared his skin as he rolled out of the way.

A strong wind pinned Jorrun down, aimed not at him but at Dryn. Kesta launched herself across the room to slash at Dryn with her dagger. The Chemman reacted with amazing speed, slamming up a shield and grabbing her wrist to pull her around and against him with her own dagger against her throat.

Jorrun's lungs froze mid-breath, his muscles went to water at the same time as blood rushed through his already hot skin. His eyes went straight to Kesta's as he pushed himself up onto his side, neither of them blinked.

Dryn Dunham laughed. 'How disappointingly easy!'

Jorrun didn't even hear his father's words, only the thundering of his heart. Kesta smiled, Jorrun took a breath.

She dropped as though every tendon had been cut, her weight surprising Dryn as she slipped from his grip; the dagger caught the side of her jaw and left a deep line of red. Jorrun scrambled to his feet as Kesta came up onto hers. She spun away and called up flame but the Overlord drew up a wind that lifted her off the ground and hurled her against the wall. Jorrun heard the crack of her skull. Dryn threw the dagger; and it embedded itself between her breasts as she slid down onto the flagstones, her eyes glazing over.

The world turned black and red. Jorrun took in a single, sharp breath, the air stabbing at his heart and lungs. Tears bled from his eyes as his skin flushed with heat. He couldn't move, couldn't tear his eyes away.

Not her!

Anyone but her!

Dryn Dunham laughed again. 'I told you *walkers* make you weak.'

A roar rose up from deep within his soul and he turned to his father whose image fragmented. He called on every ounce of his magic, feeling the muscles of his physical body strain to bursting. He ripped up every loose flagstone and sent them flying toward Dryn with fire and water. His father called up a shield but stumbled back, further and further toward the cracked wall. Jorrun gave a cry of pain, his hand going to his head and his knees buckling, but he didn't stop. His father tried to counter with fire so hot it turned blue, but Jorrun turned it away, eyes bulging with the strain. He staggered forward as he reached the end of his magic, collapsing to one knee. All around him fragments of stone hit the floor. The wind howled around the chamber and slowly died away; the air stilled. Looking up, he took in a long breath through his teeth, his father's magic had also faltered and for the first time there was fear on Dryn's face. With huge effort Jorrun stood and pulled himself up to his full height.

Osun stepped out of the fog. He swung his sword and hacked at Dryn Dunham's neck. The first blow caught in his father's spine and it took a second strike to take his head off completely.

Osun stood looking at Jorrun, covered in blood and soot. There was no smile, no triumph. The sword slipped from his hand.

Kesta!

Jorrun forced his aching legs into a run. He threw himself to her side and looked at her empty, half-closed eyes. Holding his breath, he touched the handle of the dagger and then reached out shaking fingers to move aside her wet hair and feel for a pulse in her neck.

Nothing.

Chapter Twenty-Five

Dia: Kingdom of Elden

'How many?' Dia asked. They sat in an exhausted huddle beneath the trees. About forty warriors were still with them, including those from the Fulmers.

'Too many for us to take on as we are.' Heara shook her head. 'If the fancy clothes and love for skull jewellery is anything to go by, they have two sorcerers. That and several creatures. Not many actual warriors though.'

'How far to the hold?' She turned to Merkis Vilnue.

He pulled at his greying beard. 'I'd say just over a mile. If we cut inland through the forest, we can go around those Chemmen and come at the hold from the east. That would be the sensible option.'

Dia chewed at her thumbnail, her eyes un-focusing. She had no power left, and neither did Everlyn, but she didn't like to leave those sorcerers wandering about to just attack them later.

'Let me deal with them.' Heara moved into a crouch, ready to be off.

Dia's brows moved together above the bridge of her nose as she regarded her friend. 'Are you sure?'

Heara grinned and nodded but butterflies moved about in Dia's stomach.

'Take our warriors with you.'

Heara shook her head, her grin leaving. 'They would get in the way. I'm quicker, stealthier, when alone.'

'No risks!' She reached out to touch her friend's arm. Vilnue remained silent, looking down at his hands.

Heara nodded once and was off.

'We'd best move on to the hold.' Dia reached out and squeezed one of Vilnue's hands. 'Take us east, then, Merkis.'

***

Heara rejoined them about half a mile into the forest. Dia let out a breath and forced her muscles to relax.

'I only got one.' Heara wrinkled her nose. 'The second shielded as soon as the first fell and then started throwing fire randomly into the forest. I'm afraid there'll be a lot of damage to the trees around here; hopefully not to the animals.'

'It is probably just as well to chase them away from the dead men.' She recalled the sight of half-eaten livestock on the Fulmers and shuddered. 'Take the lead?'

'Of course.' Heara skipped past Merkis Vilnue, looking him up and down with a smile. The Elden warrior's face flushed a little.

'You must find our ways strange.' Dia stepped up beside him as they proceeded through the trees.

'I find I like your ways.' Vilnue glanced at her, staying alert to everything around them. 'Everything is so much simpler with Fulmer women who say what's on their mind and, er, take what they want.'

'You never once flinched at taking command from me.'

Vilnue shrugged. 'I was told you were in charge, so you're in charge. You have never given me reason to think you shouldn't be.'

She snorted. She'd been about to say that sometimes she wondered … but the fact was that even when she did have doubts she wasn't afraid to make a decision and take its consequences. She had no reason to put herself down.

They made their way as silently as they could through the forest. Night was thick around them and several times Dia stubbed her tired feet on roots and stones.

'The walls of the hold are just ahead.' Heara came hurrying back to inform them.

They came to the edge of the clearing cautiously. The earthworks were simpler than Dia had imagined for the home of Elden's Dark Man, but there was something somehow welcoming about them; perhaps just the relief of coming to a relatively safe place in a foreign land. She could see the famous Raven Tower; it was completely dark.

'Let me go ahead so they can see we are not Chemmen,' Vilnue suggested.

Dia nodded, her eyes not leaving the tower.

Vilnue lit a torch and then stepped out into the clearing. He walked forward several yards and stopped, letting the watchers on the walls take him in. He started forward again and then halted as something caught his eye.

'What's that?' one of the warriors demanded.

Both Dia and Heara stepped out of the trees to peer into the darkness.

'Undead,' Heara hissed. She drew her short sword.

'Come on.' Dia looked around at the others. 'If they start shooting head back to the trees, if not then make for the gate. You all know how to take out an undead now, hamstring it and then take off the head. We can burn them later.'

They set off at a cautious jog across the meadow. Ten of Vilnue's men veered off to dispatch the undead warrior they'd seen. Several of them looked considerably paler as they re-joined the main party. They slowed their pace, letting the Merkis get ahead again as they came within hailing distance of the walls.

'I'm Merkis Vilnue of Taurmaline!' He held his torch aloft. 'Who keeps the hold?'

'Merkis Tantony! Come around to the gate, man!'

Dia felt a tingling in her chest muscles and her feet grew heavier. They were nearly there.

'Be careful! There are more of those monsters out there!' A woman's voice called down from above, one unused to being raised.

The men spread out a little, scanning the last few feet of meadowland. Heara, Vilnue and Everlyn all drew closer to Dia. They heard the gates open and Dia felt the back of her eyes sting and her throat tighten. Several warriors came out to guard them as they entered Northold.

A stocky man with a crooked nose and soft grey eyes presented himself to them as the gates were closed and the bars dropped. His arm was bandaged. 'I am Merkis Tantony.'

'Vilnue.' The greying warrior held out a hand. 'This is the Icante of the Fulmers, she is come from fighting the Chemmen on the river.'

He bowed. 'Icante, we are honoured and grateful.'

A woman of about Dia's age, with brown eyes and tawny hair tied neatly back, stepped forward to curtsey. 'My lady, we have food and drink in the great hall for you and your men. Please, follow me.'

Dia nodded, and they took a path through some single storied houses toward a second gate and a higher, stone reinforced wall. Dia stumbled and the woman quickly offered her arm for her to lean on. She felt a flush of embarrassment at appearing so weak.

'I'm Rosa,' the woman said quietly. 'I'm Kesta's lady ... I'm Kesta's friend.'

Dia turned to look at her, she didn't even have the strength to call upon her *knowing* yet.

'I'll take you up to the guest tower, the king's rooms.' Rosa's eyes swept gently over her face. 'I'll let you know if anything urgent happens.'

Dia nodded, glancing over her shoulder to catch Heara's eye. Rest and quiet sounded infinitely welcome.

***

Dia woke with a start, sitting up to look around the unfamiliar room. It was round. A tower. Heara lay curled up at the end of the bed, her breathing deep and audible. Dia got up carefully and padded across to the window, it looked out over the lake. There was no sign of the Chemmen or their ships, no doubt they were at Taurmaline by now.

Food had been left out, and she forced herself to eat. Her stomach didn't want it but she knew she needed the fuel. She experimented and called a few sparks to her fingertips, relieved to feel that her magic was already coming back to her.

'Dia!' Heara gave a huge yawn and flung her long limbs wide as she stretched. 'I'm starving!' She sauntered to the table and ate unselfconsciously. Dia went back to the window. Warriors lined the walls below and she was surprised to see women and children there also with bows. She hadn't thought it was the Elden way.

'What now?' Heara sat back and swallowed down a mug of water.

Dia took in a deep breath and narrowed her eyes. 'We see what news there is from Taurmaline and decide if we're going to rescue their king or not.'

Heara grunted, but she got dressed and secured all of her weapons to her belt and boots.

***

The great hall was crowded with both refugees, and warriors taking a rest from the walls. Dia couldn't see Merkis Tantony anywhere but she spotted the woman from the night before, Rosa. She had a young girl with her.

'Icante.' Rosa gave a curtsey. The young girl remained still, regarding her intently. 'Did you manage to rest?'

'I did, thank you. Any news?'

Rosa frowned and shook her head. 'Still nothing. I think all of our ravens are here though, and there is no safe way to get any into Taurmaline to bring us messages back.'

'Ravens.' Dia looked down and sucked on her bottom lip. 'They are clever birds, I might be able to get them to spy for us, even to go to the messenger in Taurmaline.'

'You're not allowed in the Raven Tower.' The young girl folded her arms across her chest.

'Catya!' Rosa blushed and flapped a hand at the girl.

'And you are?' Dia raised an eyebrow.

Catya's chin went up and her long hair fell back. 'I'm Kesta's bodyguard.'

'Really?' Dia glanced at Rosa who was pursing her lips and shaking her head.

Heara stepped forward and placed her hands on her hips. 'I'm the Icante's bodyguard.'

478

Catya looked her up and down slowly and mirrored her stance without realising she was doing so. She gave an approving nod and snorted through her nose. Heara grinned.

'Right, well.' Rosa stepped aside and gestured for them to follow. 'I should think Jorrun would allow you in his tower under the circumstances.'

Catya fell in beside Heara as they crossed the ward to the tower. Heara pulled out a long dagger and handed it to the girl who studied it with wide-eyed desire. Dia glanced over her shoulder to give her friend a warning look, but Heara just shrugged and kept on grinning.

Rosa pushed at the door and it gave way easily, the interior was disappointingly plain. Dia changed her mind when she saw the rooms through the open doors as they ascended.

'Who reads this many books?' Heara paused in one doorway, her mouth a little open.

'I hate letters,' Catya grumbled.

Heara bent down to whisper in her ear. 'Knives are better.'

Catya giggled.

'This is Jorrun's room.' Rosa pointed to the door at the top of the steps. 'The ravens roost in the loft just above.'

Dia felt a small knot of apprehension as she approached the room of the man who had all but stolen her daughter. She paused in the doorway to regard it slowly. It was the room of someone with a busy mind, clutter everywhere and such an odd array of items. The bed was small, almost an afterthought. A candle stood upon the window facing west. Dia lifted one foot, hesitating before stepping forward over the threshold. She looked through the leaded glass and saw the Ivy Tower across the ward.

'He used to light that candle when he wanted Kesta to visit. Mostly he came to her and they would, well they would just talk.' Rosa stood in the centre of the room with her hands folded together.

'They got on well together?' Dia turned to better study the woman's face.

'Oh.' A little colour came to her cheeks. 'I think they grew rather fond of each other in the short time she was here.'

Rather fond. Well, that was interesting.

'So, the ravens are up here?' Dia pointed to the hatch above the ladder.

'Oh, yes, let me open it!' Rosa darted forward but Dia waved her aside.

'I have it.' She climbed up and pushed the trapdoor back.

The ravens croaked and cawed at her interruption, she could hear the scrabbling of their claws and the ruffling of their feathers before her sight adjusted and she could see the gleam of their black eyes. She reached out her *knowing* to touch the bright sparks of their inquisitive minds. She nearly lost her balance on the ladder at their reaction. They knew her, or certainly knew who she was. They showed her images of Kesta, of Jorrun lying on the floor of the tower, of the ward changing below them. As interesting as it was Dia showed them thoughts of her own; the battered enemy ships heading up the river, Taurmaline across the lake. She demonstrated to them flying there, watching, and flying back. She tried to show them taking a message but without knowing what the person who took care of the ravens at Taurmaline looked like it was hard to explain where she needed them to go.

One of the ravens hopped down close to her. It lifted a leg and held it out.

'Quickly, write me a message!' She turned to call down the ladder. 'Write that the king's guest is with the ravens and can come to Taurmaline.'

Rosa wrote a hasty note and placed it in a cylinder. The raven waited patiently while Dia attached it to its leg. Several of the ravens hopped up to the edge of their roost, looked back at her, then flew out and away southward. Dia made her way slowly back down the ladder.

'What now?' Heara asked.

Dia drew in a deep breath. 'We wait and see what news the ravens bring us.'

***

Tantony and Rosa had the warriors and archers drilling in the ward to keep them occupied and their morale high. Even Reetha the cook had people out in the gardens working or constantly drawing up water from the well for the people and animals. Dia looked on with interest and pride, seeing her daughter's influence but also a group of people whom she could admire.

Heara had taken the little girl, Catya, under her wing and she followed the scout with shining eyes. Dia narrowed her own eyes as she watched them training together with daggers. Heara was still grieving, and she was concerned that Catya was as much a bandage for her pain as Vilnue.

The first ravens returned almost a day after leaving the tower. They showed Dia images of a closed city and a harbour in flames. Shortly after the raven who had offered to take a message came back to the tower with a cylinder still attached to its leg. It was Rosa who removed it and she picked up her skirts to run to the great hall where Dia was discussing the old Borrow raids with some of the veteran warriors. Dia took one look at Rosa's face and stood up to excuse herself.

She touched Rosa's arm. 'What is it?'

She handed Dia the cylinder. She paused for several heartbeats when she realised the wax was different than they'd used. She broke the seal and unrolled it, running her eyes over the tiny words. She let out the breath that she'd been holding and turned to Rosa.

'The message reads, *Unwanted visitors being kept out. Try to be here just before dawn tomorrow. We will come out to meet you.*'

'Will you go?' Rosa asked, her eyes wide and her chest rising with her deep breaths.

'Of course. Where's Tantony?'

'On the walls, I'll fetch him.'

Dia found Heara with Catya and after a moment's thought, sought out Vilnue as well. Merkis Tantony ushered them all up to his study, and they crowded in. She showed them the scroll.

'I'm assuming the best way to get to Taurmaline for dawn will be by water?' she asked Tantony.

'The only way to get there in that time, really.' The lines about his grey eyes seemed more pronounced than usual. 'We have a few good horses but even they would be pushing it to get there in time. We have Kurghan's boat and a few other small fishing vessels but nothing that could transport an army.'

Dia could feel them all looking at her. She gazed out of the window at the busy ward below. 'From what the ravens have shown me, the harbour is held against us and for the most part, destroyed. There will probably be dead people set against us wandering the shores of the lake. Adelphy's ships are moored out of reach of arrows from the city walls but we can't be sure he himself is still on the ships.'

'So.' Tantony sat on the edge of his desk. 'We can only send a small group to assist the king when he opens the city to attack the Chemmen. Perhaps it would be better to send him a message to give us more time?'

Dia turned to face him. 'I'm not sure he has more time. Adelphy can breach the city as soon as his magic is fully recharged. I could take out the gates without much effort and I have no doubt it would be the same for him. Once inside it would be a slaughter of the refugees and anyone else caught outside the castle itself.'

Tantony slammed the heel of his hand down on the table. 'And they become bodies for his growing army.' He drew in a long, loud breath. 'So, we must go, and quickly. What do you most need? Archers? Warriors? Those who can swim and be stealthy?'

She bit at her bottom lip. 'I like the way you're thinking, Merkis. Ideally, I need ten *walkers* and fifty of Heara.'

'I'd like to think I'm worth something.' Tantony looked down at his boots.

Rosa opened her mouth but Dia beat her to it. 'You, Tantony, are worth a lifetime of good harvests. Get as many boats together as you can hunt down. Select me strong swimmers who can do close, bloody work. It—' she winced, feeling slightly nauseous. 'It's an awful plan but we should try to kill those on watch and then trap those below before sinking or firing each ship. There will not be enough of us to take on all their warriors if they are still aboard.'

Tantony shifted on the table. No one seemed to want to meet each other's eyes.

'It's us or them.' Rosa looked up and touched Tantony's arm with just one finger. 'I don't imagine they would care about fairness or brutality if it were the other way around.'

'Get your people together then.' Dia looked from Tantony to Vilnue. 'We need to get going sooner rather than later.'

***

'As much as I love a fight,' Heara said as they went back out into the ward and headed for the Raven Tower. 'The odds aren't exactly in our favour.'

'Not yet.' Dia frowned. 'But when we were under attack by Relta and his ships Thane Jorrun was able to call on the fire-spirits and Doroquael came to help us.'

'We left Doroquael back in the Fulmers.'

Dia nodded and regarded her friend. 'There are other fire-spirits here in Elden. I'm going to see if any of them will help. There are also the ravens.'

'The ravens?' Heara frowned down at her.

Dia smiled and nodded.

They entered the tower and goosebumps rose on her arms. No matter how many times she went into the Raven Tower Dia still felt an overwhelming sense that she was intruding. The scent of jasmine was fading but the presence of the man whose tower it was hadn't lessened with his absence. She glanced back at Heara and saw that her best friend was stalking as though hunting, each step carefully placed. They heard the ravens scratching about in the loft and several croaking caws greeted them as Dia opened the hatch. Feathers rustled, and two birds alighted right before Dia's face. One of them stretched toward her and turned its head, closing and opening its eyes slowly. She reached out her *knowing,* and it showed her images of two severely damaged Chemman ships anchored at the edge of the lake and the remaining five blockading the harbour. It showed her the archers manning the walls of Taurmaline and the refugees being herded away from the main gate to make way for warriors.

She showed it images of their plan and asked if the ravens would continue to spy for them. Eagerly they consented. Ravens loved war.

Breathing rapidly, Dia climbed back down the ladder and looking around the room spotted the candle on the windowsill. Calling her magic, she lit it before taking it down and placing it on the table. Heara sat on the edge of the narrow bed watching silently. Dia made herself comfortable on one of the chairs and stared into the flame, losing herself in the hypnotic flicker. As soon as she entered the spirit realm of fire, she appealed for a drake to come forth. Almost at once she felt the presence of a sentient mind, she held herself still, allowing it to study her.

Icante. The necromansser knows that we have been helping. There are traps set against drakes on the ships.

Dia's heart sank, and she cursed. *Yes, this Adelphy seems smarter than the Chemmen we met on Fulmer. I should have gone straight after him and not waited here.*

Then you would have had insufficient power, Icante. The fire-spirit seemed to fluctuate, fading and growing like flame feeding off wood. *We cannot help you with the ships, but we will be there. Perhapss … perhaps where fire cannot go, you might use ice?*

Ice? Dia contemplated his words. Like all *walkers* she worked with all the elements and with nature, but having been chosen by fire it was to fire that they most often turned. *Yes, ice.* She smiled.

The fire-spirit crackled in what might have been a chuckle. *Watch for uss on the shores of the lake, we will be there before dawn ignitess the skies.*

Dia found herself outside of the flame. She ran her idea over in her head, not moving except to breathe and to blink.

'What are you smiling at?' Heara grumbled, leaning back on the bed.

Dia turned to regard her. 'Strap on all of your weapons. It's time to go.'

***

They had room enough for only fifty-three warriors alongside Dia, Everlyn, and Heara in the available fishing boats. Both Tantony and Merkis Vilnue insisted on being among them. With their numbers so few, Dia reluctantly decided to ignore the ships on the shore initially and concentrate on the five blockading the harbour. They sailed in darkness, relying on the knowledge and skills of the local warriors rather than risk the sound of oars or the feel of magic being detected. Their sails had been changed from undyed canvas to those coloured dark blue and deep green. Several of the ravens travelled with them, perched on rails, prows, and masts. Despite the lack of light, one of them flew ahead and came back to warn Dia when they were getting close. She signalled the other boats, and they came together to hear her.

'We'll draw close to them. Those of you who can swim well and silently must go ahead and board. Take out as many watchmen as you can and where possible close down or block any hatches from which warriors might emerge. Be aware that there will be sorcerers aboard who'll be able to blast things open with ease. Do as much as you can and then get away, make for the shore and be prepared to face the dead and the Chemmen warriors who have already landed. Once I follow and begin my magic, it will be hard for you to escape. My timing will not be precise, but I'll give about ten minutes for you to swim to the ships, five for you to do as much damage as you can, then five more to get clear. Spirits be with us.'

'Spirits be with us,' the few of them from the Fulmers chorused.

'God's have mercy.' Tantony made a sign against evil, then looked around guiltily when he realised it was also an ancient sign used to ward against witchcraft.

They proceeded across the lake, the far off watchfires on the walls of Taurmaline growing larger and brighter. Only a few lanterns were lit on the five Chemman ships and they were no more than deeper shadows against the backdrop of the city. Dia signalled for their sails to come down and those of them who were to swim quickly prepared themselves. Heara squeezed her hand and then dropped with slow control into the water, her muscles straining to hold her weight and prevent even the slightest splash. Neither Tantony nor Vilnue were foolish enough to think themselves silent enough or good enough in the water, so as much as it rankled them to remain, they took their places beside Dia as her physical protection. The absence of Shaherra was still too raw and jarring for Dia to be able to think about for long and she knew that Heara would miss her twin much more than she tonight.

Dia found herself biting her lip and clenching her fists as they waited. On one of the ships the lanterns winked out. Both Everlyn and Vilnue drew in sharp breaths when something heavy splashed into the lake. A shout went up and Dia scrambled to her feet, holding onto the mast. She called up her magic at once and created a current beneath the boat to push them rapidly toward the Chemmen. The sounds of a fight were whisked toward them on the wind and Dia found herself breathing harder, her heart pounding in her ears. She turned to Everlyn whose eyes were shadowed.

'Try to keep the temperature of the water beneath us constant. Leave the rest to me.' She leaned over the side of the boat; Tantony quickly reached forward to grab her belt and keep her from slipping. Drawing on her magic she stilled both the air and the water, sending a chill toward the towering ships. The lake water began to freeze, slowly at first and then as rapidly as though a night's frost was happening within the span of a minute. It thickened and deepened, the timber of the ships began to creak and groan.

A shower of splinters exploded upward from the deck of one of the ships. It was followed by waves of rolling flame that spilled down the side of the ship to crack and melt the ice. Steam rose and one of the ships ruptured. Despite the strain she was under, Dia's mouth opened to show her teeth in a feral grin; they were sinking their own ships! Two other ships groaned and tilted before Dia changed her tactics and sent fire of her own toward the remaining two. An almost solid wall of wind slammed into them and lifted their small boat to smack down hard again into the lake. Water came over the side and Dia was only saved by Tantony's strong grip on her belt. She was soaked through but barely noticed, scrabbling her way back to the side of the boat she created another strong current and slammed one of the ships into the side of another.

A blinding burst of flames came boiling toward them and Everlyn shielded. Both Tantony and Vilnue threw themselves to the bottom of the boat. Dia reached for the water and sent another strong current to push all five ships further toward the harbour and themselves out toward the shore. Flames ran across the deck of the ship furthest from them; their warriors must still be fighting aboard at least that vessel. She prayed it wasn't Heara but had a sickening feeling it was.

The attack against them ceased so suddenly that Everlyn fell forward. Dia quickly replaced her shield just in time as an icy blast smashed into it. She spotted a raven circling above her and realised that the sky was lightening.

'Everlyn, move us steadily toward shore!'

'Arrows!' Vilnue pointed at the sky.

Over two hundred whistled and hummed through the air from the city, but they were obliterated by a sudden wall of fire. Dia dropped her shield and sent a narrow, concentrated blast of flame at the ship of their sorcerous attacker, just above the water line. The damp planks smouldered and caught, the wood glowing with a hot white flame. She quickly drew her shield back up as she saw a fireball forming in the hands of a small figure on one of the sinking ships.

'To shore, quickly!' Dia commanded.

Tantony and Vilnue both grabbed oars while Everlyn continued to move them and Dia to shield. At the same time, she stretched out her *knowing* to find the ravens and let them know it was time for them to lead any of their remaining warriors to wherever they landed on the shore. One of the ravens came in low below her shield on the northward side to show her images of Chemmen escaping in small boats toward the same side of the lake as themselves. Her stomach muscles clenched. They'd be hugely outnumbered and a long way from the warriors of Taurmaline even if the king were to send them out immediately.

Their boat bumped against the shallows and Vilnue jumped out and reached back a hand for Everlyn. They climbed out of the boat and headed to a small stand of trees. Ravens came flying in to perch above them and Everlyn reached out her *knowing*. In all, thirty-one of them huddled together in the fading darkness; Heara was not among them.

Dia flinched when one of the ravens landed on her shoulder to show her images that made her breathe easier and her heart beat with hope.

'The king has sent his warriors out from the castle,' she whispered. 'And our *walkers* have engaged with a sorcerer who came to shore near the harbour. There are many Chemmen, and possibly dead men, scattered around the shore. We're hugely outnumbered and there could be more sorcerers about, including Adelphy himself.' She gritted her teeth. Now was when she could really do with the twins to track their way either to small numbers of Chemmen to take out, or to the safety of the king's army.

The raven tapped her cheek with its beak.

She grinned.

'The ravens will show us the best path and take us to targets we can take out.'

The birds erupted upward from the trees, not one uttering a caw or a croak. The one on her shoulder hopped off and then took to the air. Dia gestured to the others, and they followed.

They took out several lone dead men, a group of twelve Chemmen, and another of just under twenty before the sun burst upward sending bright beams through thick and fast-moving cloud. The distant sound of battle came closer and clearer, and as they stepped out into the long open stretch of land leading to the harbour and castle, they saw it for themselves. It was the Chemmen's turn to be outnumbered and yet they were winning, pushing the king's forces back. The figure of Adelphy Dunham was unmistakable. He was taller than most of his men and even from a distance Dia could still feel his power. He had more left than she'd hoped and already hers was waning.

She cupped her hands and looking up at the sky drew all of her power together to call up a storm. The ravens scattered in all directions, cawing in harsh voices before coming back to fly circles around her, forming a black feathered vortex. The rapidly expanding clouds grew darker as she took slow, deliberate steps toward her foe.

Out of the corner of her eye she spotted Heara, the scout grabbed at Vilnue and Tantony to pull them back and gestured for the warriors to stay out of the way; Dia's concentration didn't falter. Lightning flashed within the clouds and forked down to strike within the ranks of the Chemmen. She caught a brief glimpse of Adelphy's eyes before his arms went up to send flames toward her. Everlyn shielded, stumbling to one knee. Dia advanced. The ravens flew higher in their spirals and fire drakes came flying in from all around like flaming stars to join the huge thunderhead and turn the clouds to the colour of a bloody bruise.

Adelphy tried to turn the storm, leaning back as he forced a gale toward it. Dia closed her eyes and smiled, breathing in the sharp ozone smell as lighting lashed out followed by a swarm of fire drakes. She took in one, long, slow breath and stretched her *knowing* out into the storm, enraptured and enervated by it. As the drakes descended on the Chemmen and Bractius's warriors engaged their southward lines, Dia felled Adelphy Dunham with a blade made of lightning. She struck him twice.

Chapter Twenty-Six

Kesta; Covenet of Chem

Pain swept through her, making her want to vomit. All she could see was bright red and her vision refused to clear. She tried to turn her head but the shock that ran through her spine almost sent her spiralling into unconsciousness. She tried to breathe in and found that her lungs still worked. She could smell jasmine, cinnamon, and sweat. She made a small sound in her throat and reached up to grab at warm fabric, gripping it tightly.

'Kesta? Kesta!'

He shook her, and she gasped, her eyes rolling back. She felt herself being lifted, her cheek pressed against the bone of his shoulder.

Voices came from far away.

'This whole place is going to come down on us, let's try the way we came!' Jorrun, his voice so dear it hurt the muscles of her chest. She could feel the vibration of it through his ribs.

I'm dying.

'A moment, where's Milaiya?' Osun's voice.

Heat prickle her skin and she breathed in smoke. For a moment everything seemed to fade to darkness. She was jolted awake again as cold air touched her agonisingly fevered skin.

'Kessta!' Azrael was a brightness beyond her eyelids. 'Don't go, Kesta!'

She cried out as her head flopped. Jorrun tried to lift her higher and tightened his grip on her.

'Shall I take her?' Osun asked.

'No.' The word vibrated through her skin and bones. 'No, you're better with a sword than I.'

Then the world was gone.

***

The rocking and jolting penetrated her dreams before she awoke to a throbbing headache and a desperate thirst. Slowly she propped herself up on one elbow and forced her heavy eyes open.

She was in Osun's wagon.

She spotted something beside her and tried to turn, her neck and head protested, bringing pain and nausea. She dragged herself upright against one of the chests and saw that what she was lying beside was a small green book with gold runes. A dagger was still embedded deep through its pages.

She smiled to herself.

'Kessta.' Azrael shot out of the lantern and flew about madly. 'Kessta, you're awake! I'll tell the others.'

Kesta closed her eyes against his shocking glare and raised a hand. 'No, Azra, a moment. What has happened? Where are we?' She reached up and found that bandages were tightly wound about her head, her hair had been plaited back in a single braid.

'We are on our way to the coasst.' Azrael bobbed lower and she could feel the heat that radiated off him. He made himself very small. 'We thought you would die, Kessta. You were very ill.'

She swallowed, glancing down at the book and the dagger. 'Did everyone make it out?'

'Yess.' Azrael grew larger and brighter. 'Milaiya was too scared to move, but Ossun made her come. He wouldn't leave her behind.'

'Spirit, you're only giving me tiny bits.' Her pulse raced. 'What happened? Is Jorrun all right?'

'Alive, yes, and he will want to see you. Jorrun drained his father's power but his own too. It was Osun who killed Dryn Dunham, with Jorrun's sword. The palace was burning and the wallss of the room giving way, but we all got out. The guardss and those left of the covens were too busy to look for uss. Their temples were on fire. Drakess burnt their Gods.'

Kesta closed her eyes and clenched her teeth and fists. 'Blessed spirit,' she said through a tightening throat. 'I wish I had seen that.'

'We got out of the city the following morning, many people did and the guardss did not stop them. There is no one to ssit on the Seats in Arkoom; no one to rule.'

'No, but ...' she screwed up her eyes, unable to move her neck to shake her head. 'There is Adelphy still, in Elden?'

Azrael bobbed up and down. 'We don't know. Let me get Jorrun, pleasse? He has been beside himself with worry.'

She felt bad at how much that pleased her. 'All right.'

Exhaustion washed through her but when she tried to lie back down her head felt too heavy for her neck and it hurt too much to lean back, so instead she pressed her back up against a stack of crates. The wagon stopped abruptly and moments later the canvas was pulled aside. Her breath caught when she saw Jorrun, eyes wide and searching her face. He clambered up inside, Milaiya was just behind but she waited outside the wagon.

Jorrun opened his mouth but couldn't seem to speak. She reached out her hand and he stepped forward to take it, moving the book to sit beside her.

'We were worried you would never wake.' He kept hold of her hand, barely blinking as he looked at her.

'I'm not that easy to get rid of.' She smiled, and his pupils expanded, colour seemed to return to his pale face.

'How did you know he would throw the dagger?' He turned and picked up the book.

'What?' she frowned in confusion.

'You tucked this book inside your tunic and it caught the dagger.' He held it up to show her.

She shook her head, her hand flying up to her jaw as she grimaced in pain at the movement. 'I stole the book. From that slaver's library. I know you love books. It was the only place I had to hide it. I stole it for you after … after you let me know how you felt.'

He looked down at the floor, lowering the book to his lap. 'Then it's the best gift I've ever received.'

She reached out to touch his other hand with one finger, her eyelids feeling heavy and her breathing shallow. She cleared her throat against the dryness there.

'Oh, but you're still ill.' Jorrun got to his knees and then scrambled to his feet. He looked around and finding a mug and some water gave her a little. It seemed barely enough to her to fill her mouth. He rearranged the cushions and blanket on the floor of the wagon and then taking her weight against his shoulder he gently helped her lie down.

'Rest, Kesta.' He lightly stroked the side of her face and his touch seemed to linger there long after he'd left.

She awoke from time to time, but never for long. Either Milaiya or Jorrun were always with her to help her drink and eventually to eat. Sometimes she found never being alone irritating as though they were ants that crawled over her nerves. At other times she awoke covered in sweat and trembling and embarrassed herself by crying in relief to find someone there. Jorrun would hold her carefully, saying nothing, and she breathed in the scent that had woken her from death. Milaiya would hold her hand and occasionally sing. It was a while before Kesta realised that Azrael was no longer hiding around the Chemmish woman, in fact he sometimes hummed and buzzed along to her songs.

The first time Kesta was able to leave the wagon her muscles were stiff and painful, and she found herself shaking. Osun was watering the horses and looked up to smile at her but politely turned away from her struggling. She batted Jorrun away with a scowl when he kept reaching out ready to help her. When her knees did give way Jorrun quickly stepped in to grab her under the ribs and hold her up. Her neck and cheeks flushed, and she tensed every muscle in her body, her nostrils flared against the tightening of her throat and the tears that pushed behind her eyes. She pulled herself up against Jorrun and then stepped away, glancing up to make sure Osun hadn't seen her weakness.

'It won't be forever,' Jorrun said softly. 'But please give yourself time.'

She refused to look up at him. Milaiya came out of the wagon and laid a blanket down for her to sit on. She took the woman's hand as she carefully lowered herself.

'I'm glad to see you well enough to come out,' Osun said.

She regarded him and felt the flip of her heart as a stab of hatred shuddered through her, and yet ... she gazed up at his dark-blue eyes, open and clear. Azrael had said that he'd refused to leave Milaiya to die in the palace.

She looked away and down at the ground when she spoke to him. 'Where are we?'

Osun sighed. 'About two days from the coast.'

'Two days?' She turned around to face Jorrun, the movement making her dizzy. 'How long have I been ... sleeping?'

'Just over a week,' Jorrun told her.

'But ... has there not been any fighting? Has no one tried to stop us?'

Jorrun shook his head, glancing over at Osun. 'No. The country is like a smashed wasp's nest. Thanks to the fire drakes most of the populace is terrified, thinking the Gods have deserted them. The covens have already started fighting each other and the weaker sorcerers are biding their time to take what they can after. No one has time to care about a merchant and his slaves.'

Kesta swallowed. With everything in turmoil and the strongest of the coven lords dead or away in Elden, it would be the perfect time for more liberal thinkers to take control, to free women from slavery. She studied Jorrun's face, but all she saw was concern for her.

'Are you ready?' Osun asked Milaiya.

'Yes, master.' She headed back toward the wagon.

'What's happening?' Kesta straightened up to look at them all, her hands becoming fists and her heart rate increasing.

'Osun is going to sell everything he can in the nearby town.' Jorrun placed a hand briefly on her shoulder. 'We'll stay here out of the way with Azrael.'

'Oh.' She slowly relaxed her muscles and moved her legs to sit more comfortably on the blanket. She watched as Milaiya and Osun climbed up onto the wagon and headed off through a narrow copse. Jorrun moved away to fetch her a mug of water.

'Is there any news on Elden? Is Adelphy heading back as we hoped?' She took the mug from him with both hands.

'Osun has been visiting inns and markets as we moved south but there is nothing from Elden.' He sat beside her and gazed at the trees. 'We may find it more dangerous in Elden when we return than it is here.'

'We should go to the Fulmers.' She sat up straighter and shifted on the blanket to face him. 'Come with me, Jorrun. Bractius can't tell us what to do there, we could be together—'

Her anger rose as he shook his head and winced. 'If I went to the Fulmers Bractius would see it as a defection, a betrayal. It could seriously harm relations between Elden and the Islands. It's an option I've already considered. He'll never let me go.'

The muscles of her chest squeezed in tightly, making it harder to breathe in. He reached over to run a finger along her cheek and under her jaw, carefully avoiding the cut Dryn Dunham had given her. When she looked up and caught his eyes sparks of electricity ran through her to the tips of her fingers and the roots of her hair. She leaned forward and kissed him, her fingers digging into his shoulders.

When he pulled away, they were both breathing hard and the heat of her skin was not from the sun.

'Let me get you something to eat.' He stood up and went over to some bags that Osun had left them.

She gritted her teeth and wrapped her arms tightly around her body. Was he ever going to stop being sensible? It wasn't as though she was ... fragile. She uncurled her hands and watched them shaking.

He returned and placed some bowls of food down, but her stomach shrank at the sight of it. Her limbs felt heavy, and she lay down on the blanket, drawing up her legs to curl around her hands around them. Jorrun sat beside her and gently stroked her back.

'You told me once that you were a slave,' she said. 'It's true, isn't it? You're Bractius's slave. You are no more able to live without a master than Osun is.'

He withdrew his hand but didn't reply. She clenched her eyes shut and curled up tighter. Everything hurt. Especially her heart.

***

The following day they removed the bandages from her head and Milaiya washed her hair for her. It was such a relief to feel clean that she embarrassed herself by crying again. She managed to stay out of the now almost empty wagon for longer. On the final day of their journey through Chem she spent much of it sitting beside Milaiya as she drove the shaggy red bulls. Kesta opened her mouth and closed her eyes, breathing in the scent of the sea, the scent of home.

'I'll try not to be long,' Osun told them as they set up camp in the same place he'd first met them. 'But if I am to get news of Elden, then this is the best place.'

'Be careful.' Jorrun clasped his wrist.

Milaiya set about unharnessing the bulls, not looking up as Osun rode away with the horses. Jorrun set some wood for a cook fire, picking up a piece of coal which he threw for Azrael to catch. Kesta walked over to the fire and regarded the wood. Taking in a deep breath she reached for her magic and the wood burst into flames. She laughed, folding her arms about her waist. Her powers were back, and it hadn't hurt.

Azrael flew several loops around her, still eating his coal.

'How do you feel?' Jorrun was studying her face from a distance.

'All right.' She nodded and then smiled. 'And hungry!'

***

Osun didn't return until dawn. Milaiya was already up and about and Kesta heard their voices and sat up groggily. As she opened the canvas of the wagon, Azrael shot out past her. Jorrun spotted her and walked over, offering his hand to help her down.

'No news,' he said.

Kesta looked at Osun.

'Nothing at all from Elden,' the Chemman confirmed. 'No messages, no Adelphy.'

'But he must know Dryn is dead?' She turned back to Jorrun.

He drew his hand across his face to rub at his short beard. 'It could be that no message has reached him from here, either, but I find it highly unlikely that no one here has done a blood scry to him, or him to them. Let's get ourselves to the Borrows and see if my ship is still there first, we'll decide about Elden once we're underway.'

'What about me?' Milaiya asked, her eyes huge.

'You're coming, of course,' Osun replied. 'Or do you want to stay here alone?'

She shook her head.

'Well, then. Go and set your bulls free, that's the best I can do for them.'

She stood for a moment, staring after Osun. Kesta walked over to her and placed a hand on her back. 'Come on, I'll help with the bulls. Things will be very different in Elden, you won't be a slave there.' Even as she said it, she thought of Jorrun and Bractius, of Osun's inability to adapt to Elden life. Were things really better in Elden than Chem? For women, most definitely, but for men? Maybe not so much.

She realised that she was just standing there and, shaking herself, untied the rope from the nose ring of one of the bulls. 'Can these rings be taken out?'

Milaiya reached up to touch it. 'With the right tools, maybe, or someone strong.'

'Jorrun,' she called, and he stood up at once. 'Can you see if you can take these nose rings out without hurting the bulls?'

He walked over and studied the bull's nose while Milaiya and Kesta held its head. Both women drew in a sharp breath when both his hand and the metal ring glowed blue and the ring dropped away. Kesta followed him as he did the same with the other nose ring.

'How do you do that?' Kesta demanded. 'What kind of magic is it?'

He regarded her and grinned, then turned and walked away.

'Jorrun!'

He ignored her and kept going. She growled, hands on her hips. She heard a soft chuckle and narrowed her eyes.

'You're free.' Milaiya softly murmured.

Kesta went back to join her. 'I'm going to try to show them.' She stood the other side of the bull and placed a hand in its curly fur behind its ear. 'To talk to animals, you have to use feelings and images rather than words. I'll try to explain that they are free and should stay away from humans unless they are hurt or ill.'

Milaiya nodded, clasping her hands together and stepping back. Kesta relaxed and a smile spread across her face at how easily her *knowing* came back to her. She did her best to explain to the animals and when she'd finished, they went over to Milaiya to nudge and snuffle at her.

'It's time to go!' Osun called over.

Kesta felt her stomach shift and a million butterflies danced there. Time to leave Chem. Time to head back to the Raven Tower.

***

No one was as surprised as Jorrun when they found his small ship still sheltered in the sharp Borrow cove. Kesta extended her *knowing*.

'Still deserted,' she confirmed.

Jorrun frowned. 'Don't over-exert yourself. You're still recovering.'

She screwed her face up at him and he responded with one of his rare but beautiful smiles. Her heart skipped a beat.

Osun dropped his heavy chest on the deck, making her jump.

'That's it,' he panted.

Jorrun nodded and checked the rope for their small boat was securely tied. While he went to take up the anchor, Kesta loosed the sails and set them to the wind. She couldn't resist adding a little of her own to get them out of the cove and raised an eyebrow at Jorrun, challenging him to complain. He didn't react but as he walked past her, he jabbed one finger into her ribs.

'Ow!' She rubbed at her side.

He took a small green book out of his bag and took it into the cabin, she couldn't resist following. He glanced up when he realised she was behind him.

'I can't even read it,' he said.

She took the book from him and looked at the embossed silver runes on the cover; they were nothing she recognised. A large, narrow hole went almost all the way through it where it had caught her dagger. 'I only picked this one as it was small enough to hide. And I love green.'

'I love you.'

Her breath caught in her throat and goose bumps ran over her skin. She couldn't bring herself to turn around. 'I ... I could stay in Elden.'

'No!' He grabbed her shoulders and turned her to face him. 'You were right, I am a slave to Bractius, but I won't let him make you one. Or our children.' His voice broke as his throat tightened. 'You have to be free, Kesta. You have to go back to the Fulmers.'

She clenched her fists, still gripping the book in one, and refused to reach out to him. Her nose and eyes tingled, but she gritted her teeth against it. 'No one tells me what I can or can't do.'

'Exactly.' Jorrun let her go and stepped back, his eyes unblinking. 'Exactly. And that's how I want you to stay.' He looked into her mismatched eyes a moment longer before turning and ducking out of the cabin. 'Neither Osun nor Milaiya can sail,' he mumbled.

She slammed the book down on the table.

***

They approached the coast of Elden cautiously at night, searching the dark shadow of the land for any signs of smoke and flames. Kesta stretched out her *knowing* and was greeted by a confusing cacophony of emotion. It was

Azrael who brought them news, daring to fly across a narrow stretch of sea to the land to speak with the other drakes.

'Adelphy is dead!' He crackled and hissed.

'You're sure, bug?' Jorrun stood up from his seat at the rudder.

'Yess! The Icante killed him!'

Kesta sucked in a sharp breath and clutched at the fabric of her tunic at the shoulder.

'There are sstill some Shem warriors about the place being hunted down, be we have won! Elden is ssafe!'

Kesta sat down on the deck. Her vision blurred, and she had to steady her breathing. 'Is my mother okay? And my father?' She looked up at the fire-spirit.

'They wait for you at the Raven Tower.'

'We'll head straight for Taurmouth,' Jorrun called out. 'Fancy calling that wind of yours now, Kesta?'

She smiled and called up her magic.

They came rapidly into the harbour and Kesta's eyes widened at the devastation that greeted them. They had to steer slowly around several wrecked ships and many of the harbourside homes and businesses were nothing more than scorched ruins. Several of the wharves had collapsed into the water and they had to sail a long way in before they spotted somewhere that looked stable enough for them to tie up. There was no harbourmaster waiting, but a group of warriors in torn and singed clothing hurried up to see who they were.

'I'm Thane Jorrun of Northold! We come with news from Chem. Who is in charge here?'

'Jarl Hadger still lives.' One of the warriors spat onto the wooden planks. 'Although Chief Adrin has taken charge since he got back from Mantu. What's this news then?'

'Dryn Dunham, the Chemman Overlord, is dead. If you could send word to the king, I'd be grateful.' He turned to Osun and his brother reluctantly took a coin out of the purse on his belt and threw it up.

The warrior caught it. 'I'll do that. Mermaid is the only inn still standing if you want food and somewhere to stay. Land's burnt out pretty much from here to the lake.'

Kesta bit her lower lip. *Rosa and Catya!*

'We are obliged.' Jorrun gave a slight nod, dismissing them.

The talkative one narrowed his eyes but dipped in a small bow and gestured for his men to follow him.

Kesta ducked her head inside the cabin. 'Are you staying here, or do you want the lantern?'

'I'll sstay.' Azrael hissed.

She followed the two men onto the wharf and saw that Milaiya was still standing on the deck. She held out her hand and smiled. Milaiya came forward to take it and she helped her step across. She removed the woman's veil. 'You are in Elden now. You are free. Here you are no longer a slave and Osun isn't your master.'

Milaiya stood looking at her, so still that at first Kesta thought she mustn't have understood. Milaiya lunged forward, grabbing Kesta's dagger from her belt. Kesta tried to grab at her as she swung the dagger wildly at Osun. Fabric tore, and a red line opened up across his chest. Jorrun drew his sword as Osun raised his arms, using his own flesh to shield himself. Kesta grabbed Milaiya's flailing arm, and she twisted a foot around the woman's ankle to drop her to the floor just as Jorrun's sword swung around to stop, just an inch from Kesta's throat.

They froze for a moment, breathing hard, her eyes fixed on his and her heart pounding loudly in her ears.

Then Osun crumpled to the wooden planks. Jorrun quickly sheathed his sword to throw himself to his brother's side. Blood was welling up from between Osun's hands. Jorrun tore off his shirt and placed it over the wound, pressing down hard. He turned to Kesta, eyes wide, face pale.

'Help me, Kesta!'

Kesta's muscles wouldn't move, she couldn't tear her eyes away from his.

Osun or Milaiya.

Kesta grabbed Milaiya's arm and pulled her up off the ground. With a glance at Jorrun she took two steps forward, but instead of helping she snatched Osun's purse from his belt, took the former slave's wrist and ran.

Chapter Twenty-Seven

Kesta; Kingdom of Elden

The first building they came to that showed signs of life, Kesta stopped and pounded on the door. A man answered, his shirt half tucked in, his hair dishevelled, and no shoes on his feet.

'We need help.' Kesta told him. 'A man has been attacked down on the wharves by a thief. Is there a healer still alive anywhere?'

'Well, yes, I think so. They have a makeshift—'

'Will you fetch them? Or go to the wharves just down the road there and help my … my brother-in-law get to them?' She reached into Osun's purse and took out a coin.

The man looked at the strange shape and pattern of it but took it, anyway. 'I'll send my son for the healer and come with you myself to the wharves, give me just a moment.'

'No, we can't stay.' Kesta stopped him. 'They are just down this road here. Which way is it to the Mermaid inn?'

The man's brows lowered over his eyes. 'Left at the top there and then right at the well.'

'You promise you're going to help?'

'I will, miss.'

'I'll be back as soon as I can.' She grabbed Milaiya's arm and forced her to run again. They followed the man's directions and as soon as she saw the inn Kesta slowed a little to catch her breath. Milaiya was panting hard, her cheeks flushed red. Blood splattered her sleeves in small spots. She glanced up at Kesta but couldn't meet her eyes for long.

'Do as I tell you,' Kesta said, feeling sick that she was taking advantage of Milaiya's conditioning as a slave. She pushed through the inn door and quickly made an assessment as to who was in charge. It appeared to be an old warrior who still carried himself like a fighter despite being missing an arm and his remaining hair having turned white.

'Do you have a room left?' Kesta demanded.

The man grinned and looked Kesta up and down.

She drew herself up and walked forward until they were almost nose to nose. 'I am Kesta Silene and my husband is Thane Jorrun.'

The man's grin vanished, and he paled.

'Do you have a room?'

'I can make room, my lady,' he replied quickly.

'Good. This lady here will stay with you until either I return to take her, or two weeks have passed. If I am not back for her in two weeks, you will arrange her passage to the Fulmers; via Burneton if necessary. No one will harm her, and you will see that she is fed and treated as an honoured guest. If I hear otherwise, you will have my husband and the king to deal with – if you're lucky. If you're unlucky, you will deal with me. Is that understood?'

The man ground his teeth. 'Aye, lady.'

'Here.' She dug into Osun's purse and pulled out a handful of coins. 'This gold should compensate you.'

The innkeeper held out both his hands and his eyebrows raised a little. Kesta turned to Milaiya and grabbed her hands to look into her face. 'Milaiya, you must stay here at this inn. They will take care of you until either I come for you or they find you passage to my home in the Fulmers. Remember, no one here is allowed to harm you in any way—'

Milaiya threw herself to the floor and grabbed at Kesta's trouser leg. 'Mistress, don't leave me!'

Heat rose to her cheeks and Kesta's heart ached, but she kept her voice strong and her resolve iron. 'Milaiya, I have to go. Jorrun needs me. You are safe here and I'll see you soon.' She grabbed Milaiya under the arms and pulled her up, staring her in the eye and calling on her *knowing*. 'You are strong, Milaiya.' She pushed Osun's purse into her hands and, with a last glare at the innkeeper, strode to the door.

Once outside she bent over and placed her hands above her knees, drawing in several long, deep breaths. Choking back any doubts she ran back toward the wharves. She let out a small cry when she saw two men struggling toward her carrying a third. A young boy and another man jogged at their side. She stopped to wait, her heart hammering. It was hard to read Jorrun's face in the darkness. He'd grabbed another shirt from the boat, but it was badly creased.

'How is he?' she asked.

'He has taken some deep slashes but her first strike slid off his ribs. He should live. Where is she?' His voice was strained from carrying Osun's weight, his eyes red veined.

'Safe. You won't have to deal with her again. This isn't the place to talk about it but ... I want you to let her go.'

He didn't reply but readjusted his grip on his brother. As they reached the building where they were treating the wounded he finally spoke. 'I thought you had left me.'

She opened her mouth and took in several short, shallow breaths. 'No.'

They waited while the healer sewed Osun's wounds. Kesta couldn't bring herself to look up at Jorrun's pale face and she resisted the temptation to reach for his hand. The healer finally finished wrapping Osun's forearm in white bandages and went to wash his hands. He walked over to them with a thin-lipped smile and Kesta felt relief flow through her, she sagged in her seat. Jorrun stood up at once and the healer waved a hand for him to sit.

'He should be fine. He lost blood and he'll have a few scars, but he was lucky.' The healer looked from Jorrun to Kesta. 'He should stay here for a couple of days. It's not the most pleasant place but I can feed him, and I recommend you give that slash across his chest time to knit together before he starts moving about.'

Jorrun closed his eyes briefly and nodded. 'I cannot wait and must report to the king.'

'Aye, Thane, I imagine you do. Don't worry, he's safe here. Shall I send him on to the Northold when he is ready?'

Kesta sat upright and held her breath. She didn't want Osun to die, for Jorrun's sake, but the thought of having him at Northold … She still hoped that she could persuade Jorrun that they could be together somehow; she couldn't bear the thought of having his brother with them.

'Yes. Send him to me at Northold.'

Every muscle in Kesta's chest tightened and a heavy weight settled across her shoulders and in her heart.

'I will, Thane.' The healer gave a small bow and then went about his work.

'Are you coming to Northold, or will you be going to Milaiya?'

Kesta swallowed and forced herself to look around at him. His usual perfect posture and composure was gone. He slumped in his chair, dark, bruised-looking skin surrounded his puffy eyes.

'I'm coming to Northold.'

He stood up, and she followed him out of the building. The streets outside seemed completely deserted now and there was little light by which to see. The silence between them screamed at her but without her *knowing* she had no idea if he was angry with her, she had no idea what he was feeling. It made her feel sick.

Jorrun's ship was still safely where they'd left it, although with a fire-spirit on-board she supposed she shouldn't have expected anything else. As soon as she was on-board, Jorrun untied and pushed them free of the wharf.

'Once we're clear of the harbour, I can take us up river for a bit,' she suggested hesitantly. 'You look like you need some sleep.'

He turned to regard her, but instead of speaking he stepped forward and slid his arms around her to give her a fierce hug. He turned his face to breathe in the scent of her hair. She drew in the warmth of his body like a cold stone absorbing the sun. They both almost lost their balance when their drifting ship hit the wharf. They stepped apart quickly, Jorrun bending to kiss her so quickly that his lips barely brushed hers, leaving her wanting so much more. He went to the side and gave them another push away from the wharf while she went to the rudder. She had a small but constant wind ready to take them up the river as soon as he'd secured the sails.

They took turns resting and sailing the ship; Azrael kept Kesta company more often than Jorrun and when they were together one of them steered while the other created wind for as long as they could. All along the shoreline they witnessed the burnt-out remains of small hamlets and farms, and Kesta's anxiety grew. A few people seemed to be returning but most ran at the sight of their small ship. The lifting bridge across the mouth of the lake had been totally destroyed and all three of them came out onto the deck to look across the water toward Northold. Kesta caught her breath when she saw the Raven Tower. Glancing over her shoulder to where Jorrun sat at the rudder, she saw him sitting upright and tense. Azrael flew a loop around the sail.

A few ravens circled the trees and her heart lifted when she spotted a few of the hold's fishing boats out on the lake.

'It looks like the hold survived!' She shouted back to Jorrun.

Her eyes widened when she saw the figures waiting on the shore; Rosa and Catya were waving their hands above their heads and the young girl darted forward to run to the end of the wharf. Kesta's breath caught in her throat and her eyes overflowed. She climbed forward into the narrow space in front of the cabin, her vision blurring. *Could it be?*

Behind Rosa, her parents stood waiting for her beside Tantony ... and Bractius. Her heightened emotions plummeted, and she turned to look at Jorrun. He caught her eyes only briefly before himself regarding the waiting king.

'I'll talk to him,' he said so quietly the wind nearly whipped his words away. 'He owes us our freedom.'

Kesta didn't even have time to step off the ship before Catya was throwing herself at her and hugging her tightly. It was hard to step onto the wharf with a thirteen-year-old girl clinging to her waist. She kissed Rosa on the cheek and squeezed her hands and then her father was lifting her off her feet and she thought her ribs would crack he held her so tightly. She was deposited back on the ground in front of Dia and her eyes stung. Her mother regarded the cut under her chin and the now almost faded bruises on her cheek and around her throat. She hugged her as gently as if Kesta were a flower she didn't want to crush. Over her shoulder Kesta was startled to see Bractius hugging Jorrun, for once being friend before king. Hope surged through her, but her fears turned it to nausea. Surely the king would never let as valuable a weapon as the Dark Man go; but would Bractius free his friend?

Dia followed her gaze, a frown settling on her face as she turned back to study her daughter.

'Mother, please come and meet Jorrun.' She hurried across to him and interrupted him by running her hand gently down his arm.

'Ah! Kesta.' Bractius beamed at her.

She turned to look at her mother whose eyes had narrowed. There was no warmth in the way she regarded Bractius.

'Mother, this is Jorrun, my husband. Jorrun, the Icante of the Fulmers.'

Jorrun made a small bow and the corners of his mouth lifted upward. 'I am honoured to meet you.'

Dia studied his eyes and then the rest of his face. Kesta saw him swallow, but he otherwise stood up to her mother's scrutiny. She glanced at Kesta before turning back to Jorrun. 'It is good to meet you. I hope you don't mind, but I took over feeding the ravens in your absence. They have been most useful and contributed to the defence of Elden. One of them advised us of your imminent arrival.'

'It is kind of you to take care of them,' he replied.

Kesta moved closer to him, the back of her hand brushing his.

Tantony approached slowly, looking from one face to another. 'Excuse me, Thane, my lady, there are lots of people waiting in the ward to see you.'

'Tantony!' She placed her hands on his shoulders and kissed his bearded cheek. 'It's really good to see you!'

Tantony's face reddened, and he glanced at Jorrun. 'I'm glad you're both safe, lady,' he mumbled.

Jorrun offered her his arm. She bit her bottom lip and looked up at him before hesitantly slipping her hand over his forearm.

'Welcome home!' Rosa beamed at them both as they made their way into the hold.

Kesta let her eyes rove over the familiar faces and she gripped Jorrun's arm a little tighter. She spotted Kurghan standing among his family and warmth leapt up from her heart to trigger a smile. She gave him a nod, and he bowed in return. Looking up at the walls she saw women and children with bows mixed in among the warriors still. The great hall was crowded but Reetha had everything under control and she was surprised at the feast that had been laid out across the tables despite their recent siege and the burning of the river valley.

Bractius led the way to the head of the table and he pulled out a chair himself for Kesta at his right side. Both she and Jorrun hesitated and looked at each other when it became clear that the king intended to sit between them. Kesta reluctantly removed her hand, but it was Jorrun who moved away first to sit to the left of the king. Her heart sank still further when she saw her mother seated on the other side of Jorrun; however, when her father appeared at her right shoulder, she felt herself relax a little. She told herself there was still time. Time to catch up with her mother, and time to be with Jorrun.

She jumped when Bractius banged on the table with a closed fist. The room muttered its way to silence.

'Good people of Northold, of Elden, and our dearest friends of the Fulmers!' Bractius raised a hand. 'As you know, we have turned back the attack on our beloved land from the sorcerers of Chem! This afternoon, it's my honour to announce to you first that your Thane, Jorrun of Northold, and our very own Lady Kesta, have returned from Chem having defeated the Overlord himself!'

Both Jorrun and Kesta opened their mouths to protest, but the king continued.

'Raise your glasses, good people; Thane Jorrun and Lady Kesta!'

Kesta's muscles tightened, and she tried to shrink in on herself as the cheers of the room jarred her bones. She turned to look at Jorrun and found that he'd sought her eyes in return. Spirits she wished that she was standing beside him. She almost fell forward into the table when her father slapped her hard on the back.

'My urchin.' He grinned at her proudly.

To Kesta the afternoon and evening seemed endlessly long. Although it warmed her soul to be among these people again and to catch up with Rosa and Catya, she ached to be with Jorrun and desperately needed to seek the advice of her mother. Eventually, Jorrun was able to lead the king away to the Raven Tower and Kesta watched her husband until he vanished from her sight.

'Kesta?' Her mother stepped up quietly beside her.

She grabbed her mother's hand and squeezed it. 'Let's go to my room.'

They slipped away from the great hall and Kesta led the way up the stairs of the Ivy Tower to her room at the top. It was at once both familiar and alien, as though it had lost its life with her absence. As soon as the door closed behind them, Kesta turned to hug her mother tightly.

'What happened?' Kesta asked. 'Tell me everything.'

They moved two chairs together and Kesta listened as her mother told her of her hunt for Relta, of Shaherra's death, and their battle against Adelphy.

'King Bractius insisted on parading us through the city and handing out simple food to those who had been trapped within,' she finished with a wince. 'It took some persuasion, but he finally relented and let us come here to wait for news of you in peace. As soon as he received Jorrun's message that you were at Taurmouth he came here himself to tell us.' She regarded Kesta and reached out to place a hand over hers. 'And what of you? It's not like you to be so quiet.'

Kesta took in several breaths before she spoke. 'When I first came here and Bractius pronounced his price for aid, I imagined that my life would be one of despair and torment. I never expected to find friendship and a place other than the Fulmers that could feel like a home. I certainly never ...' She closed her eyes and drew air in to her lungs. 'I certainly never expected to fall in love.'

She told her mother of what had befallen her, of how Jorrun had not been what he pretended for the king. Then with a tightening throat she told her mother of Bractius's plans to use any children she might have with Jorrun to bring magic to the royal line of Elden. 'Jorrun insists I must go home to the Fulmers, but he won't come with me. I could stay, but I have a duty to the Fulmers and I wouldn't wish the life Jorrun has on any child we might have.'

'You have a duty to yourself as well as to the Fulmers.' Her mother squeezed her hand.

'I've seen the way Bractius is with Jorrun.' Kesta shook her head. She drew her shaking hands into her lap. 'He is always king first and friend only when it's convenient. He would have no qualms in treating our children and me like … well, like the lords of Chem do their slaves. Like property.'

'I don't think this is something I can solve for you, Kesta.' Dia moved her chair to face her and looked her deep in the eyes. 'I've never known you run from something difficult, not since you were old enough to walk. Neither have I ever seen you so turned inside out by a man. Only you can decide what to do, only you and Jorrun; but I will support you whatever you decide, as will the Fulmers.'

Kesta nodded. She felt as though a weight had been lifted off her shoulders at the same time as pressure still built against her chest.

Dia shifted in her seat. 'Now we know you're safe we will be returning to the Fulmers tomorrow. Please don't think you have to come, follow when you wish – or not.'

Kesta looked up, her eyes wide. Despite her mother's reassurance it did make it feel like she had only one night to decide. She steadied her breathing and forced herself to think rationally and not emotionally. 'If I don't come, will you go via Taurmouth and take Milaiya with you?'

'Of course. I should get back to your father before he drinks too much and forgets to be diplomatic.' She stood up and kissed Kesta's cheek. 'Find Jorrun and speak to him.'

Kesta couldn't face going back down to the great hall, she paced her room, occasionally going to the window to look across at the Raven Tower. She hadn't seen the king leave as yet, nor heard his booming laugh in the hall below. Night was deeply settled before she saw two figures crossing toward the keep. The king's strides were swift, Jorrun walked more slowly, head lowered. She was contemplating going down when she heard the door go far below. The careful footsteps were achingly familiar and looking around quickly she decided to sit in her usual chair and tried to look composed; however, as soon as Jorrun knocked at the door and opened it to look cautiously in, she was on her feet.

'I wasn't sure if you were on your own.'

Her legs took her quickly across the space between them and she slipped her arms around his ribs. He hugged her fiercely back before kissing her cheek and going to the window; he placed his clenched fists on the sill.

Kesta held her breath.

Jorrun bowed his head, the muscles of his jaw moved as he clenched his teeth. 'Bractius will not let me go to the Fulmers to live with you. He was very clear in his opinion that he would consider such a thing to be treason on my part and an act of aggression from the Fulmers—'

'But that's nonsense!' Kesta moved to stand behind him. 'He must know that.'

Jorrun turned to face her, his lips thin and his eyes wide and reddened. 'You don't understand how controlling he is. His throne and his power come first; always. I managed to persuade him that you need to go to the Fulmers with your mother to help her manage things after the attack there. I'll ... I'll deal with him later when you don't come back.'

She shook her head, her breathing fast and shallow. She couldn't speak but stepped forward to meet him when he bent to kiss her and wrap her hair around his fingers. 'Thank you for everything you have done, Kesta,' he said into her hair. 'Thank you for saving my life and for saving my people.'

His people, she wondered. He was a man born from all nations and yet he belonged to none of them.

'I'm so sorry for what we did to you.'

A spark of anger cut through her grief and she stepped back to look up at him, her hands resting against the back of his neck. 'I'm not sorry. I'm not sorry that we destroyed the Dunhams. I'm not sorry that I met you.'

He bowed to rest his forehead against hers. She could feel how much he wanted her, and it inflamed her own desire. Yet both Bractius and Osun stood between them, an unwanted and seemingly insurmountable wall. She could feel his heart beating against her own chest.

She closed her eyes. 'There will be a way.'

He grabbed her roughly by the arms and pushed her away, almost shaking her with each word that he spoke. 'Don't you dare wait for me, Kesta! You are stronger than that. If you're not going to live your life, then you might as well be a slave.' His skin and eyes had turned red and tears fell as he blinked.

She stared up at him wide-eyed, but before she could make a reply he kissed her again, this time very slowly as though memorising every sensation. He was saying goodbye. A thousand splinters pierced her heart, and she buried her face in his neck and shoulder to hide her tears.

Please stay. Please stay just for tonight! She pushed her thoughts toward him but was too proud to say them aloud, too scared that he would say no.

His arms withdrew from around her and he touched her face to kiss her one last time before stepping away. She could barely breathe her chest and throat were so tight.

'I won't come out to say goodbye tomorrow.' His blue eyes, as hot as a flame, searched hers. 'I'm sorry to be a coward but it will be easier for us both.' His voice almost failed as he walked toward the door. 'You'll have a wonderful life, Kesta; stay free for both of us.'

She opened her mouth to gasp in air, her vision splintered into rainbows through her tears as he vanished through the door. For several, painful heartbeats she stood frozen before her feet jerked into motion and she ran to the window to look across at the Raven Tower; at its dark and empty windows. She sank to the carpet, her cheek pressed against the stone of the wall below the window, her arms wrapped tightly around her shaking body. Tears snaked down her hot cheeks.

'Kessta.'

She wiped her eyes with the backs of her hands and looked around to see Azrael hovering between herself and the bed.

'I hate seeing you and Jorrun hurting sso much.' The fire-spirit made himself small and pale.

'It isn't very pleasant from my side, either.' She moved her hands down to her stomach to try to hold in the feeling of nausea. Her heart still raced. She sniffed and swallowed, trying to pull herself together. 'Would you like a story, Azra?'

'I will read you one, Kesta.' He came closer and made himself larger.

'But you can't read a book.'

'I have books inside me, Kesta.'

They heard voices below and she got unsteadily to her feet. There was a soft knock, but she couldn't find her voice. It was Azrael who invited them in.

'Azra.' Catya grinned.

Rosa went straight to Kesta and wrapped her in a warm and gentle hug. Kesta bit hard at her lower lip to fight against the sting of her eyes and the awful pain in her chest.

'Jorrun told us to come up and see you.' Rosa studied her face with her kind eyes.

Kesta sniffed and drew herself up. 'I'm leaving tomorrow, Rosa. I would love you to come but that would be selfish. As long as the queen allows it you must stay here with Tantony. Whatever you do, you must tell him how you feel. Don't waste a minute more of your life with politeness and shyness.'

Rosa's cheeks flushed, and she looked away. 'I'm not sure that Tantony even likes me.'

Kesta grabbed the tops of her arms and gripped tightly. 'Of course, he does! You know it really, too.'

Rosa regarded her, eyes wide. She nodded.

'But I'm coming with you.' Catya announced, hands on her hips. 'I'm your bodyguard and Heara is going to teach me.'

Rosa and Kesta looked at each other and smiled.

'Get Jorrun's permission and you can come.' Kesta nodded her agreement. 'Now, Azrael has just promised me a story.'

Kesta settled on the floor against the bed and Catya snuggled against her. Rosa sat up against the pillows, but it wasn't long before she was asleep and breathing loudly. Azrael spun his tale and Kesta tried hard to lose herself in it and forget that her soul was weeping, and her heart was breaking.

She couldn't stop shaking.

***

The first thing she did when she rose was go to the window and look at the Raven Tower. The windows looked dark and empty, but the ravens were more active than she'd ever seen them, circling the tower and diving down at the ward. She spotted the source of their excitement at once; her mother had gone out to feed them and they squabbled over who could sit on her shoulders and outstretched arms.

Gritting her teeth and tensing her shoulders, Kesta set about packing her few possessions. Her heart caught as she touched the cold metal of the silver leaf necklace Jorrun had given her. Her anger rose to defend her from pain, but her hand would not unclench to let the necklace go, nor move to throw it. Instead, she secured it about her neck. She was done in less than ten minutes, her hand brushed over the back of the chair in which Jorrun had always sat as she passed it to head for the door. She couldn't help a last glance out of the window toward the tower.

When she reached the ward Catya came running after her, breathing hard.

'He said yes!' she panted. 'Will you wait a moment for me to get my things?'

'I'll wait.' She smiled, a ghostly mask across her real emotions.

She dropped her bag and hurried across to the stables, finding Griffon's stall and feeling guilt creep across her skin like a chill at abandoning the nervous, intelligent horse. She tried to let him know he would be safe, that he could trust Nerim and bright little Nip. Nerim walked quietly up to her and waited in patient silence as she said goodbye to the horse. He reached out a hand, and she clasped his wrist, not looking up once before turning to head toward the gate and the small wharf.

She clenched her fists when she saw Bractius was there among the people of the hold waiting to see them off. Catya was already scrambling aboard the ship that would take them down the river Taur; Heara was there to help her on. It was Jorrun's ship. Her feet faltered. Her eyes searched the waiting crowd. He wasn't there.

She passed Kurghan and reached out a hand. With a grin he shook it. His sister turned her head slightly to wipe at the corner of her eye. Reetha stepped forward to hand her something warm wrapped in cloth; she could smell that it was her wonderful thyme bread. The old woman looked down coyly when Kesta kissed her soft, wrinkled cheek.

She stopped when she reached Rosa and Tantony. She regarded them both, trying to burn their faces in to her memory so they could stay as strongly there as they stood in her heart. Tantony took a startled step back as she dropped her bag to hug him and kiss his bearded cheek. She took Rosa's hands and looked in to her eyes for a long time before giving her a hug.

'I'll miss you both.' A painful lump formed in her throat.

'I'll miss you too.' Rosa dabbed at her reddening eyes.

Tantony scratched at his beard. 'It's going to be rather quiet without you. Too quiet.'

She grinned despite herself.

When she reached Bractius, the king stood beaming at her. She had no doubt that he had some prepared speech ready to entertain those wanting to believe it. She bared her teeth in a snarl. 'Anyone can make people fear them,' she said. 'Respect is much harder to earn. You don't deserve the loyalty you have.'

She didn't wait for a reply but strode towards the wooden planking of the wharf. Everyone was ready and waiting on the ship. Her mother stood watching, her hands folded together before her although her shoulders were tensed. Kesta turned to look back at Northold and its people. Her eyes travelled up to the Raven Tower and then searched the crowd. She could feel her blood pulsing through the vein in her neck and every breath seemed harder to take than the last. He wasn't there.

'Kesta?'

It was her father who spoke but when she turned, it was her mother's eyes she caught. Her legs didn't want to move. Her mother lifted her chin and narrowed her eyes. 'Cast off,' she said.

'No!' Kesta choked out the word and forced her legs to move. Her feet were hard to lift, as though weights had been tied to her ankles. Her heart shrank and shattered, her pulse thundered in her ears and sweat trickled down her back. But she moved forward and took her father's hand as she stepped over onto the deck.

She didn't move as the ship – his ship – took them away from the wharf. She held her mother's eyes, frozen, barely breathing. As they moved out onto the lake her muscles seemed to come alive and she ran back to look toward the wharf, at the waving people, at the walls of the hold; at the Raven Tower. She watched as it all grew smaller, as the trees seemed to spring up to hide her view of everything but the highest windows and the sharply slanted roof around which the ravens flew. She took in a deep, painful breath, her heart hammering against her ribs. With a rush of willpower, she turned away to face forward toward the mouth of the river, toward the way home.

Behind her, unseen, the windows of the Raven Tower blazed suddenly with candlelight.

Acknowledgements

Firstly, a big thank you to you, the reader, for choosing this book and taking the time to read it. I hope you enjoyed it, if you did please leave me a review, reviews are incredibly important to us authors. I would love it if you said hello, come and find me in one of the places below:

Facebook   www.facebook.com/EmmaMilesShadow

Twitter @EmmaMilesShadow

Instagram @emmamshadow

Thank you also to my loyal Facebook 'likers', for your constant support in reading and 'liking' my posts. Val Coote, Alan Pearson and of course my Aunty Karolyn; your encouragement is noticed and very much appreciated.

Thank you to the amazing authors who are a part of the FictionCafe family, your advice, company and support has made a big impact on my life, not just as a writer. A fond hello also to my Spoonie family. Rosie Cranie-Higgs, I learned a lot from your editing advice. Ta for the goats Kiltie!

And a big thank you to the lovely Emma Mitchell, my editor.

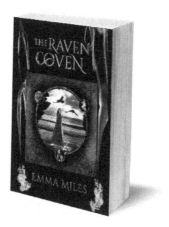

Would you dare to change the world?
Fire-Walker part two.

Kesta had left her heart across the sea, choosing her people, retaining her freedom. They were at peace, her islands saved from slavery, and yet... her soul was uneasy.

To the north cruel Chem lies in chaos, its people suffering as a result of the death of the ruling sorcerers. Refugees flee the cursed Borrows, begging for help from those they have made their enemy. A Queen unknowingly makes a dark, deadly pact, and new powers rise to fill the seats left empty by the Dunham necromancers.

In the seclusion of the Raven Tower both Jorrun and Osun search their hearts, and their conscience, and the brothers come up with a daring plan. They have a chance to change the world, but how can they break free of Bractius's control to take it?

'This is a thrilling read, the pacing is perfect. The latter stages of the book were very intense, going from one crises to another. There are some real heart in the mouth moments and you will feel all the feels.' – The Midnight Review.

'an amazing journey into a fantasy world that was brilliantly constructed.' – Jess Bookish Life

'Awesome. It also broke my heart, but hey, it wouldn't be a good book if it didn't. We're treated to an intrinsic lore which mystifies and awakens a mood within fantasy lovers only the unusual can conjure. Every single one of us have a selection of authors whose style sings to our souls. Be it Stephen King, Neil Gaiman, etc, and Emma is one of those authors for me.' – Radzy writes.

UK https://www.amazon.co.uk/Raven-Coven-Fire-Walker-Book-ebook/dp/B07Q4K623S

US https://www.amazon.com/Raven-Coven-Fire-Walker-Book-ebook/dp/B07Q4K623S

Also by the same author...

Valley of the Fey books

Hall of Pillars

Hall of Night

Fire-Walker Saga

The Raven Tower

The Raven Coven

Raven Storm

Raven Fire

Land Beneath the Sky; Companion books to the Fire-Walker Saga.

Queen of Ice. (Fits chronologically between books 3 and 4 of Fire-Walker)

Made in the USA
Columbia, SC
11 October 2021